MW00638575

THE UKINHAN WILDS

WARDER

THE UKINHAN WILDS

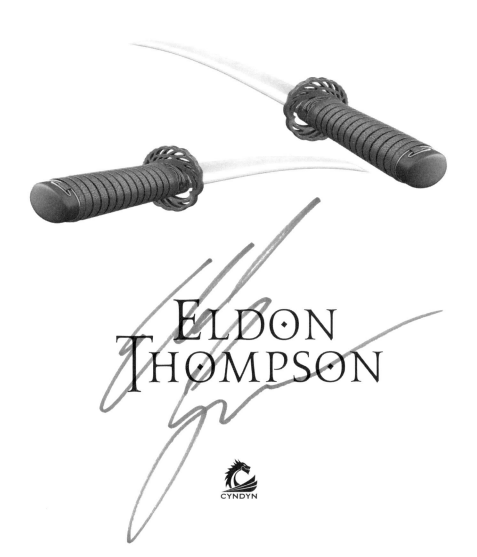

ELDON THOMPSON

CYNDYN

THE UKINHAN WILDS
Copyright © 2018 by Eldon Thompson
All rights reserved

Cover illustration by Daren Horley
Addaranth map by Maxime Plasse

Library of Congress Control Number: 2018903345

ISBN 978-1-948825-00-9
Trade Hardcover – Limited Edition

Published by Cyndyn; Irvine, California
Printed in the United States of America

ADDARANTH
The Sundered Isle

PROLOGUE

THE DARKNESS MOVED, and Ledron's hackles pricked in alarm.

By then, he was already too late.

The blackness grew limbs, springing from the invisible depths of the open cargo hold. A clawed swipe struck Demin, beside him. Ledron sprawled backward, down against the decking. A severed sword arm—Demin's—hit the planks near his feet.

His lungs drew breath, bellowed a warning. "Groll!"

Demin's cries were muffled as the mutant's teeth ravaged his throat. Blood sprayed, black in the mooncast dark. Ledron felt its warm splatter upon his face and brow. He searched for his sword, found it still gripped in his palm. As he looked up again, Demin's body was thrust aside, and the groll's baleful eyes fixed on him.

He'd have been dead before he could rise, but the others were already there, converging on the creature with ready blades. The groll hissed at them. It flared, seeming twice their size, then shrank into shadow as the swords began to bite. It was there, and yet it wasn't, a constantly shifting form almost too quick for the eye to follow.

Ledron scrambled to his feet, heart hammering. He tried not to look too closely at the flayed ruin of Demin's neck, the horror in his paralyzed gaze . . .

Another of his soldiers fell with a sharp cry. Otho. The Blackfist

dropped his weapon to hunker over his bloody wrist. Bite marks
pierced his flesh. Already, the venom sizzled through his veins, crawling toward his heart in darkening streams. His death would be painful,
yet quick.

"New moon!" Ledron commanded, and his Shadowguard responded with the desired formation. "Pin it to the forecastle!"

Their execution was flawless. Endless hours of drill had forged
movements instinctive and precise. Their courage and discipline
would not waver.

But the mutant recognized the tightening noose. It slashed and
lunged and circled with increasing desperation. Another Blackfist
crumpled, splintered leg bones protruding below the knee. The groll
pressed the breach. When a fellow guardian stepped forward to fill
it, the groll suddenly reversed direction, slipping instead toward
the starboard flank. Nethreal stood his ground, scoring a hit on the
mutant's shoulder.

The groll screeched, but tore its way free.

The Shadowguard shifted as one, mending the broken formation.
But they no longer had the shelf of the forecastle to serve as their
base wall. The groll backed across the ship's decking, gaining space.

"Redirect! Full press!"

Ledron himself anchored the charge. Already, the mutant's wound
was healing, its blood filling the gash and curing like mortar. Virgin
scales would cover the wound by daybreak. Were it to survive the
week, it would not even bear a scar.

Ledron was determined not to allow that. The mutant had surprised them, yes, but his regiment had been prepared for the possibility.
The mercenary's report had proven correct on all counts. And though
the creature before him represented his worst fears, he wasn't about
to let it plague his sleep another night.

The Blackfist to his left stumbled, gargling blood. Another, to his
right, pitched forward with a grunt. But his men were landing blows
now, as well. Ledron heard the hacks and pricks against the mutant's
scaled flesh, and relished the groll's snarling cries. It was difficult to
tell which of them held the upper hand.

Ledron feinted, then executed another thrust. The groll met his strike, slapping down against his blade. Ledron ducked, felt the swish of a clawed hand graze his naked skull, then drove forward with his dagger, plunging deep into meaty flesh.

The groll shrieked, bringing a fierce grin to Ledron's face.

His grin vanished as the mutant plucked the dagger from its gut and flung it back at its assailants. The blade found Fuldor's thigh and, smeared with the groll's venomous blood, marked the man's end.

Ledron growled and cursed. His muscles burned with exertion. His lungs strained. It was all he could to do hold his position, to refrain from flinching whenever the groll lashed out at him. If the creature was tiring, it showed no signs.

Finally, they pressed it from the shadows and into a patch of moon-light, where its mottled hide seemed to shimmer. Another step, and it was backed against the starboard rail. The ring of his remaining Shadowguard was at least three deep. The creature had nowhere to go.

It tossed its head, wailing in fury. A harpoon that must have come from the ship's own lockers pierced its side. The groll seized the shaft and tried to yank it free, but the barbed head hooked against its ribs. A pair of arrows, fired from atop the wheelhouse, struck it in the chest.

Again the groll roared, its all-too-human cries curdling Ledron's blood.

"Finish it!"

The first man to try had his arm snapped at the elbow and his body snatched forward to be used as a shield. An arrow pierced his stomach, while a friendly sword bit deep into his neck. The remaining Shadowguard hesitated but a breath—all the time that was needed for the groll to lean backward sharply over the rail.

Flinging Errahn's body overboard like an anchor, the mutant held fast, catapulting itself over the gunwale.

Ledron rushed forward, his Shadowguard beside him. The black waters rippled and sloshed, reflecting the dim gleam of starlight. He searched a moment longer, jaw clenched, then spun away in disgust.

"First team, all eyes! If it surfaces, kill it!"

He marched back across the deck, careful not to tread on the bodies of the slain. He took note: Demin, Otho, Hamric, Thoros, Fuldor, Errahn. And Inmon wasn't going anywhere on that splintered stump. Seven lost. Seven of his king's best, against a single adversary. If battle belowdecks had gone as poorly . . .

He caught sight of Jahant, emerging sweaty and winded from the central stair. Ledron lengthened his stride.

"Report."

His lieutenant saluted. "Fourteen renegades slain, Captain. All aboard, save our mole."

"Merrec put their number at a score."

"The weasel tells me Ulflund and four others went ashore already."

Ledron cursed. "And the princess?"

"Drugged, but whole. Trajan wards her now."

"Casualties?"

Jahant inspected a gash on his forearm, as if seeing it for the first time. "Three dead, sir, though Haeg is too stubborn to count himself among them. Half a dozen wounded, but not badly enough to slow us."

Ledron breathed deep, and his stomach roiled. It might have been the smell of carnage mingling with the fetor of the sea. Or it might have been that he had lost half a score—an entire squad—of the king's Shadowguard without achieving his full objective. Until Ulflund and his fellow renegades were brought to heel, they would remain a thorn underfoot. Had he at least been able to finish off the groll . . .

"Too many frayed edges," Ledron muttered.

There were shouts now from the docks. The clamor of their struggle would soon raise an alarm within the city—if it hadn't already. Though he had prepaid Wingport's authorities to have their watch turn a blind eye to this night's incursion, the wharf would soon be crawling with human vultures, come to catch a glimpse of the disturbance. Patrols would be dispatched to restore order. Ledron wished to be well away by then.

Percel approached. "Colven sends report. No trace of the Ukinh, sir."

If only that meant it were dead. His heart still drumming, Ledron took one last look around the moored vessel. "Form up. Three squads. Divergent routes through the city. We sail on the Sparrow's Hour. I want the dawn's light riding our wake."

Lᴇᴅʀᴏɴ's ɢᴀᴢᴇ swept the rutted street as he trudged along, senses alert to any approach. His hand gripped the pommel of his sword. The dockside roadway appeared empty in its westerly course. But then, so had the deck of Ulflund's ship, once they had shot the lone sentry hunkered in its crow's nest.

He did not relish having to report to his king that Ulflund had eluded him. And he could only imagine His Majesty's ire when it was confirmed that the rogue company that had made off with his daughter had consorted with a Ukinh. The king tolerated the mutants better than most, but only insofar as they kept to themselves.

Behind him, Nara moaned softly. Ledron turned at once, but found her still unconscious, bundled in her cloak and draped over Trajan's shoulder. The towering Blackfist gave a reassuring nod without breaking stride, which was good enough for Ledron. He cast a quick glance over the rest of his encircling squad. Their vigilant stares probed the night, weapons at the ready.

He reflected momentarily on the missing faces of Haeg and Inmon. As their captain, it had been his personal duty to dismiss them from service. Haeg had been defiant at first, but was eventually persuaded to let his wounds bleed out. Better that than waiting for the rot to claim him. Inmon stood a chance, given a successful amputation, but how long could a proud soldier bear life as a crippled outlander? A dagger across the throat had been the kinder end.

They knew the perils, Ledron thought, but with their final expressions etched in his mind, the sentiment rang hollow.

Ships in the harbor creaked and groaned as the slumbering ocean rose and fell in steady breaths. A nightbird cried as it dove from its roost, toward a flash of sea life in the waves below. Ledron could not wait to be away from this foreign land. A small continent, no larger than their own, yet said to bear forty times the population. To the north, climbing the slopes that overlooked the southside harbor, watchfires burned in hundreds, perhaps thousands, of windows and streetlamps. Hearthfire smoke sullied the skies, like a permanent stain of soot. In the heavens above this sprawling city, he could scarcely see the stars.

His focus shifted as they approached an alley between a pair of shops shuttered for the night. A diminutive figure, fully hooded, emerged from the shadowed crease. The stranger took two steps before flashing a quick light signal from a tiny mirror. He took two more steps, paused to hold both arms out wide, then crossed them over his chest. Percel, serving point on the near flank, signaled in return. Bows were lowered, and their man approached.

"I was wondering when you meant to rejoin us," Ledron extended grimly, nodding for the newcomer to fall into place. "You've disappointed me, Sallun."

The fresh-faced youth looked up in surprise. "Sir?"

"Tell him, Merrec."

Merrec grinned his gold-toothed smile. "Seems a handful of rats slipped right under your nose . . . led by Ulflund himself."

Ledron frowned at Merrec's smugness. Did the betrayer fancy himself a hero in this?

Sallun turned to Ledron in horror.

"Did you know of this?" Ledron asked him.

"No! Sir, no. I . . . I sent word as soon as they arrived, and kept sharp watch—"

"A blind lookout, then," Merrec snickered.

Ledron bristled, but would deal with that one later. "You are only as good to me as your eyes," he admonished Sallun, all but affirming Merrec's assessment. "Fail me again, and I'll have them plucked from your skull by a flock of starving crows."

"Yes, Captain."

The youth fell back, a step behind Trajan in the center of their company. In truth, Ledron wasn't as sore as he pretended. Ulflund was a snake, when he needed to be. It was said he could slither through a cornfield without bending a stalk. An exaggeration, surely, but one who failed to learn stealth did not long serve as Ulflund had in his earliest patrol days, hunting Ukinha along the borders of their wilderness. Had he wanted to go ashore unseen, then he—and those who followed him—would have done so, no matter how many eyes

Ledron had set upon them.

Thankfully, the former Shadowguard captain had chosen not to take the princess with him, else Ledron and his men would still be hunting for her now. Most likely, Ulflund had scouted ahead to secure whatever arrangements he had plotted for her ashore. Ledron wondered if, by now, Ulflund had returned to his vessel to learn that his prize was gone.

"How much farther is our ship?" Merrec asked.

Ledron hissed at him to be silent—if only because it grated on him to hear the conspirator's voice. *Our* ship? The rat's greed had aided them in their rescue of the princess, yes. But Ledron was a lifelong soldier, and didn't like sharing air with those he knew he couldn't trust.

"I was to receive payment the moment the princess was safely in hand," Merrec groused.

"You're fortunate the king's command wasn't to flay you on sight." Had the scoundrel truly wished to serve, he'd have given word of the plot before Nara had departed their shores. Instead, he had left his warning via courier, selling out Ulflund's crew after the fact. He had claimed in his message that it was too late to marshal a proper pursuit, and that he was setting sail with the other renegades in order to oversee the princess's safety. But if that were so, why demand payment for his service? "You'll have your gold," Ledron promised, "because His Majesty is a man of his word. But not before *I* deem Her Highness to be safe."

Merrec scowled, yet must have realized what little room he had to argue. Indeed, this opportunistic parlay of his would never have worked with a less honorable lord—or if His Majesty Kendarrion hadn't wished to interrogate the mercenary about these dealings personally. Merrec had to know that he would be relieved of his commission in the king's army and made outcast the moment he collected his reward. But even that was better than he deserved.

The mercenary's sullen silence caused Ledron to brighten inwardly. Despite their losses, the many loose ends, and the long voyage that lay ahead, they had in fact achieved the first phase of their mission. With Nara's safe retrieval, they had what was most important to their king. All else, he assured himself, was mere seasoning.

The winds shifted, blowing into their faces from the west. Briny gusts gave way to a thickening taste of smoke. Ledron coughed and spat. He could not leave these polluted shores quickly enough. He hastened pace. Without command, his Shadowguard did so alongside.

A strange crackle grew in his ears, overtaking the murmurs of the sea. To the west, around a rugged promontory, an orange light began to rise. Without quite knowing why, Ledron felt his confidence slip.

There were shouts now, as well, echoing from the area of their destination. The unknown crackle grew louder, and with it, the reddish orange halo strengthened, risen up from where an evening sun would normally set.

At last, their road rounded the promontory, bending northward. Through curtains of black smoke, Ledron gazed down upon the wharf with sickening realization.

The harbor before them was astir, its docks swarming with men. Flames lit the sky, devouring sails and rigging and racing with an angry roar up the masts of a clutch of moored ships. At the heart of the blaze, a great bark listed to one side. Its masthead—an image of his queen riding a pod of dolphins—shimmered in a veil of heat.

Lytherial's Chariot.

Despite the efforts of the harbor patrols, the ship would not be saved. Nor did Ledron need to see the bodies to know that all left aboard had been killed. The groll had wasted no time in striking back at them. *Else Ulflund and his rogues,* Ledron thought, but did not believe that to be possible. Only the Ukinh could have sniffed out their vessel this quickly, and wrought such destruction upon it.

It scarcely mattered, the one or the other. The result was the same. Without their ship, they were stranded.

"What now, Captain?" Trajan prompted.

Ledron only shook his head, eyes tearing amid the smoke and cinders as he watched his king's ship burn to its hull upon the shoreline of this forsaken land.

1

"What's your name, lad?"

"Rydan."

"And what sailing experience do you have, Rydan?"

"Little of note, sir," he replied honestly.

"Meaning none whatsoever."

"No, sir. But I work hard, will serve as commanded . . . and I do have skills."

"Oh? What sort of skills would those be?"

Rydan glanced around at the handful of seamen bustling about the harbormaster's office. This one, he sensed, was mocking him. And he didn't want to let one man's amusement ruin his chances with the others, even if this one *was* the captain of his own ship.

"I'm good at hunting rats," Rydan said finally.

The captain smiled. "Let's see your palms."

Rydan showed him.

"You've got some healthy calluses, I grant you. But you'd find that ship rats are much sprier than your fattened sewer rats, lad. Besides, I already got me more rat-chasers than I can feed. Most of them'll be eating only what they can catch."

The captain turned away, back to his ledger.

"I may not look it, sir, but I've a fair hand with the knives. I could peel potatoes, skin a fish, or drop a pirate at twenty paces."

"I'm sure you could." The captain smiled benignly, yet without looking up from his paperwork. "Luck to you lad, but I've business to finish here."

Despite his condescending tone, he remained the best lead Rydan had come across in three days of search. He was considering how to press further when one of the clerks drew up behind him.

"The master wishes to see you," the clerk drawled.

Finding *himself* the target of the newcomer's attention, Rydan bridled his surprise. The harbormaster? He noted the clerk's stern face and cross-armed stance. "Did he say why?"

"I'm to show you to him, or show you out."

He mulled it over. Though he might come to regret it, an audience with the city's harbormaster might be exactly the opportunity he was seeking. He glanced once more at the captain before turning back to the clerk. "As he wishes."

The clerk led him past the main service counter and through a door beyond. A narrow flight of wooden steps carried them upstairs. There they followed a hall flanked on one side with offices, and papered on the other with maps and charts and schedules that Rydan could scarcely begin to decipher. Upon reaching the fourth and final office door, the clerk knocked. A resonant voice from within bade them enter.

The harbormaster's desk was perhaps large enough to be oceanworthy itself. But if so, its cargo of scrolls and tomes could have weighed it down to the sea floor. When its would-be captain looked up, his hunch-shouldered bulk was all but blocked from view.

"The boy I spoke of," said the clerk.

The man behind the desk squinted hard at Rydan, as if attempting to recognize his grubby face. Or perhaps the old master was merely going blind from his work. Whether rolled, bound, tied, or left loose, it flooded the windowless room, filling the full-length shelves and cubbies that encircled the walls, and spilling out into stacks upon the floor.

After a moment, the harbormaster dismissed his clerk with a wave.

"I'm told you've been pestering my patrons for three days now.

What's your story?"

Rydan shrugged. "No story, sir. Just looking to move on from these shores."

"You've no parents? No kin? How old *are* you, boy?"

He replied deliberately, careful to match the other's more proper style of speech. "I was spring-born, or so I'm told. Drawing near my seventeenth. As to family, I cannot be certain."

"Victims of the war?"

"Not that I know of, sir. Been on my own for almost four years now."

The harbormaster frowned. "Hailing from?"

"Partha, sir."

"Then here is your story. Your father was a soldier-in-training, freshly conscripted from the southern borderlands. That way, he could've been killed by the dragonspawn 'fore his name and rank were officially registered. You lost him at Dirrk, let's say. Or perhaps Crylag. You take this story to the local ministry of war orphans, here in Wingport," he continued, scribbling something on a scrap of parchment. "They may end up transferring you, possibly all the way to Atharvan. But at least you will be cared for and given a chance at a fair future." When finished scribbling, he looked up and extended the parchment.

Rydan remained where he stood. "But sir, I'm not looking to go home. I want to try a life at sea."

"From which I would spare you, if I can. The sea takes more'n she gives—that I promise. Especially from boys your age, who fancy themselves invincible." He shook the parchment. "Try this first. If in a few years you haven't settled into a life that pleases you, maybe then you scratch your sea itch. She ain't going nowhere, I assure you."

Rydan reluctantly stepped forward, all the while trying to measure the old harbormaster's true intent. He reached up over a stack of papers and took the one offered him, which bore crude directions to the aforementioned orphan ministry. "If you'll pardon the observation, sir, you appear a busy man. Why interest yourself in my affairs?"

"Truth be told, I was hoping you were someone else. But as long as you're here . . ." He fiddled with his quill as his pause lengthened, his squinted stare becoming momentarily distant. "Let's just say I've paid to that fathomless deep more'n my share, and count myself richer every time I can deprive her of another young soul."

There was a tale here, but Rydan wasn't inclined to seek it. "I'm sorry for your losses. But supposing I had my will set, is there any chance—"

"Winter's peak draws nigh," the old master snapped, his visage souring. "The sailing season is at its ebb. Captains have their pick of the roster, and any man who would take you over an experienced seaman is someone you'd best avoid."

Rydan looked to the floor, making his disappointment plain. After three days, he'd heard some form of this refrain more times than he cared to count.

"Cry if you must, lad, and curse me if it helps. But I'll not try to wedge you into a circumstance you—and surely I—may come to regret. Try your luck at the ministry. Give this other aim a rest at least until the high season."

"Thank you for your counsel, sir. Your concerns are most kind."

He turned to leave, pausing as the harbormaster's words caught him at the door. "Whatever you do, stop begging 'round these offices. Some trolling slaver is liable to lure you in and snatch you up."

Rydan nodded glumly, hopeful yet that the obvious softness of the man's heart would warm through his crusty exterior. Glancing back, however, he saw that the harbormaster had already returned to work.

Never one to foster disenchantment, Rydan shook his head at the encounter and started down the hall. Wingport was a large city. An opportunity was bound to turn up—and long before the summer season.

He slowed as a cloaked figure crested the stair and turned toward him. The figure shied to one side as it passed Rydan and shuffled on, continuing to the harbormaster's office with hood drawn. Made curious by the newcomer's secretive manner, Rydan hesitated at the top of the stair, then crept back down the hall in pursuit.

The door closed, but Rydan heard clearly the harbormaster's voice within.

" . . . this conversation yesterday, did we not?"

"And the day before that." The response was quiet, but Rydan's ears were keen. "Yet my captain wishes to know what progress has been made."

"Your vessel is being prepared as quickly as possible. You can tell your captain—"

"It's been half a week already. I fear I'm festering in that diseased pit, waiting for your man to contact me."

"Your man chose the place, not mine. My page will have to burn his shoes upon return."

"We've paid a princely sum, as you'll recall."

"Which is why you've found a ship at all—particularly given your long list of demands. What you ask for cannot be conjured from driftwood and seaweed."

"My benefactor—"

"May be the only king on his isle, but 'round here, they ain't so rare. I've my own to answer to—not to mention that spineless carp of a city governor." There was a moment's pause in which the harbormaster muttered unintelligibly, likely to himself. "When your ship is ready, I'll send word."

"Can you at least—"

"Buzzing 'round my ear ain't going to speed things along. So unless you have some further request I must see to, I suggest we conclude this conversation here and now."

By comparison, Rydan's own chat seemed now to have gone rather well. Whoever this stranger was, he was out of his element, as evidenced by his cowed silence. A moment later, the door opened. Rydan ducked into the adjacent office—a darkened storage room crammed with even more paper. Crouched within the shadows, he watched the hooded stranger slink sullenly down the hall.

Out of his element, but not without means. *A princely sum,* he'd said, to commission a ship for a royal benefactor hailing from foreign shores.

When the stranger had reached the stair, Rydan set forth, trailing the scent of opportunity.

He didn't have to travel far.

Wending a narrow, back-alley path, Rydan tracked the mysterious messenger's steps west and north to a nearby dungeon of a tavern—rooted at sewer level beneath the cracked foundation of a derelict slaughterhouse. It was the kind of place even rats avoided, stinking of spoiled ale, rancid meat, old vomit . . . and the befouled spirits of men whose only far-reaching goal was to scrape, beg, or steal enough coin for their next mug. Gazing down the crudely chiseled steps at the dank hole of a doorway, Rydan questioned the necessity of persisting along this course. With curiosity overruling caution, he mustered a deep breath and descended.

His first observation was of the grease-stained barkeep staring at the hooded stranger as the latter claimed a corner table to the right of entry. After a moment of lingering scrutiny, the barkeep nodded at another patron, seated at the bar, who promptly headed for the exit. He sidestepped Rydan on his way out, eyes lit with a feral gleam. Rydan drew a mental portrait of the patron's pocked face, then headed toward the abandoned barstool.

"Back again, are we?" the barkeep asked, and Rydan was unsurprised to see him addressing the skulking messenger. "You actually gonna buy something today?"

Skulks dropped a coin onto the table. "Just the usual."

The barkeep shook his head, chuckling. "Something on the house, then. You've already paid me thrice over what that table is worth."

A toothless drunkard was slumped over the left end of the bar in drooling, openmouthed slumber. A dog lay curled at his feet, trying to sleep even as it clawed at its patchy, flea-ridden coat. Aside from that, Rydan noted, the tavern was empty. He'd be surprised if it could hold a score—and shocked if it ever drew half that.

"I don't need your swill," Skulks assured the barkeep. Despite the harsh words, his voice bore the softness of youth. "Just a corner undisturbed."

Again the barkeep chuckled. "This be the place, then." He turned to Rydan. "What about you, boy? Got any coin stuffed in those rags of yours?"

"Enough for an ale, I should hope. Or maybe I'll just finish this one," Rydan said, peering into the mug left half full by the departed patron.

The barkeep scowled, casting a reflexive glance at Skulks. Just as quick, he forced his grin to return. "Sure. Special for the day. Half drinks at half price."

"But this one's warm."

"Street rat like you wouldn't know what a cold one tasted like. What makes you think to learn here?"

Rydan smirked sourly at the gibe, looking properly abashed as he fished an ivory knuckle from his pockets and let it clatter atop the bar.

"Ha! See? Barely enough to top you off."

As the barkeep filled Rydan's mug from the nearest keg, the slumbering drunkard stirred. His blinking eyes, red and swollen, opened on Rydan's ivory, as if he'd been wakened by its telltale sound.

"Got another of those?" the drunkard wheezed.

Rydan looked at the man's dog, which yawned and stretched at the sound of its master's voice. "Mayhap. Have you something to offer?"

The barkeep chuckled anew as he delivered Rydan's drink and pocketed his payment.

The drunkard, meanwhile, grinned wide and scooted near. "The latest word. Tidings most foul and dangerous. A warning to those wise enough to heed it."

Despite an odorous breath, Rydan couldn't help but smile at the rumormonger's theatrics. "Are you peddling whispers or ravings?"

"'Tis my trade to sift truth from falsehood, and my solemn oath to never sell one for the other. A wise man does not pay twice for deceit."

If wealth was the measure of his success, then, judging by his appearance, the man was no master of his craft. Of course, Rydan knew as well as anyone that appearances were often deceiving. "So give me a taste. What does this fell warning entail?"

The beggar consulted his dog, which looked up and scratched itself. "Elves," he rasped, "spotted in the mountains."

"What sort of elves?"

"Ghastly ones, with faces all black and shriveled."

The dog whimpered. Rydan frowned, skeptical.

"Goblins, too."

"Goblins?" Rydan laughed and took a drink. "Next, you'll be telling me you believe in dragons."

"'Course I do . . . though not no more. That Allion and Kylac went and killed the last. 'Less you're talking the 'spawn, but they died off when the big one did. Turned to dust, I hear."

Boulders, according to the witnesses Rydan had encountered. But it wasn't worth correcting. The beggar's tale had more of the truth than most.

The barkeep stepped away, moving off to collect the coin from Skulks's table. The young stranger, his cowl still drawn, said nothing.

Rydan spoke to him. "What say you, friend? Should I give ear to this beggar's chatter?"

"Save your coin," Skulks responded. "He speaks the same gibberish everyone on these shores is talking."

"*These* shores. Then you're an outlander?"

"Mind your drink, *friend*."

"Must be an outlander yourself," the barkeep surmised, "if you ain't heard the tale of the dragon-slayers."

"Maybe I have. Maybe I just wanted to hear *him* tell it."

"Fine, so pay Dareth here his knuckle and quit baiting him."

Rydan looked from the frowning barkeep to the grinning drunkard, Dareth. "But I haven't decided which story to hear yet."

"Would you hear tell of King Torin and his quest for the Crimson Sword?" Dareth asked.

"Bah. I could probably tell that one myself, heard it so many times. Didn't think much of it from the first."

The dog gave a loud yip, forcing Rydan to meet its indignant stare. Evidently, the little mongrel favored that particular tale.

"What I really enjoy," Rydan continued, raising his voice so Skulks could hear, "are adventures set at sea." He shifted his gaze to the messenger's corner. "Pardon my interest, sir, but which land are *you* from?"

The question met with silence.

"Sir?"

"A land where others know how to leave a man be."

"Prefers his solitude, boy," the barkeep interjected, "and has paid for the privilege. Pester off, or get out."

Rydan bit the inside of his cheek. It seemed he would need a new strategy if he was to crack this one's shell. Fortunately, his quarry was anchored to this hole for the time being, given what Rydan had overheard in the harbormaster's office.

"All right," he said, turning to Dareth with the promised ivory, "tell me more of your elves and goblins."

"Ghosts of the ancient dead, some say," Dareth replied, snatching up the piece and reaching down to pet his dog's head. The animal licked his fingers, panting with excitement. "But what ghost still wears its skin? Alive, they are, with flesh and movement, but in the ragged state of rotted death."

"Oh? And where do these walking corpses hail from?"

"From the east, they says. Killangrathor's revenge, or Spithaera's. For dragons and demons cannot truly be killed. They merely change form."

"Is that so?"

"True as I'm sitting before you, the threat to Pentania has only just begun. It is all part of the great purge, in which this land will be scoured of man and returned to the races of old."

Rydan took another drink. *Creative,* he thought. But then, the wilder the imaginings, the more attention they drew. He wondered if the beggar had conceived these ills on his own, or if he was merely echoing the lunacy of others.

"The boy hears, but he doesn't listen," Dareth said to his dog. The pathetic creature wagged its tail and then looked at Rydan, issuing a low growl.

"Or perhaps I'm just thinking we should leave this cursed land before it's too late."

"Running from one trouble often puts us in the path of another."

Rydan smiled and raised his mug in salute. "Then let them come, and we shall weather them as best we may."

He was about to drink to his own words when he saw the barkeep stiffen and lower the tankard he'd been cleaning. Rydan felt a twinge at the nape of his neck as a shadow stole the light from the open doorway at his back. Heavy footsteps struck the tavern floor—first one pair, then another—with the telltale thud of armor.

The barkeep tossed his head to one side, pointing out Skulks to the new arrivals. Rydan half turned, peering over his right shoulder. Of thick build these two, wrapped in heavy cloaks, hands perched on the pommels of their swords. One was dark-haired, the other fair. Aside from that, they might have been brothers, with their jutting chins, stubbled beards, and a similar assortment of nicks and scars marring their weathered faces.

"Sallun," the dark-haired one addressed Skulks. "Is that you?"

Skulks froze, a deer reacting to the snap of a twig beneath the huntsman's boot.

"Ah, I thought so."

Sallun remained stricken, poised to flee, but the only exit lay behind the two swordsmen.

"Come, my friend, this don't have to hurt."

The silent, fair-haired brute drew his sword halfway from its sheath. Both weapon and mail were well worn, but of serviceable quality.

The dog barked once, then growled. Dareth plucked it from the floor and shied back to his own corner, holding the animal close. The barkeep sought similar refuge behind his counter. Rydan hunkered in his seat.

"The captain's patience grows short," the dark-haired thug continued. Clearly the voice of the pair. "Were I you, I'd not keep him waiting."

"Ulflund no longer commands the Shadowguard," Sallun managed defiantly.

"Giving us leave to slit your throat without reprimand," the thug countered. "Wait for Grathe to draw his blade, and I daresay he'll be sheathing it wet. Or have you forgotten the report of yours that sent him to the stocks for three days?"

"Followed by a week of pig's rations," the fair-haired brute—Grathe—added.

Sallun's fear was palpable, but he held it in check, refusing to rise. His cowl shifted ever so slightly, and Rydan imagined the cornered man's gaze flitting about, seeking escape.

Grathe stepped forward suddenly, sword rasping another hand's breadth from its scabbard. Sallun snapped to his feet, backing against the tavern wall.

"Just a chat, now," the unnamed thug promised. "You'll see."

He strode ahead until he stood shoulders above the diminutive Sallun, then reached out and seized the younger man by the meat of his arm. Sallun gasped and stiffened further, but made no attempt to pull away.

Grathe sneered.

"Come," the lead thug urged, almost gently. With a firm grasp, he coaxed Sallun from the corner.

Rydan thought he caught a glint of the desperation in Sallun's eye as he was guided toward the open doorway. Grathe assumed a rearguard position, casting warning glances at the tavern's remaining occupants. The dog barked once more as Grathe backed through the exit. Grathe bared his teeth in response.

When the three had gone, an uncomfortable silence settled over the tiny tavern. Rydan peered up at the barkeep.

"What was that about?" he asked.

"How should I know?"

"Thought he paid well enough not to be disturbed."

"Don't know what you're talking about, boy. And neither do you."

"As you say," Rydan allowed, looking at his shared mug as evidence to the contrary.

The barkeep's scowl became threatening. Rydan turned and hopped from his stool. It scarcely mattered, what this one might admit to. If need be, he could return to question the greasy toad later. As dangerous as it might seem, the truth could be found just as easily by following events as they unfolded. No sense in missing the action.

"Take the stranger's advice, boy," the barkeep called after him. "Leave him be."

Dareth's dog yipped.

"Just need some air," Rydan said, and stepped out in search of Sallun and his friends.

2

THE ALLEYWAY VEERED NORTH another thirty or forty paces, but Grathe and his fellow ruffian cut off well before that into a side alley branching west. Rydan raced after, only to pause and peer cautiously around the bend. Rash, he might be, but not foolish.

The new alley proved to be a dead-end stub, little more than a niche between the sagging structures to either side. Though wider than the parent alley, its crumbling rear wall lay less than ten paces away, heaped high with refuse. Three more men awaited, armed like the two that had snatched Sallun. Of the three, one stood front and center, flanked by his comrades as he stepped forward to meet the new arrivals. Rydan pegged him the leader of this crew.

The leader regarded Sallun bluntly. "Where is she?"

His words met with silence.

"Torman and Grathe will tear your arms from their sockets if I have to ask again."

As if to validate the threat, the pair of thugs handling Sallun shook him roughly. Grathe kicked the back of his legs, dropping him to his knees, while the dark-haired Torman yanked the hood from his head.

"She's safe," Sallun sputtered. "No debt to *you*."

"And where is Ledron keeping her?"

"Have you no honor? His Majesty will have your head."

Torman dropped low, wrenching one of Sallun's arms painfully behind his back. He bent to whisper in the youth's ear. "I told you this don't have to hurt, but it *will* if you don't answer the captain's questions."

Ulflund, Sallun had named him—this captain who no longer commanded the so-called Shadowguard.

"Better that than defy my king and break my oath," Sallun said, grimacing.

A dagger rasped from Torman's sheath to lie against the young man's throat.

"Do not confuse bravery with foolishness," Ulflund said. "Would you have me give you over to the mutant?"

Sallun held his breath, clenching with renewed alarm.

"Best you answer me now, don't you think?"

Rydan had witnessed enough. Completing his study of the cramped, filthy ground, he cleared the corner and strode into view at Sallun's back.

Ulflund and those flanking him looked up at once. Following their gazes, Torman and Grathe turned their heads.

"Move along, rat," Ulflund snapped. "This ain't your hole."

"Is it yours, then? Bit small for the six of you, I'd say."

Grathe sneered, eyes narrowing in recognition. "You was in the tavern."

Despite the blade tickling his throat, Sallun turned his own head now, fearful eyes growing wider with surprise.

Rydan met his gaze. "You never told me where you're from . . . or where you're headed."

"Bugger off, boy," Grathe snapped.

"The name's Rydan. The young sir and I were having a pleasant enough chat before you came and interrupted. Were we not?"

Sallun squinted in confusion.

"Were we not? Tell 'em."

"Yeah. Sure." Sallun swallowed and nodded. "Sea stories, was it?"

"It will have to wait, boy," Ulflund said. "Our mutual friend here has more pressing business at present."

"Name's Rydan," he repeated. To Torman, he added, "You ain't

going to cut his throat before he answers your question, so you might
as well lower the blade."

"Boy—"

"*Rydan.*" He focused on Sallun. "Your friends don't hear too good—
do they."

"Rydan, then," Ulflund allowed. "I don't know what game you're
playing, but you'd best carry it elsewhere before I lose my patience."

"Game? A simple one, really. Sallun here was going to offer me a
ride on his ship, but only if I agreed to dispatch any ruffians come
to harass him."

The nameless thugs flanking Ulflund sniggered, while Ulflund
himself cracked a smile. Grathe smirked. Torman frowned, wary.

"Is that so?" the renegade captain asked. "Sallun? Is this beardless
lad your warder?"

While the others laughed, Sallun gaped at Rydan, glanced at
Ulflund, then looked back at Rydan.

"Well, then, perhaps *he* has the answer to my questions," said
Ulflund, who then nodded at Torman.

Torman's blade pressed Sallun's throat.

"The boy knows nothing," Sallun gasped. "He's foaming mad, is
all."

"Mad or not, I'll have your pledge," Rydan said, picking at the dirt
beneath a fingernail. He stopped to face Sallun squarely. "I relieve
you of these thugs, you guarantee me a place on your ship."

Sallun remained pinned by Rydan's gaze, unable to turn his head
now without slicing his own neck. There was confusion in his eyes,
a flicker of desperate hope warring with the same scoffing disbelief
that clouded the faces of the others. More than anything, however,
Rydan recognized an overwhelming sense of helplessness, leading to
the only response Sallun could truly give.

"Yes. Yes, of course." The captive man gulped.

"On your oath?"

"You have my word."

"There," Rydan said, as if the matter had been settled. "You all
heard it. So I reckon you should be on your way."

Again the incredulous laughter, louder and harsher this time. Even

Torman shook his head in wry amusement.

"Last chance to scurry off, *boy*, before I have Grathe do it for you."

Grathe grinned.

"Him? Doubt he could chase a fish into water."

The grin vanished. Grathe looked to his captain, who nodded.

Leaving Sallun in Torman's clutches, the fair-haired brute stalked toward him. "Hope your feet are as fast as your tongue, boy."

But Rydan had no intention of running. His blood began to tingle, the familiar euphoria creeping over him.

It took a moment longer for Grathe to realize that threats were not going to cow him. When understanding finally struck, the brute frowned, then lunged ahead with a low growl, fist leading. Rydan caught it with fluid calm, seizing the thick wrist and twisting the arm inward. Elbow and shoulder went up, and Grathe cried out, his body forced low and to the side as his palm was bent forcefully back toward him.

The ruffian winced and squirmed, but Rydan's hold was secure. Unless he was willing to break his own wrist, Grathe wasn't going anywhere.

The pair flanking Ulflund took a reflexive step forward, smiles forgotten. The captain held them back, but must have seen or sensed something that concerned him, for he let them go just as quickly.

"Bring the runt to me," he commanded.

They came on in split formation. Like Grathe, their movement showed them to be skilled fighters. Grathe had simply underestimated him. These two weren't likely to do the same.

When they converged on him, they did so simultaneously. One attacked from the front, the other from behind. The front man came high, looking to break his hold on Grathe, while the rear man went low, no doubt thinking to take his legs from beneath him.

Rydan reverse pivoted to his left. The shift forced Grathe back, creating a shield against the rear assailant. Meanwhile, Rydan threw an elbow to deflect the forward attack, following with an inside kick to the man's calf. By the time the front man hit the ground with a sprained knee, Rydan had spun a half circuit in order to place a pair of kicks to the rear man's face—all without relinquishing his hold on Grathe.

The soldiers looked up at him from the ground, eyes wide with astonishment as they checked their wounds. Grathe hissed and snarled, but remained paralyzed with pain. A glance at Torman saw him turning to his captain, who now gritted his teeth.

"Cut this rat off of me!" Grathe pleaded, enraged.

The rear man was the first to draw weapon—a dagger. The front man trumped him by drawing his longsword.

"I'd leave the blades out of this," Rydan cautioned, "lest bruises give way to wounds more grievous."

The dagger struck first, aimed to take a bite of his kidney. Rydan sidestepped that lunge, then hopped a hamstring swipe from the swordsman. He threw a side kick as his feet came down, catching the swordsman square in the chest and sending the man stumbling back in search of breath. He let go of Grathe then, who instinctively straightened by rolling right. The shift broke another charge from the dagger wielder, whose weapon arm was left exposed. With a strike and a twist, Rydan sent the dagger clattering to the ground. A foot sweep sent it skittering away.

Grathe was the first to reengage, roaring as his own dagger slid free, gripped in his left hand. The man was seasoned enough not to go for his sword, which he would have been lucky to heft with his strained wrist. His dagger strike, however, was hurried and therefore off the mark. Rydan did not even have to dodge before kicking him in the chin, which also forced the previous dagger wielder to fall back toward the mouth of the alley, where he too was now incensed enough to go for his sword.

"Last chance, Captain," Rydan called out to Ulflund. "Leash your dogs before they hurt themselves."

But it had gone too far for that. Rydan was familiar with the looks now aimed his way. These men's pride had been damaged, an affront much less forgivable than any physical injury.

"Shadowguard!" Ulflund snapped. His voice arrested the men where they stood. For a moment, Rydan thought he might call them back. Instead, he stepped forward, seized Sallun by his cloak, and flung the speechless young man back toward the rear of the alley, where he would be hemmed in. The captain then drew his own sword and nodded for Torman to do the same. "We bleed this whelp," he continued, glaring at Rydan.

Inwardly, Rydan sighed. He would have preferred it hadn't come to this.

Then why provoke them as you did? a voice within him demanded.

"Fair enough," he replied aloud. So maybe he *had* goaded them. But it wasn't as if he hadn't given them ample warning.

Being the only one unarmed among the Shadowguard, Grathe circled around to where the first man to draw a sword handed him a new dagger. Rydan let him go. He would let them make the first move, and thereby allay his sometimes troublesome conscience.

The five men, blades ready, formed a closing circle. Rydan knew the routine. Really no different than that used by village huntsmen to skewer wild boar. In combat, simpler was usually better, and against any normal adversary, there was no reason to anticipate failure. One pair would hold his attention. The other would drive in from his blind spots. Grathe, with his shorter blade and damaged wrist, would stand ready to make sure he didn't slip the noose. The remaining four would strike low and hard and fast.

Rydan crouched deep, focused on Ulflund. The rest would await their captain's signal. Their hungry swords were nearly within reach.

Ulflund gave a slight nod to those behind him. He needn't have bothered. The drawback of his driving sword arm signaled the impending lunge. Rydan sprang, flipping up and back. The blades missed him, stabbing at empty air. He came down on the outstretched arms of the two behind him. His weight unbalanced them. One—Torman— found his blade pinned to the ground by Rydan's foot. The other lost his grip entirely. Rydan punched this one in the throat, then spun behind him and shoved him forward.

The first man to draw his sword was also the first to see it covered in blood, as his second thrust missed Rydan and slipped into his own comrade's stomach.

Rydan was still moving, snatching Torman's dagger from its sheath. Torman felt him at his back and whipped his sword around in a low arc. Rydan leapt the blow and slashed an "X" in Torman's throat.

He vaulted to the side then, as Ulflund swept in. The overhead strike would have cleaved his collarbone, except Rydan was no longer there. Using the alley wall as a springboard, he leapt up and over the captain's shoulder. Ulflund was quick enough to execute a reverse lunge, but Rydan leaned left to avoid the blade, then used his borrowed dagger to sever the tendons of the captain's wrist.

While Ulflund grunted and hunched over his wound, Grathe dove in like a rabid dog. Rydan parried the brute's dagger and spun around to bury his own in the back of Grathe's neck.

He left the borrowed blade there, for the lone uninjured swordsman had finally drawn his weapon from the belly of his companion and now brought it to bear. Rydan was quicker, diving in to attack the man's sword arm with a flurry of openhanded, forearm strikes. The third sent the man's elbow buckling toward the sky. He howled and dropped his sword, which Rydan caught by the hilt before the tip could scratch the ground.

Rydan ducked low, for Ulflund had reengaged with a left-handed dagger thrust, his bloody sword hand clutched protectively close. Spinning behind the soldier with the dislocated elbow, Rydan once again had himself a human shield. Instead of shoving this one forward, Rydan held him close so that Ulflund had to raise his dagger high, arcing over the other's shoulder to reach him.

Rydan shoved his sword clear through his shield's back and into Ulflund's stomach, impaling both together.

He let them fall, watching the blood bubble from their mouths and the light fade from their eyes. Their faces, like those of so many others, contorted through an emotional array of shock and agony before settling upon useless denial.

As he cast about to confirm that none of the five would rise, Rydan felt a chill drape about his shoulders. He looked skyward at once, toward the source of the sensation. Upon the north rooftop, he detected a whisper of movement, accompanied by the scratch of claws. By the time he blinked, it was gone.

He turned away, then glanced back again to be sure. But the chill had passed. Whatever had seen him had moved on.

He shifted his attention to Sallun, who crouched against the alley's rear wall with an expression of utter amazement.

"Are there any more after you?" Rydan asked him.

Sallun gaped.

"Either way, best not to remain here. Wouldn't return to that tavern either, if I were you. Got anyplace else to go?"

"You . . . you killed them. You killed them all."

"Seems that way. Care to tell me who they were?"

Sallun only managed to stare at the bodies.

"All right. Later then." He stepped toward the startled young man, who recoiled at his approach. "Come. This corner smells worse than a dragon's den, and when the sun hits these corpses, it'll only get worse."

Sallun seemed at first not to hear him, until he echoed, "Dragon?"

Then his eyes—wide already—opened further with lid-stretching realization. "Your name isn't Rydan—is it."

"No," Kylac admitted. "It's not."

3

He'd put off using his real name, Kylac explained as he accompanied Sallun though the streets, because his own drew far too much attention these days—ever since that little affair in the mountains.

"The dragon," Sallun marveled. "You killed it. Just like they're saying."

"Would that I had. Most I can says for Allion and I is that we *confronted* the beast. Seems enough to make every minstrel in the land sing our praises."

To go unnoticed, he'd even started minding the way he spoke, mimicking the local accents instead of using his own. After a few weeks, the stiffer, more formal dialect almost felt natural.

He couldn't wait to shed it.

"Are the rest of this land's tales true?" Sallun pressed. "The sword of fire? The queen of demons? The armies of dragonspawn?"

"Depends on the telling, I'd reckon. Though I'll wager more's true than any sane man'd like to believe."

"You're a hero in some accounts, a god in the rest. Some suggest this woodsman-king owes you his kingdom at the very least."

"Bah. Torin himself likely started that one. Lad won't claim the merit he deserves." Kylac looked at Sallun. "Your point?"

"The people call down blessed graces whenever your name is uttered.

You could rule this island, if you wished. Why leave?"

Kylac shrugged. "Already got more graces than I knows what to do with. Why let 'em go to rot in some drafty castle?"

That put a stop to the questions for a time, as they continued to slip through the wharfside district en route to a promised meeting with Sallun's captain. Just another pair of wretched dock maggots they must have appeared, sprung up to feed on the rotting underbelly of Pentania's greatest port city. Kylac had spent a week here already, following three weeks of mostly aimless travel through Kuuria, and had tasted his fill of Wingport itself. Had he known just how difficult it would be to secure passage at sea, he might have tarried at Krynwall as Torin, Allion, and Marisha had begged. But a week in Alson's tumbledown capital had left him anxious for sport. He'd also wanted a firsthand look at the devastation wrought against Morethil and Souaris by the dragonspawn—a struggle he'd missed due to his own scrap with Killangrathor—while the scars of those conflicts were fresh. After that, he'd followed his itch south, having seen all he cared to, and wondering what the lands beyond might have to offer.

"Is it true you were raised an assassin?" Sallun asked.

Kylac wrinkled his nose as they neared a warehouse, from which the rank smell of fish permeated the air. "If'n we're going to explore every rumor on the wind, ya'd best be willing to tells me more 'bout your business here, first."

The young man proved suddenly tight-lipped. "I think it better that my captain explain."

"Have ya something to hide?"

"We still have enemies on the loose," Sallun hedged. "I'd rather not risk my tongue by wagging it about."

Kylac could respect that—part of why he hadn't pressed the lad sooner. He'd pieced together a sufficient understanding of circumstances on his own. As long as Sallun's master was willing to fill in the holes, he saw no reason to tug at the lad's shroud of secrecy.

Yet Kylac had his own secrets. And he'd long ago learned that the fastest way to deflect attention from himself was to turn tables and become the inquisitor.

"So be it," he agreed. "But ya *will* keep your promise, yes?"

"Something tells me that if you're *that* determined to board our ship, we couldn't stop you if we tried."

"You're a bright lad, Sallun. Seems we ought to fare just fine."

Instead of leaving the rank-smelling warehouse behind, Sallun turned a corner and started down a narrow corridor between jutting wings. Kylac sensed those who marked his approach from the rooftop on either side, but remained calm. These were sentries, not assassins.

The approach was littered with crates and barrels, some stacked precariously high. Beyond stood a dilapidated entry, where a large, wheeled door sagged in its rusted track, open just a slit to one side. A shelter to urchins, given the nature of the alley debris. But if Sallun's crew had taken up residence, the occupying rabble would have been swept clear.

As they neared the door, a lean shadow emerged from behind a stack of pallets stained with fish guts. Tall to begin with, the shadow only grew taller, matching the man who cast it as he rose from his seated perch.

Sallun stopped. "Trajan," he greeted, with a fist-to-heart salute.

Trajan wore no hood, and made no other attempt to mask his displeasure. His sandy hair was long and loose, his tangled brows sharply raked in a menacing glare. As close to seven heads as a man could get without surpassing it, Kylac decided, though his movements had shown none of the awkwardness typical in men of such stature.

"Best have a good explanation, Sallun," Trajan grumbled. "Captain's orders were to leave even your own shadow behind."

Despite the soldier's fierce expression and penetrating eyes, Kylac detected a hint of amusement in his tone.

"He saved my life," Sallun offered, gesturing vaguely at Kylac.

One of the tangled brows arched. "From what? A pack of feral kittens?"

"His name . . ." Sallun stopped himself and turned to Kylac for permission. Kylac nodded. "His name is Kylac Kronus."

Trajan's mocking scowl smoothed in surprise. "Kronus. The dragon-slayer?" He measured Kylac up and down with renewed interest. "Looks and smells like gutter filth. What makes you believe his claim?"

"Because Ulflund and his renegades will be too busy breeding maggots to trouble us further—thanks to him."

Trajan remained skeptical. "You saw this?"

Sallun nodded. "Slew five armed Shadowguard. Without drawing a blade of his own."

Trajan's fingers danced on the hilt of his sword. "What's he want with you?"

"A ride on our ship. And since we're short a few hands . . ."

The towering soldier appeared to mull it over. "Perhaps he'd be good enough to wait here while you brief the captain. If Ledron wishes to see him, I'll send him in."

Again, Sallun consulted Kylac with a questioning glance.

"Less time I have to spend in there, the better," Kylac said.

"I'll return in a moment," Sallun assured him. To Trajan, he added, "Try not to test him."

When Sallun had slipped through the slit in the doorway, Kylac sat himself on a nearby crate. "Ya might wants to has your bowmen stand down. A weary shoulder can affect aim, and o' the two of us, you're the larger target."

Trajan smiled slightly, then signaled to his rooftop archers to relax their drawn bows. "You're not what I envisioned."

"No?"

"You're much more . . . *real*."

Kylac smirked. "Meat and bone."

"Is it true, then? Did you slay yourself a dragon?"

"A whole nest of 'em at once, some say. But ya'll never hear such a claim from me."

"I thought not. But you did kill Ulflund?"

"If your man Sallun named him correctly. His brood didn't seem much interested in any formal introductions."

Trajan laughed. "I suspect not." He stepped back, crossing his arms while leaning against the far wall. "Kronus. Is that a family name?"

"More like a title, won in the sight o' my peers."

"Oh? These would be the fighters you trained with, I suppose."

"Something like that."

"Has the ring of Old Entian."

Kylac nodded.

"What's the translation?"

"Unbowed."

Despite his word, Sallun was gone for nearly a full hour before returning for Kylac. He did so accompanied by a Lieutenant Jahant and a squad of Shadowguard whose individual names were not given. Jahant frowned at Trajan, who by then was chatting with Kylac as if the pair were old friends. While neither had relayed anything about his more private history or business, Kylac had seen plenty of misadventure in his wanderings over the past three and a half years—tales he deemed innocent and amusing enough to share. Such stories prompted Trajan to tell some of his own, a few from his days of recruitment and training, but most stemming from his time as a young rogue growing up in what he merely described as an "untamed" region of his homeland isle. With just a few shared laughs, Kylac felt at ease—more so with Trajan than the skittish Sallun. While Trajan remembered himself quickly enough when the others arrived, saluting his superior officer and begging apology for his slack behavior, he offered a parting wink of encouragement as Kylac was led away.

The warehouse interior was dark, lit only by the faint rays streaming in through high, open windows. The smell, at least, was somewhat less than Kylac had feared. The place actually seemed fresher within than without. Or mayhap he was merely growing accustomed to its flavor.

His escort led him past tubs and stalls toward a flight of steps that climbed to a loft, where dim candlelight guttered softly. A pair of sentries warded these stairs top and bottom. Instead of leading him up, however, Kylac's escort guided him into an empty office to the right, directly beneath the loft.

"Wait here," Jahant ordered him.

The lieutenant and his soldiers filed out. Kylac heard them forming a line just beyond the door. He felt around until he found the rough edge of a worktable, on which he sat.

And waited.

It wasn't more than a minute or two before another man entered, carrying a lantern. He was lean, but well muscled, with a shorn head and a prominent peak in his throat. He eyed Kylac in obvious appraisal. Despite the descriptions he'd doubtless been given, he seemed surprised.

"Captain Ledron, I presume."

The captain remembered himself, and scowled. "You risked your life to save my man. Why?"

"Risk? No, sir. None that I recall."

Ledron's scowl deepened. "The men you killed . . . those were no mere alley thugs, but a pack of highly trained Blackfists, Shadowguard, the royal elite."

"If'n so, they was no longer fit for duty. Your king should thank me for removing them from his family's service."

"So it's gold you're after?"

Kylac sighed. "Your man was in trouble. Seemed the right thing to do. A ship is all I require, as I'm sure Sallun told you."

Ledron weighed the answer. "He claims you've no specific destination in mind."

"No, sir. Anyplace off this island continent should do fine."

"Then you've got trouble on your heels."

"Boredom, actually." He found it strange, what so many others failed to see. This land had proven exciting beyond expectation, yes. But after all it had recently endured, chances were that matters on its shores would be quiet for a while—notwithstanding the admonitions spouted by a drunken Dareth and his doomsaying ilk. The friends he'd left behind in Alson and those he'd encountered since . . . all seemed to ask the same question, the answer to which should have been obvious.

"A man who seeks danger will eventually find more than he can handle," Ledron warned.

"As others may have told ya, I'm not quite old enough to calls myself a man."

Ledron considered, his expression unreadable. Finally, he asked,

"What do you know about the people of Addaranth?"

"Addaranth. That the one they calls the Sundered Isle?"

Ledron nodded.

"Ain't part o' the Finlorian string. Too far south. Addarans would be ancestral cousins to the Kuurians, or some such. That where we're headed?"

"We Addarans are under siege. Have been for years, from a fleet of seafaring marauders who call themselves the Grenarr."

When the captain's pause lengthened, Kylac decided to nudge him along. "Distant island. Ocean raiders. Is that all?"

"The Grenarr have long sought a toehold upon my people's shores, hoping eventually to overrun the island and depose my lord ruler, King Kendarrion."

"But the men who nabbed Sallun—Ulflund and his gang—were yours." He thought he knew where this was going, and so was trying to press Ledron's oration . . . without aggravating the captain into silence.

"Ulflund was my captain, the king's personal shadow. He and others betrayed Kendarrion by abducting his royal daughter, Princess Denariel, at the behest of the Grenarr—for what amount of gold, I cannot fathom. They brought her north to hide her here, among the Kuurian populace, until a ransom of land was met."

Something felt askew. The mere recounting of Ulflund's disloyalty, mayhap? Kylac couldn't say for certain, but noted the way Ledron had suddenly become distracted by the floor, the far wall, and the handle of his lantern.

"Ulflund was *seeking* the princess," Kylac reminded the captain.

That drew Ledron's gaze again. "Only because his treachery was doomed by another's. One of the mercenaries Ulflund employed sold word of the plot to King Kendarrion. It came too late for us to prevent their departure, but knowing their destination, we raced ahead aboard a faster vessel to lie in wait for their arrival."

"Here in Wingport."

"We raided their ship that very night, retrieving the princess—blessed be the Mother's mercy—before harm was done to her."

"But lost your own ship somewhere 'long the way."

"Razed in its berth," Ledron confirmed.

"So ya purchases another, and we escort this maiden home. Simple enough," Kylac said, knowing that it wasn't.

His goad seemed to work, as Ledron's visage soured. "It will relieve me to learn that Ulflund and his renegades are dead—assuming my men return with confirmation of Sallun's tale. But the greater threat remains."

"The mutant."

"Sallun spoke of it?"

Kylac shook his head. "Was the only threat Ulflund uttered that truly spooked the young man."

Ledron paused, but seemed pleased by this. "*Ukinh*, it was named by its creators, though we call them grolls. Bred by an ancient sect of magi, now extinct."

"Gorrethrehn," Kylac echoed, recalling his history of that former age. "*Breeders*, as they was commonly known."

"The Ukinha are relentless creatures, once set upon a task. Deadly in ways a mortal man can scarcely fathom. This one wants Denariel. It slew ten of my Shadowguard that night, and nine crewmen when it destroyed my ship. It will seek to hunt us."

Ledron stepped forward abruptly, raising his lantern. Kylac didn't flinch.

"Dragon-slayer or charlatan, I care not. But this I tell you in fair warning. If you sail with us, you do so under my command, a warder to the princess, knowing that a mutant of nightmarish creation will shred your bowels to chum if you stand in its way."

Kylac chuckled. "My, my, captain. A perilous voyage, a monstrous adversary, a maiden in need . . . despite your lengthy chatter, I believe ya's gone and roused my interest."

"This is no game, boy. I'll not risk my mission on a rakehell, no matter how quick and sharp his blades."

Kylac spied a roach skittering along the floor at the edge of Ledron's light. "Pardon my saying so, Captain, but you need me more'n I need you. I can't swears ya an oath, 'cause I gots nothing to swears on. But if this princess o' yours don't feel again her father's embrace, may the bards make me a liar and a leper."

Ledron appeared to grind his teeth. "Are you truly as skilled as Sallun boasts?"

Kylac shrugged, then swiped the dagger from Ledron's belt and threw it at the floor, pinning the unfortunate roach in place. When he turned back, the captain stood frozen, a hand on his empty sheath and a look of shock on his face.

Kylac hopped to his feet. "Let's find out, shall we?"

4

"WHERE ARE YOU . . . ?" Sallun asked in confusion, as Kylac cut left down a goose-necked alley. "The Bilge lies farther north."

"I've an errand to run," Kylac replied without slowing. He sensed his companion's lingering hesitation, followed by the shuffling footfalls as Sallun made his decision and hurried to catch up.

"What errand?"

"Some belongings I means to retrieve."

Sallun's gaze tracked along the alley's north wall like the needle of a compass. His body may have been following, but his mind was not. "I'd give a diamond fist," he muttered grimly, "for a carving of that slug's expression when we stroll back in there."

Ah, thought Kylac. That would explain the lookout's magnetic focus. His own gaze lifted as they emerged from the crooked alley onto a cliffside lane offering a mostly unobstructed view of the fog-shrouded harbor. "Going to asks him to returns your money?"

"Let him keep it," Sallun said, beaming cruelly. "I'll wager that mine and Ulflund's coin together won't stop him from soiling his breeches."

Kylac chuckled. He couldn't fault the lad his petty vengeance. Whatever shock that toad barkeep and his pock-faced snitch suffered upon Sallun's return to their lair was well earned.

There had been considerable debate as to whether Sallun—or
Kylac, for that matter—should return there at all. An inquiry into
the deaths of Ulflund and his renegade Shadowguard might have
readily led back to the Thirsty Bilge—the name, Kylac had learned
from Sallun, of that festering hole. As far as Ledron was concerned, it
would be like sending them right back into a cloud of angry hornets
that *they* had stirred up.

Kylac had argued it unlikely. There wouldn't be much Wingport's
authorities could accuse the barkeep of, even if his role in matters were
confessed or uncovered. It was Kylac—or Rydan, rather—who alone
could be proven guilty of the killings. And only Sallun could attest
to even that. Besides, the victims had been outlanders. There would
be an unofficial tax on Ulflund's payment to the barkeep, mayhap.
After that, whatever ruckus might be raised over their deaths was
liable to quiet quickly.

Perhaps, Ledron had agreed. Even so, Ulflund's men had obviously
been sniffing about the wharfside watering holes, offering bribes
to anyone who could direct them to a man of Sallun's description.
Though the renegade captain had been dispatched, Sallun was a
marked man whose presence could only invite curiosity and trouble.

Which suggested that one location was as good as the next, Kylac
had pressed. They still needed to await the harbormaster's page *somewhere*, and returning to the scene of the crime might be the last
thing anyone would anticipate. To switch meeting locations—or to
send some other man in Sallun's stead—would itself present certain
difficulties. Though Sallun had been compromised, none were left
to trouble him. Well, save for the mysterious mutant, of course. But
Kylac had already proven able and willing to keep the young lookout
safe, and would do so again.

Ledron, seeming unconvinced where this mutant was concerned—
or mayhap where *Kylac* was concerned—had nevertheless conceded.
Better that, Kylac had sensed, than to risk sending any others out,
which would only weaken the captain's cordon around the princess.
Nor was Kylac naive enough to believe himself truly welcome amid
that inner circle. A friend he'd been named, but only at pike's length.
Sallun had almost assuredly been instructed to keep a watchful eye

on him, to see if there was anything more to be gleaned of his intentions. Until then, the farther he was kept from Her Royal Highness, the better.

"What can ya tells me 'bout this princess o' yours?"

Sallun squirmed within his cloak. "What did the captain tell you?"

"Nothing. But then, I didn't ask."

"So why are you asking me?"

Kylac chuckled wryly. "Forgets I did. Tell me instead about these enemies—the ones who hired Ulflund to take her. Grenarr, Ledron named them."

Again, that tense hesitation. "What would you know?"

"Whatever there is to tell." A screech drew his attention to a roadside gutter, where a pair of gulls pecked at each other over a skeletal fish tail. "Their ransom demands. What o' that?"

"What of it?"

"How much o' your lord's kingdom did they expect, exactly, for the princess's return?"

"I don't . . . Listen, I'm just a lookout."

He was a bit more than that, Kylac knew, or he wouldn't be here. "Are lookouts not supposed to *spy* matters of interest?"

Sallun scratched at his shock of red hair. His fidgeting gaze never seemed to rest. It swept the road, the fence along that sandswept ridge, ships below as they drifted in their berths, the sagging storefront to their left, a gull roosting atop a barren lamppost, the post itself worn by wind and painted in droppings. He saw everything while seeming to see nothing. Kylac knew this because he'd been trained to do the same. Sallun's efforts were far less natural than his own, but that was most likely a matter of inexperience. The lad, no more than a year or two older than himself, had yet to completely grow into his skin. Kylac might be able to help him with that, were he so inclined, with a lesson or two in confidence. But, for now, it seemed they were still playing games.

"Just now, I'm supposed to be keeping an eye out for the groll," Sallun answered finally. "You would, too, if you knew the first thing about them."

"So tell me," Kylac said. He'd been meaning to ask about the creature anyway. For now, Sallun could believe himself successful in having deflected the prior questions.

Sallun seemed to consider, then shook his head. "Monsters. Abominations. To even think of them curdles the blood."

"O' fine use that knowledge will be in defending you against one," Kylac said pointedly. "Tell me something useful. Strengths? Shortcomings?"

"All and none," Sallun replied, until Kylac gave him a prodding look. "Bred to kill, and to survive where nothing else could. Deadlier than any creation nature alone could devise."

Kylac waited for Sallun to offer something further . . . and waited . . . and waited. Finally, he halted his stride. "Ya know, it may be I's tired o' your company after all."

"What would you have of me?"

"You're not a lackwit. And, not being a lackwit, you know better than to fence with me. So stop sputtering as if'n I's just asked your hand in marriage, and tell me about the groll—in fixed terms."

Sallun waited as an elderly man pushing a cart full of old fishing nets passed down a rutted crossroad. "Nothing about them is fixed. They were human once, too long ago to remember. The Gorrethrehn twisted and tortured them, bred and cross-bred them with animals, lizards, insects—whatever unholy ingredients they could concoct with their perverse blend of magic. Of the magi sects, the Breeders were the most foul, the most mistrusted and disdained."

Kylac crossed his arms over his chest. "Only, I asked about the groll—not about ancient masters dead and gone. I'm assuming it's fast?"

"As a river viper."

"Strong?"

"Like a rampaging grackal."

"Stealthy? Armored? Intelligent?"

"Yes, yes, and yes. You won't think of an attribute the Breeders didn't. Speed, strength, camouflage, cunning—their aim was to perfect the human animal. They can be shadows or berserkers. Size, shape, and color shift according to their needs. Their wounds are self-healing, so if you *are* going to kill one, you'd best do it swiftly. Their venom? Touch it, and your mind will drift toward madness. Taste it, and you will die a slow, stomach-wrenching death. Find a drop of it in your veins, and . . . well, at least your death will be swift."

Kylac did well not to laugh. All that effort to pry forth a few words, and now Sallun was raving as if fevered. "Land creatures only? Or can they breathe underwater?"

Sallun grinned. "Now you're seeing it. Any terrain, any weather, any temperature, is theirs. One is as natural as the next."

"Except for the sky. Were they able to fly, I'll wager it would have swooped down upon us by now."

Sallun glanced up as if the notion might prove a reality. But only gulls and herons wheeled overhead. "No. They do not fly."

"There. Ya see? That would be a shortcoming."

"So it would," Sallun agreed reluctantly. "But hardly a disadvantage, since we don't either."

"Have you ever actually seen one?"

"No."

"I thought not." Kylac clapped his companion on the shoulder and started forward once more.

"What? So now you don't believe me?"

It wasn't disbelief, exactly, but to Kylac's ears, Sallun's account weighed heavy with exaggeration. No matter. Truth was seldom gleaned from a single source. He would ask the others as the opportunity arose, and piece together what he could from their various renditions.

"Everything I've told you has been borne out by those who've studied the creatures."

"Any o' those in our company?"

"Trajan grew up in the wilds, and witnessed them on occasion— mostly at a distance. Ulflund was the real expert," Sallun snorted. "Hunted them along the borderlands for years, but saw many more of his own slain than theirs. Much of what we know, in fact, is from examining their corpses—just about the only time to get a fair look at one. Few have encountered one face to face and lived to tell of it. Just peer into the gazes of the men in our company," he added, "and you'll know those who fought abovedecks against the groll we now face, and those who fought below to secure Her Highness."

"Mayhap *she* can tells us something 'bout this particular beastie," Kylac observed. "Has Ledron questioned her 'bout it?"

A coarse breeze gusted along the ridge, stirring sand and grit with icy teeth and briny breath. Sallun drew his cowl, retreating like a turtle into its shell. "I wouldn't know about that."

Something in his tone suggested elsewise. *Muzzled by Ledron,* Kylac thought. He considered pressing the issue, certain he could loosen the lad's tongue by any number of means. But Sallun was only following orders. Of primary concern to Kylac, at this juncture, was leaving these shores. No reason to do anything that might jeopardize his departure.

He decided to pacify his nervous companion instead. Often, the surest way to elicit a man's confidence was to take him into yours. A bloodless method, but an effective one. "In any case, I'll wager you're safe enough, as long as this one fears me."

"Fear?" Sallun scoffed. "Fear has long since been bred out of them."

"Then why has it not attacked us?"

"Because it hasn't yet found us, I'd guess."

"But it has. I's already sensed the creature."

Sallun froze. "What, now?" His voice was a panicked whisper as he searched the road, the sandswept cliffs to his right, and the smattering of structures perched haphazardly on the chiseled hills to his left.

"No, not now. Must I starts calling ya Flinch?"

Behind those overactive eyes, Sallun's mind raced. His face paled in realization. "The alley." He gulped. "When Ulflund . . ."

Kylac nodded. "I was weaponless, outnumbered. If'n fear didn't hold your mutant in check, what did?"

It was Sallun's turn to stop in his tracks, as if paralyzed by the implications. "Ledron made no mention."

"I didn't tells him."

The lookout's gaze turned accusing. "How could you not? Her Highness—"

"Might be a phantom, for all I's seen o' her. Regardless, your captain's already taken every precaution. The foulest-smelling warehouse he could find . . . thirty men, give or take, where a dozen might do . . . sentries, decoys . . . the greasiest cesspit in which to stash his gopher . . . Did I miss anything?"

"All of which you might have undone. If it saw us in the alley, it could have followed—"

"It didn't. It left the moment I caught its wind."

Sallun searched his face with those darting eyes. "I suppose you might be mistaken. It could have been something else."

"And I might have been wrong to thinks I could save you from Ulflund's hounds."

Their gazes locked. Sallun's was the first to break. "Well, then, it is only because the groll wished to let its presence be known."

"Why would it do that," Kylac challenged, "if it could has remained hidden as ya suggest?"

Sallun shook his head. "A warning, perchance, to let you know this isn't over. Or a test, to see if you would divine it at all. But, dragon-slayer or no, I'll not believe for a moment that you or any other man could sense a Ukinh that did not permit it."

What the lad believed about him didn't much matter to Kylac. His skills and abilities had been honed, tested, and proven in ways that few could fathom. "Ya still hasn't told me why it didn't attack."

"I should know? Maybe it recognized your skills where Ulflund did not. Grolls are clever enough to seek every advantage. They're not prone to impulsiveness, reacting out of pride . . . or being goaded by personal affront as the others were."

Kylac considered. The latter might be true enough.

"Besides," Sallun added, his confidence mounting, "you're not its target. Her Highness is. If your death or mine would have brought it any closer to reclaiming her, the rats in that alley would still be bloated with our remains."

Kylac smirked at the notion. Still, Sallun's appraisal held possibilities worth conceding, lest he underestimate the mutant's prowess the way so many others underestimated his. "Then ya truly believes this creature is a match for me?"

"Don't misunderstand me," Sallun replied, missing the jape. "I've never seen a man move and react and anticipate as swiftly as you did in that alley. But our enemy isn't human—or at least hasn't been in more than a thousand years."

Kylac reached a switchback stair hewn along the cliff, and started down. It wouldn't be the first inhuman creature he'd faced. Nor even the most daunting, from all he'd heard thus far. But nothing he said was going to sway his companion, so he opted to save his breath.

"Anyway, you should have told the captain," Sallun insisted. "Keeping secrets endangers us all, and will make it more difficult for you to win his trust."

Though tempted to expose the hypocrisy in that statement, Kylac let it go. "I'll just has to hope ya fashion your reports on me with a favorable eye, won't I?"

He tossed Sallun a wink in emphasis. Sallun opened his mouth as if to disavow any such orders, but just as hurriedly snapped it shut and lowered his gaze, to focus on the crude path at his feet.

That path continued in winding, twisting, ragged fashion—overgrown in some patches, completely eroded in others—until they'd descended the upper cliff to reach the wharfside level of the city. Instead of proceeding toward the wharf proper, however, Kylac veered west, following along the rutted track of a rainwater spillway. Sallun was likely wondering by now where, exactly, Kylac was leading him. More than once, the lad's head turned to study the trail they were leaving behind, as if seeking some recognizable pattern or landmark that might serve as clue. But he refrained from asking anything more, mayhap worried that further discussion would only invite more questions he wasn't permitted to answer.

Or mayhap he was just worried now about the groll ambushing him the moment his back was turned.

The spillway led to a canal, which Kylac followed toward the harbor. The scent of brine, already pervasive, grew stronger as the winds swept inland. A few hucksters peddled wares from their carts and stalls—mostly fish and urchins and hard-shelled creatures harvested from the sea. Kylac politely declined their second-rate offerings, lowering his head as he pushed through a thickening curtain of brume. He may have appeared desperate enough to eat whatever was set under his nose, but he'd learned from painful experience not to trust seafoods sold this far beyond the fringe of the marketplace.

With the harbor shore still several hundred paces out, he reached another spillway, this one tunneling out from the side of a derelict watchtower. It was also grated—or had been. Its remaining bars now hung rusted and broken, its dark maw like a mouthful of missing teeth.

"We're not going in there," Sallun objected, when Kylac stooped beside the opening. "Are we?"

"And why not?"

"It smells of sewage."

"A powerful deterrent, wouldn't ya say?" With no more explanation than that, he slipped through the narrow opening, careful not to snag his clothes—tattered as they were—on any of the iron half-bars. Sallun was welcome to follow. Or not.

Inside was cramped and dank. Kylac moved quickly, nimbly, holding his breath against the stench, and trying not to give too much thought to the coating of slime beneath his hands and feet. Behind him, the dim light from the mouth of the tunnel was eclipsed. That and a muttered oath announced Sallun's entry behind him.

The channeling track elevated slightly, then branched left and right. Kylac followed the left fork, feeling his way now by touch alone. The darkness was absolute . . . but didn't last long. Veering sharply right, he emerged from the duct into a much wider tunnel—this one a shallow, flat-bottomed river that burrowed beneath a courtyard overhead. Grates in the ceiling shed pools of meager light from above, like fragile tethers to the outside world.

"Whoa," Sallun remarked as he half stepped, and half slipped, into the sewer canal. "We're beneath the tower, aren't we?"

Kylac nodded. "The south wing."

"Now what?"

"This way."

They headed in a southwesterly direction, keeping to the edges of the tunnel, where the placid waters were shallowest. The sludge was also thickest here, where the current was weak, so Kylac took extra care with his step. Sallun slipped once, marked by a splash and a curse. But the lad kept pace dutifully, so Kylac let him be.

They followed this course until they came to a break in the sewer wall—a natural breach caused by erosion. Here, Kylac reached down behind a loose pile of jagged rocks to find a sack full of firebrands.

He lit one, then stepped into the cleft, which soon became its own tunnel, rough-hewn by centuries of pounding, probing waves. Its waters deepened as they progressed, but these were seawaters, cold and fresh. The walls were sharp in areas with encrusting barnacles, and slick in others with patches of algae and tufts of seaweed. Ordinarily, this particular offshoot was completely inaccessible, flooded by ocean. But the tides this month had been particularly low, and—for the next half hour—at their day's furthest ebb.

Even so, their crushing echo grew louder, swirling now around Kylac's ankles. Behind him, Sallun was shivering.

"Like crawling through a whale's intestines," the lookout groused. His hood had fallen back, revealing matted hair and a face smeared with grime. "If it weren't so biting cold, that is."

Kylac chuckled. "Knows this from experience, do ya?"

"Aren't there easier ways to drown a man?"

Several, Kylac thought, but only winked and said, "Almost there."

He wasn't entirely insensitive to Sallun's condition. If there was one thing Kylac feared, it was confinement. The very notion was anathema to his adventurous spirit. In such tight quarters, beneath the crushing weight of this limestone bedrock, even he felt a gnawing agitation. But if the sea had found a way in, then there was also a way out. And knowing that was enough to keep his panic in check.

The tunnel narrowed, then widened. To one side, an alcove opened up. Chains of iron hooks had been hammered into the stone of one wall, dangling like empty manacles in a torture chamber. From several of these hung netted sacks, the mouths of which were sewn around iron rings that clipped onto the hooks in such a way as to resist the push and drag of inconstant tides.

"What is this?" Sallun marveled, with blue-tinged lips and quivering jaw.

"Smuggler's cache," Kylac replied, handing Sallun the firebrand.

"How did you know this was here?"

"I didn't," Kylac said, grasping one of the chains and drawing it in like an anchor. "But every city has its bowels. Just gots to know where to look."

Another netted sack, submerged beneath the waterline, came free.

Kylac gripped its mouth ring and unlatched it from its hook. He released the tether, then slung the sack over his shoulder.

"That's it?" Sallun asked, peering suspiciously at the waterlogged bundle of cloth inside.

"We can heads back now."

The lookout frowned. "Tremendous pains, I'd say, to stash some moldy breeches."

"Supposing there's gold inside?" Kylac teased. "Gems?"

"It's no dragon's hoard," Sallun huffed, as if to deny his curiosity. "And I'd have gladly given you one to spare me this journey."

"Shall we let the tides roll in while ya lament it?" Kylac beckoned for the torch, which Sallun surrendered.

"To the Bilge, then?"

"I've one more bundle to retrieve," Kylac admitted. No matter the precautions, it was seldom wise to store all of one's possessions in a single place.

"What must we crawl through this time? Nails? Shards? Flaming coals?"

Kylac smiled. "Dust and cobwebs, more like. Might see a roach or two. Nothing worse than a splinter, I promise."

"I was kind of hoping for fire of some sort," Sallun said through chattering teeth. "My limbs are about frozen through."

Kylac found the chill invigorating, but doubted his companion would care to hear that. "I know a good roaring hearth nearby," he replied, slowing as he came upon the breach connecting their trail to the main sewer tunnel. "A warm stew and a tankard of hot cider should be just what ya need to—"

The darkness fell like a headsman's axe. Kylac snapped back, feeling the wind of the swipe that whipped past his nose. An adderlike strike forced him to twist and withdraw further, flattening himself against the jagged wall of the narrow cavern. He thrust forward with his torch at the same time, but its meager gleam caught just the hint of a black-scaled hand before the brand was torn from his grasp—seized by its flaming head—and thrown into the sewer waters, where it died with a hiss.

The attacker pressed into the breach, relentless. Kylac was trapped,

hemmed in by walls of rock and Sallun at his back. He dodged the
first two strikes, then brought his netted sack to bear, using it to
parry two more. The third sought to rip it from him the way it had
his torch—but this time, Kylac was ready. A knife sheathed against
the small of his back was already in hand, and as his assailant latched
onto his makeshift shield, the blade cut hard and fast. A gash, a shriek
of surprise, and the darkness withdrew.

It returned at once, swifter than thought. There was no time taken
to inspect its wound—mayhap no need. The groll—for what else
could it be—had struck with the element of surprise, and refused to
relinquish its advantage. If anything, its darting swipes came faster,
forcing Kylac back another step. He heard Sallun sputter—finally
realizing what was happening—and stumble in reflexive panic, landing on his tailbone in the rising waters of that cramped tunnel. But
he was on his own, as Kylac wasn't yet offered an instant to breathe.
Block, slash, parry, twist, duck, lunge in rapid succession. He could
see almost nothing, the only light a faint glow from the tunnel mouth,
blocked in intermittent spurts by the groll's quicksilver strikes.

Then his shield ripped, its netting torn asunder. Kylac's heart danced
as the bundle was juggled between them—slapped, swatted, spun,
and partially unfurled. A lost cause for now. Kylac drew a second
knife. The groll pressed forward, its uncertain size seeming to swell
now, eclipsing the dim light utterly. Kylac feinted high, then drove
low, but came away without scoring a hit. He hadn't truly meant to,
but it troubled him that he had yet to detect a pattern in his enemy's
attacks. Mayhap it was too skilled for that. Certainly, it was too close.
Kylac needed more room to maneuver, and a longer weapon to keep
it at bay. Neither was likely to happen if he didn't somehow gain the
upper hand.

But, try as he might, he could discover no tendencies to its movements—no stance or form it favored, no part of its body it sought
to protect. Though Kylac fought with his own movements to lure
it into some recognizable rhythm, he found himself still completely
on the defensive.

Fortune intervened. After barely slipping one strike, Kylac caught
the next between his daggers in scissor formation. Ripping the blades

apart, he severed the groll's hand at the wrist. The beast recoiled with a wail—only to lash out at Kylac's exposed flank with its opposite hand. Here at last was a predictable response. Kylac spun low, ducking the swipe and following its arc with a reverse-handed strike of his own. Stabbing hard, he pierced the creature through the center of its wrist bones, then drove his dagger tip clear into the limestone wall, pinning its good arm in place.

He aimed to finish it with a lunge to the throat, but in the instant it took him to discern where that throat might be, the groll surprised him yet again by ripping downward on the edge of the buried knife, snapping its own bone and cutting through tendons and ligaments without hesitation. Somehow, Kylac was once again on the defensive, forced to leave his knife in the wall while he dodged a blood-filled punch to the face.

"My bundle!" Kylac yelled at Sallun, fending off his enemy's two mangled appendages with just the one dagger now. He was fighting for an opening with which to retrieve the other, but the groll, having tasted the blade's unnatural sting, was making sure that didn't happen. "Inside!"

But Sallun was still on his backside, thrashing and scrabbling to put more distance between himself and the combatants. Kylac, hard-pressed as he was, couldn't expect help from that quarter. And the groll wasn't giving up. Despite its wounds, it continued to press its attack, kicking with clawed feet and punching with ruined hand and stump. Wary of venomous blood spatter, Kylac was forced to give ground.

Before it escaped his reach altogether, Kylac made a diving grab at the sprawled ruin of his clothes roll. The groll seemed to anticipate this—and why not, when Kylac had announced his intention to retrieve it? As he dipped low, a foot pinned the bundle in place. With Kylac reluctant to let go, he may as well have been pinned himself. When the groll launched its follow-up strike, Kylac had no choice but to roll aside.

He jammed his dagger into the splayed bundle as he did so, thinking the groll's next move would be to yank it free as it had tried before. He guessed correctly. His tunic unfolded and tore, but the true treasure remained in place on the tideswept floor. Kylac flung a throwing knife from his belt. It missed the groll, but caused the beast to hesitate, allowing Kylac to slip forward, stealing back a few steps of precious ground.

He growled as he advanced, alternating between ducks and one-armed slashes. Though thrilled by the challenge, he was angry that he hadn't seen it coming. He never should have allowed himself to be caught so unawares. Why hadn't he sensed the groll sooner? Neither scent nor sound had betrayed its ambush. Even his instincts had failed him. Reflex alone had kept him alive. Grateful as he was, it never should have come to that.

So he hacked and spun and slashed at his sudden nemesis, refusing to die in this sewer offshoot, or to lose a fight he'd clearly been winning. That the groll was strengthening seemed obvious. Its wounds no longer bled freely. Even the severed wrist had scabbed over. Kylac didn't know if it would grow a new hand, but he wasn't waiting around to find out.

Then he lost his remaining dagger. Managing somehow to invert itself in those cramped confines, the groll lashed out with a clawed foot where Kylac was expecting a stump. It latched onto the blade itself, wrenching and twisting. Kylac might have clung to the weapon or sliced free, but sensed the bite aimed at his calf. A hop, pivot, and kick met with a satisfying crunch to the creature's face, but it also meant releasing his dagger in order to extricate himself from what might have elsewise been a killing hold.

As the weapon flew away in a clanging skitter, Kylac turned for the one stuck in the tunnel wall. The groll was already there, jaws snapping at the air where Kylac's hand would have been had he followed through. Instead, he spun and launched another kick, smashing the groll's head against stone.

Behind him, Sallun was fishing through his scattered clothes roll. *Good lad,* Kylac thought, concentrating on the splashing of Sallun's search—even over the snarling rasp of the groll's movements.

"What am I . . . ? Wait, I—"

Kylac spun, relying on his preternatural sense of sound and space to tell him the position and stance of his comrade, as well as the orientation of the objects Sallun had retrieved. He might still have misjudged slightly, but the groll lunged after him with a throaty hiss, allowing a dim halo from the sewer to light the cavern tunnel.

It was more than Kylac needed.

His hands flew to the hilts of his twin shortswords, clutched by their scabbards in Sallun's shivering fists. Freed from the center of the discarded clothes, the weapons could now be brought to bear.

Kylac did so with a whirring, dicing flourish, feeling suddenly reborn. The groll wove and snapped and thrashed, but in its wounded condition was no match for Kylac's blades. Spinning, stabbing, and slicing with flawless precision, Kylac thwarted the beast's desperate counterstrikes and grinned with a growing sense of triumph as its injuries began to mount.

And then it fled. Swifter than Kylac would have believed possible, it reversed through the breach as if sucked free by a funnel cloud. A shriek, splash, flap, and slither—and it was gone.

Kylac darted after it, entering the sewer with blades at the ready. He crouched and cast about, searching with eyes, ears, and every finely honed warrior's instinct he could muster. He saw ripples, heard a scrabbling echo, and smelled its blood amid the filth. But those signs were fleeting and contradictory—save that all left him feeling the same thing.

Emptiness.

He waited a few moments more. The beast couldn't hide from him forever. And, fast as it was, it couldn't really be gone.

Could it?

A splashing rustle drew his attention. But it wasn't the mutant poking its head so tentatively from the tunnel breach. Sallun. The young lookout was pale as wax, and hugged himself against a wracking chill. Nonetheless, the fierce grin that broke across his face burned with redemptive satisfaction.

"Believe me now?"

5

KYLAC CAST ABOUT the sewer tunnel, still seeking some sight, scent, or whisper of the departed groll. Finding none, he turned back to Sallun. "Not its target, eh?"

The shivering lookout shrugged. "Unpredictable creatures. At best."

Unpredictable. Invisible. Swift, strong . . . everything Sallun had claimed them to be, and more. Frustration and fascination gnawed at Kylac in equal measure. The encounter could have gone worse. And yet he felt cheated by its abrupt conclusion.

Thinking he might lure the mutant back by dropping his guard, Kylac did just that, lowering his shortswords as he waded toward Sallun. He nodded at his blades' sheaths, clutched in the lookout's whitened fists.

"I'll have those back now."

Sallun seemed surprised to find the items still in hand. When he extended them, Kylac tossed his swords in the air, snatched the scabbards by the throat, and caught his blades cleanly as they descended.

"Ya did well, by the way." Tucking the weapons in his belt, Kylac clapped the stunned lookout on the shoulder. "I'm indebted." While Sallun groped for a response, Kylac slipped past, back through the tunnel breach to collect his knives.

The first was still embedded in the limestone wall. Kylac slid it free with a yank, briefly inspecting it for damage. Unmarred, as expected.

"What manner of steel pierces rock like raw meat?" Sallun asked, raising his voice over the growl of churning surf.

"Must've caught a cleft. This wall is riddled with 'em."

But Sallun wasn't biting. "And the groll? I saw how you cleaved its flesh. No ordinary blade cuts them so easily."

"Mayhap not," Kylac admitted with a smirk. "Find the other, and ya'll see for yourself."

He turned to gather his tunic and breeches, swirling more or less where he'd left them in the shallow tide. These, he noted, hadn't fared as well, suffering numerous rents and tears. It remained to be seen whether they could be salvaged.

Sallun, meanwhile, was splashing though the frigid waters in search of the knife that had been wrenched from Kylac's grasp. Though Kylac wasn't certain where precisely the blade had landed, his companion was sweeping the right area.

He'd just finished wringing and rerolling his stashed clothes when Sallun gave a triumphant shout.

"I'm impressed," Kylac admitted.

Sallun stopped beaming long enough to examine his find. "It lacks the shine of steel."

"More like pearl."

"There are no scratches," Sallun marveled, "no nicks." He raised his thumb to test the edge's sharpness.

"Ah," Kylac warned. "I wouldn't."

"So, what is it?"

"Still seeking the smith or armorer who can tells me. Though I's come to doubt they're forged by man."

"What does that mean?"

"Means, if'n ya were to remove the grips I fashioned for 'em, you'd find what looks more like a giant quill than anything else. Mayhap the spine of a fish."

"Fish?"

"They was littering the beach of a mountain cove, far to the northeast, where nary a man dares tread. Thousands . . . some no bigger than a finger, others tall as century-old granitewood. Like shards fallen from the heavens, or dredged up from the oceans below."

Sallun might have laughed, but didn't. The skepticism in his expression couldn't quite break free—overruled, mayhap, by what he'd already witnessed of their inexplicable nature. "Are these the swords that slew the dragon?"

Kylac smiled. "After a fashion," he replied, having not the heart to dash the lookout's awed sense of imagination.

"Hence your pains to hide them," Sallun surmised, regarding the longer blades sheathed at Kylac's waist. "Though I'm curious you should part with them at all."

"A street rat wouldn't carry such claws," Kylac explained, referring to his urchin guise. "Nor did I imagine I'd need 'em." Not in Wingport. The daggers he'd kept on him—the ones most easily concealed in the rags he'd been wearing—were more than sufficient for the drunken thugs and clumsy thieves in this wharfside quarter. He'd proven as much in the fight against Ulflund, where even those daggers had remained sheathed.

"And now?"

Now, his decision to ferret away his larger blades seemed a foolish risk. "We fetch my longsword from *its* hiding place, and dare your beastie try me again."

Sallun glanced behind him, his smile slipping. This time, he caught himself mid reflex, and turned back in mild chagrin. "I'll attend the first. The latter is yours alone." He held forth Kylac's knife.

"Keep it."

"What?"

"I's got others. And it'll serve ya better than the hunting knife buried in your boot."

"I barely know how to wield the thing."

"All the more reason to carry a blade ya can trust."

Sallun remained hesitant. "I couldn't begin to pay you—"

"Ya's earned it already. One o' these, even." He patted his shortswords. "But longer is less wieldy. Nerves tight as yours, ya mights lose something vital 'fore the groll can takes it from ya."

Sallun grinned at the slight, and for a moment, all of his carefully guarded defenses evaporated like smoke. "Fair enough." He bowed in gratitude, staring even then at his new weapon, marveling at the treasure he'd been given.

A cheap price, really, for the lad's devotion.

Sallun looked up abruptly, as if having the same thought. Kylac clapped him on the arm in reassurance. Regardless, Sallun seemed suddenly refocused on his duty.

"I should report back to the captain straightaway."

"What of our return to the Bilge?"

"Captain Ledron should know the groll is here, tracking us."

"He knows it already. Or has positioned himself so. We spoke o' this?"

"I know, but . . ." The look Sallun gave was almost pleading. "If I were to fail to report this attack . . ."

"Come, then. I wouldn't have ya in the captain's disfavor. Just sheathe that blade 'fore ya cut yourself, eh?"

"I'd rather keep it ready—at least until we're in the open."

"Ya thinks it would attack again in its condition?"

"I think I have no idea what it might do. And neither do you."

"Fair enough," Kylac mimicked, drawing a meager smile from the chill-wracked lookout as they left the sea-breached tunnel behind them.

"COME," JAHANT BADE in his gravelly voice. "The captain's waiting."

Kylac started to follow Sallun, but stopped as the burly lieutenant thrust forth a meaty arm to block his path.

"You're to remain here."

Kylac considered the outstretched paw that hovered before his chest, wondering if Ledron's second-in-command could sense how close he'd come to losing that hand at the wrist. "Am I to root in this very spot? Or mights I stretch my legs while you confer?"

"The captain may wish to speak with you once he's finished with Sallun."

With his head and beard of spiky gray-and-black hair, and his cheeks pocked and scarred, Jahant had the look of a battle-worn mace. Only, Kylac had never met a mace with so stern a disposition. "Why not save time, then, and meet with us together?"

"That wasn't the captain's command, now—was it." Jahant lowered his arm, but leaned forward, staring Kylac down.

Kylac tilted his head. Sallun must have recognized something in the gesture, because he hurried to intervene. "You said he's waiting." The lookout cast a glance at Kylac before striding swiftly away, forcing Jahant to follow.

Only when the lieutenant turned his gaze did Kylac do the same, shaking his head at the unnecessary rudeness. The retreating pair slipped past an expressionless sentry, into the little room where Ledron had interrogated Kylac previously. Jahant slid the door shut behind them.

Kylac looked up at the loft above, where he was certain the princess was quartered. When that drew scowls from both the near sentry and those posted at the base of the stair, he turned instead to survey the line of stalls to his right. Most were filled with overturned tubs, piled haphazardly, each encrusted with the dried guts of slaughtered fish. His roaming gaze settled on a patch of daylight. Though boards had been hammered over the lower windows, those higher up allowed a thin wash to pool over a small stack of crates. It would be warmer in that pool, and drier than in the rest of this dank warehouse. As long as he had time, he might as well make use of it.

Ignoring those watching him, Kylac strolled over to the crates and shrugged free of the wet clothes roll slung over his shoulder. He then removed his outer travel cloak—retrieved with his longsword from the rafter hollow of that burned-out church house. Doing so revealed the hilts of his primary blades—a shortsword on each hip complementing the longsword on his left—but there was no reason to shroud them here. The secret of who he was had already been shared. And now that Sallun knew of his weapons, soon too would the others. Mayhap the hilts—along with the stories accompanying them—would give Jahant and his less amiable cohorts an apt measure of pause.

Fair warning should any be tempted to strong-arm him.

With the cloak set aside, he went about unrolling his tunic and breeches, draping them across the sunlit crates to dry. The damage, he was pleased to see, wasn't as extensive as he'd feared. The groll's claws had cut cleanly. He could stitch the rents himself, given a chance to acquire needle and thread. It wouldn't be pretty, but his was light-weight, loose-fitting garb worn for comfort and mobility, not for vanity.

He'd finished inspecting his tunic and just about spread out his breeches when he heard the approach of two—no, three—pairs of feet. Kylac had long ago learned to identify a man by his gait, mea-suring variable factors such as weight, length of stride, and cadence. A critical skill, as a man's movements could reveal things his appearance did not. Two of these men, Kylac quickly determined, he hadn't yet met. The other, if he wasn't mistaken, belonged to . . .

"There you are," Trajan greeted, as he ducked beneath a low beam and fixed his arched brow on Kylac. "Returned early, I hear. Thought we weren't to see you again until nightfall."

Kylac nodded. "And yourself? In charge of the outer watch, yet it was some lad by the name of Nethreal camped out in your alley when I arrived."

"Rotations. Keeps the eyes fresh. Just returned from a western perimeter sweep with Ahlman and Ahren here."

Brothers, Kylac surmised, and twins at that. He couldn't tell from their faces, for each was hidden beneath a deeply shadowed cowl, with mouth and chin masked by a cloth wrap. But their build, stance, and bearing—not to mention a gait so similar that he'd initially thought it to belong to a single man—told Kylac all he needed to know. Bowmen, judging by their matching wrist guards. He wondered idly if this Ahlman and Ahren were better at their craft than the brutish brothers Grathe and Torman had been at theirs.

"So," Trajan said, "Nethreal says you got a look at our mutant friend."

"Does he? A fair stretch from what we told him."

"Saw it in your faces. Man can read truth like no other. How close did you get?"

"Close enough to smell its breakfast."

Ahlman and Ahren glanced at one another. Though he couldn't
see their expressions, Kylac sensed their doubt.

"Either o' ya lads got a voice?"

The hoods turned as one, their attention snapping back to him.

"They don't, actually," Trajan answered for them. "But their story's
not a pleasant one."

"Ah. Forgive my clumsy tongue." He bowed to each of the brothers.

Ahlman gestured with his hands. Ahren responded in kind. Though
sign languages had been an integral part of his studies in stealth, Kylac
didn't recognize theirs.

Whatever passed between them caused Trajan to chuckle. "Wouldn't
be the first time," he said. Of Kylac, he asked in jest, "You didn't
kill it, did you?"

"Maimed."

This time, all three Blackfists shared a look. "There must be some
truth to your reputation," Trajan decided. "I've seen as few as three
men face a Ukinh. Drove it off before two of the three died of injury.
This was just you and Sallun?"

"And the terrain," Kylac admitted. "Ground hemmed its attacks.
I suspect it would have fared better in the open."

"I'd lay wager on a Ukinh on any ground." Trajan's scowl showed
that, despite his friendly banter, he too was having difficulty digesting
the account. At a gesture from Ahren, he added, "Are we to believe
it was those slivers in your belt that kept it at bay?"

"They're stronger than they look."

"They'd have to be—wouldn't they." Trajan took a seat on one of
the nearby fish tubs. Ahlman and Ahren remained where they stood.
"Care to tell us about it?"

He didn't, really. But with little else to do while his clothes dried,
he supposed he had scant reason not to. Mayhap in reporting first
to the others, he would have some forewarning of what Ledron's
reaction would be.

So he shared with them everything that had happened, including
the admission of having withheld mention of his earlier brush with
the groll. It made no sense to leave anything out that Sallun was
sure to tell his captain—and Sallun was sure to tell all. During the

oration, two more pairs of Shadowguard returned from their prior rounds, rotating in to rest. Like Trajan, they were anxious to hear what news of the groll Sallun and Kylac had returned with. Was it closing in on them? Was it dead? Could they sleep any easier this night than they had the last?

There were seven men in all gathered round, listening with rapt attention, by the time he spoke of the groll's ambush. He did so in what detail he could, though Kylac had never fancied himself a storyteller. Lacking the talent for embellishment, he'd always felt his recountings too plain, matter-of-fact. In either case, what drama could be squeezed from a fight whose outcome was already known?

Besides, he could see that most of these men were privately questioning every word that escaped his mouth. Forthright as he'd always been, Kylac had little patience for doubters. Why should he have to prove himself? Disbelief didn't change the truth.

When finished, he met with a momentary silence, facing a range of expressions—awe, confusion, wariness, even outright disdain.

"Sure," the disdainful one sneered. "And my piss tastes like wine."

"Yours just might," said Trajan, drawing snickers from some of the others. Presumably, the man enjoyed his time in the barrel.

"I don't suppose you'd spare us a look at these unnatural blades of yours." A challenge, yes. But the whiskered veteran uttering it did so calmly, and wore a look favoring genuine curiosity.

"Certainly," Kylac agreed. With startling speed, he unleashed one of his shortswords. Smirking at those who tensed, recoiled, or fumbled their own weapon hilts in reflex, he extended the blade to Whiskers hilt-first.

The veteran accepted it tentatively. "Doesn't weigh much," he observed. "This severed a groll's wrist?"

"A pair o' smaller ones like it."

As he tested the weapon's balance, Whiskers glanced around at his fellow soldiers, who all seemed to be awaiting his verdict. When his gaze settled on one of the fish tubs, a gleam filled his eye. "Would it cut through this, then?"

The tubs looked to be made of lightweight spruce, banded with thick rings of teak around the top and bottom rims. "Try it."

The veteran hesitated, as if expecting to call Kylac's bluff.

"Come, Brenth," the disdainful one urged. "Let's see it bite."

The urging was taken up by some of the others. Trajan cocked a brow toward Kylac in question.

"Mayhap you're unfamiliar with how a blade works," Kylac prodded. "It commonly involves a slice, thrust, or chop."

Trajan chuckled. Two others smirked. The rest frowned or glared, mayhap mistaking his playfulness for arrogance. Brenth was among the latter. Looking first as if he might turn the weapon on Kylac, he instead drew back and took an overhand hack at the thick edge of the wooden tub. Instead of lodging to a halt near the rim, as one would expect, the blade cut completely through the teak ring, and carved a gash fully the length of a hand's breadth into the underlying spruce.

Brenth was suddenly impressed, releasing the hilt and lurching back in surprise. "Dawning winds," another whispered in exclamation. An awed hush stole over the group.

But the disdainful one only sneered. "Proving what? Wood looks half rotted, to me."

"Show us," Trajan challenged.

"Eh?"

"Match that stroke, if you can." He looked to Kylac, once again seeking his consent.

"If'n there's a blade here that can best it," Kylac agreed, "I'd love to sees it."

"There," said Trajan. "Any blade you like, eh, Ribach? I'll even throw in my axe."

"Like anyone but you could heft the bloody thing," Ribach replied, adding a harsh laugh.

None laughed with him, suggesting that it was too late to withdraw the challenge he'd raised. Judging by their reactions, this wasn't the first time Ribach had carried off at the mouth—and likely not the first time they'd called on him to back those words.

"Very well, you laggards. Step aside."

Giving Brenth a shove, Ribach drew a heavy broadsword. Once given a wide berth by his comrades, he checked his weapon's edge, rolled his shoulders as if to loosen them, shook his neck from side to side, and adjusted his stance.

"Are you going to split the bloody thing, or dance with it all day?"

Ribach glared at the new speaker, a cleft-jawed youth with auburn locks fair and flowing enough to belong to a maiden. But the withering look was wasted on the lad, who grinned at his own jape with unflappable confidence. Mayhap it lay in knowing the majority of the others had his back in this. Or mayhap it was his nature. Kylac noted either possibility, continuing to learn what he could of these men with whom he intended to brave the seas.

With a grimace, Ribach raised his blade and heaved downward. The heavy steel made a dull thud as it bit into the teak—at a depth that covered only half of the blade's width.

"Ho!" the others roared, laughs and cheers mixing with wide eyes and openmouthed stares. Glances shifted between Kylac, his embedded sword, and the disgruntled Ribach as he wrested his blade free in disgust. Brenth clapped his faithless comrade on the shoulder, then stepped forward and yanked Kylac's weapon from the wood—nearly stumbling when it slid free with unexpected ease.

The clamor drew the attention of the nearest sentry, who craned his neck in curiosity before looking over his shoulder to see if Sallun's conference with Ledron and Jahant had been disturbed. Wondering the same, Kylac watched for their potential emergence from behind the heavy sliding door—until he sensed the approach of another from behind him.

"What game are we at here?"

The newcomer grinned broadly, arms outstretched as if to embrace the group. His arrival, however, had a less-than-warming effect. As abruptly as a thunderhead might eclipse the sun, all merriment ceased. Expressions tightened. Laughs faded. Men rose and turned away with mumbles or groans, awe giving way to disinterest. Brenth offered Kylac his blade with barely a grunt before departing on Ribach's heels. The mute Ahlman and Ahren shadowed him, leaving only Trajan. As the rest cleared out before him, the big man, too, took his feet.

"What? Is the fun over already?" the newcomer asked.

"Rest is short," Trajan said to Kylac. "Best get to it." He turned and stalked away.

"No lie there," the newcomer told Kylac. "Got us sleeping in four-hour snatches. Wears a man thin. Name's Merrec," he added. He extended his hand in greeting, flashing again his gold-toothed grin.

"Merrec," Kylac echoed, sheathing his shortsword. "Ya sailed here with the renegades."

"Just doing my duty to king and country."

"By abducting the royal daughter?"

"I was brought on too late to prevent matters. And I knew it would take Darr time to organize a proper pursuit."

"Darr?"

"King Kendarrion. Though I'm no Blackfist, I thought it best to carry on and keep watch over Nara, make sure no harm came to her."

"Nara. That would be Her Highness." The king and now the princess—he'd heard no other refer to them in so familiar a fashion.

"And you're Kronus, yes? Heard me some stories about you." Merrec laughed. "Outlandish, really. Tales even your mother wouldn't believe."

"Ya knows my mother, do ya?"

"Well, not in the wedded sense." The mercenary nudged Kylac with an elbow, winking as he did so. "Shame. I'll bet she's a comely lass."

Kylac had only his father's word to go by—though that would seem a good deal more than Merrec had. He instinctively brushed his sleeve where the mercenary had touched him.

"I heard you demanded a reward."

"Demanded? Of course not. I only asked that if my efforts should please the king, he might show me a measure of gratitude."

"A lesser ransom, mayhap, but a ransom nonetheless."

"Is that what they're telling you? Ungrateful louts. Were it not for the risks I took, they'd still be hunting for Nara now."

"I suppose that's one way to sees it."

"They're likely jealous it's me Nara owes her life to, and not them. Shadowguard, outshone by a Redfist. Had they done their duty better, I'd not have had to do it for them."

"Redfist?"

"Soldier of the Stonewatch. Grunts, they call us. Though, in defending our lands, we do most of the fighting and dying, while the Blackfists, they spend their time lurking in shadow, buzzing about their royal charges like houseflies. It's us and the Whitefists who make their task easy."

"And the Whitefists would be . . ."

"Seawatch. Barnacles, we call them. Barely more useful than the houseflies, really, for all they do is get buggered by the Grenarr. But at least their burning ships can serve as beacon warning. No one's told you this?"

Kylac regarded the mercenary with cool appraisal. He preferred to form his own opinions of people, rather than blindly accept those fed to him by others. Merrec, however, was making that terribly difficult. He was affable, sure. Even now, his smile was broad, and his eyes bright. The mop of dark curls atop his head lent him an almost boyish innocence. But he was much too forward for Kylac's liking, and seemed far too pleased with himself, given the circumstances. Nor could Kylac see where this denigration of the others was warranted. "Dare I inquire about the Bluefists? Greenfists? Yellowfists?"

Merrec laughed. "It's just the three. Names sprang from the color of glove worn in uniform during ceremonial occasions."

"I see. Alas for the budding rainbow."

The mercenary continued to smile, even though Kylac didn't. When his amusement finally seemed set to wither, Merrec asked, "Why all the fuss just now?"

A clumsy shift meant to feel casual. Though he'd seemed oblivious to the slight paid him by the others, his prodding interest suggested now a keener awareness and a deeper motive.

"Just a test o' arms between Brenth and Ribach, if'n I caught their names correctly."

Merrec eyed the gashes in the teak-rimmed tub. "Who won?"

"Brenth."

"The old hound. After all these years, I can't believe he still serves. Darr would be safer dismissing him and appointing me."

Now who's jealous? "Seems to me, there'll be plenty o' new positions to be had by the time y'all return."

"More yet, as long as the mutant prowls free."

"Knows the beastie well, do ya?"

"I sailed with it, didn't I?"

"I's not been led to believe it the companionable sort."

Merrec laughed. "It didn't join us 'round the capstan at dice or bones, no. In all those weeks, I saw it only twice. But I know it fancies Nara. One dawn, I was asked to bring her breakfast. Scarcely uttered 'good morning' before it hissed at me from the shadows. I turned, and there it was, slavering beside me. Damn near soiled myself when I looked into its eyes."

"That terrifying, is it? What about the second time?"

"Just a glimpse. But that's more than most can say—including half these liars, who will talk as if they got scores of Ukinh heads mounted on their barrack walls."

"Was it Ulflund recruited the thing?"

"Didn't deny it when I asked him. But didn't seem too merry about it, neither, so I didn't press."

"Must've been desperate indeed, to keep such treacherous company."

The pointed remark could have been taken as another slight, but Merrec just laughed, assuming he was still talking about the groll. "Like swimming with a tarrock," he agreed.

Whatever that was. "What made him thinks he could tame the creature?"

Merrec shrugged. "Beasts have a mind of their own. But if anyone spent enough time with them to crack it, it was Ulflund. Say, is it true Grathe begged for his life like a plucked hen?"

"'Fraid the tale's been a mite overcooked."

"Pity. I'd love to have seen that. Man was a cheat."

Snorts the pig to the swine, Kylac suspected. "Mayhap ya can stake a claim with the authorities for his coin purse."

"I should, the buggerer. But I'll settle for knowing he ain't ever going to spend it."

"How do ya suppose the princess is faring?" Kylac asked. As long as he was enduring this chatter, he was determined to steer it in a more meaningful direction.

"Tough as granitewood, she is. If any of us survive this, she will."

"What could the groll want with her, now that Ulflund's gone?"

"What does any beast want, once freed from its tether?" Merrec's grin became wolfish.

"That's it?"

"What else?"

"Vengeance, mayhap, for Ulflund's crew?"

"Ulflund had no love for the beast. Why would it love him?"

"Does it serve these Grenarr raiders?"

"Grenarr or Addarans, why should it care who rules its shores?"

"Then why persist in hunting us?"

"It's a beast, I tell you. One that serves its own beastly desires."

Sallun had suggested elsewise. And Merrec's own account from the time at sea seemed to suggest it had been protecting Denariel. Mayhap that was the job Ulflund had assigned it—to keep any like Merrec from exercising their baser desires. Still, if it owed no allegiance to Ulflund, and none to the Grenarr, then mayhap the mercenary was right. For what else could explain its continued pursuit?

He would have to ask the others. Merrec, he'd already decided, was far less reliable than he boasted. Lies or witlessness—or a combination of both—seasoned his words. Yet he spoke so smoothly, so confidently, that Kylac couldn't discern one from the next. With time, he might learn to detect the specific ticks or habits that would betray the mercenary's attempts at deception. But that meant time spent in the man's presence that Kylac would sooner avoid.

"Look here, boy. If you're half as good as they say, you may have a fighting chance to make it out of this alive. But to do that, you're going to need someone who sees things the way they are."

"The way they are?"

"About the groll, and about this group. These Shadowguard, they're sworn to die for her, you know. Means they ain't always going to make the wisest choice. They're going to make whatever choice favors her, even at risk to themselves."

"As *you* did in following her?"

"Just so." Merrec grinned, then leaned in, lowering his voice conspiratorially. "Only, things have changed. With Ulflund's crew, the groll was 'tamed,' as you put it. Now, it's off its leash. It wants what we have, and nothing short of death will stop it. If it means sacrificing you for her, they'll do it, don't you doubt."

"Ledron made that plain."

"An easy agreement now, while we're ensconced like this, confident in our combined strength. But there'll come a time—mark it—when the choice may not be so simple. What I'm saying is, you and me, we don't owe this girl nothing. I've paid more than my share of risk already. And you . . . you don't know her from my bastard sister. It ain't like she's the crown heir, you see."

"I see. Siblings?"

"A brother. Thane." The mercenary brushed past the topic as if shooing a fly. "These others, they may play at friendship. But when there's that choice to be made . . . Well, if we're not careful, it'll be you and me cast out in the same small boat."

"You and me," Kylac echoed.

"Your blades. My eyes, ears, and experience. As good a marriage as we'll find before this is done."

Kylac did well to suppress laughter. Not only at the offer, but at the wholly transparent way it had been presented. *Don't trust them. Trust me.* Did Merrec believe him fool enough to even consider such a ridiculous proposition?

Outwardly, however, Kylac nodded, his expression showing the expected amount of earnestness. He *was* still an outsider here, and might indeed have need of further information. Unreliable as it was, Merrec's had proven to be the only loose tongue among them.

Thankfully, the door to Ledron's office slid open just then, and the captain himself emerged with Jahant and Sallun in tow. Jahant's scowl deepened considerably when he saw Kylac standing with Merrec, while Ledron and even Sallun frowned with clear disapproval. The trio marched straight up to them.

"Have you anything to add to Sallun's report?" Ledron asked directly.

"Doubtful," Kylac replied. "Lad seems to know his business."

"Can't say much of it pleases me," Ledron admitted. "But I can't say I'm much surprised, either." He cast a sidelong glance at Merrec before addressing Kylac again. "Your orders are unchanged. You will escort Sallun to the Bilge each day, returning at night to report. If you do not, you will be presumed dead, necessitating other plans. So, make sure you return."

Jahant interjected. "What of leading the groll here?"

"Surely, it knows where we are already. All we can do is hunker down, remain vigilant, and hope word of our ready vessel comes soon." To Kylac, he added, "If the mutant tries you again, see if you can't finish the job, hmm?"

Merrec stiffened in surprise. "Wait. You've seen the beast?"

Though all ignored the mercenary, Ledron relaxed almost imperceptibly—pleased, no doubt, to realize that Kylac had kept Merrec in the dark.

"O' that," Kylac said, "ya needn't fear."

6

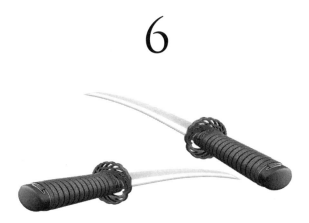

Six days later, Kylac found himself in roughly the same place, summoned along with the rest of the Shadowguard company to what all hoped would be their last meeting on these shores.

"We make for the docks just after sunset," Ledron announced, when all—save for the invisible Denariel and her personal sentries—had gathered. "Iron Star formation, with the princess at its heart."

Kylac, seated on a barrel apart from the others, twiddled a knife as the captain spread a city map across the table.

"We'll march east first, along Wendway, then south, cutting through the Storm Quarter along Sliver Street."

"I count at least three major plazas along that route," grumbled Trajan, "making us visible from half the rooftops in the city."

"Open enough to alert us to any approach, and space in which our numbers can be brought to bear. Better that than some webwork of close-knit alleys, where the groll could ambush us at any turn."

The groll. Nerves tightened at the mere mention, though it was already on every man's mind. Kylac himself had thought of little else over the past week. By day, he'd hunkered down with Sallun at the Thirsty Bilge, awaiting word from Wingport's harbormaster. By night, after delivering their empty report, he'd patrolled the area around their hideout, privately hoping the mutant would become foolish or desperate enough to make an attempt at the princess.

So that he could finish the business they'd begun.

Alas, he'd crossed neither sign nor trace of the Ukinh, leading him to wonder aloud if, considering its wounds, it might have given up. The others had laughed grimly at the possibility. When questioned as packs or individuals, the response remained the same. First, its wounds would heal. Even its lost hand would regenerate, though this could take weeks, rather than hours or days. Second, grolls didn't give up. They did not barter, yield, reconsider, or lose interest. It was out there, they'd assured him. Hiding, watching, waiting for its next opportunity to strike.

Why? Kylac had asked, as he had of Merrec. At this juncture, what could it mean to achieve? But the answers he'd received had been no more useful than the mercenary's. Some had shrugged, others had offered jests, while still others had reacted nervously, hedging their response or ducking the question altogether. Trajan, whom he'd come to trust more than the rest of this brood, had replied simply, *Only the groll could know.*

Kylac cleared his throat. "Not that anyone has asked me, but why not run a separate squad in diversion?"

Ledron eyed him cautiously. The Head, Kylac had nicknamed him, for his shorn pate and commanding role. "I'll not risk splitting our already diminished numbers. A single unit is more formidable than two."

"Depends on its members," Kylac argued. "Your princess would be safe with me. Toss in one or two o' yours, if'n ya like. The rest o' ya, escorting a decoy, should draw the beastie."

"*Second*, the groll knows the princess's scent. A hundred decoys would not throw it off once we have her in the open."

If so, the Head's strategy was sound. Overly cautious, mayhap, but after his own encounter in that sewer tunnel, Kylac was less inclined than before to suggest as much. In either case, he let the argument go. He'd not made it with any expectation of Ledron agreeing to it. He'd merely wanted to gauge the captain's reaction.

"Our ship is moored offshore . . . here," Ledron continued, pointing at the map. "*Denariel's Return.* When we reach the harbor, we'll

board a set of skiffs and slip out to where she waits for us. Should
the mutant attempt to follow, her tending crew will feather it with
a rain of iron-tipped shafts."

Kylac frowned. Unless the descriptions he'd gathered about this
creature were greatly embellished—and he had little reason now to
believe that they were—it could simply swim out beneath the dark
waters, cling to the ship's rudder, and slither aboard the moment the
lookouts turned their heads.

"What's to keep it from swimming after us?" asked Merrec. The
cagey mercenary had evidently had the same thought.

"That's where our renowned little rogue earns his keep," Ledron
said, turning his gaze upon Kylac.

Kylac arched his brow in question. "Oh?"

"The rest of us—how did you say it—tread too heavy."

A handful of Shadowguard bristled at the reminder. Mayhap he
should have let one or two of them accompany him on his nightly
patrols. The truth, it seemed, too often drew offense.

"Since you claim to be more dangerous unencumbered, I'm appointing you as our hunter. As we are the groll's quarry, it will be yours.
You'll trail us at a distance, to make sure the mutant doesn't. You spy
it, you kill it . . . or at least throw it off our scent. Agreed?"

He caught a knowing look from Merrec, but ignored it. If he'd
been itching for another chance to engage the beast, this was it. Countering that . . .

"Ya won't just leave me behind?"

"If I must. My duty is to Her Highness."

Kylac scowled, providing the outward response Ledron expected.
In truth, the answer pleased him, as it was the only one he could trust.

"We'll leave a skiff for you. If it is safe to do so, you'll board on
our heels."

Kylac mulled his options. The plan wasn't without flaws, but what
plan was? So much depended on execution—and blind chance, of
course. If this was the role Ledron wanted him to play in this game,
so be it. Kylac would just have to make sure the dice tumbled in his
favor.

And if Ledron thought to cross him . . . well, Kylac would make sure the captain lived just long enough to regret it.

He sensed Sallun and a few others turn their gazes on him, made uncertain by his lengthening silence. Sallun's was nervous. Trajan's was reassuring. Merrec's . . . Merrec's eye had the gleam of a vulture, looking always for some scrap to feed on.

"I'll has your backs," Kylac agreed, wondering who—if anyone—might have his.

The sun bled, and night's shroud fell across the sky. The pulse of the city slowed, raucous echoes of voice and movement softening to murmurs as its citizens retreated to their nocturnal dens. A fog-filled darkness pressed heavily upon the seaside hills, homes, and streets, despite the countless fires from lamp and torch that sought vainly to keep it at bay.

Kylac turned his gaze to the south. From his vantage atop the abandoned warehouse, he could just make out the dim line between cloud-choked heavens and the distant sea. The ocean had taken on an obsidian cast, smooth with slumber. A ruse. Like the calm of the night. Like the calm of his flesh. Look closer, and one would find the dangerous forces churning beneath.

He closed his eyes, seeking to still his growing anticipation. The purest focus, he'd learned, could best be found in losing oneself utterly . . . setting adrift upon the currents of life's energies. A man could fight those currents by perfecting his command over the principles of motion, honing flesh and practicing physical routines until they became reflex. But all of life was an ocean. Boundless. Inexorable. A rigid vessel, no matter its strength, would eventually founder beneath the waves stirred by the passage of other living beings. The smoothest course was cut when one stopped attempting to bend, control, or resist nature's interweaving forces, and learned instead to navigate their inconstant flow.

His hand slipped instinctively to the hilt of his slender longsword, fingers caressing the wood- and leather-wrapped haft, thumb lightly

brushing the small, disc-shaped crosspiece. He'd scarcely let go of
it or his other blades since their retrieval, reflecting too often on
how close he'd come to never holding them again. He might tell
himself elsewise, but the crudely stitched tears in his breeches and
tunic served as a constant reminder of the groll's attack. This time,
he would be ready.

In his mind's eye, he retraced the steps that lay ahead of them. So
many precautions. So much wariness and fear. And all of it just to
escort Denariel safely to her ship, to say nothing of the voyage beyond.

His stomach knotted strangely. Not a warning, exactly, but a
discomfort bred from uncertainty. Unsurprising, given all that was
still unknown. Despite a week of probing both subtle and direct,
he'd managed to draw little about this journey that Ledron hadn't
already revealed. The same command that had jailed Sallun's tongue
had shackled the others' as well. Lingering questions regarding the
Addarans, the Grenarr, and the conflict between them had gone
unanswered. Mayhap the matter really was as simple as Ledron had
painted it—a desperate land grab by the seabound Grenarr. But if
that were so, why the need for such guarded silence?

Let them keep it. Experience told Kylac that most secrets men
hoarded were valuable only to them. And he trusted in his own
ability to ride matters out, regardless of any untamed reservations.

Inland, bells began to toll, proclaiming the Crow's Hour. Kylac
felt the reverberations penetrate his flesh, rolling through him in
eddies of expectation.

Time to move.

As he opened his eyes, he caught Sallun, nearly invisible in the
dark, slipping from the warehouse. Hooded as the lad was, Kylac
discerned the sudden shifts of Sallun's head as his gaze darted every
which way like an anxious bird. Upon reaching the end of the alley,
he flashed a signal from a small mirror, aimed back in the direction
from which he'd come. With that, the Shadowguard emerged.

Ahlman and Ahren led, a single body before splitting into two.
Hood and Cowl, as he'd come to think of them, their ravaged faces
hidden at all times. Their bows were strung, in hand, an arrow nocked
to each. Quiver caps hung open, dangling by leather thongs, exposing

the fletching of ready reserves. They too looked ahead and behind them, from side to side, from foundation to rooftop, sweeping for any sign of their enemy as they ventured into the night.

Jahant the Mace, Nethreal the Truth, and two whose names had been given only as Moles and Grimes, came next, followed by two more pairs. The last of these, Kylac hadn't seen before. Denariel's personal sentries, he decided, kept from the outer rotations. Which likely meant . . .

He leaned forward ever so slightly as she appeared, flanked by Ledron on one side, dwarfed by Trajan, whom the others aptly called the Tower, on the other. Though cloaked like the rest, it had to be her, Denariel. The one for whom all—save Merrec—would lay down their lives, with the expectation that Kylac would do the same. A dubious assumption. For while he would gladly shield her from the Ukinh, he did so more to test himself, not because he believed her life to be worth any more than another's.

Royalty or no.

The rearguard followed. Colven, nicknamed Gallop for the hitch in his stride, and Percel, of the tree-trunk legs and lopsided grimace that had inspired Kylac to dub him Fishhook. Brenth, called Salts, and Obren, of the cleft chin and silken hair that had earned him the moniker Locks. Sour Ribach, hot-blooded Hadrum, and more. Kylac counted thirty-one Shadowguard in all—what remained of the forty-one who'd set sail along with ten sailors of the Seawatch to recapture the princess. Mix in Sallun as the lone surviving Whitefist, the Redfist Merrec, and himself, and they were thirty-four, warding Her Highness. Near enough twoscore. If that was insufficient to keep a single wounded groll at bay, well then, the beast deserved its prize.

At the end of the alley, the line fanned into its Iron Star formation. Five wedges of six men each that walled Denariel off at the base and spread to a point covering rear flanks, forward flanks, and the road ahead. A point man—Faban—split the fifty paces between Sallun and the formation's central tip, while a lone Blackfist—"Twitch" Davins—trailed at roughly the same distance. More bait than guard, really. Just an outer alarm, waiting to be triggered. For behind him came only the darkness and fog.

And high above, Kylac Kronus.

He rose from his crouch as Davins reached the corner and twisted down a cobbled bypass that emptied farther ahead onto the east-curling Wendway. Still he waited, eyes, ears, and nose attuned to the night, in search of anything out of place. Ledron and the others had sought to convince him that the question was not *if* the groll would attack, but when, how, and where. Kylac had a hard time imagining it. No matter the direction from which it might approach, it would face a two-pronged defense designed to entrap it like an insect's pincers. The formation itself would not stop the groll from claiming its share of victims, but the discipline of this company's members, in addition to their superior numbers, would surely keep the mutant engaged long enough for Kylac to join the fray.

At which point, it would meet its end, or be forced to flee as it had before.

Only a mindless creature, then, would make the attempt. And the groll was too smart for that. Or would bestial urge in this instance overrule rational thought?

When Davins had just about faded behind a deepening curtain of brume, Kylac took a running leap onto a rooftop across the way. There he crouched again, waiting momentarily before dashing along the roof's peak and leaping to the next. From there, he leapt to an adjacent balcony, then scrambled higher in order to jump a wider gap that awaited.

He felt foolish, in a sense, navigating these rooftops like a court tumbler performing for his supper. The groll had *his* scent, too. It would know he was there. Aware by now that Kylac presented the greater obstacle, it would not be misled into thinking it could kill or slip past Davins and make a free charge at the others. Were their roles reversed, Kylac would have aimed to take the groll out first, and only then set his sights on those blanketing Denariel. That, or he would have taken a sewer route, looking to steal up from below into the heart of their defense. But Ledron fully anticipated the latter, and was veering far from any grates or conduits from which the groll could attempt such an ambush. So mayhap the Shadowguard captain was hoping for the former, as it offered the strongest explanation for keeping their best sword so far from the main company.

Still, the elevated vantage did offer a clearer visual than what he would find on the ground, allowing him to keep an eye on the company's progression through the streets. And Kylac was not averse to hanging back in the shadows. Should it tempt the groll to face him, so be it. He would just have to finish the beast quickly enough to not miss his boat.

Their march was drawing notice now, as they continued along Wendway and made their approach to the first plaza along their charted route. Heads turned, fingers pointed, and whispers were exchanged, as onlookers took stock of the large, battle-ready crew. A pair of city watchmen looked up as they entered the plaza square, observing closely . . . but didn't approach. Though banned in many of the larger, walled cities of Kuuria by decree of the Imperial Council, bared arms were not uncommon in the more open, coastal communities such as Wingport. Here, one did not draw the ire of the watch until blood was spilled.

Curiosity, however, was another matter. It clung to them like webbing as they pushed past the inns, alehouses, fountains, and pavilions—wherever the city's denizens had gathered. Even here, among a people accustomed to an eclectic mix of every known nation and culture from these shores and beyond, it was impossible not to raise excitement or suspicion. Such a guard ring surely indicated wealth of some sort. Royalty, mayhap, or mercenaries ready to defend their stolen treasure. *Or both,* thought Kylac. He could see these and myriad other possibilities flitting through the onlookers' minds—people who didn't know whether to press in for a closer look, or seek shelter as swiftly as possible.

For the moment, at least, most seemed content with gawking or speculating among themselves. None yet had dared approach, and those in the company's path quickly stepped aside. Kylac kept tight watch regardless. He had to assume that any one of the robed figures could be the groll. Else it might be skulking among them, using them as cover from which to spring. The creature would surely need a diversion of some sort to make its move—chaos in which to work. In that respect, the course Ledron had plotted for them favored their enemy, providing the human pawns it might use to its advantage.

Not here, however. They reached the east end of the square and left it behind them, continuing along Wendway as it funneled onward, deeper into the heart of the city. Light, sound, and movement dimmed somewhat from that found in the plaza. Though strangers still walked the streets, they kept mostly to its edges, giving Denariel's company wide berth as it marched down the center of the road.

Kylac kept pace along the broken line of rooftops, at one with the shadows. The groll might know he was there, but no one else would. He would dash along for a spell, then tiptoe or crouch the next. Leaps and climbs were timed so that none could spy him—not even those who knew he followed. His pace was intentionally erratic, without discernible rhythm. Just to make it harder for anyone—or anything—to draw bead on his movements.

Despite the obstacles and challenges inherent in his uneven course, Kylac's focus never wavered. If he wasn't watching the company's progress, he was listening to its echoes. Should something cause their pace to falter, he would know it from their movements. More than either sight or sound, however, he relied on his instincts—his sense of the night and the things within it as they enveloped him. The world had a feel to it that he'd always found difficult to describe, or for others to comprehend. It really was like waves and ripples of emotional energy, unseen, that triggered similar sentiments within. He could be walking along and feel a sudden hunger, moments before he turned the corner and found the starving cripple who begged for a meal. He could be overwhelmed with joy, before cathedral bells heralded the emergence of a newly wedded couple from its vaulted doors.

If that weren't unusual enough, at times, he felt these emotions even before the person had projected them. The murderous rage of the cheated gambler—before the dice had been cast. The sadness of the mite lass who wept over her lost pastry—before she'd fumbled it to the ground. Such signals were everywhere, so prevalent that the greatest challenge often came in sifting through them. But Kylac had felt these emotional reverberations all his life, and so had become well versed in filtering distraction.

The road carried them for several hundred paces in relative quiet before traffic began thickening. They were coming upon another plaza—the largest along their planned route. Kylac tensed as a pack of six mounted swordsmen—a merchant guard ring—rode into view at the head of an oncoming trio of wagons. Along either flank rode another six. They too had lain claim to the center of the street, expecting any in their path to make way. Nor did they appear of a mien to yield now. Though clearly outnumbered, they came apace, their direction unaltered.

Kylac could sense the rising hackles among some in Ledron's company. Some, he knew, were spoiling for a fight, frustrated at having been cooped up for so long, and by their fear of an enemy they couldn't face. All it would take was a spark.

But Ledron wasn't going to let pride jeopardize his commitment to Denariel's safety. A quiet command swept outward, and the entire company veered to the right, skirting the line of storefronts that Kylac traversed. Kylac half expected the groll to come lunging out of the dark, leaping from an alcove or one of the shuttered windows on that side. But Ledron, he was sure, had already weighed that risk. And the men were ready.

Members of the passing troop exchanged glances with the Shadowguard on the near flank. Some nodded in courtesy, while others puffed their chests in perceived victory.

They should have counted themselves fortunate.

As the groups finished passing each other, the plaza opened up. Sallun, Kylac noticed, was already deep within the milling crowd. A pair of women approached him, their easy smiles and lack of dress betraying a wanton intent. Sallun shook his head, then feigned a cough that had them stepping away. Thirty paces back, Faban brushed past a peddler plying him with silks. Twenty paces behind him, the main company had an easier time of it, as once again the crowds parted with wary curiosity. Musicians, acrobats, vendors, patrons—none wished to interfere with such a sizable force, fully cloaked and bristling with drawn steel. For the attention it drew them, they could as well have paraded a herd of bleating sheep before them. Any attempt at secrecy may have been wasted on the groll, but did they have to alert the entire city to their passage this night?

That concern manifested a moment later when a small patrol of soldiers took notice. Imperial Army, not city watchmen. Which technically meant they had no particular authority here, as they were sworn to the land of Kuuria, not the city of Wingport. But Imperial soldiers were widely known to enjoy certain liberties with their position, interpreting a lack of local allegiance as a right to conduct themselves in whatever manner pleased them. Whether a magistrate found a man in violation of city ordinance became mostly irrelevant when the soldier could simply claim his actions to be in the greater interest of the empire's safety.

The soldiers approached. Ten in all, Kylac noted. Not too many to overcome, but a fight would mean making a mad dash toward the docks before the city watch *did* respond. Though Ledron had already bribed a pair of city ministers and the master of the watch to look the other way regarding their departure this night, Governor Kardan himself would not be able to pardon them should they resist or kill a full Imperial squad.

Ledron called a halt when it was clear there was no other choice. He further commanded his Blackfists to lower their blades, then left Trajan with Denariel at the heart of their star while he stepped forward alone to the edge of the formation. Kylac scanned the surrounding crowds, which thickened in anticipation. An attack by the groll at this moment might easily result in swords between Shadowguard and Imperials a bloodbath of confusion in which to execute its own purpose.

Men on either side eyed one another with more ease than they felt. Kylac, crouched atop a corner balcony, read it in their stances. The Imperials had their cloaks pushed back, so that hilts were in easy reach, while the Shadowguard weapons, though lowered, danced with itchy movements. Heads swiveled and turned, searching for that small clue or signal that would trigger their ready response.

The captain of the Imperial squad, in conference with Ledron beside two of his lieutenants, threw his head back in sudden laughter. Kylac wondered how that could happen, as he'd yet to hear Ledron utter anything one might consider amusing. Then came the quick exchange of a coin purse, passed from Ledron to the Imperial corporal, who just as quickly slipped it to the lieutenant on his left. Ledron permitted the corporal to clap him on the shoulder, after which he turned and made his way back to Denariel.

As easy as that, thought Kylac.

Would that their enemy could be purchased so cheaply.

The Shadowguard march resumed, while the Imperial squad went about dispersing the gathered crowd. Sallun, Faban, and Davins, still holding their remote positions, fell into step. Davins eyed the area around him with a particularly nervous air—more so even than Sallun, which was no small feat. Doubtless, he felt especially vulnerable out there in his trailing position, and it couldn't have helped to be standing around, wondering as Kylac had if this was the moment the groll would strike.

As it approached a fountain near the heart of the plaza, the main company veered right, cutting south along an intersecting roadway. Sliver Street. Two more plazas—including one nearly the size of this one—lay in their path. Then, on to the docks and the skiffs that would carry them to their offshore vessel. In terms of distance, they were already more than halfway home. As Kylac slipped along in pursuit, he began to wonder, what was the groll waiting for?

Though smaller than Wendway, Sliver Street proved to be more heavily trafficked. Horses, carts, and wagons clogged the cobblestone path, which was further narrowed by awnings and verandas that reached out from either side. A street fair, Kylac realized. As the winds turned, the scents of roasted meats, grilled vegetables, and freshly baked breads—as well as the ever-present assortment of fish and shell creatures both raw and boiled—filled the briny air. Music and merriment, peppered with drunken cheers and the squeals of delighted children, echoed within the cramped corridor. Sallun and Faban had stopped, seeking some indication from Ledron of what they should do—suggesting that this hadn't been part of the plan.

The captain wasted no time signaling his desire. They were to push through. Though he'd specifically hoped to avoid any narrow or overly crowded confines, he clearly wasn't willing to deviate from the chosen path. Better to remain in the open, it seemed, than attempt to redirect down any of the smaller alleys and byways.

They made few friends as they carved their path, their formation squeezing only slightly, pushing all else aside. Some looked on with smiles at first, thinking them part of the fair—a theater troupe on parade, about to unveil a live performance. But souring expressions gave way to boos and jeers when it became clear that they were merely a band of haughty ruffians forcing their way without any regard for the festivities or its participants.

A stumbling drunkard ventured too near one of the rear wedges, and had to be shoved away. A pack of gypsies, indignant at the interruption of their coin-grubbing dance performance, reached for weapons until deterred by Ahlman's and Ahren's bows. All along the festival route, music and song and feasting ground to a premature halt.

The crowd's animosity, however, was short-lived. Like a knife through a stream of water, their passage did no real harm. Celebration resumed swiftly in their wake, healed by laughter and music and the determination of entertainers and vendors seeking to make a profit. Save for a smattering of half-eaten bread rolls, vegetable scraps, and slurs that rained after them, the Shadowguard emerged on the far side of the motley gathering unscathed.

Kylac's disappointment grew more acute.

From there they encountered only dregs—the late, the lost, the uninitiated, or the unwelcome—before reaching the low, pitted wall marking the Storm Quarter. So named for its exposure to the elements of an untamed ocean, this crescent-shaped, low-lying district served as the southernmost buffer between the inner city and the great, churning beyond. More than once in its history had its weathered slopes been scraped clean by surging waves and tempest winds—devoured by the hungry sea. But mankind thus far had proven equally possessive, stubbornly working to chisel, hammer, and rope their feeble structures back together, borrowing every inch of stony shore their cantankerous neighbor would allow them—knowing even as they did so that it would return to feed again.

Among the busiest by day, this district was all but empty at night. A few scattered watchmen could be found here or there, but served no real purpose other than to hassle the occasional urchin into finding some other corner in which to while away his night. The main docks, farther east, were still astir, but this area belonged mostly to the poor, the wretched, and the vermin who preyed upon them.

Kylac took one last, lingering overview before descending from his rooftop position. There were few remaining heights between here and the breakwater, and those that *did* stand did so aloof of one another. He took up a position about twenty paces to the rear of Davins, creeping along in soundless pursuit. Davins himself cast frequent backward glances—in search of the groll, or mayhap Kylac. Whichever, it seemed the Blackfist and he might be sharing much the same thought: The groll had declined to attack them amid the noise and lights and the open-air crowds; mayhap it would do so now, amid the faint moon and almost eerie solitude.

But nothing troubled them as they navigated the ramshackle spread of pens, hovels, and unpaved roadways that marked land's end. Kylac remained vigilant, marking every corner, every alley, every dip, bend, ditch, and overhang that they passed. Still, no sign of the mutant. His senses told him it was out there. He couldn't see, hear, or smell it, but he felt certain it hadn't so easily surrendered its prize. It hadn't simply accepted defeat in the sewer and moved on to other pursuits.

Had it?

He was forced to question his own assumptions—fueled largely by these Shadowguard—when their group neared the final stretch. An earthen jetty reached out into the inkwell surface of the night-cloaked sea. At its far end, a weathered lighthouse. Sallun reached it first and vanished inside. Moments later, its lantern flashed a signal to the ghostly shadow of a ship anchored offshore. When that signal was promptly returned, the company moved ahead, while Kylac crouched in wait.

Around the lighthouse they curved, down to where the promised skiffs were moored amid the surfswept rocks at the jetty's base. This was it. At any moment, the groll would launch itself from a crevice within those barnacle-encrusted boulders. Or from beneath the waves themselves, Kylac thought, as the first of the boats set free to ride their swell. Now, while their company was segmented. Mayhap it didn't even care about the soldiers. Mayhap it would simply rise up to snatch the princess and drag her into the depths.

He remained motionless while, instead, four boats carried Denariel, Sallun, thirty-one Shadowguard, and the mercenary Merrec off to their waiting vessel. The only sounds were the chewing of the surf, the shriek of seabirds, and the echoes of city activity too far distant to be of any concern to them here. Kylac watched the shore, the lighthouse, the waves, the boats, seeking any sign of pursuit, and found none. Was the groll already aboard the ship? If so, there was little he could do about it from here.

When the boats returned, they did so filled with the harbormaster's tending crew, relieved now by Ledron and his Shadowguard. Kylac moved to the end of the jetty to greet them.

"You's the one I'm to ferry over?" asked a scowling, silver-bearded brute with what looked like a barnacle on the side of his nose.

Kylac nodded, pleasantly surprised that Ledron would keep their bargain. "No sign o' trouble aboard?"

"What kind you expecting?"

"Just some business unfinished." He knew not how much his ferryman had been told about their undertaking, but guessed it hadn't been much.

The ferryman snorted as Kylac settled into the skiff with him and three other oarsmen. "Folks what finish their business don't steal off in the tail of the night."

Kylac smiled, wondering how often the crusty sailor had been tasked with this sort of affair. "We baited the hook. The fish simply didn't bite."

Their little vessel shoved off as the other crews settled ashore. Kylac felt their passing gazes upon him, but sensed only varying degrees of disinterest. Nonetheless, he remained alert, hoping against hope that his night hadn't ended yet.

Alas, all he felt was the slap of the oars, the rhythm of the waves, the cold seawater pooled at his feet—nothing to suggest the groll stalked him.

Leaving his thirst unslaked.

Sallun saw this in his eyes when he boarded *Denariel's Return*. The young lookout met him at the rail—along with Ahlman and Ahren and their still-ready bows—as he ascended the rope ladder and waved a sardonic farewell to Barnacle-nose.

"Seems your beastie ain't so beastly after all," Kylac groused.

"And blessed be the graces if you're right."

"Rather dull way to put spurs to this adventure." He turned to Ahlman, and then to Ahren. "Tell me I'm wrong."

They, of course, remained mute. But Sallun quickly disagreed. "We've still a storm-wracked ocean to cross, infested with man-eating creatures, ridden with pirates who would make a sail out of your skin. With the perils that lie ahead, I wouldn't weep for the one left behind."

7

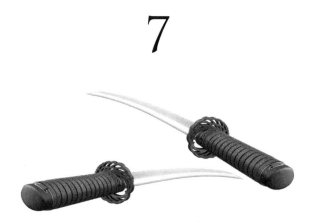

Few took any rest that night. Instead, they searched *Denariel's Return* from bow to stern, larboard to starboard, topmast to bilge, and back again. They scoured her cabins and holds, checking every crate, every sack, every barrel. They combed sails, spars, rigging, and ballast. They inspected weapons closets and supply lockers, probing every hollow they could find. All in an effort to uncover a hair, a scale, a claw mark—anything to indicate that the groll might have somehow slithered aboard.

When finished, they began the process anew. It mattered not that the harbormaster's crew had been paid handsomely to ensure a clean vessel. It mattered not, the precautions they had taken while ashore, or that Kylac had sensed nothing of the groll during their embarkation. Ledron's order to rake the ship a third time when the first two sweeps turned up nothing went unquestioned. If, despite everything, there was any chance the mutant was among them, the Shadowguard were determined to ferret it out.

Until they had, none would lie easy.

Kylac was as anxious as any of them, albeit for different reasons. One never knew where the winds might blow him. But he understood it quite possible that he would never return to Pentanian shores. To leave them without having settled matters between himself and the

Ukinh left an unfamiliar hollowness in his stomach.

With the dawn's rays spilling across the horizon in a blinding shimmer of molten hues, and the smudge of Wingport no longer visible behind them, Ledron finally sent a third of their crew to find sleep. The remainder of those not charged with keeping their vessel on course were asked to continue the search. Kylac himself knew nothing of hoisting sails, running out rigging, tacking, frapping, trimming, tricing, reefing, reeving, or any of the other myriad sailing tasks that seemed to be ongoing at all times. Thus, he found himself patrolling the decks above and below in an endless circuit—mostly working to keep clear of sliding ropes, swinging spars, and shuffling crewmen—clinging to the dwindling hope that his enemy might be discovered.

The one place he wasn't allowed was the captain's quarters, where Denariel had sequestered herself along with her private sentries by the time Kylac had boarded. Or *been sequestered*, mayhap. Kylac had yet to discern whether her privacy was by personal choice or by Ledron's orders. It was one of those answers he'd fished for, only to draw up empty. To a man, the Shadowguard deferred such inquiries to their captain. And Ledron . . . well, when not in hiding himself in the navigation room, Ledron would grunt and frown as if he'd just as soon have Kylac tossed overboard. Kylac couldn't have said how many he might have to kill to prevent that. He knew only that dead men made poor sailors, and he wasn't inclined to try to steer this beast by himself.

Moreover, Ledron had made plain the terms of his authority on this voyage, and Kylac had agreed to them as such. It would be disingenuous of him to complain now.

It was midafternoon before Colven, Ledron's third-in-command, offered to relieve him. Kylac declined. He waited until the next rotation, at midnight, before succumbing to weariness and disappointment. Eschewing the cramped confines of the crew's cabin, he ventured astern and climbed the poop deck, granting himself a reasonable overlook of the decks below. There he claimed an open stretch against the taffrail, beneath the limitless expanse of the starlit sky, and closed his eyes in search of slumber.

HE AWOKE to the sound of retching.

There were a dozen other noises that filled his ears—a cacophony of creaking, snapping, splashing, groaning, whistling, rattling, and more—formed by the interplay of churning ocean, gusting winds, and rollicking vessel. But these he'd acquainted himself with readily enough to push to the background. *This* was something new.

He rolled to his feet and sprang upright, experiencing none of the stiffness or cramps that most men complained of when waking. His body responded as it always did, triggered by mental command, primed for any challenge.

He targeted the source of the disturbance almost at once, two levels down, on the quarterdeck. There, a pair of men flanked a diminutive form leaning over the larboard rail and spasming in the telltale manner of stomach sickness. Straightaway, Kylac recognized the trio for who they were, and grinned in spite of himself.

Here at last, Her Royal Highness, the Princess Denariel.

A forward glance down the length of the ship revealed but a skeletal crew: Colven at the wheel, Nethreal in the crow's nest, and Obren stationed atop the forecastle. He spied Ahlman roaming the starboard rail, and knew that meant Ahren would be found patrolling their vessel in silent circuit as well. Faban was climbing the ratlines of the mainmast— for what purpose, only he and the gods of sailing knew— while Brenth and Ribach were on the maindeck, wrestling a length of sail. The remainder of the crew, it seemed, was busy below. Else slumbering. Though clouded skies glowed with a hint of the dawn's coming, the sun itself had yet to crest the horizon.

The retching came again. Kylac cast about once more for Ledron, but saw no trace of the captain. With a spring in his step, he descended.

The sentries took no notice of him until he was nearly upon them. Even then, he had to alert them to his arrival, so as not to startle them.

"Mights I be of any—"

The smaller of the two sentries wheeled defensively, daggers in hand. The larger hovered more closely to the vomiting Denariel, shielding her with his bulk.

The princess herself only heaved again.

"Ah," the dagger-wielder realized. "It's you."

"Expecting the mutant, I gather?" The soldier's daggers, Kylac noted, were still raised.

"What do you want?"

"Only to aid, if'n I may." He folded his arms, trying to minimize any apparent threat.

"We require no aid," the larger one sneered, chest puffing like that of a blowfish. His dark hair was gray at the temple, and his face clean-shaven, while his companion's hair burned red, growing also in a carefully trimmed ring about the mouth. Each carried a healthy paunch at the waist, and slack skin about the throat, neither of which was common among the Shadowguard. Ranson and Jekks were the names he'd been given for this pair, though he knew not one from the other. "We know our business."

"I see," Kylac said, wiping a stray drop of windblown vomit from his cheek. "That why ya's got her retching into the wind?"

Their superior expressions turned contemptuous.

"Has ya tried ginger root? I's heard sailors talk about—"

"Of course we've given her—"

"I am not your concern, mercenary," came Denariel's own muffled retort, followed by yet another heave.

"Begging pardon, Your Highness, but I's been led to believe that your well-being is my utmost concern."

The blowfish doubled over abruptly. An elbow to the gullet from Denariel herself, Kylac realized, as the princess squirmed about. Dagger-man extended a warding arm, but offered little fight when she shoved him aside to place her upturned face as close as she could to Kylac's.

"Do not ply me with your cheap loyalty. Were I a three-legged goat infected with rot, you would care the same, provided the weight of the purse met with your satisfaction."

Seldom speechless, Kylac found himself tongue-tied here. This royal waif was not at all as he'd envisioned. For one, her darker skin suggested a different mix of blood than these, her people. That carried with it any number of possibilities—irrelevant mayhap, or mayhap not. No less obvious was her revulsion of who she perceived him to be—a general judgment he had little reason to take offense at, but which suggested a history here that might prove difficult to overcome. Then there was the interaction between her and her sentries—Daggers and Blowfish. Neither jailors, nor confidantes, but something in between. Was it their overprotectiveness that vexed her, or something more? Or was it all merely a reaction to the discomfort from her sea illness?

The latter seemed most likely in that moment, as her petulant expression gave way suddenly to telltale alarm, an instant before she bucked forward and heaved again, this time at Kylac's chest. Kylac stepped aside to avoid most of it. In truth, there wasn't much to avoid. The lass had all but emptied her stomach already. Her poor body just hadn't realized it.

As she stood there, bent forward, strings of bile dripping from her mouth, the dark-haired sentry stepped forward to place a hand on her shoulder. She straightened at once, slapping him away.

"Ranson! I swear to Eriyah, if you lay hand on me again without leave, I'll have it lopped off and served to you for breakfast on a bed of sun-dried maggots."

Ranson. The Blowfish. That would make Daggers Jekks. Both glared now at Kylac as if he were the sole cause of their current distress.

"Your Highness," Jekks dared, "he's only trying to comfort you."

"And his comfort I treasure . . ." she began, with an expression of devoted appreciation. "As I do yours, you fur-faced vermin." The mask crumbled like an avalanche. "Why don't the two of you coddle each other and leave me"—another pause as she retched once more at her own feet—"out of it."

Upon straightening, she reached up to shove Kylac forcibly aside. He allowed her to do so. Had he avoided the contact, she might have pitched to the deck face-first. She glared at him as she went, as if daring him to say something more. But Kylac kept his words to himself, as he did his hands, though he feared she wasn't going to make it far on her own with that stumbling gait.

Jekks and Ranson must have agreed, because they too glared once more at Kylac before hastening after the departing princess. Though they looked as if they wanted to support her, they wisely waited instead for Denariel to reach out for them—which she did, reaching up to grab a shoulder on either side, sagging in between.

As they crossed the quarterdeck, a door opened on the sterncastle deck above. From the navigation room, footsteps emerged. Kylac looked up as Ledron, in conversation with Trajan, approached Colven at the wheel. Their talk ceased as Ledron caught sight of the scene below.

"Is Her Highness unwell?" the captain asked of Ranson and Jekks.

"Can 'Her Highness' not speak for herself?" Denariel snapped.

Even at this distance, Kylac could see Ledron's jaw clench.

"Forgive me. Is *Your* Highness unwell?"

"Emboldened by the prospect of death. Thank you, Captain, for asking. I am favored to be surrounded by so many dutiful protectors."

The sarcastic retort was punctuated with another angry glance in Kylac's direction, which Ledron didn't miss. The grim-faced captain bowed slightly. "If there is aught Your Highness requires . . ."

The offer met with a dismissive wave and a disgusted snort. Ranson and Jekks saluted their captain before venturing through the door leading back to her quarters in the great cabin. No sooner had they disappeared than Ledron beckoned to Kylac.

While Kylac climbed the narrow wooden stair to the higher deck, Colven was relieved of the wheel by Trajan—making the Tower the only witness as Kylac joined Ledron beside him.

"Captain?"

"Have you some worry I've not addressed?"

"Worry? No, sir. Not as such."

"Have your duties been made unclear?"

"Sir?"

"I presume you had cause to trouble Her Highness just now, or you'd not have done so."

"She seemed to be in some distress."

"Distress." The Head's jaw tightened with that nervous clenching of teeth. "And do you find that odd, given her ordeal?"

"I suppose not. I only meant—"

"You are not to bother or elsewise concern yourself with Her

Highness beyond her basic safety. Is that plain-spoken enough?"

Kylac glanced at Trajan, but the Tower was pretending to mind his focus on the ship's wheel. "How can I know she's worth risking my life for?"

"Because that's the job you agreed to," Ledron snapped. He followed this with a hard stare, as if daring Kylac to contradict him.

Kylac couldn't, of course, for the captain was right.

Accepting his lengthening silence as a capitulation, Ledron added, "I trust we'll needn't have this conversation again."

The Head didn't wait for further confirmation, but nodded at Trajan before turning on a heel, back toward the navigation room. Activity was increasing on the decks below, as Blackfists filed out from belowdecks for the shift change. Lieutenant Jahant barked at those who didn't move quickly enough, or who lingered in idle chatter. Kylac observed with only passing interest, his attention fixed on the ocean as the sun crested the rolling horizon in an explosive shimmer of reflective light.

"About as welcoming as a saber rat," Trajan offered abruptly. "Wouldn't you say?"

"The captain?"

"Her Highness. Captain's just doing his duty."

"So she's always this cordial?"

"Not my place to judge, you see. Just didn't want you to take offense."

Kylac shrugged. "Been misjudged myself a time or two," he said, still drawn to the play of fresh daylight amid the sparkling waves. "Though I admit to some difficulty deciding who aboard despises me most."

Trajan chuckled with understanding. "A Blackfist is trained to be suspicious of all, and at all times. If it's friends you seek, you've taken up with the wrong crew."

"You seem comfortable enough."

"Do I? Perhaps I'm slack in my duty." He leaned in, his brow arching. "Or might it be a ruse meant to engage your confidence?"

It was Kylac's turn to chuckle. He'd considered the possibility, of course, but trusted his instincts better than that.

"As for the princess, well, she despises most everyone, best as I've seen. But it's a stifling existence, that of a royal daughter, so who can blame her?"

A dozen new questions regarding Denariel came to Kylac's mind, but he settled for the only one that truly mattered. "Will she be all right?"

"The sickness? Must have weathered it on the voyage here. She'll do so again."

Tough as granitewood, Merrec had described her. She certainly *seemed* strong enough to look after herself. But, if so, then what purpose did Kylac truly serve here?

"Anyway, you can't expect all aboard to idolize you as he does," Trajan added with a smirk. Kylac traced the direction of the Blackfist's nod, to where Sallun climbed the mainmast toward the crow's nest. "Boy gives praise to the earth beneath your heel."

Kylac smiled faintly. He couldn't argue the lookout's obvious admiration of him. Nor would he deny the brotherly fondness he'd come to realize in turn. It reminded him of the kinship he'd developed with Torin and Allion throughout their unlikely adventures—particularly Torin, whose staunch sense of unspoiled hope and dreamlike wonder had fascinated Kylac.

Mayhap because he'd never known such innocence himself.

"Pity, then, that we won't see earth again for some time."

"And is it pity that causes you to watch over him?"

In part. He'd always had an affinity for the weak. *There are the strong, and there are the prey,* Kylac's father had liked to say. But, if that were truly the bedrock of nature's preferred order, then why had Kylac never felt more satisfied, more alive, than he did when coming to the aid of someone in need? Despite years of torturous conditioning—both mental and physical—his father had failed to cure him of his instinctive desire to balance the scales where nature hadn't. It wasn't so much a reverence toward life, or any moral compunction regarding good and evil. Merely a respect for basic fairness. If two men wished to kill each other, it seemed to Kylac they ought to do so on even ground.

"He does seem a minnow among sharks," Kylac admitted, as Sallun reached the nest and Nethreal began his descent.

Trajan's grin was mocking. "Ours is not a world for soft hearts."

Suffer the weak and you will suffer their weakness. Another of his father's pearls. Thus far, however, he regretted none of the risks he might have taken, or any of the lives he'd saved. Should every other facet of this undertaking prove regrettable, mayhap he could pride himself in having spared this one, unsuspecting soul a gruesome fate.

"Regardless," Trajan added, "with that kind of devotion, you ought to be able to stomach a little derision."

"Speaking o' derision, I wonder at the princess's handlers."

Trajan seemed to wince. "Oh?"

"Slow and portly next to the rest o' ya. I figured them Her Highness's favorites, but if'n so, I pity them more'n I do Sallun."

"And you should, by my thinking." Trajan glanced behind him, to make sure no one else was listening. "Ranson and Jekks, they have a unique quality that makes them ideally suited to safeguarding the princess—from more threat than one."

His tone told Kylac all he needed to know, even before Trajan emphasized the words by adjusting his codpiece.

"Ah," Kylac replied, feeling suddenly vulnerable himself. "And how is one chosen for that honor?"

"They volunteered. Saw it as the ultimate sacrifice, and you won't find many men to disagree. Ranson served Queen Lytherial, Mother keep her, before our treasured Denariel. Jekks is newer. Only one way to earn their respect, and I wouldn't recommend it."

"How long has the queen been gone?"

"Ten years, or near enough. The king worshipped her. So did Denariel. Her passing changed them."

And not for the better, Kylac inferred. "And the prince?"

Trajan's gaze shifted momentarily, turned forward as if rocks had been spotted ahead. The sudden intensity struck Kylac as odd, but it vanished before he could make anything of it. "Dethaniel has a scholar's temperament. I think he sees death—even the unexpected—as a curiosity. His was the voice of reason that might have kept father and sister from surrendering fully to despair."

"Reason?"

"She was gone. Sad, yes, but no cause for letting their own lives be destroyed alongside. When an anchor is dragging you down, you cut it loose and sail on."

"Sounds a mite cold."

"Reason often is. Still, I'd sooner trust a rational commander than one who gives rein to his emotions."

"Kendarrion's an emotional one, then?"

"I didn't say that. Only that Dethaniel has shown himself to be more pragmatic than either his sister or father—by my eyes, anyway."

Of scant issue here, Kylac decided. Neither the prince nor the king his father would have any hand in this voyage. Nor did he expect to meet them when it was over. Learning about them gave some insight into Denariel and these Shadowguard, but not enough to have any bearing on his actions—or lack thereof. He was naturally inquisitive, because knowledge helped keep one alive. But the more he probed here, the less important it all seemed.

Making this chatter only so much noise.

"Suppose I should sees to my rounds," he said, "before Jahant finds some less savory task to sets me on."

"Nah. Jahant's smarter than that. He'll not risk his own neck with the mutant for the petty satisfaction of watching you scrub the bilge."

"The mutant? Ya still thinks it could be aboard?"

"I only know I wouldn't wager anything of consequence elsewise."

"And it's waiting for what?"

Trajan shrugged those massive shoulders, his loose mane whipped by the wind. "Full moon? Southern gale? For a one-eyed cormorant to lay egg in the hole of a jade whale? I'm not saying it likely. I'm only saying, I'll believe us clear of that danger when we're home and Her Highness delivered to her father—and maybe not even then. Best would be to see it spitted on those unnatural blades of yours."

"Only, if'n it's as smart as they says, it knows better than to engage me twice."

"Making you the most popular man on this vessel," Trajan suggested. He tossed in a wink. "Despised or no."

8

"I'M GOING TO PEEL the ears from your skull," the Blackfist spat, as he picked himself off the deck.

"All right, Hadrum," Colven said, "I think we—"

Hadrum's roar cut the lieutenant short. A snaking strike from his spiked flail arced toward Kylac's face, but found only ocean breeze by the time it reached him.

"Keep grinning," the enraged Blackfist snarled, brandishing his flail and a murderous gaze in Kylac's direction. "We'll see how pretty it looks when I'm playing Rattlebones with your teeth."

"Well, which are we playing for?" Kylac asked. "Ears or teeth?"

Hadrum whipped another strike, which Kylac avoided with a slight lean. He then slid forward, spinning the wooden hand-stave gripped in each fist. The first, he used to parry Hadrum's gauntleted backhand. He jabbed with the other, a directed shot at the corner of Hadrum's mouth. The soldier stumbled back, spitting blood, while a clatter hit the deck.

Hadrum checked his mouth, finding a gap where his left fang should have been.

Gasps and shouts arose from the Shadowguard gathered loosely around them—Colven, Percel, Brenth, Ribach, Faban, Davins, and the droop-eyed Eytan. Beneath their murmurs and stifled laughter,

Kylac spoke privately to his opponent.

"Give it back," he said, "and I'll let you keep the other."

Hadrum drove at him in a berserker frenzy. Kylac shuffled and spun from side to side, circling in the middle of the ring formed there on the foredeck by their surrounding shipmates.

"Hadrum!" Colven barked, seeking to rein the other in.

But the Blackfist was like a mad horse with the bit in its teeth. Ignoring his commanding officer, he proceeded to chase Kylac around that small space, tying himself in knots as Kylac danced one way and then another, never more than an arm's length away.

"No?" Kylac asked. "You'll find it a mite harder to tears your meat."

Hadrum growled. A desperate lunge resulted in a wayward swipe that would have crushed Faban's knee had he not skittered clear.

"Whoa!" exclaimed the nearby Davins.

"Mind your weapon!" Faban himself shouted.

Others merely laughed. A narrow miss, yes, but no harm done.

"Enough!" Colven tried again.

"Very well," Kylac said, as Hadrum whirled about and came barreling in. Instead of dodging, he caught the flail around one of his hand-staves. He then dropped low with a sweeping leg kick. Hadrum hit the deck, rolled and pinned with an arm locked behind his back and the right side of his face exposed. A precise strike from Kylac's free hand knocked the right fang from its socket.

Once more, gasps and exclamations erupted from the gathered Shadowguard.

"Fangs is what we'll call you from now on, I think."

That drew a chuckle from Brenth and a scornful laugh from Ribach. The overall mood, however, had darkened with tension. They'd had their sport, but the time had come to end this before it got out of hand.

Instead of rising, Kylac pressed the armlock, so that he could hiss in Hadrum's ear. "I'll take your tusks next, and all the rest, one by one." The threat only caused Hadrum to buck and squirm more savagely beneath him, forcing Kylac to tighten his hold even further. "Come, man, would you spend the rest of your days gumming gruel?"

It had started as just another morning sparring session—Kylac's favorite time of day, as it gave him his best opportunity for keeping his muscles honed and his reflexes sharp. Ledron had forbade him from leaping and scrambling about the rigging, so, aside from the various porting, cleaning, and patrol duties, sparring was the only activity to be had. A spectator at first, Kylac had soon found himself the center of these sessions, instructing anywhere from a handful to a dozen of his shipmates in various fighting techniques: disarming opponents, how to defend against group attacks, nonlethal strikes that would incapacitate, or how to ensure—when necessary—that even a single blow was a lethal one.

This morning, however, a week into their voyage, he'd happened upon Sallun and found the lad to be sporting an unusually glum disposition. When pressed, Sallun had revealed that his dagger—the one Kylac had given him—had gone missing. Probably lost while climbing the rigging or going about his duties, Sallun had added. Kylac suspected elsewise. He'd seen more than a few of the men eyeing the treasure greedily—especially after they'd had a chance to see more of Kylac's blades in action.

Toting his suspicions, he'd made his rounds. He hadn't bothered with general inquiries, because he hadn't needed to. Positioned near enough, he could *smell* the distinct nature of his blades—whatever their composition—and so knew when he came upon the boot in which Sallun's missing dagger had been stashed. Since that boot was being worn at the time by Hadrum—one of those he'd scarcely encountered before their time at sea—he might have shaken the brute down then and there. Instead, he'd simply asked if Hadrum had observed anything concerning the whereabouts of the item.

The Blackfist had promptly disavowed any knowledge, snickering openly at Sallun's expense and asking Kylac if he was going to start wiping the lookout's nose for him, too. Kylac had ignored the slight—until it came time to issue sparring challenges an hour or so later, when he promptly singled out Hadrum. After a few exchanges designed to rile and humiliate, Hadrum had done what any proud soldier would do in calling Kylac out for a fight with real weapons. Kylac had declined to set aside his practice hand-staves, but had invited Hadrum to arm himself however he chose.

Had Ledron or Jahant been overseeing the session, it would have likely ended there. But Colven was the ranking officer present, and was, as Kylac had learned, less stern than the other commanders. Accepting Kylac's promise that none would be seriously hurt, the second lieutenant agreed to let them play it out for the sake of everyone's amusement. With Hadrum wielding his spiked flail and matching gauntlet, they'd continued, hailed by an assortment of cheers and heckles—and now, a growing fear among some present that matters might have gone too far.

"You're dead, boy," Hadrum snarled, continuing to writhe and snort helplessly beneath Kylac's pinning hold. "When I'm through with you, your own mother won't recognize what's left."

"Take what doesn't belong to ya," Kylac replied evenly, "and I'll give ya what does."

"Release him, Kronus," Colven ordered, though he didn't sound entirely certain of himself.

Kylac obeyed the command anyway, rolling aside and springing to his feet. As soon as he could gather his twisted arm beneath him, Hadrum pushed himself up, albeit more gingerly than before. He kept his head lowered, as if too embarrassed to face anyone directly. His chest heaved, but his arms hung slack in a posture of submission. Those gathered eyed him warily, unconvinced.

"We're finished here," Colven said. "Agreed?" When neither combatant responded, he addressed his fellow Blackfist. "Hadrum?"

"For now," Hadrum seethed, raising his brow just enough to direct that crazed glare at Kylac.

"Now or later, only one way this ends favorably for ya."

"Silence, Kronus," Colven snapped in exasperation. "You've goaded him enough."

"If you wish to accuse me, do it," Hadrum growled, his words whistling through the fresh gaps in his bloodied teeth. "And I'll see you hanged for false witness."

Men turned to one another, questioning their fellows with grunts and murmurs.

"I make no accusations for just that reason," Kylac replied. "Though it's not my own neck I'm looking to spare."

There, in his eyes, Hadrum's confidence slipped. It returned swiftly.

"You should, 'cause I'm going to wring it like a festival hen's."

The Blackfist spat blood at Kylac's feet, then threw his flail to the deck. The unbuckled gauntlet followed. Afterward, he turned and made for the stair leading down from the forecastle, reflexively tonguing the holes in his bite.

Before he'd gone three paces, however, he found Ledron climbing that same stair. Merrec shadowed him a pace back, leaving but one guess as to who had alerted the captain to their scuffle. Hadrum halted, while the other Shadowguard quieted and straightened as if they'd been caught filching wine from the king's goblet. Kylac kept his poise, but chose to lower his hands—and the staves still gripped within—to his waist, crossing his wrists casually before him.

Cornered there atop the forecastle, the group's members held their ground, weathering their captain's scrutiny.

"Report, Lieutenant."

Colven cleared his throat. "Training, sir. A bit spirited, perhaps, but no cause for alarm." He glanced at Kylac.

That look, more than anything, seemed to anger Ledron. "I said *report*, Lieutenant. You stand gaping while Kronus beats one of ours bloody. I would hear your reasons."

"The fault is mine, Captain," Kylac offered.

"I'll decide fault," Ledron snapped, "and mete punishment as it's due. Lieutenant? If I must ask again, yours will be the sack of bones raked across our keel."

Colven sighed. "There is some matter between them. I can't speak to it, save that it spurred Hadrum to an imprudent challenge."

"Which our young rogue was most reluctant to accept, I'm sure."

As he stood there drawing the heat of the captain's ire, Kylac caught Hadrum grinning, no doubt thinking himself in a position to exact some immediate revenge.

"Thinks I stole the blade he gave to Sallun," the Blackfist explained.

"And did you?" Ledron asked.

Hadrum's smile vanished. "Even Sallun says he misplaced it."

"Answer the charge."

"I'm no thief."

"I never claimed as such," Kylac interjected. "I only asked if'n ya'd seen it."

"And what cause have you to single him out?" Ledron asked.

Kylac held his tongue. For Hadrum's sake, this was the spectacle he'd hoped to avoid.

"Answer," Ledron insisted, "or I'll have Sallun hung from the yardarm while you think on it."

A more effective threat than any he could have made against Kylac himself—and one that Kylac didn't doubt. "Because it seems to have found its way into his left boot."

Kylac hadn't thought Hadrum's gaze could narrow any further. Though, it was less a furious squint, and more a reptilian one. Seeming to promise that, even now, he wasn't ready to submit without a fight.

"Oh?" Hadrum asked as all eyes turned his way. "What are you willing to wager on it?"

Kylac readied a retort, but Ledron raised his hands to silence them both.

"This ends now," the captain declared. To Kylac, he said, "Stow your tongue, rogue, until I give you leave to loose it." To Hadrum, "Remove the boot and place it on the deck."

With a forced smile, Hadrum complied.

"Lieutenant."

Colven, still lacking the customary presence of a commanding officer, stepped forward and inspected the boot, peering inside. He shook his head, turning the article upside down. "Nothing, Captain."

Hadrum's smile broadened. "See, Captain? A false accusation."

"So it seems," Ledron agreed, turning his attention back to Kylac. Kylac remained silent as he'd been bade. "But then, perhaps I'll have a look myself."

Hadrum had already half slipped the boot back over his heel, but froze now, his triumphant, gap-toothed grin becoming brittle. "Captain?"

"Is it the ceaseless wind that's deafened everyone? The boot."

Behind Ledron, Merrec was now grinning broad enough for all, thoroughly enjoying the proceedings. Kylac was glad Sallun was currently belowdecks, for he was sure the lad would have been mortified by all the fuss.

After a lingering hesitation, Hadrum removed the boot again. "Certainly, Captain."

Ledron stood his ground, forcing Hadrum to hobble over to deliver the item personally. Upon receiving it, he stared at Hadrum while fishing a hand around inside. After a moment's rummaging, he turned his gaze on Kylac.

"Appears empty."

Hadrum smiled again, with more than a little relief. "Whelp took two of my teeth for nothing."

Again he reached for the boot, mayhap too quickly. For Ledron half turned, withdrawing it suddenly. "You're lucky he didn't take your leg at the knee."

"What?"

"You'll be luckier still if I don't." Ledron rummaged again, more forcefully this time, tearing into a hidden pocket formed of boiled leather flaps covered over by the thick woolen lining. From out of this secret pouch, he yanked Sallun's missing dagger, which he immediately placed at Hadrum's throat.

"But . . . but I . . . I didn't . . ." Hadrum stammered. "He must have planted it there. He must have—"

"Take heed, soldier. Lie to him? That's one matter. Lie to me, and you'll lose more than your fangs. Lieutenant."

"Sir."

"Have Brenth and Ribach escort him to the hold. A week with the rats to reflect on his conduct, while I decide what further reprimand is necessary." He faced Hadrum squarely. "Is this acceptable?"

The disgraced Blackfist remained defiant at first . . . then wisely hung his head.

"Good. Because if our need for bodies were not so great, I would use yours to bait a shark here and now."

He gestured in disgust. Colven, Brenth, and Ribach responded, hurriedly hauling the prisoner away. When they'd gone, Ledron looked over those who remained.

"We're not a fifth of the way home, and already unraveling." He stepped toward Kylac. "The next time you take issue with one of my men, you bring it to me. Understood?" After waiting for Kylac's nod, he added, "And you train alone from now on." He raised his voice for the sake of the others. "Spread the word. The next man I see engaged with him for so much as a Tarly jig will be draped from the bowsprit by his own entrails."

Clever, thought Kylac. While Ledron understood the futility of threatening him directly, there was more than one way to ground a hawk.

So much for the popularity Trajan had predicted—correctly so, these past seven days. While few aboard would trust him at their back, it seemed there wasn't a man among them who wouldn't want him at his side should the time come for battle. The sole exceptions had been Denariel and her eunuch warders, Ranson and Jekks, who still managed to disappear whenever he came within sight of them. With this new edict, however . . .

Ledron waited a moment for objections to be raised. When of course none were, he turned and shouldered past the still-smirking Merrec, who gave Kylac a telling look. The remainder then dispersed in silence—even the smug mercenary—leaving Kylac to wonder if, mayhap, he should have handled the entire matter differently.

TIME GROUND to a crawl.

Though his specific banishment applied only to training, most of the Shadowguard erred on the side of caution by having nothing to do with him whatsoever. Trajan would still converse with him, but only sparingly, with an eye always on who might be watching. The Shadowguard were not without their petty differences, the soldier explained, and there were more than one who wouldn't mind clawing higher in their captain's estimation by bringing down one already there. Even Sallun had grown icy, ducking aside whenever he approached as if wary of plague. If appreciative for the return of his dagger, he never said as much.

Kylac refused to be troubled, at first. He'd expected it, after all, and didn't begrudge them their need to keep him at arm's length.

But as the days coupled to spawn one week, and then another, his continued isolation began to take on the eerie feel of confinement. Here he was, surrounded by boundless ocean, his only playground a wooden crate measuring barely forty-five paces long and ten paces across. His rounds were endless, but had also become pointless. He kept waiting for some threat to manifest, but after three weeks at sea, nothing had.

How could that be? Tales of ocean travel were always fraught with peril. Where were the sky-blackening tempests that could grind a ship to splinters with their sail-shredding winds, fiery lightning, and crushing waves? Where were the monstrous denizens of the lurking deep, who would erupt without warning from the churning swells to gnash at their vessel and drag the men to a watery grave? Where were the fearless, ocean-borne savages who would reave them of their possessions and use their mutilated bodies as chum?

For all the excitement encountered thus far, he could have remained in Alson as his friends had pleaded, reading petitions, attending hearings, and elsewise assisting with all of the mundane tasks required in the rebuilding of their tumbledown kingdom. Shards, a gopher outbreak would have generated more excitement than this.

He hated to think like that, to second-guess his life's path. A man couldn't see where he was going while studying the ground left behind. But the prolonged tedium seemed to intensify with each passing day—made worse by the lack of a foreseeable conclusion. Just how much of his life would be paid to this endeavor?

He wondered this now as he did most evenings, alone at the bow rail, peering southward at the infinite horizon while watching the sun melt like liquid gold into the sea. There was something about the rise and fall of the great flaming orb that captivated him. When all the world stood at that tipping point between darkness and light . . . before one was engulfed by the other. The most eternal of conflicts, for which there could be no resolution. The only purpose? The battle itself.

"Heavy thoughts?"

Merrec. Kylac ignored him, trusting him to keep his distance pending invitation. Instead, the mercenary approached, to stand at his shoulder.

"What do you stare at out there? Looks the same as it did yesterday. Same as it will for weeks hence."

Kylac let the winds answer for him.

"Forgive me for neglecting your company," Merrec went on, misinterpreting the cause of his silence. "The captain's still raw with you. And I'm not all that well respected among these oafs as is."

Tame words if ever Kylac had heard them. At least his own status as outcast had come under order. Merrec was genuinely and universally reviled. Wherever he went, the men shunned him. He carried on blithely enough, interjecting himself in others' conversations with smiles and jests, then pretending not to notice as the men would abruptly disperse—at times with feigned cause, and at other times with open derision. It had come to where Kylac pitied the mercenary—from afar. Whenever their paths actually crossed, such as now, his flesh prickled with irritation, as if a roach had wormed beneath his tunic to naggle at his skin.

"I did warn you about them," the Roach went on, seemingly unperturbed by Kylac's lack of response. "Witless hounds care for naught but their precious charge. Eye them crosswise, and this is the treatment you get."

Kylac couldn't bring himself to agree. However harsh the judgment, if he and Merrec were victims, it was in no small measure by their own hand.

The mercenary proved undaunted by his continued silence. "So here we are, you and I. Just like I told you it would be."

Kylac smirked at the absurdity.

Merrec took it as a sign of companionship. "Have you seen Hadrum since they released him from the hold?"

"Only at a distance," Kylac said, surrendering at last.

The Roach leaned in conspiratorially. "Begged the captain's apology, from what I hear. Claims the matter is forgotten. But I've seen him looking your way more than once, and I'm telling you, it ain't forgiveness he regards you with."

"No?" He didn't bother to tell Merrec that he'd felt those stares at thirty paces, burning with the heat of a blacksmith's poker. Nor had he needed them to know a reckoning lay ahead. Hadrum wasn't just proud. His eyes had marked in him a bloodlust that would not be sated until one or the other of them was dead. "If'n that's his choice, he's welcome to it. I gave him plenty o' chances to emerge unscathed."

"How did you know?" Merrec asked, grinning companionably. "Did you see him take the blade?"

"A suspicion. A man'll tells ya more'n he cares to, if'n ya learn to listen."

"Boldly played, for a suspicion."

Kylac shrugged. "Mayhap. But then, some say boldness is the root of achievement."

"And we are brothers in boldness, you and I."

Kylac scowled—refraining from harsher reaction—as the Roach clasped his shoulder. "Are we, now?"

"I told you it would come to this."

"Is there an echo on this wind, or did ya say that already?"

Merrec released him, but the mercenary's grin was unabashed. "So I did. It's just . . . even I didn't expect them to be so obvious."

"About what?"

"Us. You and me."

Kylac arched a brow in confusion.

"Our fate."

"Fate?"

"Come, boy, are your blades that much sharper than your wits? Once Nara is delivered to her father, safe and sound, what are the odds they're going to pay you your promised reward?"

"I's been promised no reward."

"Your fee, then."

"I's been promised no fee, because I's asked for none."

Merrec's smile slipped. For once, he seemed too confused to even pretend elsewhere. "But . . . surely you negotiated payment—"

"My services were exchanged for passage, nothing more."

"To Addaranth?" The mercenary shook his head. "Got yourself more twisted than I thought. I'd have settled for half my reward if they'd have paid me there in Kuuria. Alas."

"What's your concern, Merrec? They may not pay ya as promised?"

"Why would they? I mean, all I really have is Darr's promise to go by. Once he has what he wants . . ."

He might stab ya in the back, 'cause that's what ya'd do to him. "It's a risk," Kylac admitted. "Though, Ledron suggested that his lord's word was clear and good on this one."

"Ha! The word of a king. He'd say or do anything to get his daughter back." The Roach leaned closer. "But that's the key, isn't it?"

"The key to what?"

"Our safety. Our freedom. The only way to assure our rightful reward."

Ah. Kylac nodded with understanding. He should have spotted this from the first—and likely would have, had he allowed anything escaping the mercenary's mouth to merit his full attention. All right. He would play. "There's bold," he said, "and then there's foolish."

It was part warning, part goad. Merrec seized upon the latter. "Foolish would be strolling into Darr's hall, outcasts among this crew, and trusting to his gratitude. The Shadowguard will be hailed triumphant, of course. But what of me, a rank-and-file soldier, and yourself, a rogue of—shall we say—questionable origins and intent? Who will be there to recognize and reward our contributions? Who's to say they won't simply shackle us on sight?"

Were the mercenary to mention *reward* one more time, Kylac might have to flip the conniving fool over the rail then and there. Privately, who would complain? Officially, however, Ledron would be furious. Were it not against his king's orders, the Shadowguard captain would have long since done it himself. "Is there a particular plot ya had in mind?"

Merrec cast a nervous gaze aft along the length of the ship, noting the positions of the crew. "Plot? You make me sound the villain. Justice. Survival. That's all I'm talking here. You believe in justice, do you not?"

"After a fashion, yes."

"And survival?"

"A natural instinct. Sure."

"Then we're agreed. I'm not saying we must plan anything now. I'm only alerting you to the fact that, before this is done, we'd do well to devise a strategy that will ensure our safety and just recompense."

"A strategy involving the princess."

"She's the only thing they care about. The only thing Darr cares about. It's an all-or-nothing game, you see?"

Kylac nodded. What else was he to do? Expose the mercenary to Ledron? Surely the captain needed no forewarning as to the possibility of Merrec—and himself, for that matter—resorting to treachery in the name of self-preservation. And, without any specific details, what was there really to offer up? The Roach would deny any such conversation had ever taken place, and the mistrust toward both of them would only intensify.

Better to be patient. Kylac suspected that, in truth, Merrec had given this a lot of thought, and likely did have a plan or two sketched out in his mind. But he'd come at this juncture merely to gauge Kylac's reaction. Startle him, and he might not approach again later, when he had something of consequence to reveal.

And those were merely the considerations to be had if the mercenary's proposed course was as wrong as it first seemed. What if the scoundrel was right?

"How much longer do we have, anyway?"

"At sea? Difficult to say. Ledron has taken us well off the regular routes, hoping to avoid any run-ins with the Grenarr."

"Is he that fearful of them?"

"At home? On land? No. But the sea belongs to them. We're but one ship, outmanned by all save the smallest of theirs. If they're hunting us—and it's a wise bet they are—our best hope is to slip past unseen."

Lengthening the overall voyage—in both time and tedium. Kylac would have preferred the fight. Whatever the outcome, at least it would be swift.

"Is it weeks we're facing? Or months?"

The Roach smirked at his obvious discomfort. "Depends on how much circumnavigating lies ahead. Thus far, we're making blessed time, actually. I'd wager that, as the sparrow flies, we're more than halfway home. An eternity it may seem, but the land . . . she steals upon you quite suddenly. If we wait to see it before we contemplate our next move, it'll likely be too late."

The mercenary clapped him again on the shoulder, grinning that unsavory grin and eyeing him with that vulture's gaze. He then turned and marched away, boots clopping against the deck, a lively tune whistling from his lips.

The fool can't help it, Kylac supposed, swallowing his annoyance. A snake might shed its skin, but not the serpent underneath.

He kept his own gaze on the sea, cast now in the metallic tint of reflected moonlight, the sun but a seared memory at the far edge of the fallen horizon. In the endless conflict, another turn toward darkness.

Let the darkness take it. For but a glimpse of shoreline, the darkness could have it all.

9

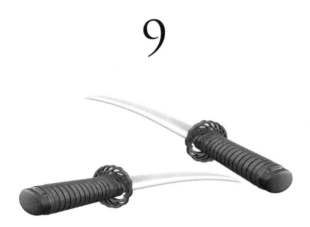

THE FIRST STORM STRUCK a week later, overtaking them on a south-easterly course. Long overdue, it carried a pent-up rage both sudden and powerful. Even iron stomachs turned soft as *Denariel's Return* rose and fell time and again, tossed and battered by the heaving swells. Lightning cracked until it seemed the sky itself must crumble, while gusting winds rent sails and sent lines whipping about in a frenzy. Ribach was nearly lost when he was washed overboard, saved only by his entanglement amid a stretch of rigging that Trajan, Nethreal, and Brenth were able to draw back in.

For all its fury, however, the tempest was mercifully short-lived, lasting mere hours. Clear seas and calm skies emerged promptly in its wake. Though it took some additional time to assess and repair damages and to right their course, the total cost in terms of delay was estimated at less than a day.

Alas, that first squall proved to be but a harbinger of winter's wrath. The chain of storms that followed was long and violent. Though the intensity of any individual blow did not quite reach that of the ushering gale, the relentless hammering of one after the next had a debilitating effect on both vessel and crew. Spirits grew gray and sodden to match the surroundings, raked by winds turned icy and mournful. The sun, when it appeared, did so behind thundering veils of rain and mist, its fires extinguished by the ceaseless downpour. Landfall? What hope of that? The world, it seemed, had already drowned.

Kylac weathered the bleak circumstances better than most. It wasn't the sort of battle he was accustomed to, and not one they appeared to be winning. He, like the others, was perpetually waterlogged, claimed by a chill that had settled in his bones. Still shunned by the crew, he was disallowed all but the most base, solitary duties—sanding decks, pumping water from the bilge, patching seams, securing loose stays at perilous heights, and, as always, keeping a lookout for any enemy, within or without, that might threaten. But a battle it was, at last. A set of challenges that, once overcome, would strengthen him in ways he could foresee—and in ways he couldn't.

More easily imagined than accomplished, of course. Nature's fury cared nothing for the sharpness of his blades, nor the speed, stamina, and dexterity with which he wielded them. It cared not for Trajan's size, Obren's wit, Sallun's vision, or Ledron's stone-faced dedication. Here and now, in this watery cage, they were all of them one and the same, regardless of skill or strength. At times, it seemed they were no different than the rats in the hold, scrabbling from one corner of the ship to the next, clinging where they could to whatever they could, and hoping that the sea would lose interest before it devoured them.

Their overall progress suffered, week after grueling week, as the storms continued to assail them. There was no help for it. Though it made Kylac feel increasingly helpless to admit it, the only way to combat the foul elements was to withstand them, and sail on.

KYLAC LAY in his hammock, swishing gently to the rollicking sway of the vessel to which it was attached. He should have been sleeping, but the swells were high this night, the ship's course erratic. He didn't like the feel of it.

Or mayhap it was the clamor above. He'd crawled belowdecks that evening, the rains heavy enough to chase him from his preferred

place atop the sterncastle. In doing so, he found himself in a position
to hear not only the ceaseless thrum of those rains, but the muted
shouts and frenetic scuffle of those tasked with keeping *Denariel's
Return* on course during the night. By all indications, that challenge
was proving more arduous than usual.

Had he been able to distance himself from those sounds, there
were still others more immediate to contend with. Trajan snored
loudly, wrapped in his own hammock nearby. Brenth's wind whistled
through his nose—broken years ago as a fresh-faced recruit. Every so
often, Percel would moan irritably, swatting at his elbow as if shooing
a bothersome fly. And, of course, there was no escaping the creaks
and groans of their storm-tossed vessel.

A peal of thunder rattled the unseen heavens. The ship shook in
response. Kylac half hoped that a mighty lightning bolt would cleave
her in two and end his present misery.

He was still imagining how that might unfold when there came
a stomp of booted feet overhead. A moment later, the hatch was
wrenched open, allowing a gust of wind and rain to sweep eagerly
into the hold.

"Ho!" Jahant shouted as he came thumping down the narrow
wooden stair. "Up! Up!"

Kylac rolled from his hammock in a swish of fabric, feet kissing
the floor with a soundless touch. The others grunted or groaned as
they wrested themselves from slumber.

"Trajan, Hadrum, with me. Topside, the rest of you. Ho! Now!
Now!"

The awakened Shadowguard lurched or swayed, but found their
bearings quickly. Kylac stood aside, giving way as they rushed to
respond. The men divided themselves as ordered. Jahant was already
pressing aft, the appointed duo in tow. Hadrum, as was his habit,
spared Kylac a glare before pursuing his commander.

Kylac hesitated. He must have received a hundred such looks from
the vengeful Blackfist over the past month and a half. But something
in this one triggered an inner warning that, while having nothing to
do with Hadrum himself, was one Kylac knew better than to ignore.
Rather than follow the others topside, he decided as suddenly as that

to see first what business Jahant was about.

He trailed them invisibly along a flanking route through the piled clutter of the aft hold. All around him, the ship issued complaint, rocking and shuddering and groaning in lament. Jahant paused to inspect a vertical shaft—part of the steering mechanism that connected to the wheel above.

"What's wrong?" Trajan asked.

"She's sluggish," Jahant grumbled. "We're losing control up there."

They descended another level, continuing onward until they reached the tiller room. Kylac paused at the entry as the three larger men bent close to take a look.

"Sangho's Tempest," Jahant swore, with an edge of fear in his voice.

"It's snapped clear free," Hadrum exclaimed.

The deck lurched—tilting from one side to the other—as a powerful swell rolled beneath them.

"Snapped?" Trajan added, in a suggestive tone. "Or severed?"

Kylac entered, to see for himself. Hadrum was the last to turn, but the first to protest.

"Lieutenant sent you topside."

Kylac slipped past before the other could block him, using Trajan as a shield to avoid confrontation. Neither Jahant nor Trajan seemed to much notice him, focused as they were on the splintered stump of the tiller where it should have been connected to the rudder. Kylac leaned in to where Trajan brushed at the damaged wood. The Tower was fingering a crosswise gash—one of many marking the broken tiller. Kylac's stomach knotted. Even before Trajan looked at him, he knew the word upon the Blackfist's lips.

"Groll."

"The princess," Kylac countered, and dashed from the room.

The others gave chase in an urgent scramble. Kylac didn't wait, but surged on ahead, blowing through the narrow, unsteady confines like a stray gust, speeding his way abovedecks.

A fiendish gale confronted him as he reached and opened the hatch, but Kylac pressed through almost as quickly. Outside, the sky was black—moon and stars smothered by roiling storm clouds, layers of midnight fog, and heavy sheets of rainfall.

Kylac crouched there momentarily, waiting for his eyes to adjust and for his remaining senses to attune themselves to the night. Shrill winds and thrumming rains filled his ears, along with the shouts and activity of the crew as they trimmed and heaved and elsewise wrestled with their runaway ship. Shards of driven rain clawed through his damp layers of clothing. He smelled the sea and the wood of their vessel and the pitch that helped seal her together. Physically, he sensed nothing of their enemy. But he no longer had any doubt that it lurked among them.

A flash of distant lightning revealed the outline of the hooded sentry posted outside the door to the captain's quarters. Ribach, given the figure's height and the hunch of his shoulders. Kylac drifted toward him, left hand resting lightly on the pommel of a hidden shortsword, treading with slow, crossing strides that allowed him to rotate as he went. His chief objective was to ensure the princess was safe, but the groll knew this. He wasn't going to rush headlong into another ambush.

Colven manned the wheel, spinning hard left against a powerful broadside current. He did so instinctively, for it was clear the vessel offered no response. She was at the mercy of the waves, until such time as they could bring her to heel.

In the crow's nest above, another poorly sheltered head hung low, bowed against the elements. Sallun. What the lookout was expected to spy in this void was anyone's guess.

Lightning flashed again, nearer than before, judging by the roll of thunder that echoed in its wake. Ribach turned toward Kylac as he reached the outer door to the great cabin.

"Stand aside," Kylac said.

The bearded Blackfist peered at him in confusion, then shook his head, reaching forth a halting hand. Kylac put a fist in his stomach and a heel in his shin, before rolling him out of the way. Leaving him slumped to one side, Kylac tested the door. He found it locked.

A fresh shout went up as Jahant emerged from the hold. The lieutenant gestured to where Kylac stood outside the great cabin.

"The princess!"

While Ribach drew a scraping gasp of breath, Kylac turned back to the door with a spinning kick that snapped the latch on the other side, revealing a darkened antechamber. Before he could enter, an arrow struck the doorframe near his head. Kylac looked back, tracing the arrow's trajectory in reverse to find Ahlman—or mayhap it was Ahren—some dozen paces below on the maindeck, nocking another arrow to his string.

Not me, ya lackwits, Kylac thought, then darted inside.

He was met by a diving swipe from Ranson and a lunging charge from Jekks. He blocked the first and sidestepped the second, searching even then for sign of Denariel. She was there, he saw, in a lamplit corner near the rear windows overlooking their wake, sitting up in bed.

Though relieved, he had no chance to show it, for Ranson and Jekks pressed their attack. The pair was skilled—no arguing that. Nonetheless, it took only a duck, parry, and twist to disarm Ranson, and a block, leap, and leg sweep to unbalance Jekks. A kick sent Ranson tumbling backward, while a blade pointed at Jekks's throat kept him on his knees.

"Yield!" Kylac shouted. "The groll is among us."

Ranson might still have retaliated, but stopped short at the sight of Kylac's dagger pricking his companion's neck. Jekks swallowed thickly.

"Groll?"

A hammering on the deck outside announced the arriving ship-mates. Kylac wondered whether to let them enter, or give them another moment to calm themselves. He'd just kicked the door shut when a window at the rear of the room shattered, unleashing a wind that caused lamps to gutter and candles to blow out.

Through the breach came the groll.

The dagger at Jekks's neck flew to meet it. A man would have caught it in the chest. The mutant, however, shrank suddenly, while raising a wiry arm to swat it away. It *did* hiss sharply—more in surprise than in pain—as the blade drew a gash upon its forearm. But it wasn't the wound Kylac had hoped for.

Denariel squealed, recoiling instinctively. Jekks was no longer on his knees, but on his buttocks, mouth agape. Ranson was similarly stunned, pressed against the cabin's front wall, his body seeking to catch up to his thoughts. Kylac left them there, vaulting toward the intruder with longsword in his right hand and shortsword in his left.

The groll hissed again, crouched uncertainly. It hadn't expected him, Kylac realized, taking grim pleasure in the thought.

Then the cabin door burst open, with a knot of Shadowguard fighting to pour in. The Ukinh made its decision. With a glance at Denariel, it reversed direction, leaping back through the broken window, gone as suddenly as it had appeared.

Kylac's blades just missed the beast as it vanished over the empty casement. He thrust his own head through the opening. Slapped by winds and clawed by rains, he saw only black waves below.

The stretch of a bowstring caused him to whirl about.

"No!" Jekks managed to shout—too late to arrest the flight of another arrow from Ahlman's eager bow.

Kylac dodged to his right, intentionally moving farther from Denariel while letting the missile sail harmlessly through the shattered window.

"Hold!" Ranson shouted, finally bringing himself to step in front of the new arrivals with upraised arms. He waved those arms for emphasis, crying again, "Hold!"

"Stopper that bow of yours," Trajan agreed.

"Kronus is not the enemy," Jahant said.

Kylac would never have guessed the lieutenant felt that way, given his furious look. But the others—most notably Ahlman—seemed to give more weight to their leader's words than his expression.

"Then why—" Ribach's cough cut his argument short. He winced, rubbing his sore abdomen. Evidently, he, like Ahlman, had failed to witness the groll during its abrupt escape, while Jahant, Trajan, and Hadrum—first through the door—must have caught at least a glimpse. As with Ranson and Jekks, it was the only thing that could have stemmed them.

Others were entering now—Percel, Nethreal, Obren, Eytan, and Merrec on their heels. Kylac, however, shifted back toward Denariel, who'd crawled forward for a closer look at the broken window.

"I wouldn't, Your Highness," Kylac cautioned, extending the flat of his longsword to intercept her.

Denariel swatted at the weapon with indignation. "Do not presume to tell me where I may venture and where I may not. How dare you barge in here as you did? I ought to have you hurled right out that—"

"Highness!" a new voice barked.

Kylac turned to find that Ledron had shoved his way through the clutch of Shadowguard. It couldn't have looked favorable, Kylac standing there by that shattered portal, sword raised toward Denariel. But the captain seemed to recognize by the stance of his men that the situation was more or less under control.

"Ranson, Jekks, secure Her Highness." While the personal warders moved to obey, Ledron faced Jahant, who responded to the unspoken question at once.

"Groll."

"It was here? You saw it?"

"Seems someone failed his task," Hadrum growled, with a pointed look in Kylac's direction.

"Kronus flushed the beast," Trajan added, only slightly less pointedly.

Kylac made room as Ranson and Jekks—having retrieved their weapons—hastened now toward the damaged aft wall, through which the storm continued to gust and swirl. Still petulant, Denariel moved from the window and back toward her bed, nightgown fluttering about her diminutive frame.

"Our ship is sabotaged," Hadrum reminded them all.

Ledron, previously more interested in the princess and Kylac, spun now toward Hadrum. "You say?"

"The beast sheared tiller from rudder. We're a wingless gull."

The captain turned to Jahant, who nodded. Ledron gritted his teeth, then wiped an angry hand across the top of his bald head. "Then time a'wastes." Lightning flashed again, drawing Kylac's attention to the darkness beyond the open window. "Lieutenant, take a squad and secure that rudder. All other hands on the lines. We'll tame this wind, else sleep tonight with the crabs. Kronus."

Kylac heard his name, but his focus just now was on the blackened horizon. Out there, beyond the rolling waveline, he saw what looked like . . . Could it be?

"Kronus!"

"Uh, Captain, it may be too late for all o' that."

Ledron tromped near. "Why? What do you see?"

The lightning came again, and there it was, limned if only briefly in frightening clarity.

Land.

A mirage, it seemed, but there was no reason for Kylac to imagine it. A ridge of mountainous coastline jutted from the roiling sea, black rocks all but invisible in the night. And though it hung astern, hundreds of strokes distant, Kylac knew at once from the roll and sway of the ship that the currents were carrying them directly toward it.

He waited for Ledron to convince him elsewhere. But the captain seemed to draw the same conclusion. "Drop anchor."

Jahant stepped forward. "Sir?"

"Drop anchor," he repeated, still staring at the dim outline of that looming landmass. "Now."

Jahant hesitated, clearly unnerved by the deathly calm in his captain's voice. A moment later, he was barreling toward the exit, pushing past those who didn't stand aside quickly enough on their own. "Anchor!" he yelled. "Drop anchor!"

The shout was taken up by others outside, echoing as it passed forward from man to man until it was lost to the wind's wail. Kylac had seen the crew carry out enough orders to imagine the flurry of movement now. Sails would have to be lowered and furled. Lines would be loosened while others were belayed. Somewhere near the bow, one of his shipmates was already tripping the capstan, freeing the anchor for its descent to the ocean floor.

"All hands," Ledron said, turning at last to address those still gathered in the great cabin.

Most filed out as quickly as they'd entered. Hadrum lingered, with Trajan beside him, until Kylac moved to obey, leaving Denariel in the hands of Ranson and Jekks.

"Not you, Kronus," Ledron amended. He found Kylac's gaze. "I'd have you stay with Her Highness, if you would."

Kylac checked reactions throughout the room. Denariel crossed her arms and looked away. Ranson and Jekks scowled, but held their tongues. Hadrum froze in the doorway, making no attempt to mask his disdain.

"As ya will, Captain."

Hadrum was about to open his mouth, when Trajan gripped his arm and drew him outside.

The pair was gone only briefly. A string of shouts approached, a reverse echo from the one sent forth moments before. After a muted confirmation of some sort, Trajan ducked his rain-drenched mane back inside, with Hadrum on his heels.

"No anchor, Captain. She's been gnawed free."

Ledron blanched, letting slip his alarm. "It can chew through iron? And none noticed?"

Trajan could only shake his head. "We've got an empty line is what I know. But I'm wagering it wasn't rust that took her from us."

Their anchor had been affixed by chain, not rope. And though she dangled overboard at an obscured angle, it would have been no small feat to tear her loose. Kylac couldn't quite envision it—the groll clinging to the outside of their hull in the dead of night, while the ship heaved and rolled upon the swells. But it was easy enough to picture the broken end of chain hanging limply in the anchor's place, and easier still to feel their unimpeded progress toward the nearing shore.

"Anything else we can use?" Kylac asked, thinking there must be some makeshift way to produce the necessary drag.

"Hadrum, have Jahant see to it," Ledron agreed.

Hadrum's surprise was followed immediately by suspicion, evident in the glances cast first at his captain, and then at Trajan beside him. He seemed ready to challenge the order, but must have thought better of it. "Aye, Captain."

"And me, Captain?" Trajan asked, when Hadrum had gone.

"I want you and Colven to ready the longboats. If we still have them, that is."

Trajan answered with a nod before ducking back out into the storm.

"How many will the boats carry?" Kylac asked.

"A dozen each," Ledron answered.

Leaving eleven of their overall number aboard, Kylac figured, as there were but two boats, and thirty-five crew.

The captain read his thoughts. "Let us pray we don't need them."

The boats, or the men? Kylac thought grimly.

"You may as well dress, Your Highness," Ledron suggested.

"Indeed, Captain. You've chosen a divine night for a swim."

To her credit, she didn't seem afraid—nor abashed, Kylac noted, as she stripped of her nightshirt in full view. He averted his gaze anyway, though he didn't turn his back to her as Ranson and Jekks did. At this point, it seemed unwise to let her fully out of sight.

Ledron must have agreed, because he didn't so much as blink while watching her rifle through her clothes chest.

"That's the north shore out there—isn't it," Denariel said, as she slipped into a pair of woolen breeches.

"If our charts are true," Ledron admitted.

The princess laughed. "So it won't much matter if we survive the landing or not—will it."

"One fight at a time, Your Highness."

Kylac might have asked a question in follow-up, but he happened to agree with Ledron. Whatever dangers Denariel alluded to would have to wait. Apart from that, the very notion of standing again on dry, steady earth appealed to him in a way he could scarcely describe. North shore, south shore, Addaranth, or threshold to the Abyss, he wasn't going to complain.

Provided, of course, he lived to feel its soil beneath his feet.

For that reason, he was more concerned just now with the activity beyond their cabin. Though being here to shield Denariel freed up a dozen Shadowguard crewmen better equipped than he to salvage their injured vessel, he wasn't accustomed to standing idle while blindly entrusting his fate to another man's labors.

He was wondering what criteria the captain might use when choosing to save one man over another . . . when racing footsteps hammered on the deck outside, and there came a fresh, furious knocking at the cabin door.

"Come," Ledron said. Denariel was just now pulling a silken tunic over her naked torso. But if she cared nothing for her modesty, there seemed little enough reason for her captain to safeguard it.

The door opened to reveal a white-faced Nethreal. "Sir! Trajan reports we've only the starboard longboat."

"The other?"

"Riddled with holes. No better than flotsam."

Ledron's silent fury drew another snicker from Denariel. "You were expecting elsewise, Captain?"

"It wants her in the boat," Kylac realized, "with but a handful left to guard her."

The princess spared him a haughty smile. "Reckon that, do you? Were diving in here to snatch me away its only hope, it would not have departed so quickly."

"Ya seem rather amused by all o' this."

"Ineptitude *is* amusing, don't you think, mercenary?"

Rather than trade barbs, Kylac turned to Ledron. "Is there time to ferry the crew ashore in shifts?"

"In these swells? We'll be lucky if a single boatload slides aground upright."

"So which is it, Captain?" Denariel asked. "Will you cull a third of your men and set forth as the Ukinh desires? Or shall we ride this tub to splinters and let the sea sort it out?"

10

Hᴇʀ ᴀᴄɪᴅ ᴛᴏɴᴇ notwithstanding, Denariel seemed to have a clear understanding of matters. Already, the jagged shoreline was coming into focus. White waters churned at the base of great, glistening rocks, while the broken pieces of waves that slipped past were chewed to foam by the underlying reef. As of yet, nothing the crew had tried appeared to be working. Seized by the currents, their ship was still being driven relentlessly inland, carried inextricably toward that iron-edged bed of stone.

Kylac regarded Ledron expectantly, awaiting an answer to the princess's challenge. The captain, in turn, was slow to respond, choosing instead to stare out the shattered aft window—as if, by refusing to acknowledge it, he might change the truth of things.

"Her Highness takes the longboat," he said at last, turning to face Nethreal. "Trajan and Hadrum at the oars, along with lieutenants Jahant and Colven. We'll need Ahlman and Ahren for their bows . . . and that dog Merrec," he added, as if spitting poison, "per His Majesty's wishes."

"And the remaining seats?" Nethreal asked, when Ledron paused.

"Myself to command, and the three you see here." He gestured to Ranson, Jekks, and Kylac. "Forgive me, Nethreal."

"As you will, sir."

"Hold there," Kylac interjected, before Nethreal had finished his salute. "It ain't my custom, Captain, to seek safety while another faces peril in my stead."

"I care not a whit for your safety," Ledron snapped, "only that of my charge. I need your blades."

"Come, Ledron," Denariel offered mockingly, "let a soulless rogue commit an act of nobility before he dies."

"Guardian," the captain reminded Nethreal, "you have your orders."

When the Blackfist had exited, Ledron said to Kylac, "Refuse me, and I'll gladly appoint another in your stead. But you vowed to see her delivered to her father, and I'm asking you to do so."

So he had. But did that vow justify preserving himself while Sallun, Obren, Brenth, Ribach, and so many others were left to the mercy of the sea?

"The oath of a mercenary?" Denariel scoffed, then rolled her eyes and set to tying a leather vest.

It would serve her just, Kylac thought, were he to step aside and let the groll claim her. But, as in most battles, justice wasn't the issue here. Men fought and died, each with his own reasons, and only the gods, if gods there were, might be able to sort through the carnage. Right and wrong were shifting targets, relying heavily on where one stood. The only constant a man could truly hope to find, the only integrity, was that which he created for himself by matching deeds to words—be they kind, cruel, or something in between.

"So be it, Captain. The boat it is."

Ledron met his gaze expressionlessly, then turned on a heel and followed Nethreal from the cabin.

"You waged a desperate fight there, didn't you?" Denariel snickered. "I trust your conscience can bear the burden when your abandoned crewmates start washing ashore drowned and broken."

I'd more likely weep for them than you, Kylac thought, dipping his head in a polite bow.

He looked then to Ranson, who scowled down at him over a raised chin, and Jekks, who was smirking—presumably at the princess's ceaseless attempts to berate him. "Ya disapprove, I imagine?"

"We follow the captain's orders," said Ranson. "But you've a long road to merit the esteem he's given you. And that road is about to grow longer."

Denariel laughed while pulling on her boots. "Grand words from a man who was just slapped about like a pastry-thieving butcher's boy."

Kylac suppressed a smile. He might have even thanked her—had the words been uttered in any way as a compliment toward him and not merely as an insult toward Blowfish.

She came to her feet with boots in place, and wrapped a travel cloak about her shoulders. "Let's put an end to this, shall we?"

She marched toward the cabin exit, nimbly navigating the floor that angled beneath her feet. Clearly, she had found her sea legs at some point during the past few weeks. She paused upon reaching the door. "Must I lead myself out?" she asked.

"Your Highness," Ranson replied, "I believe the captain intended—"

With a roll of her eyes, the princess yanked open the door and pushed out into the storm.

A moment later, Kylac, Ranson, and Jekks stood alongside her atop the sterncastle deck, where they were immediately thrashed by winds and pummeled by rain. The mad struggles Kylac had been listening to were now visible—and even more chaotic than he'd envisioned. Waves sloshed over the lurching decks, causing skittering crewmen to slip or stumble. Sails had been furled or cut loose in an effort to sap the wind, so that masts and spars reached forth now like leafless trees in a barren wood. Lightning still forked through the heavens, flashing its ghostly radiance before peals of thunder ushered back the darkness. Near the bow, Ribach led a team in heaving a fallen boom—weighted with iron chains and tied to a deck rope—over the rail. Another would-be anchor. Judging by the number of ropes and nets draped already along those rails, it was but another wasted effort.

Though inured since childhood to the prospect of death, Kylac felt disheartened by the futility of it all. He searched for Sallun, and found the lookout still clinging to his perch in the crow's nest, swaying back and forth at the peak of the ship's motion. He thought to shout at the lad, but saw as well the uselessness in that. Even if Sallun were to hear him, what was he to say? Farewell?

Fate be kind, he thought instead, hoping that if any made it out of this alive, Sallun did.

But the lad's destiny was out of his hands. Denariel had fixed her squinted gaze already on the knot of bodies gathered around the starboard longboat, and was starting toward it. Kylac dutifully followed, helping the princess to keep her feet as she went. For once, she uttered no complaint. Ranson and Jekks kept pace behind them, gripping the rail. As they reached the stair leading down to the quarterdeck, Kylac happened to glance over at the empty wheel. It turned loosely left, then right, manned only by the winds, waves, and the shifting leans of their vessel—an eerie reminder of their helplessness.

Ledron burst from the navigation room at their backs, weighed down by leather satchels. He saw them at once and rushed to join them, lowering his bald head against a shrill burst of wind. He caught up to them at the forward edge of the quarterdeck, and they reached the maindeck together. There the longboat was prepped, though rocking heavily within its davits. Jahant and Colven, Ahlman and Ahren, Hadrum and Merrec, were already seated. Trajan stood at the rail beside her, along with Nethreal and Percel, who Kylac presumed would be tasked with lowering them once all were aboard.

"Make way, Merrec!" Ledron shouted over the whistling gale. "To the bow with you!"

The mercenary had claimed a seat at the exact center of the boat. Typically cheerful, he appeared downright sullen, wrapped tightly within his hood and cloak, hunkered against the rains. His gaze narrowed at the command, but he knew better than to argue.

"Kronus! You're our eyes!"

Kylac nodded, springing to the head of the bow, balanced atop the swinging gunwales and facing aft. Merrec moved more quickly now—no doubt feeling better about being stashed at the front of their boat as long as Kylac was warding his back. As soon as he'd relinquished his seat, Trajan helped to place Denariel there—flanked by Ranson and Jekks—before taking up the aft oar position on the near side.

The captain himself was the last to board, lingering beside Nethreal and Percel as if considering giving up his seat.

"We'll await you on the beach!" he shouted to the pair. His gaze tracked across the rest of the ship. "All of you!"

While most of the Shadowguard were engaged in their assigned duties, some of the men had surrendered their hopeless tasks and allowed their attention to be drawn to the departing group. Though they couldn't likely hear their captain's words, more than one of these offered salute. Kylac found himself nodding in fascination. Whether brave or foolish, a true soldier didn't gripe, beg, or squeal. He simply performed as requested, took pride in doing so, and thanked his commanders for the opportunity to serve.

Even when it was time to die.

As soon as the captain had claimed his seat in the stern between Ahlman and Ahren, Nethreal and Percel—one on each line fore and aft—released the locks and began lowering the longboat. It wasn't the steadiest of journeys, given the rocking of the boat amid the storm-tossed swells. More than once, the longboat swung wide only to come crashing back against the side of hull. After the second such collision, Trajan and Jahant used the oars on that side to help cushion further blows. Throughout it all, Kylac maintained his aft-facing crouch at the head of their little escape vessel, weathering the unpredictable motions while watching even now for any hint of the groll.

Their landing promised to be even rockier. A swell rose to catch their stern, then rolled on. Another hammered them amidships. To Kylac, it felt as if attempting to mount a bucking horse. He was more concerned, however, with their shifting orientation. They'd started out with starboard to the east, placing their longboat on a seaward side of the ship. But the storm had caused *Denariel's Return* to rotate during the descent, so that now, Kylac found their breakaway group pinched between the ship to the north and the oncoming shore to the south. The thrust of the waves was pushing the larger vessel into them, threatening to roll them beneath its hull.

"Hold the lines!" Ledron shouted, signaling to his men above.

But the lean of the ship was such that those above could no longer see or hear him. As the longboat bottomed out within a sloping trough, first the stern line, and then the bow line, went slack.

"It's too late, Captain!" Colven hollered.

Had the ropes continued to hold them aloft, their crew might have hung there with the hope of the ship circling about. But with the tension in the lines gone, the ropes were serving now merely as tethers to the ship barreling down on them.

Ledron saw the truth. "Release!"

Kylac unhooked them at the bow. Ahren disengaged the stern. While Hadrum and Colven set their oars in the oarlocks, Trajan and Jahant continued to push against the hull of the ship with theirs.

"Heave!" Ledron shouted. "Get us turned!"

Kylac saw the strain in Colven's face as the lieutenant dug deep against the rising sea. His strength, along with Hadrum's to aid him, had them twisting quickly, swinging the bow southward. That put their stern firmly in the shadow of the ship's hull, and killed Jahant's warding reach. Fortunately, the larger ship rocked back the other way with a groan, giving them a glimpse of its black underside—encrusted with barnacles and seaweed below the waterline.

Jahant grappled with his oar, fighting to fit it within the lock. They couldn't get clear with rowers on only one side.

The looming ship came rolling back toward them, as if to bury them beneath the swells.

"Heave!" Ledron roared again.

Trajan, seated astern, raised his oar like a spear to meet the ship. He succeeded only in scraping a small patch of sea growth from its belly before it slapped that oar down against the transom. The others in the aft section of the boat leaned forward instinctively as the hulking vessel bore down upon them. Denariel let slip a frightened squeal.

But Trajan's effort did provide a slight push to their longboat that—together with the deep pulls by Colven and Hadrum on one side, and Jahant on the other—helped them slide clear of the ship as it came crashing down, grinding against their stern. Their bow went up, high enough nearly to throw Kylac from his perch. His balance served him, however, even when the waves dropped out from beneath their boat, causing it to lean sharply to larboard before crashing down again.

"Heave! Heave!"

It was all they could do now. Trajan threaded his oar in place to join the other rowers. Kylac, trusting to the strength of his crewmates, continued to observe the ship as it seethed like some monstrous beast over its escaping prey. When convinced that enough water lay between them, he turned forward, to oversee what dangers lay ahead.

We'll await you on the beach, Ledron had said. An audacious sentiment to begin with, but more so now, as Kylac surveyed the staggered array of giant, freestanding rock formations that littered this broken shoreline. Beyond, the cliffs of the mainland rose and fell in steep climbs and sharp descents, the high swells churning at their base. He saw crevasses and folds that hid narrow coves, and a larger break or two that might serve as a gateway inland. By and large, however, the stretch before them reminded him of a siege-ready fortress, prepared to withstand any assault.

"Larboard tap!" Ledron yelled, acting as coxswain from his aft position.

Jahant and Trajan, the oarsmen on that side, checked their stroke, causing the boat to shift in their direction.

"Even it out!" came the follow-up command a moment later.

They were taking aim, Kylac realized, at one of the larger clefts in the base of the cliffs. It was really their only choice. Here, in their smaller vessel, Kylac could better feel the incredible power of the current driving them toward shore. There would be no fighting it—not for any meaningful length of time, anyway. And even if they could resist its push, it seemed foolish to believe they could weather these seas for long. The storm-fueled waves were tossing them about like cork, foaming tips whipped into further frenzy by the prevailing winds. It seemed but a matter of time before a broadside hit picked them up and hurled them over.

It was this, as much as anything, that threatened to undermine their approach. As rogue waves came at them, Ledron was forced to realign their bow to meet them head-on, else risk being capsized. Now and then, they would catch a rising crest that helped propel them forward, but just as often they found themselves swept off course, or caught within a deep trough while the strikingly tepid waters of a neighboring crest poured in atop them, threatening to drown their boat along with them.

While others rowed, bailed, or bellowed commands, Kylac rode the bow as it bucked and fell, searching the black swells for sign of hidden danger. Was the groll still aboard *Denariel's Return*? Or was it somewhere alongside them, waiting to spring an attack? Would it truly trust its quarry's fate to the furious whims of a tempestuous sea?

Their lurching, ragged path brought them within the looming shadow of one of the renegade rock formations. Seldom had Kylac felt so small and insignificant. Were the ocean to raise them up and dash them against that jagged, encrusted stone, they might not leave so much as scratch or stain while their little party was reduced to splinters.

But captain and oarsmen guided them true. Though tossed and twisted, they managed to veer past at a safe distance, avoiding damage and pressing on toward their goal.

Their luck held out against the next two monoliths that arose before them. Under as sure a guiding hand as could be mustered, their longboat slipped by as if passing between a pair of massive watchtowers. A third, smaller rock in the shadow of its larger brother caught them by surprise, but again the waves favored and allowed them to maneuver safely.

Could the ship they'd left behind fare as well?

Kylac glanced back periodically to check its progress. It was now about a hundred strokes astern, and mayhap half that distance to the west. Pushed and spun haphazardly by the storm, it managed to brush past the first monolith it encountered without making contact. The second, however, snapped off her bowsprit with a thunderous crack that triggered desperate shouts from the crew still clinging to her rails.

"Mind your oars!" Ledron shouted.

Hadrum lowered his wayward gaze, regaining the control he'd lost with his lapse in focus. It was difficult to fault him. The doomed carrack had taken aim at mayhap the largest of the offshore cliffs. The distant shouts of her brave crew rose now in a panicked chorus of alarm. Even Denariel betrayed concern, biting her fist to stifle her anxious cry.

Wood and stone met in a great, rending crash, the sound of which reached Kylac's ears only after the vessel had caved at its center. As if the first blow weren't sufficient, the sea snatched up the shuddering vessel as it tried to recoil and hurled it at the giant rock a second time.

At that point, it split apart, bow and stern tearing from one another, each to seek its own path around the interceding mountain.

Of course, neither could remain afloat on its own. While the bow section disappeared momentarily behind the rock that had claimed her, the stern leaned back at a precipitous angle, ocean waters rushing in. Men were shaken from the rails and ratlines as the stricken vessel twisted and bobbed, yanked one way and then the other, bashed and wrenched and dragged all at the same time by the sea's savage forces.

Like wolves at a carcass, Kylac thought, turning away. It felt wrong to do so—like he was abandoning them a second time. But he had his own crew now to tend to, and nothing he could do from here would be of any help to those beyond his reach.

A violent thud struck the underside of their boat at almost dead center. It jolted a yelp from Denariel and sent a wracking shiver through the vessel. Hadrum mishandled his oar again, and had to grip the gunwale to keep from tumbling backward. Ahlman and Ahren turned to examine their wake. They signaled to each other, and then to Ledron.

"Shoal!" the captain hollered.

Kylac could see it now—not with any visual clarity, but well enough to recognize that their situation had just grown more perilous. As they neared the shore, the ocean floor had risen to greet them. Not with smooth sands or flat, wave-worn reef, but with even more sharp mounds and jutting crags. Lurking beneath the water line, these smaller rocks were invisible unless exposed by a passing wave trough, making them that much harder to circumnavigate.

"Three strokes to larboard, thirty degrees!" Kylac shouted, pointing out one such hazard.

"Larboard tap! Starboard dig!" Ledron barked in response.

At first, Kylac wondered if the captain had heard him correctly, as the command had them shifting *toward* the hazard, rather than away from it. Then he realized that Ledron was accounting for the easterly drift of the south-running current. Had they turned to starboard as reflex would dictate, they likely would have been carried straight into the submerged stone.

As it was, their starboard oars clipped its glistening skin as they scraped by and on to the next.

"Dead ahead, two strokes!" Kylac signaled.

Again they angled to larboard, riding the current rather than fighting it. The oarsmen, Kylac realized, were showing signs of fatigue. Though they'd come a fair distance, they were still mayhap two hundred strokes from the shoreline break that Ledron had targeted. Should they prove unable to maintain pace, only the gods knew where they might end up.

Thunder shook the heavens and the rains continued to pour. Waves slapped and sprayed over and around them. Kylac wondered how many men from the carrack were out there now, clinging to bits of flotsam, kicking or paddling their way toward shore. He wondered if any would be able to traverse this churning, razor-edged shoal—or if the groll was out there hunting them, one by one. He wondered this and more even as he continued to seek out the hazards before him, doing what he could to increase his own party's chances of reaching land alive.

Still sixty or seventy strokes from shore, the roiling waves turned to foaming surf. Shortly thereafter, their longboat ran aground, bottoming out and then scraping to a halt on a shelf of reef. A white-capped crest threatened to pick them up again and carry them past, but failed to do more than roll them to starboard. When a pair of following waves offered similar result, Ledron gave the order to disembark.

"Trajan carries Her Highness!" the captain commanded. "Jahant, Colven, Hadrum, Merrec—provisions. Ahlman, Ahren, you'll have the point. Kronus, rearguard."

Kylac stood in place, resisting the drag of the calf-deep surf while waiting for the group to form up. Jahant and Colven saddled Merrec and Hadrum with sacks, skins, and pouches from the seat lockers before loading themselves up with more of the same. Ahlman and Ahren loosened their quiver caps and tested their wet bows.

"I can carry myself, Captain," Denariel said when Trajan reached for her.

"You'll be carried," Ledron insisted, "conscious or elsewise."

Denariel opened her mouth to argue further, but must have decided against it. "At least let me ride humpback," she suggested tartly. "I'm not a sack of grain."

Ledron considered briefly before nodding.

"As you will, Your Highness," Trajan agreed.

Ranson and Jekks flanked her, naturally, as the party set forth, with the others taking up positions before and after. Kylac fell in at the rear.

He didn't envy Ahlman's and Ahren's task of selecting their path. The reef was slick with urchins, seaweed, and beds of thick-bladed kelp, all of which hampered visibility and threatened their footing. Treacherous waves barreled in from behind as if to hamstring them, only to form dragging riptides when pulled back to sea. Tolerable challenges, mayhap, on even ground. But the reef was a patchwork of mounds and grottos, making the waters ankle-deep in some areas and waist-deep in others. The brothers did their best, Kylac assumed, to keep all out of the deeper channels. But, as with any maze, they were forced more than once to double back and seek another path.

Then Ahlman disappeared. It happened so abruptly that even Kylac blinked to be sure. There one moment and gone the next, sucked beneath the waves as if he'd stepped off a cliff.

When Ahren fired an arrow into that watery void, Kylac knew it was something more.

He was thinking groll until a lizard's tail, roughly four feet in length, broke the water's surface. Spiked and armored, it whipped in a circuit before slapping down again.

"Tarrock!" Trajan shouted in warning.

"Move!" Ledron roared, drawing his sword and splashing forward to the head of their troop.

Ahren hadn't budged, still searching the waters that had claimed his brother. He remained there when Ledron reached him and when the rest of the party had joined up, knotting together defensively. Kylac, maintaining his role as rearguard, was the last to arrive, to find the pool in question filled with blooming clouds of telltale crimson.

"Go!" Ledron shouted. "Jahant, keep them moving!"

The lieutenant obeyed, taking point as Ahren continued to stand there, rooted in place. Amid the bloody murk, an arm floated to the surface, bitten off at the elbow.

It still wore the leather wristguard to match Ahren's.

"I didn't bring you both to die as one!" Ledron snarled, seizing the paralyzed archer and propelling him forward. "To the shore, now!"

Their passage now was much more reckless, resulting in a greater number of slips and stumbles. Most trudged along with sword in one hand, and the other clinging to the nearest companion. Only Trajan went without weapon, his arms hooked underneath Denariel's legs. With a ready blade in each hand, Kylac had the Tower covered.

They were mayhap twenty paces from shore—so tantalizingly close. It could as well have been a hundred leagues. Colven was the next to fall, stepping into a hidden pool on his right. Jahant reached for him, but the junior lieutenant was ripped from his grasp by something else within those waters. Before the Mace could react further, a tarrock lunged from a second pool behind him, snapping jaws erupting from the surf to clamp about his lower leg.

Jahant howled. The tarrock twisted, ripping tendons and snapping bones. Kylac arrived as the beast attempted to drag the Mace away. Though its body was submerged, he scored hits to the creature's face with both blades, loosening its hold on the lieutenant and driving it back amid snarls of pain and fury.

Hadrum slogged past both Kylac and the half-submerged Jahant, kicking at the waves in his path, taking the lead without regard for those behind him. Merrec splashed hard and fast on his heels.

"Go! Go!" Ledron shouted at Trajan, waving the rest onward before stopping to clutch at Jahant. He seized the lieutenant by the forearms, pulling hard as the tarrock returned to tug from the other end.

Kylac slashed at the waters, but the creature was beyond his long-sword's reach. He was about to make a lunging stab when the tarrock let go and Jahant came suddenly free. Ledron pitched backward, the lieutenant falling atop him—both legs ripped to bloody stumps at the knee.

"Leave me," Jahant rasped at his captain, face purple with agony.

Kylac took the Mace's head with a clean stroke, giving him the mercy of a quick death.

Ledron recoiled instinctively, nearly falling back into the pool that had claimed Colven. When a tarrock's gaping jaws shot this time from the water, Kylac met them with a left-handed thrust of his shortsword through the mouth, punching back at an angle to pierce its dragonlike skull.

He let the beast convulse while sheathing his longsword to grab a fistful of cloak at Ledron's chest. He then ripped his killing blade clear and hauled the captain to his feet with one swift movement.

"We're lagging, Captain."

Jahant's headless body was yanked away behind them. Despite the bitter taste, Kylac would waste no more time here. He dashed onward instead, trusting Ledron to follow. The captain did. Together, they watched another tarrock emerge behind Trajan, the spikes on its ridged back protruding above the waterline as it gave chase through the surf.

"At your back!" Ledron shouted.

Jekks turned, diving at the beast to intercept its snapping lunge. While the dagger in his left hand was knocked from his grasp, the dagger in his right found its throat. Still, the weight of the creature carried it forward, and Jekks was pinned beneath its thrashing bulk.

Not even the thunder could drown out his screams.

The wounded tarrock had slithered away by the time Kylac reached it. Jekks remained, staring sightlessly amid bloody waters, his body ground to pulp against the reef's jagged surface.

Kylac lunged past. He could see not just one, but two of the creatures angling toward Trajan and Denariel on an intercept course from the west. Hadrum and Merrec had reached the shore. So too might Trajan and his precious cargo. But not if—

The tarrocks stopped suddenly—first one, and then the other—as if snagged by their tails. One vanished instantly beneath the foaming waves. The second bent skyward instead, arching its back with a deep-throated yelp. It then gnashed its jaws and circled away, ducking swiftly from sight.

Kylac veered in that direction as Trajan covered the last few strides to climb free of the reaching tide—Denariel on his back, Ahren and Ranson at his side. Hadrum and Merrec hadn't stopped, but continued to stumble their way up the rocky beach.

"Kronus!" Ledron shouted, as Kylac drifted farther from him, falling again to the rear.

Kylac stopped—not because of the captain's call, but because he'd reached the lip of the reef overlooking that final pool, and saw neither the tarrocks nor the shadow of anything else beneath the storm-whipped surface.

The sea rolled in and Kylac moved on, dancing nimbly amid the smaller wavelets to join Ledron in reaching dry land. Like those in their party before them, they kept going, glancing back to see if anything gave chase. Kylac saw one tarrock staring after them at the tide's edge, its yawning mouth full of teeth as frothing waves washed over it. But it didn't seem inclined to follow.

When he looked back, it was gone, swallowed by the surf.

11

"PUT ME DOWN," Denariel groused, as Trajan continued to climb the stony shore.

The Tower ignored her, huffing as he trudged onward amid the rains. He was gaining quickly on Hadrum and Merrec, who were staggering to an exhausted halt some twenty paces ahead. With him were Ahren and Ranson—the latter of whom appeared to be favoring a cramp on his right side. Ledron was doing well to keep pace beside Kylac, though his breathing was labored, and his brow and cheeks red with fatigue.

"Captain!" Denariel called out. "Must I be carried all the way to Avenell?"

Here beyond the heaving seas, churning waves, and monstrous tarrocks, the storm's threat had abated. Ledron glanced back at the foaming breakers, some thirty paces behind them now, and slowed. "Halt!"

Kylac stopped beside the winded captain. Farther on, the order caught up to Ahren, Trajan, and a grateful Ranson, who doubled over, hands on his knees, sucking for breath.

"Halt!" Trajan echoed ahead to Hadrum and Merrec. Labored as their own movements were, it appeared the pair might continue through the night, crawling if need be over the shards of stone that littered this rocky shore.

"Well," Denariel said, chuckling as she detached herself from Trajan's back. "A fine bit of strategy that was, Captain."

Ledron remained where he stood, jaw clenched as he gazed out over the incoming surf, watching for . . . well, Kylac couldn't be sure. Pursuing tarrocks? Survivors from *Denariel's Return*? A pod of seamaids bearing cakes of honeycomb and casks of summer wine? Kylac saw none of these and little else, though with charcoal clouds still hoarding the dim light of a sliver moon, he couldn't expect to see much of anything.

"I mean, even the Grenarr know better than to enter the Widow Strait this time of year," Denariel continued as she came up to them, heedless of the persistent winds and steady rainfall. "Or might that be precisely what drove you to such madness?"

"Had the beast not taken our rudder . . ." Ledron mumbled.

The princess laughed. "Weep if you will, Captain, but you presented the opportunity. Had our rudder failed farther north, we might yet be drifting—with a chance, at least, to salvage our ship before the Toshanni Current snagged her."

Ledron's only response was to grind his teeth, suggesting to Kylac that, once again, Denariel had the truth of it.

"So, now that your boldness has brought us here, what course do you propose?"

A fair question, and the one on everyone's mind, Kylac saw, as they came trickling back down—Ahren, Trajan, Ranson, Hadrum, and Merrec. A company of thirty-five reduced to just eight in a span of minutes. Weary and waterlogged, stunned by what had happened, looking for someone to make sense of a senseless situation.

"We wait here until daybreak," their captain announced, surveying their bleak surroundings with a suitably gloomy eye, "for survivors and supplies to come ashore."

A practical start, Kylac agreed. The majority of their provisions had disappeared with Jahant and Colven. The remainder, slung across the backs of Hadrum and Merrec, looked to be minimal, even for this small group.

Survivors seemed less likely.

"Where is *here*, anyway?" Merrec asked.

The cove looked to be three hundred paces across; mayhap twice that in depth. Broken bluffs rose up to either side, joined at the center by a deep, sloping fold clogged with patches of leafless growth and carpeted with jagged scree.

"The Shattered Fingers," Trajan answered, when Ledron didn't. "First or second, maybe, but north of the Knuckle and west of the sound."

With the exception of Denariel, who remained strangely giddy, and Ledron, whose teeth were surely being reduced to nubs, a collective wind seemed to be sucked from the listeners.

"The north shore?" Merrec rasped. "We're dead men."

Kylac waited for someone to refute the mercenary, but only the storm gave voice. "Is this the Abyss, then?"

"Near enough," Hadrum muttered.

Ledron whirled on him. "You would snivel like him?" the captain snarled, nodding at Merrec. "We are Shadowguard. We have a duty, and will not shirk it."

"My brave protectors," Denariel snickered. "Does your courage wax only in the south, behind your walls and fences?"

"It must be sixty leagues to the northernmost settlement," Merrec complained. "And that a'wing. Sixty leagues across the most savage, inhospitable stretch of—"

"You're welcome to swim it, if you prefer," Ledron offered.

"We don't have to walk sixty leagues," Trajan said. "Thirty should bring us to the outpost of Faer Ungen, at the horn of the Reach. Bitterwood, we call it. Amid the Edgelands along the sound. From there, we can ride a barge south along the Myrdin, clear to Avenell."

Merrec scoffed. "Thirty leagues. I'll call us blessed if we last three."

"You'll call yourself mute if you wag your tongue again," Ledron threatened.

"This territory we must cross . . ." said Kylac. "I gather it's some sort o' wilderness?"

"The Ukinhan Wilds," Trajan replied. "Or the Harrows, if you prefer. Homeland to the mutants."

"But land it is. No more boats—at least until boarding this barge ya speak of." He faced Ledron. "Captain, be it a thousand leagues, ya'll hear no gripes from me."

Predictably, Ledron scowled, seeming no more charmed by Kylac's brashness than by Merrec's cowardice.

Denariel laughed. "Congratulations, Captain. You combed your company for both spineless *and* brazen, I see."

"As it pleases, Your Highness," Kylac said, "your grolls are not the most fearsome creatures I's faced."

"Nothing about you pleases me," Denariel snapped. "Though the manner of your death might provide some small amusement. I wonder, which will it—"

"Enough!" Ledron shouted, scrambling to unbuckle one of his satchels. "There! Is that one of ours?"

They turned as one to face the midnight ocean. Debris from the shipwreck had indeed reached the reef, some of it even now being carried in by the shoreline breakers. Floating fragments stretched from one side of their cove to the other, but as to whether any of it might prove to be . . .

"It's Brenth!" Ledron cried.

Kylac found the captain peering through a spyglass drawn from a dripping pouch. Following the aim of the instrument, he turned his gaze to the east, where he saw what appeared to be a pair of bodies draped over a scrap of hull, kicking toward the shore.

Kylac shed his outer cloak and bolted for the water's edge.

"No!" Ledron shouted after him. "Stop! Kronus! Ahren! Come back!"

A backward glance found Ahren on his heels. Behind the archer, Ledron was wrestling Trajan to a halt, preventing the Tower from following.

"Ahren!" Ledron roared again.

Kylac raced on, as did Ahren. Evidently, the captain didn't wish for them to risk their own lives, worried that their company of eight might only be further reduced. Sensible, but so was lending his skills where he knew he could help.

At this distance, he couldn't see the faces of the men upon the oncoming waves. Mayhap one was indeed the salty veteran, Brenth. It didn't matter. If any had managed to ride out the wreckage and swim this far, he was determined to give them a fair chance to straggle ashore.

Before the tarrocks claimed them.

He didn't slow as he reached the water, but raised his knees to high-step through their rolling press. That bought him a half dozen strides before he was forced to wade through deeper waters along a ridge of submerged limestone, searching left and right for gaps in the reef wherein the tarrocks might be lurking. He didn't know how many of the beasts filled these waters, or what drew them. He might hope that however many there were, they'd gathered by now to fight over the bodies of the Shadowguard already taken. But his father had taught him to never assume the better of two likelihoods.

Now seemed a good time to heed that advice.

The oncoming pair hadn't yet reached standing ground when Kylac sighted another group, farther out, clinging to a splintered length of mast. Four men, this time, looking half drowned, attached like a clump of wave-worn mussels to the netted strands wrapped around their makeshift float. A resourceful bit of work. But then, whatever their comparative shortcomings, these were resourceful men.

The near pair hit the reef and climbed doggedly to their feet. One went down again at once, barreled over by a pursuing wave. But the larger figure caught his partner by the elbow and helped pull him to his feet. Lightning brightened the sky, and, at twenty paces, Kylac got a clear look at their faces. The larger of the two was indeed Brenth.

The other was Sallun.

Kylac grinned as he hastened his pace. Ahren, he realized, had paused at the surf's edge, though his bow was loaded and ready. Of limited use the weapon seemed at that distance, given the relentless rains and gusting winds that raked this shore—never mind that the tarrocks were almost fully submerged. But who could say what the Cowl actually intended?

"Fine o' ya to join us," Kylac welcomed with a hearty smile.

The pair staggered into him, Brenth nearly impaling himself on Kylac's readied shortsword. Somehow, Kylac managed to catch both men and keep them propped upright. But it was clear they were at the end of their strength, and he couldn't well carry them across the reef and defend them at the same time.

"Whoa, there. All right, lads. Let's get your legs under ya, shall we?"

Sallun sucked for breath, sagging with exhaustion. Like Brenth, his cheeks were waxen.

"Why the blades?" Brenth wondered aloud. He pushed back, swaying on his feet, but managed not to fall.

"Calls it a precaution," Kylac said, gently pushing Sallun back as well. His gaze swept the surf at their feet, eyeing the shifting swirl of dark waters and cresting foam. He didn't want to alarm them if he could avoid it, but he wasn't going to lower his guard, either.

"The groll," Sallun assumed. "It's . . . it's . . ." The attempt at words ended in a choking gush of water spilled from the lookout's lungs.

"Save your strength, lad." Warm as the waves and the rains might be, the length of time these two had spent in the sea had obviously taken a dangerous toll. "Your beastie hasn't shown itself," he added encouragingly. "Mayhap it perished in the wreck."

Their sour expressions killed that single-seeded hope before it took root.

The next handful of moments spanned an eon as the float of four drifted toward them. Though a couple of the riders tried once or twice to paddle, it was clearly all they could do to maintain their clenched grips. As a result, the current seized them, hauling them well east of where Kylac stood.

He was still eyeing the widening span, estimating a distance of fifty paces or more, when one of the four was yanked beneath the waters. Only his arm, caught within the netting, prevented him from disappearing entirely. The entire piece of mast dug deeply in that direction, causing the other riders to cry out in alarm. A tail that might have belonged to a small dragon thrashed amid the waters. A moment later, the submerged end of the mast bucked back to the surface, the entangled arm missing the man that should have been attached at the shoulder.

"Whenever ya lads are ready," Kylac prompted.

Neither needed additional urging. The thrashing and screams of their comrades, muted by the ceaseless thunder of storm and surf, prodded them onward at a frantic pace. Kylac trailed closely on their heels, darting from one flank to the next as deeper pools arose to either side. A game of guesses, as there was really no way to anticipate which grotto might hide one of the monsters. In placid waters, there might be ripples or shadows to betray their movements. In this murk, there was only instinct and blind chance.

An arrow whizzed past, followed by another. Kylac didn't know if Ahren had spotted something that pursued them, or was firing at ghosts. He glanced back long enough to see the first shaft pierce the waves. The second struck something hard, from which it ricocheted and fell away broken. A rock, he guessed, rather than tarrock skin— though the two didn't seem entirely dissimilar.

The one tarrock he thought he spied turned out to be a clump of eelgrass. Evading that, his little trio stumbled ashore. Brenth took but two steps before slipping on a loose stone and hitting hard. Sallun bent at once to help.

"Get away from the water," Kylac advised as he sped off to the east.

Ahren had already turned in that direction, firing arrows in a covering pattern near the second group. There were only two now. Kylac could only guess when the third had fallen, as he'd been too busy focusing on his own retreat with Brenth and Sallun. Efficient predators, these tarrocks. Stealthy, armored, powerful. Not unlike the Ukinha said to populate these wild shores.

When he'd closed to within a dozen paces, Kylac veered back into the waves along an intercept course. He recognized these men now—"Fishhook" Percel, with his lopsided grimace, and "Locks" Obren. Locks was favoring his left arm, using his right hand to cradle it against his chest. Percel, Kylac saw as he reached them, was bleeding freely from a gash on his brow.

Lads look like ya's come from a shipwreck, Kylac thought to say. But it seemed wrong to jest—especially when he saw the outline of the eight-foot-long tarrock swimming up on Percel's heels.

"Ankles!" he barked in warning, before spinning to catch the creature mid-lunge with both blades. The first pierced it just behind the gaping jaws, while the other hacked down from overhead, opening a cleft in its armored neck. Though it failed to cut through completely, the blow must have severed some critical nerves, for the tarrock went limp without so much as a whimper, its black eye rolling back in its triple-lidded socket.

Ahren was there, then, reaching forth a hand to help guide the exhausted men forward. Kylac released the dead tarrock as convulsions rolled through its lizard-shaped body. He then backed away in the shadow of his companions, searching for any last strikes from the reef's denizens. Moments later, he followed the others as they limped from the sea, boots crunching against the shore.

"Go on," he urged the group. His gaze stretched farther out across the churning reef, seeking sign of any more survivors. The ship's debris had spread, with hundreds of pieces bobbing amid the swells, snagging against the reef's jagged mounds, or rolling in upon the surf. None that he could see looked to be human.

Ahren gripped his shoulder. The wrap that the archer normally wore around the lower portion of his face had slipped free, revealing a glimpse of the horrific burn scars that marred the man's mouth and chin beneath his ever-drawn cowl. Kylac half expected him to speak. Instead, Ahren just gave his shoulder a squeeze, then turned to lead the others up the beach.

Kylac maintained his surfside vigil for another hour, long enough for the thunder to roll east and for the rains to slacken. Two bodies washed ashore in that time—Nethreal and Davins. A severed hand turned up, as well—Faban's, given the thick patch of red hair on the back of it. It didn't appear to have been chewed free by tarrocks. More likely severed at some point during the splintering of *Denariel's Return*.

He gathered both bodies and the grisly remainder, and patrolled the shore looking for more. He also snatched up and formed a small pile of potentially useful supplies—empty pouches, a length of rope, a sack of firebrands. A barrel of ale rolled in, but its hole had been sprung, leaking most of its contents into the sea.

By that time, a bonfire crackled farther up the beach, near the cove's southern crease. How Ledron's crew had managed to find enough scrub and driftwood to serve as fuel, let alone set flame to the soaked pieces, was a minor mystery. But he was glad they had, for the beacon it might serve to any still struggling out there.

Sunrise was still hours off when Trajan approached, with Ahren beside him.

"Captain asked us to relieve you," the Tower said.

"Thought he didn't want any o' ya venturing back into the waves."

"Didn't exactly ask *you* to, either, as I recall."

"So if'n ya sees someone out there?"

"Won't be any others coming in that we can help."

That wasn't callousness talking. Nor a justification born of fear. Merely grim acceptance. After this much time, those who hadn't been smashed, drowned, or devoured would have succumbed to exhaustion—and *then* been smashed, drowned, or devoured. Mayhap one or two had been carried by the currents and found shore somewhere to the east. But if that were so, they would likely have to fend for themselves.

"And these?" Kylac asked, gesturing to the bodies of Nethreal and Davins laid nearby.

"There'll be no burial in this ground," Trajan replied, scuffing his boot on the broken bits of limestone. "Ahren and I will put stones in their bellies and let the fish fight the tarrocks for them."

A shame it seemed. Though neither man would much care, he supposed. Kylac took another look at their faces. Nethreal the Truth. "Twitch" Davins. He wondered idly how long either would be remembered.

"Get some rest," Trajan urged. "For tomorrow, our trials begin in earnest."

"Will the trek be so perilous?"

The Tower shrugged. "Few have crossed the Harrows and lived to tell of it. Those who have are hailed as legends, or dismissed as madmen."

"*You* don't seem frightened."

"I would indeed, if that fear served better shield. When my turn comes, it comes. I've already had more time than some." He nodded toward the younger Nethreal.

True enough, thought Kylac. Whether it marked the end of a man's adventures or merely the gateway to another, death had never seemed to him anything to fret over. It was death that made life special.

Not that he had any intention of submitting to it.

"Being a legend is tiresome business," Kylac cautioned, glancing over to include Ahren. "But given the alternatives, I guess it's legends we'll be."

12

Dawn saw the storm venture east, leaving behind leaden skies that strained now to hold back the sunlight clawing at their seams. Of small consolation this was to the decimated troop that awoke beside Kylac in that shattered cove. What might have been a terrible dream revealed instead an all-too-stark reality. Were there not the sober faces of his fellow survivors, there were still the pieces of wreckage that had washed ashore throughout the night to remind him of all they'd lost, and all they had yet to overcome.

Still, there was an air of resiliency among the men as they combed through that wreckage a final time, salvaging what they could in the form of provisions. Mayhap it was as simple as the long-awaited relief from winds and rain. Or mayhap it was the realization that, despite the incredible odds, their lives had been spared—permitting hope that it might happen again. It could have been a soldier's natural resilience pushing to the fore, or merely that their tasks provided sufficient distraction from dwelling too deeply on what couldn't be helped. Whatever the cause, Kylac sensed little disconsolation when Ledron at last called them together, and more of a collective determination.

"We've but four waterskins," the Head announced. Though two more had been brought in by the waves, their contents had been befouled, and would be useless until refilled. "One belongs to Her

Highness. The others we share for likely the next two days. Barring rain, get used to parched throats and swollen tongues. That should make eating less comfortable—which is good, since our only food-stuffs are some pickled olives and weevil-infested tack. We may be able to hunt and forage for more, but I wouldn't touch anything unless Trajan says it is safe. Questions?"

The men looked around at one another, as if measuring themselves and those upon whom they might best depend. Denariel still wore the smirk she'd unveiled last night, seeming amused by the entire endeavor. Merrec peered at Kylac from beneath a lowered brow, a surreptitious stare that suggested he still saw them as private partners in this. Ahren might have been a statue beneath his cowl, slightly aloof of the others. Still in denial, Kylac was certain, over the death of his brother. Sallun was a wrack of jittery movements and edgy expressions. Unsettled by the ordeal of the prior night, or by that which lay before—or both. None among them, Kylac included, had any words.

"Then let us bid farewell to our fallen," Ledron said with stinging finality, "and do our best not to join them."

They gathered their meager possessions and fell into line behind Trajan, who marched them south into the crease between the cove's walls. What looked from the bottom like nothing more than a rock-slide evolved into a narrow, switchback trail that climbed steeply through the scrub vegetation. Despite his size, the Tower proved to be as sure-footed as a mountain goat as he followed its meandering path along the pitted face of the eastern cliff, cutting generally deeper into the south-running cleft. After navigating this uncertain ascent for nearly an hour, including a pair of difficult stretches that had them hoisting one another up over bald gaps in the cliff face, they entered a defile that cleaved the rim of the bluff, providing them a gateway passage through the isle's outer wall.

Kylac was surprised to discover just how thin that wall really was. It couldn't have been more than a hundred paces before the defile widened, then flattened out to either side. Growth began to crop up amid the wind-raked stone, stunted and scraggly at first, then larger, all of it dry and misshapen. A little farther on, the cliff crested and fell away completely, sloping downward over a rugged stretch of a league or more into a gnarled jungle that even at a distance stank of rotting brush and brackish water.

A hush fell over the group as its members stopped to absorb the view.

"She looks innocent enough," Kylac offered.

"So does the shark," Percel chuckled, "judged solely by its fin."

"Run on down there," Hadrum sneered in agreement. "See how innocent she really is."

Kylac ignored them, amused by their disdain and their inability to hear sarcasm. Were he really that close-minded to the possibility of danger, he'd have perished long ago.

"Far from the worst of it, in any case," Trajan said. "What you see there is the Grayslake. Still part of the Edgelands. Tough country, but not quite lethal. Even so, we'll keep clear as long as we can."

To do so, they hugged the inner ridge as it curled eastward, keeping to the windworn slopes of salted limestone a hundred paces or so below the coastal crest. The ground was smoother there than at the zenith, with fewer fissures and crevasses to negotiate. It also gave them some protection from the breezes blowing off the north sea—warm gusts filled with eye-clawing grit. Alone, Kylac might have climbed a little higher, where he could use the ocean as a marker to track how far they were bending inland. Countering that, he might be just as happy if he never saw the ocean again.

They marched in almost utter silence, attuning their ears to the song of this land, that they might better sense anything amiss. It was a mostly empty tune, driven by the wind that carved through the narrow clefts and canyons, underscored by the scrape of their feet on the desolate surface. The occasional bird shriek would punctuate the stillness, from either those that hunted the seaward bluffs, or those that roosted in the sickly-looking depths of the deadwood jungle below. At one time or another, Kylac heard a stuttering caw, a chorus of croaks, and a throaty growl from the same murky tangle. In all, however, the landscape was remarkably lifeless, with the relative stillness seeming to lament its solitude.

After an hour's march, the ground started to dip, angling steadily downward. The scattered growth thickened, as if the Grayslake had finally warmed to their presence and decided to reach out in welcome. In a matter of moments, they were enveloped by a profusion of exotic plants and bushes, most of it parched and twisted and drained of color.

"Avoid this one," Trajan said, pointing out a shrub whose leaves were covered on the underside by tiny bristles. "Lady hair. Her nettles will sting like acid, and don't pluck free easily. Manchineel," he added a little farther on, indicating a tree whose moldy bark was dotted with tufts of grass. "Touching the glaze on its leaves will cause severe blistering."

He introduced them to these and a dozen others as they went along—some to beware, and others benign. There was the maiden plum, a tree whose poisonous sap didn't wash off with water. Beyond that stood a copse of voyager trees, so named because their red, peeling bark resembled the skin of visiting outlanders unaccustomed to the strength of this land's sun. There seemed to be no shortage of blood birch, and a healthy sprinkling of segmented shag trees, tall and bowed, with tufted foliage consisting of large, shredded leaves. Kylac failed to see the difference between silver thatch and bull thatch, and wasn't sure how the Tower discerned logwood from whitewood—both of which looked like ironwood. Unable to track them all, Kylac dismissed from his attentions those with fair scents, and those with foul, and concentrated instead on those with thorns or barbs or telltale poison sheens, determining in general to follow closely the steps of those who trekked before him.

As the plant life thickened, so too did the wildlife that dashed, flew, or skittered amid the intertwining boughs and leaves. Kylac caught flashes of tiny birds, lizards, crabs, and rodents, and heard the cautious rummaging of many more than he saw.

"Is there truly nothing to be foraged from this region?" he asked. Recalling Ledron's warning, he looked to Trajan for an answer.

"Little your bowels could keep. And less that is large or meaty enough to warrant the risk. Be content nothing yet has tried to eat *you*."

The Tower was obviously not factoring insects into his appraisal. By that score, their troop was already under siege, ambushed at every turn by gathering clouds of bees, blood gnats, and great, colorful flies that seemed drawn to the sweat of their bodies.

This irritation worsened as the sun finally cracked through the gray dome of the sky, giving Kylac a taste of the oppressive heat said to dominate these shores. Gone were the chill ocean breezes, and absent were the towering shade trees that might have helped provide relief. The burning rays descended, and the mostly thin, twining brush did little to shelter them. Sweat pooled and cloaks were shed, but that left even more skin exposed to the stinging insect swarms. Almost as vexing were the dust, spores, pollen, and splinters that seemed now to fill the air, little bits of growth that caused their flesh, lungs, and eyes to itch. Lacking sufficient water to wash themselves with, little could be done about any of it.

Sallun seemed particularly affected, coughing and sneezing and rubbing his eyes until the whites bled redder than his hair. Others shared his torment, to one degree or another—all save Percel, who seemed strangely immune, and who mocked any who expended the energy to mutter complaint. Before long, those who dared do so were shamed into silence.

If this was the mild terrain, then Kylac didn't care to imagine the rest. He'd been trained to repress physical discomforts such as heat, cold, hunger, thirst, breathlessness, illness, and more—to withdraw inside himself and thus mitigate any adverse effect on his body's ability to function. His proud companions would surely claim much the same, making them better suited here than most. Yet even Kylac, after just a few short hours, understood how taxing this journey promised to be, and wondered how many of them could endure it.

Now and then, the jungle would break apart, thinned by snaking trails of barren stone. By and large, however, they were forced to hack and claw their way through unforgiving thickets that tore back at them with thorns and burs and innocent-looking leaves that none-theless left their skin itching and raw. The sweat that stung their eyes couldn't be wiped away, due to the grime of bark, soil, and plant oils that covered their hands. Cloaks were donned again for protection, giving the heat that much more strength. The breathing of Kylac's companions grew labored, coming in rasping huffs. Bodies leaned, limbs drooped, feet dragged . . . and still the jungle wore on.

Shortly after midday, Kylac finally detected the hint of a returning breeze, and with it the familiar scent of the sea. The jungle opened up again—not all at once, but with a subtle thinning of its growth and a gentle rising of the ground from which it sprouted. Kylac heard the distinct roar of surf, dim at first, then louder. The ocean was near, though what that might mean to their overall progress, he couldn't say.

A curtain of brush clogged the gaps in a wide wall of narrow tree trunks. Pushing through this, Kylac found their troop atop a cliff overlooking an immense swath of water that severed the ground on which they stood from what looked like a rocky beach on the opposite side, several leagues distant. The swath opened to the ocean north, and carried south for as far as Kylac could see, effectively cutting them off from the eastern half of the isle.

"The Gorrethrian Sound," Trajan announced. "Never thought I'd be happier to see her."

"Why's that?" Kylac asked, breathing deeply of the crisp, salty air.

"Because it tells me we crashed upon the first of the Shattered Fingers, and not the second. It means we can turn south now without having to grind eastward another full day."

"A measure of fortune, at last," Hadrum grumbled.

Denariel scoffed. "Never mind, then, the good grace that carried you this far."

Hadrum gave her a withering glare. In response, Denariel dropped cross-legged to the earth with her back to him, where she set to combing a hand through her shoulder-length hair.

Others, Kylac noticed, were quick to follow the princess's lead, settling down to stretch and spell their weary legs.

"It's an impressive sight," Kylac said, turning back to the sound. Before this, he'd seen it only on maps. The great rift from which the Sundered Isle drew name, it cut from the northern sea some ninety leagues through the land's center, dividing her nearly in half.

Obren joined him. "Caused by a terrible battle, they say, waged between rival mage factions a thousand years ago during the War of the Magi."

"Religious folk claim it to be the result of a cataclysm cast down by the Fair Mother Eriyah upon the Gorrethrehn," offered Sallun, "as punishment for their foul creation practices."

Kylac chuckled. "Or naught but a natural shifting o' the restless earth, mayhap?"

"Whichever you believe," added Brenth, "the isle was cleaved and the Breeders overrun by their own mutant creations, which then scattered and withdrew into the wilds before we recolonized the land."

"We?" Denariel laughed and shook her head. "That's the magic of history. The victors write it as they please."

"I care little enough for history," Ledron interjected, "only that we're trapped here on the western shore, with no way to cross to the east."

"Is the eastern shore easier to traverse?" Kylac asked.

"Most would say so," Trajan replied, "if only for the reduced Ukinh population. But unless you can fly or outswim the sharks, eels, and tarrocks, it's this shore we'll be dealing with."

"The mutants should be easy enough to avoid," Ledron said, "provided we cling to the shoreline as planned."

Trajan nodded.

"And what of the Ukinh that is surely chasing us?" Merrec asked.

None before had indicated any interest in hearing the mercenary speak, and with the collection of expressions that fell upon him, it seemed they would have preferred his silence now.

"We'll deal with it when we must," Ledron answered him, then glanced around at his men. "To your feet. We find food before we rest."

It took them another hour to do so. Thrashing their way southward through the woodland tangle that hugged the sound's western shore, they came at last upon a collection of fruit-bearing trees that Trajan declared palatable. The shape and color differed from anything Kylac knew. One looked like the offspring of an apple and a pear, with an orange skin and yellow heart. The other was smaller and rounder, with a fuzzy brown rind warding the green flesh beneath. Kylac didn't care for the taste of either, finding one too bitter and the other too sweet. But the sugary juices were a welcome relief to his parched throat, and the meaty pulp preferable to his insistent hunger.

They encountered an even greater number of insects in this area—unsurprising, given the bright colors and attractive scents of the accompanying flowers and nectars. Ranson suffered a sting on his palm when he happened to pluck a fruit already claimed by a large wasp. The injury swelled viciously in a matter of moments, leading Ranson to seek Trajan's assessment. The Tower looked at it, then assured him the sting was of no threat—provided he could tolerate the pain.

When Ranson continued to whine, Percel, true to form, demanded that he stop sniveling. This sparked a challenge that led to Percel locating a nearby wasp nest, giving it a savage shake, and standing amid the resulting cloud. While the others withdrew in a flurry, Fishhook suffered stings to his arms, neck, and shoulder.

"Satisfied?" Percel asked.

"What does that prove?" Ranson moped. "We all know you don't feel pain."

"And we all know you do. So you needn't keep reminding us."

"Enough," Ledron snapped. "Or does this squabbling serve some purpose?"

It didn't, from what Kylac saw, except to further illuminate the tenuous nature of their companionship. Tight as these guardian soldiers were trained to be, they were still a long way from home, and faced with an irregular task. The shipwreck and subsequent slaughter of so many had exacted a price greater than the obvious. Whatever their collective strength, it was clearly frayed at the edges.

While the rest looked on, Ranson and Percel glared at one another in heated silence.

"I'll not remind you of your oath," Ledron said at last, "any of you. You know your station. Prove yourself unworthy, and I'll relieve you of it, if it means I must see Her Highness home by myself."

He circled the grove with his gaze, but sought no acknowledgment before turning on a heel and resuming his march through the brush.

As suddenly as that, they were on the move once more.

Their trek continued throughout the afternoon, the bulk of it spent beneath a blistering heat that had them sweating rivers of precious moisture down chest and limbs. Twice, the skies blackened with the promise of rainfall, but the taunting clouds proved stingy with their blessed brew. An oppressive humidity lingered in the wake of these near-storms, mitigated only by the breezes that stole in off the sound.

Now and again, they happened upon additional fruit-bearing trees, hidden amid the deadwood brush. Each time, they ate their fill, simultaneously dulling their thirst without taxing their paltry water supplies. When Kylac asked why they didn't stock their pouches for later, a couple of the men snickered, while others shook their heads.

"When the grackal is stalking you," Trajan answered kindly enough, "you don't drape bloody meat around your neck."

As dusk fell, their path intersected another body of water, this time the bay of an east-flowing river emptying into the sound.

"The Navandi," Trajan announced as he gazed across its wind-churned sweep. "Our best hope for food and water lie beyond, amid the higher elevations south. Another day, perhaps, depending on how far we have to track the river west before crossing."

"Why not cross here?" Kylac asked. The bay was not so vast. A mile at most. And the waters were much calmer than those that churned through the sound.

In response, Ledron picked up a loose rock and tossed it into the shallow waters lapping at the near bank. When the stone struck, the waters erupted in spray, as a pair of submerged tarrocks reacted to the disturbance. Even Kylac retreated a step, amazed at their size. The largest he'd seen upon landing had been mayhap twelve feet in length. These snapping monsters were each closer to thirty.

"It's only the smaller tarrocks that inhabit the reefs where they are hatched. As they mature, they migrate into the sound, and from there to the bays and rivers inland."

"Is no body of water safe, then?"

"The beasts prefer saltwater, so they'll travel only so far upstream. When the river turns fresh, it should be safe to cross."

"Except west will carry us deeper into the Harrows," Brenth reminded them. "Groll territory."

"Which cannot be helped," said Ledron, pointedly turning his back to where the agitated tarrocks were just now settling beneath the waters.

No, Kylac thought, staring at their baleful, multi-lidded eyes. *I reckon not.*

13

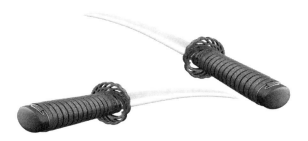

THEY JOURNEYED NO FARTHER that day, electing instead to set camp in the woodland fringe overlooking the sound and adjoining bay. Trajan had persuaded Ledron that, unless pressed to do so, they wouldn't travel after dusk.

"Your blades may hew down a dragon," Trajan explained to Kylac, "but the nights 'round here bring forth things small enough to kill you without ever being seen—especially as you venture inland."

Riddled with insect bites from the day's march, Kylac took the warning seriously. Only because those insufferable blood gnats were venomless had any of their company made it this far. He found it discomfiting, now as ever, to consider that there were threats out there that cared nothing for all his finely honed talents.

In meager defense, three small fires were lit in a triangle pattern at the farthest corners of their campsite, to help draw attention from the bodies huddled in the center. A sentry was posted near each—Brenth, Ahren, and Obren drawing first watch. Finally, Trajan directed that a circle of salt salvaged from *Denariel's Return* be poured around their site's perimeter, as further deterrent, he said, to any curious crawlers.

"I'd rather the stray spider or serpent than attract every Ukinh from here to the western Oloron," Merrec muttered, as he lay down near Kylac.

Kylac shifted, increasing the space between them. "I'd rather a warm mattress with silken coverlets and a pillow o' down. But I reckon I'll be glad for what I have."

There was little conversation after that—a whisper here or a murmur there as the companions settled into what comfort they could find, but nothing of consequence. Weariness had sapped their strength, and wariness kept them quiet. There wasn't much to discuss, in any case. Had he been able to draw Trajan aside, Kylac might have pressed for more information about the terrain and its denizens. But he didn't want to instigate any group discussions, and had already decided he would learn what he must as he went. It seemed he knew the situation as well as any of them, and the goal at this moment was simple.

Sleep while he could, and hope to wake upon the dawn.

It took some time to accomplish the first, keen as he was to every unfamiliar scrape, flap, and skittering beyond their camp, and to the restless snorting, grunting, and shifting of those within. Eventually, however, he managed to find the necessary inner stillness to accept his surroundings and put his overactive senses to rest. By the time Ahren woke him for his turn at watch, he felt as he normally did—alert and ready to confront whatever challenge the winds might bring.

He found his place at the eastern watchfire, positioning himself at the edge of its revealing halo—just beyond the hovering swarms of blood gnats. His flesh itched where they'd pierced him throughout the day, but he resisted the urge to scratch. With his back to the flame, he peered out into the moonlit dark, gaze shifting in a loose circuit.

Aside from the itching and his growling hunger, he felt better than he had in weeks. The relative solitude was refreshing. Removed from his constant companions, blanketed by nightfall, looking out over the broad expanse of both bay and sound with his feet set firmly upon the land . . . there was a peace here that had eluded him during all those weeks at sea. His veins simmered with excitement—the promise of a mysterious land, full of mysterious challenges. Unknown inhabitants, unknown dangers, unknown adventure. If there was a better reason for living, he hadn't discovered it.

Over the next three hours, disturbances were few. He watched a wandering crab crawl nearly to the edge of camp before changing its mind and burrowing away beneath a ground cover of dead leaves and twining, rootlike vines. He heard the ripples set off by a restive tarrock, down upon the muddy banks of the bay. He saw a preening swift take flight out over the sound, only to be brought down by a crested spearwing that had been circling overhead. If anything threatened his slumbering companions, it did so without his notice.

He would have been happy to extend his watch, but Ledron himself came to relieve him, with Ranson and Sallun spelling Percel and Hadrum from their respective posts.

Kylac greeted the Head with a nod. "Captain Ledron the sentry? I expected Merrec or Trajan."

"I wouldn't trust Merrec to watch my chamber pot. And I like our chances better if Trajan is rested and alert."

"This may be the first time I's seen Ranson more than five paces from Her Highness."

"And if you would take his place beside her, I'd thank you for it."

Kylac faced the Head in mild surprise. "Why, captain, I hope ya hasn't mistaken me for a eunuch."

"I'll *make* you one," Ledron promised, "if I catch so much as a gleam in your eye."

Kylac scoffed at the notion. With her scathing tongue and belligerent demeanor, Denariel wasn't what he might consider beautiful. Regardless, he'd seen the dulling effect a woman could have on a man, and—knowing too well the cost—could scarcely envision one worth blunting his edge for.

A residual pang nipped at his chest. Last of all would be one he'd agreed to protect.

"Were that a concern, I'd do the carving myself," he said, turning away.

"Kronus."

"Captain?"

"I know not how many of us will survive this. But I suspect your chances are better than most."

"With Trajan to point out a pitfall or two, sure."

"You *will* see her home, will you not? With or without us?"

"Barring suitable option? I reckon so."

Despite his predictable frown, Ledron's expression was almost plaintive.

"If I's the breath and strength, yes."

The Head nodded. Kylac waited for something more to be said, but it seemed Ledron had gathered what confirmation he'd been seeking. After another moment, Kylac turned back to camp, stepping soundlessly amid the sleeping forms to sit cross-legged beside Denariel. Even in slumber, the woman's expression was harsh—her brows raked, her dark face pinched. Whatever fueled her anger, she carried it with her in her dreams.

That, he could do nothing to help, Kylac told himself. But the rest . . . the rest would likely prove challenge enough.

THEY AROSE with the sun, battling thirst, stiffness, and angry stomachs to collect themselves and be on their way. However odd their defensive precautions might have seemed the night before, they must have worked, for none had suffered lethal bite or sting. Kylac received an ugly look from Ranson when the Blowfish returned from his watch to find Kylac so near Denariel, and a disgusted grimace from the princess herself upon waking, but no flame or ring of salt, he supposed, could defend against that.

As he'd promised the night before, Trajan led them westward along the river's swath, treading the line between its tarrock-infested waters and the deadwood forest that hugged its banks. The sun burned with a renewed strength, but the slight breezes blowing off the river worked to sap a measure of its intensity. Countering that, those same, slow-moving waters seemed to draw an increased number of blood gnats. At times, the swarms were thick enough to taste.

"They breed in the still pools at the river's edges," Trajan explained, when others had raised similar complaint. "If you wish, we can venture into the forest, but this is the swifter, safer path."

Kylac saw minimal difference. As often as not, the twisted growth they were trying to skirt encroached upon their trail, with thick mangroves that sprouted out into the river—or from the river onto land; it was difficult to discern which. Whenever this happened, they were forced to veer further aground, hacking into the jungle's unforgiving mesh, to find their way around.

Though they kept a sharp eye out for food, the trees edging this route were barren. According to Trajan, the salt and minerals carried by the river along this stretch served to counteract whatever nourishment the waters might have elsewise provided. What little fruit did sprout here was quickly picked clean by the birds and rodents whose habitat this was.

"What about fishing?" Kylac asked. "We's got a few hooks and lines."

"And should you snag anything large enough to eat," Brenth replied, "rest assured it'll have a tarrock attached to it when you try to drag it ashore."

"So mayhap we eat *it*, too."

"Not without beating a host of its brothers off the carcass." Trajan's grin was rueful. "Trust me, it's not worth the fight."

Kylac wasn't so sure. His hunger had grown quite acute. And with all of the other, more subtle contests being waged, it would be refreshing to engage in an open battle. Of his current companions, only Sallun and Trajan could be considered friends—and Ledron, mayhap, though the captain was too grudging to ever admit it. Merrec the Roach was still playing at friendship, but Kylac knew better.

As to the rest, well, Ahren had withdrawn to the extent where he engaged no one, save to seek permission now and again to stray from the main group entirely—ranging short distances to inspect various sights or sounds. Brenth, Obren, and Percel were dangerously indifferent. Were he to stumble, Kylac wasn't certain any of the three would bother to break his fall, let alone help him up again. That left Denariel, Ranson, and Hadrum, all of whom would just as soon see him as a corpse—the latter by his own hand, should the opportunity present itself.

"Has ya ever tasted tarrock?"

Trajan nodded. "Once. Took twelve of us to land the beast, and another twelve to stave off those that came after. Even then, we managed to keep only its tail while the rest was stolen."

"How was it?"

"Tough as they look. And even drier than you'd expect."

"Belly's softer," Merrec interjected.

Percel scoffed. "And *you* would know this."

"Not saying I tasted it myself."

"'Cause it'd be too great a lie, even for you."

"Silence," Ledron snapped from the rear.

Trajan halted. "Did you hear something?"

"No. Nor will I, over this chatter."

That curbed the developing discussion quickly enough. Attentions turned back to whatever they'd been prior. For Kylac, this entailed a watchful study of his surroundings, a constant awareness of the movements of his companions, and an ongoing attempt not to think about his thirst, his hunger, or the sun beating down upon him.

The last was mayhap the most difficult, given the waxing heat and the proximity of the river. As the morning drew on, Kylac found himself looking ever more longingly at the calmly flowing waters, imagining the relief he might find by dipping his body within.

Save that he might never get it out again.

Another hour passed, dragging yet another on its heels. The day was quickly becoming a reflection of the one before—a tiresome march marked only by monotony and irritation. Kylac kept his patience, refusing to let it all wear at him where it truly mattered. He'd been in worse situations ones that had been more laborious, more hazardous, more tedious. Though, now that he reflected on it, he wasn't certain any trial in his past had weighed as heavily with all three.

When Ahren went down, he did so abruptly. He'd been venturing roughly a dozen paces ahead, edging to their north flank, exploring a thicket of shriveled berries. Kylac, marching near Sallun just a few steps back of Trajan, had a clear view of the solitary archer through a thin screen of underbrush, dropping to one knee. At first, he thought Ahren had sensed something before them, and had crouched in caution. A moment later, however, the Cowl was on his back, arching in agony.

Kylac bolted forward, beating Trajan by a stride. By then, Ahren's hood had fallen free as a result of his spasms. His mutilated face was purple, veins bulging black. Wild eyes peered up at Kylac with horrid comprehension, while a gaping, tongueless mouth filled with foam.

"Keep back!" Trajan warned, stretching his arms wide to block those rushing forward at his heels. Several had drawn swords, for all the good it would do them. Kylac could see no enemy, nothing that a weapon might—

A scorpion the size of an open hand crawled out from under Ahren's convulsing form, drawing up between the Cowl's legs. Black, but tinged red about its head and stinger, it perched upon Ahren's belly, pincers extended. Trajan reached for his own sword at that point, but Kylac was swifter, whipping out a shortsword and driving its tip through the scorpion's shell, stopping a mere finger's breadth from piercing the Cowl's flesh.

He'd have driven on through, had he thought it would help speed Ahren's passing. The Cowl seemed unable to scream—as though his lungs had seized. But that didn't stop him from hacking with every spasm, spewing foam about his chest and the earth upon which he lay. Seeing this, the others withdrew now, giving the doomed man the space he needed to die.

Seconds later, the coughing ended and a rasping sigh eked its way through Ahren's clenched throat. Kylac waited for the body to relax, but the muscles remained rigid, locked in full strain.

"What is it?" Kylac asked, presenting the insect skewered upon his blade.

His companions—even Trajan—recoiled from the still-squirming crawler.

"Galamandrytch," said Ledron, the only one to stand his ground. The captain pushed forward to look down on Ahren. "Blood scorpion. The source, some say, of the groll's venom."

"One source, anyway," Sallun muttered.

Ledron knelt, closing the lids over Ahren's eyes, replacing the cowl to mask his disfigurement.

"They also say blood scorpions are nocturnal," said Hadrum, a tremor in his voice.

"They are," Trajan confirmed, his own voice deep and steady as he studied the crawler, which had finally curled up and gone still on the end of Kylac's shortsword. When their gazes met, Kylac saw in the Tower's eyes a suggestive look, which he deciphered at once.

"Unless something drove it from its nest."

Trajan nodded. The others began casting about as if the groll itself might emerge at any moment. Except for Denariel, Kylac noted. The princess just stared at the fallen Ahren, her expression unreadable.

Trajan turned to Ledron as the captain rose. "The galamandrytch is rare," the Tower said. "It may be that . . ."

Ledron waved him off, seeming more concerned with the pall that had settled over their troop. "We knew this would happen," he said. "And that it will likely happen again. All we can do is remain vigilant, for ourselves and one another."

Would that be enough? Though larger than most scorpions Kylac knew of, the galamandrytch was indeed small enough that, in this underbrush, even he might have failed to spy it before it was too late. But for the whims of chance, it could have been any of them lying there now in Ahren's stead.

"Form up," Ledron commanded.

"What do I do with this?" Kylac asked, brandishing the blood scorpion.

"Let it serve as Ahren's marker, since we have no time to bury him. It will help to keep the scavengers at bay."

"Pity the scavenger that tastes his poisoned flesh," muttered Brenth.

"And clean your weapon," Ledron added, ignoring the comment. "Do not let its blood touch your skin."

"His bow and daggers?" Kylac asked.

"Bring them."

The others gave him a wide berth, veering to either side as he knelt to carry out the orders. After stripping the slain Blackfist of his weapons, Kylac lay the dead crawler on Ahren's chest.

May ya find your brother swiftly, he offered, wiping his blade on the dead man's cloak.

Despite Ledron's stirring speech—or mayhap *because* of it—the pall over Ahren's death lingered. Silence ruled, due in part to somber reflection, but in greater measure, Kylac suspected, to a fearful caution.

The eyes of most of his companions swept the ground. Feet became itchy, lifting suddenly for every strange leaf, suspicious root, or rogue stone. And fate forbid a roach, centipede, or leafhopper should skitter, crawl, or bound across their path. Vigilance was well and proper, but this, Kylac feared, was edging closer to panic.

Spirits brightened somewhat when they came across a scattering of fruit trees. But that hopeful enthusiasm was swiftly stolen, as they found the bulk of it infested with purple worms whose disease-ridden forms, Trajan warned, made it inedible. Nor would he trust the fruit that appeared to be untouched. So they moved on, leaving it be.

Shortly after midday, they came across a swiftly rushing narrows in the river, marked by a series of short falls. A hundred paces farther on, the river widened again, its waters slowing to a pondlike stillness.

Trajan paused, looking out over the shallows.

"Here?" asked Ledron.

"We've gone a good deal farther than we likely needed to," the Tower replied. "To the west lie rapids, if our maps are true. We'll be hard-pressed to find a better crossing."

As he had before, down at the bay's edge, Ledron hurled a stone into the waters. All waited, watching for movement. When the ripples from his throw died, he tossed another.

"Seems clear," Kylac said.

"Water this fresh could make them listless," Trajan cautioned.

"Do we even know it's fresh?" Ranson asked.

"I'll have a taste," the Head determined.

"Let me, Captain," Brenth interjected.

Ledron seemed hesitant.

"I'll accompany him," Kylac offered, drawing both longsword and shortsword.

Finally, the captain nodded. "Do not lower those blades for any reason."

"And don't swallow," Trajan advised. "No matter the freshness, these lowland waters are not suitable for drinking."

Brenth nodded, and started down. Kylac found his shoulder. His defensive instincts were raw and tingling, but that might have been due to the others' anxiety.

Salts's bold approach became tentative as he neared the river's edge. Kylac slipped ahead to assure him it was safe—not at all certain that it was. He scanned the dark waters, seeing nothing of what lay beneath.

Brenth drew his own sword, and held it beside him as he knelt there on the muddy bank. With Kylac standing at his left, warding his downstream shoulder, he dipped his free hand into the waters and drew a cupped handful. He sniffed it, then swished it in his mouth before spitting it free.

"Fresh," he announced to those awaiting verdict.

An eddy drew Kylac's attention downstream. Betraying a slithering advance toward the ripples unleashed by Brenth's hand. "Left flank," he cautioned.

Salts shied back, even as his gaze intently marked the disturbance. When the whiskered mouth of a small, rose-lipped fish broke the water's surface, he relaxed, exhaling audibly. "Just a snickergill," he said, while the fish groped soundlessly before him. Taking a fresh look around, he added, "Not a tarrock in—"

"There!" Kylac called, as the familiar armored eyes emerged above the waterline, no more than two paces upstream.

The tarrock covered that distance in a mighty, serpent-swift lunge. Brenth lurched to his feet, but his right foot slipped in the mud beneath him, landing him on his buttocks. With Kylac on the guardian's left, and the tarrock striking from the right, there was no way to intercept it in time.

Brenth howled as the massive, gaping snout clamped down on his extended right leg. Kylac hurdled the downed Blackfist, longsword jabbing. He caught the tarrock in one eye, and a gout of fleshy juices burst forth as that eye popped. The tarrock bucked backward, but the strike hadn't loosened its clenched jaws. As the creature tore free, the lower half of Brenth's leg went with it.

The river itself seemed to heave, then, as three, four, five more tarrocks bore down on their position. Shouts from above urged Kylac to clear. Nonetheless, he remained at Brenth's side as the Blackfist clutched and stared at his torn stump. The first two tarrocks that lunged tasted only the edges of Kylac's blades—one he pierced through the tongue, and the other he slashed across the muscled cheek at the corner of its jaw.

The third slipped in to snag Brenth's remaining foot. With an upward yank, the creature flung Salts into the air like a hooked fish. The clustered tarrocks—including one of the wounded ones—clambered all over one another, jaws snapping skyward to claim a piece as the Blackfist fell. Kylac caught a final, frantic look from the veteran guardian before the family of giant river dragons tore him apart.

Kylac was dancing backward, then, pressed from either side by a pair of tarrocks who'd been shoved aside by their feasting brethren and now viewed Kylac as their likeliest food source. His swords hacked at them, but the incited beasts shrugged through the blows. A rancid breath assailed him with their ragged growls.

As he withdrew, he caught sight of the squat, powerful legs that propelled them after, up the muddy bank. Their armored bulk was incredible, and belied their formidable speed. The ones encountered before had shown no interest in leaving the water for the shore, but these displayed no hesitation in coming after.

His companions must have seen this, for suddenly Trajan was beside him, swinging a heavy axe. With him came Hadrum, brandishing that savage flail. Kylac was able then to stand his ground, and take the offensive. Within moments, the ravening tarrocks had suffered enough stabs and slashes to retreat, snarling in frustration as they slipped back into the now-churning river.

Kylac stood for a moment between the pair of Shadowguard as the tarrocks rolled back and forth in the shallow waters, thrashing and snorting, churning up sediment and foam.

Listless, indeed.

"Come," Trajan urged, swatting Kylac on the arm.

Hadrum was already backing away. Alongside Trajan, Kylac did the same. Another tarrock emerged from that bloodbath—the first, Kylac realized, upon seeing its wounded eye. Instead of coming on, however, it plopped down at the river's edge, mouth wide, its wet, green-black hide glistening in the sun.

Kylac stopped.

"It will come no further," Trajan said.

"And them?" Kylac asked, as two others crawled forth to flank the first.

"They'll lie there while they digest."

The commotion in the river began to settle, tarrocks turning away as those fighting for scraps realized there were no more to be found. Rather than stand there as further temptation, Kylac followed Trajan farther up the bank, to where their companions huddled at the edge of the tangled wood.

He kept one eye on the river, and the other on the trio of basking tarrocks.

14

"Farther than we needed to, eh?" Ranson asked bitterly, as Trajan and Kylac rejoined the others.

The Tower matched Blowfish's glare. "We're five leagues upriver—miles beyond where any tarrock has been known to lurk."

"He said the water was fresh," a slack-jawed Obren added, still staring at the spot where Brenth had been so viciously devoured.

Denariel chuckled. "You may as well forget the river. He's not going to let us cross."

He. The Ukinh?

"For the tarrocks to suffer these waters," Trajan agreed, "the groll must be herding them upstream."

Kylac's memory flashed back to their struggle to reach the north shore, when a tarrock had been forcibly snagged upon approaching Denariel. He'd wondered then if it could be the groll's work, or merely a rival tarrock. Even if it *were* the groll . . . "It can drive an entire pack o' them?"

"Tarrocks have an instinctive loathing of the beasts."

"If we can't cross, how are we to get home?" Obren asked.

But it wasn't merely about preventing them from crossing. Had there been any question concerning the galamandrytch, this seemed to answer it.

"It's using the land's perils to hunt us," Kylac said. "Picking us off, one by one."

"Because of you," Hadrum growled.

"How is it his fault?" asked Percel.

"Had the whelp done his job, the groll would never have been able to sabotage our ship, let alone stalk us now."

"That's unfair," Sallun piped. "You can't possibly expect—"

"Fair or not," Ledron snapped, "it changes nothing about our present situation. So we press on."

"Press on?" Ranson echoed. "How are we to endure without food and water?"

A sensible question. Mayhap the only one that mattered—particularly with regard to water. Even rationing as they had, supplemented the day before by the occasional fruit trove, they'd all but drained their skins already, both the one for Denariel and the three shared by the rest of them. Given the heat and their exertions, what remained to them would not suffice.

"Water must be our first priority," Ledron agreed. "How long to bypass the river's headwaters?"

"At least a day," Trajan replied. "To wrap east again, to where we might find safe drinking water, would cost us another."

"Two days." Ledron glanced at the sun, burning brilliantly overhead without a cloud in view. His frown deepened. "Too long."

"We could drink from Eshla's Tears," Denariel suggested.

After all they'd endured, Kylac wouldn't have guessed that anything could stun this group into silence. But this did.

"Eshla's Tears?" he asked.

The silence persisted. Ranson and Hadrum cast nervous glances at ghosts in the wood. Obren gulped and made a warding sign against his chest. Even the iron-skinned Percel stared sourly at his feet.

It was Sallun who finally answered. "A depthless rainwater basin atop the Cindercrag, rising high above the headwaters of the Navandi. At the heart of a region once lush and vibrant. The Breeders held it a holy place, until—"

"The rock is cursed," Hadrum spat. "The Cindercrag *and* that drink in its throat. The entire land around it . . . anything touched by its foul waters."

"The font that poisoned the land," Obren said, in ominous recitation, "and seeded the Harrows."

Kylac turned back to Sallun for explanation.

"Legend has it, during a terrible storm lasting more than a month, the pool overflowed, spilling into the river and the drowned earth below. Some say it was the Breeders' work, carrying a disease they spawned there throughout the land. Others say it was the Fair Mother seeking to cleanse herself of their taint. Either way, the region died, becoming what it is today."

"Fireside drivel," Percel said, though his typically brutish tone lacked conviction.

"The land may have gone to rot," Ledron conceded, "but the pool itself is fresh, by all accounts."

Merrec snorted. "The accounts of madmen."

"We must bypass the 'Crag in any case," Trajan reminded them, "if we are to bridge the river."

"And bypass it we should," Ranson chimed in. "The Redfist is right. All who partake of the Tears find madness."

Trajan stroked his beard, quickly grown unruly, then turned to his captain. "The mutant would anticipate this move," he warned. "It might be steering us along this very track."

That much seemed obvious. At the very least, the creature was forcing them farther west, deeper into Ukinhan territory. But it also knew their needs. If they couldn't cross the river, and if this Eshla's Tears was in fact the only available water source of any reasonable proximity, then it would know precisely where to spring its next ambush.

"Our best hope, in any case," Ledron determined. "To travel two full days without water—not knowing what obstacles might arise—is too much to risk." He gave Denariel a hard, discerning look. "If any know a viable alternative, speak it now."

The only response was a growling yawn from one of the mighty tarrocks sunning openmouthed at the river's edge.

"Then we march."

And so they did, the tension among them thickening with every step. How could it not? Having lost two members of their company in a matter of hours—and this *before* they'd entered the deadlier region they were venturing into now—gave even Kylac pause.

"These Ukinha," he asked quietly of Trajan, pacing the Tower at the front of their troop, "how many o' them are there?"

"Scores. Hundreds, maybe. Reclusive as they are, no one really knows."

"Any chance they could gather against us?" One of the creatures, he didn't fear. But he wasn't certain he could repel a pack of them.

"That's not their habit, no. When two meet, one usually dies—or so the signs with the carcass have always suggested."

"So we needn't worry about any but the one harrying us?"

"I can't say that. With the direction we're headed, it's quite possible we draw another's interest. Might be preferable that we did."

"Oh?"

"Always a chance they rip each other's throats out, rather than ours."

"But ya thinks it unlikely."

Trajan shook his head. "It's not the popular opinion, mind you, but to my eye's record, grolls are mostly evasive creatures. As adept as they are at killing, they seem not to have much of a taste for it."

Kylac took the Tower's meaning. In his experience, few predators of the wild were nearly the ravening, bloodthirsty beasts men made them out to be. Animals hunted. Animals killed. That didn't make it the primary purpose of their existence.

"This one seems willing enough to leave the bloodletting to others," Kylac observed.

"Why face us when it doesn't have to? Above all, the beasts are calculating, as you've seen. This one, it won't move until it knows the outcome will fall in its favor."

Kylac fell silent after that, and remained so for several hours thereafter, respecting the quiet concentration of his companions. Challenged by thirst, hunger, heat, exhaustion, and the images of their slaughtered comrades, they could ill afford any unnecessary distraction.

He busied himself instead as they did, in constant observation of the land through which they journeyed. By midafternoon, that land had undergone a marked change. The farther they delved inland, the more the forest seemed to trap the humidity—and the stronger effect that moisture seemed to have. The ground, so hard and unyielding, had grown soft and spongy, dotted with salt marshes and pools of brackish water. The growth, so dry and brittle, became thicker and more fleshy, sprouting molds, mushrooms, and other forms of diseased growth. In a cruel twist, berries and fruits were now plentiful, as well, but were all poisonous, inedible, suitable only for the stray lizards and cruel-eyed birds spotted in stray flashes of dark color and frantic movement.

The smell of rot became increasingly pungent as the wetland tangle thickened. Wilted leaves clung to drooping branches and to curtains of withering vines. Trees fallen along the edge of the river or bowed over its dark rush forced them inland, where stagnant swamps and lurking sinkholes caused them to reroute with mounting frequency. The crumbling remains of logs and stumps drew new breeds of ant, spider, beetle, and snake. And each step was ushered by those clinging clouds of blood gnats, which took turns nipping at their flesh while the rest buzzed about their ears, hovering like vultures, as if waiting for them to fall.

Dusk arrived earlier than it had the day before, due to the shadowing canopy that had sprouted overhead. With the shielding foliage interwoven thickly enough to block out the sky in all but small patches, the darkness gathered quickly, forcing Trajan to slow, then finally grind to a halt in a small clearing. Looking less than pleased, Ledron stepped forward, signaling for a defensive huddle.

"I had hoped to reach the Cindercrag tonight," the Head admitted.

"As had I," Trajan replied. "Would you have us continue in this murk?"

"How far is it?"

"Difficult to say." The Tower's gaze drifted southward. "What markers we have are all from the Navandi."

They'd lost the river some time ago. It had happened gradually, as various hazards and pitfalls in the unpredictable landscape forced them to divert time and again. For a while, the sound of its rushing waters had lent reassurance, but that too was gone now.

"How far would you guess?" Ledron pressed.

"On the winds? A league. Maybe two. But that might mean ten, on ground such as this."

"We're lost?" Ranson asked, a queer tremor in his voice.

"I didn't say that. Only that we lack the markers by which to measure our progress."

Blowfish laughed, his expression tinged with panic. "A matter of time, then, isn't it? We may never find the river again, let alone the Cindercrag or Eshla's Tears."

"Enough, Sergeant," Ledron snapped.

But Ranson wasn't finished. "A league, he says. Or maybe two. Yet we blindly trust him to lead us through this festering wasteland?"

"Sergeant!"

"He can't see us clear. No one can." Ranson's eyes were wide, and his voice shrill. It was obvious some madness gripped him, but as to its source, Kylac could only guess.

Ledron lowered his own voice to a growl. "Compose yourself, Sergeant, or I'll have you composed."

"What difference, another mile or camp here? We're groll fodder, either way."

"Obren, Hadrum," Ledron said crisply, nodding at each.

Obren was nearest. "Come, my friend—"

Ranson shoved free. As Locks and Fangs approached him from either flank, Blowfish retreated, backing into a hedge of mismatched brush. "Hadrum was right. We doomed ourselves the moment we took on this lordless rogue. We should have left him on the wharf back in Wingport, else used him as an anchor in the storm. Perhaps then he would have served some use!"

Amid his ranting, Ranson's heel kicked a tendril root that jerked away, withdrawing abruptly into shadow. Kylac thought it curious—a heartbeat before his senses screamed an alarm.

"At your back!"

The hedge collapsed, curling inward like a giant thistle bud. In its place appeared a mass of thorn-encrusted vines, which lashed out to clutch at Ranson's form. One slapped across his chest, while others looped around waist and limbs, quickly coiling. As Hadrum and Obren froze, Ranson's eyes bulged in startled fright.

Kylac drew his blades, but Trajan's hand upon his shoulder gave him pause.

"Stand clear!" the Tower shouted.

Ranson shrieked as the whipping vines continued to slither and thread around him, thorns digging for purchase. The harder he fought to wrest free, the tighter they gripped—which in turn made him even more frantic. When a snaking vine grabbed his throat and began to squeeze, drawing blood with its barbed thorns, Obren raised his sword with a primal yell.

"No!" Trajan shouted.

His warning couldn't arrest Obren's swing. Locks's blade hacked into the vine. Though he failed to sever the fleshy stalk, a white pulp sprayed from within, much of which splattered upon Obren's face.

With his next breath, Locks dropped his weapon and wailed in agony, clawing at the flesh melting from his cheeks. Hadrum scrambled back at that point, risking no further contact. It was good that he did, for he only narrowly hopped the whipping reach of a vine that seized Obren by the ankle and yanked him to the earth.

Kylac stood in place among the others, mesmerized by the horrific display. Obren bucked and rolled as he was dragged into that writhing nest, squealing uncontrollably while the plant's acids devoured his flesh and bored holes in the bone beneath. Ranson's own muffled shrieks had ceased. His face was purple, his eyes still wide. The vines had entangled him so completely that more of him was covered now than exposed. Yet still they squeezed and tugged, pulling his limbs askew, slowly crushing.

A squirming tendril twisted his right forefinger until it broke. Another snapped the bone in his forearm. His left leg was wrenched from the hip with a loud pop. Veins in his cheeks and forehead bulged with unimaginable strain. Yet all Ranson could do was stare in mute agony.

When a probing vine forced its way down Obren's throat, his screams, too, were muffled, and then muted. Though his body still thrashed in denial, there was no escaping the horrid truth.

At that, Denariel turned away. "Shall we set camp then, Captain, and watch their throes all night?"

Ledron looked at Trajan, who shook his head. "To the next clearing, then."

They made no attempt to retrieve Obren's sword or anything else before departing the area. Kylac kept his own blades drawn and ready. Like the others, he scanned the ground carefully for twitching roots, and trusted none of the hedges he brushed up against. Progress came at a crawl, but none seemed to care.

After a time, hearts and nerves quickened by the ordeal settled into a more natural rhythm. But the overall heaviness remained, fueled by a mounting sense of despair. Two more dead, in about as much time as it had taken them to don their boots that morning. The groll, the galamandrytch, the tarrocks, their increasingly unbearable thirst . . . and now the jungle itself out to consume them. Though some might deny it, Kylac imagined easily enough the prevailing question echoing through each man's mind: What chance did they have?

Their sluggish trek brought them eventually to the edge of a bog. Trajan stepped in it before he saw it, so still and hidden were its stagnant waters amid the knee-high thrushes at its edge. A brief inspection found it to stretch in both directions, filling the air with its brackish stench.

"Far enough," Ledron decided.

They thrashed out a patch of ground to ensure it was safe, and huddled closer than any of them felt toward one another. Starting out, there had been a camaraderie, a belief that, if they banded closely enough, they might see themselves through this. With death claiming them at such a rapid pace, however, it seemed almost a competition now as to which—if any of them—would survive.

"That demon bush," said Ledron, shattering the uncomfortable silence. "What was it?"

Trajan gave him a brooding look. "Stricthyus krahl, as Rashad the Mad Wanderer named it. Great banethistle. Before tonight, I'd have told you it didn't really exist."

"They would have felt nothing," the Head offered consolingly, "once the breath left their lungs."

"By Rashad's observations, the thistle's toxins work to keep the victim's brain alive. Enough to sense pain, anyway."

Merrec snorted and shook his head. Ledron frowned.

"Apologies, Captain," Trajan added, voice hardened with accusation. "But a man lost vigilance today, and three paid the price. I'll not baste the truth in honey and risk it happening again."

"No," Ledron agreed. "But Ranson did more than lose vigilance. He panicked, where we will not."

And there it was. As discouraging and inexplicable as a plant that preyed on men was the madness that had claimed Ranson just before his death. Kylac understood, then, the Head's purpose in forcing this conversation. As commander, he recognized the lingering effect that the banethistle episode would have if the topic weren't dealt with. Raw and painful as it was, he meant to scrub that wound, in hopes of allowing it to heal.

"It is indeed a hostile environment," Kylac admitted, seeking only to encourage further talk. "I's not seen its like."

"Nor will you," Sallun said glumly. "The sickness that prevails here was cultivated by the ancient Breeders, as a proving ground for their foul creations."

"Maybe," Percel agreed. "Or maybe the land was already in this state, and thus chosen by the Breeders for its lethal aspects."

"Either way, the grolls adapted," Ledron said. "Thrived, even. And if a mutant can do it, so can we."

Stirring declaration, or hollow boast? Kylac marked the reactions of his companions to decide which. Only Percel and Hadrum seemed to accept the former. Trajan, Sallun, Merrec, and Denariel were not so easily swayed.

"We're stronger than anything in this jungle," Kylac agreed, "until the jungle proves elsewise."

"Right he is," said Percel. When he clapped Hadrum on the back, Fangs grunted reluctantly. Denariel rolled her eyes, while Merrec offered a sour smirk. Trajan seemed to consider before giving a shrug.

"Makes sense enough to me," the Tower said.

Sallun's glum expression took on a plaintive cast, so Kylac gave him a quick, confident nod.

Denariel snickered. "We lost four lives today. At that pace, half of us have but one more dawn to greet. The remainder will be gone by the after-morrow's sunset. But do go on," she said, lying back with hands locked beneath her head. "Let us hear more of how strong you are."

Ledron's grimace was wasted on the princess, as she didn't bother to look for his reaction. "Two men per watch," he determined, "three-hour shifts. That includes you tonight, Merrec, with Kronus to catch what your eyes miss. Sallun and I will relieve; Percel and Hadrum will follow. Trajan, you and Her Highness sleep."

"If you're done with your nattering, Captain," Denariel agreed, eyes closed already against her ring of warders and the surrounding dark.

15

Few found any sleep. Those who did discovered it only in fitful snatches ruled by nightmare. Most tossed restlessly, casting about every time an insect chirped, a bird shrieked, or a toad croaked. The air was warm and windless, heavy with humidity and the stink of their stagnant surroundings. Stray breezes brought temporary relief, but also rustled leaves, shook branches, or set vines to flapping in the brush. With fear magnifying every minor disturbance, and hunger and thirst waging war on their bodies, the night brought no respite from their travails.

As the hours passed, even Kylac grew edgy. Resistant he was to others' dread paranoia, but not immune. Surrounded by their restive spirits, he found himself increasingly anxious for the dawn.

When it finally arrived, he stood ready as the others hauled stiff limbs and aching joints from the moist earth to stretch and deplete themselves of what little water their bodies still held. Eyes were red and deeply shadowed, while cracked lips and raspy voices betrayed the extent to which they were parched. They would find water today, Kylac told himself, else some of them would not see the morrow.

The morning light was dim, shrouded in mist and cloud cover—lending hope that rainfall might serve answer to their most glaring need. But a false promise it proved to be. An hour into their plodding trek, the clouds dispersed and the brume burned away. Steam wafted from the wet ground and the various waters pooled atop it, carrying off with their foolish optimism.

As it had the previous day, the unpredictable landscape forced them along a circuitous route over, around, or through the streams, ponds, and bogs that carved its surface. It seemed that each mile gained forced them to tread three. Minutes gathered and passed, dragging the hours on their heels. Observing his companions, Kylac saw the fatigue and dizziness resulting from starvation and lack of sleep weighing heavier with each step. And none but mayhap Trajan knew if any reasonable progress was actually being made. They were heading generally westward, yes. But without knowing the location of their destination, it was impossible to discern how close they might be.

Of larger wildlife, they saw no sign—until they stumbled across the carcass of what looked something like a giant cat, lying half submerged with ruptured belly at the edge of a stagnant pool, the hide stripped from its body.

"Looks fresh," said Hadrum. He sniffed hopefully. "No smell of rot."

A bristling creature, despite its lack of fur. A broken tusk protruded from the curled lip at the corner of its mouth, with a wall of sharper teeth angling toward the tip of its elongated snout. Three long, curving claws extended from each of its four paws, while smaller, barbed spines clung in spiraling rows down the length of its rodent-like tail.

"Its flesh is poisoned," Kylac said.

Fangs snorted. "You don't even know what it is."

"He's right, though," said Trajan. "There's not a fly on it. Were it edible, every insect and scavenger within a mile would be converging."

So they let the beast be, and moved on. A strangletail, the Tower named it. They lived in the trees, using those tails as a noose to ensnare passing prey. What had killed it, and why its skin had been taken, were questions Trajan couldn't answer. Ultimately, a useless discovery, except to remind them that, despite appearances, they weren't alone in this jungle. It was solely by grace that whatever creatures prowled the vicinity were thus far proving wary of them.

The Tower wasn't merely seeking to frighten them. Kylac could sense some of the cruel things out there, beyond the reaches of sight, smell, or sound, that tracked their arduous passage. *As alien we must seem to them,* he supposed, *as they to us.* But he also understood the natural order well enough to know that the caginess of these native denizens would keep them at bay only so long.

Much the same held true of the less animate plant life. That they hadn't yet suffered further injury didn't mean those threats had somehow been eluded. They waded past natural snares with almost every step, evading tripping roots, sucking mud seeps, venomous flowers, clawing thorns, pricking darts, scratching leaves, stinging nettles, and more in abundance. Trajan had done well in educating them on what to avoid, and what clues to search for. Traveling in a tight cluster, with all on their utmost guard, they'd thus far this day kept themselves safe—but only thus far.

"We're getting close," the Tower announced, as midday overtook them and the Dove's Hour drew near. He pointed to a gnarled tree with smooth, paper-thin bark. "Hiltwood. And there, at its base, a skirt of thrushleaf. That means weaker salts in the groundwater. The swamp will soon lose grip."

It did so swiftly over the next mile, the earth rising like the humped back of a breaching whale. Frequent pools became stray puddles, while streams dried to a trickle. The ground turned stony, taking on an ashen cast. Jungle growth grew scant. Farther on, the rock became pitted and craggy, with sharp ridges and deep grooves. The ashen gray became peppered with black. It seemed to Kylac like walking across the charred remains of a fire—save for the unforgiving hardness of the rock, which dug and scratched at his boots rather than crumbling beneath them.

A mile after that, the remaining jungle split off to either side, at the base of a mound of rock that jutted skyward four hundred heads or more. Its skin was black and gray like the earth over which it loomed, its jagged slopes raked through by narrow clefts and folded creases. Those slopes didn't climb in a smooth taper, but in a chopped array of wedged hollows and protruding shelves—like the stump of a mammoth tree hacked at by some drunken woodsman.

"Cindercrag," Trajan announced.

An unimaginative name, Kylac decided, peering up at its rugged shoulders and toothy spires. A mournful whistle filled the air, formed of breezes scraping over and through the Cindercrag's scarred hide. He could hear the river again, as well, though its rush lay somewhere on the far side, springing from a throaty hollow at the Crag's broken base. He looked for some evidence of Eshla's Tears—a reflective gleam dancing near the peak, a sliver falls, a ribbon scar that might mark the path of its occasional spillover. If present, then these clues, too, lay somewhere beyond his view.

"How are we doing this?" asked Merrec. When the others turned to him, he seemed to squirm. "It makes little sense for all to make the climb."

"Do you count heights among your many fears, then?" Percel snickered.

"I was thinking of Nara."

"Her Highness," Ledron corrected. "But the Redfist is right. I'll not risk her life on this ascent."

Kylac saw no point in delaying the inevitable. "If'n it's a nimble climber needed, I'm your man."

"Not alone, you're not." The Head looked over the remainder of their troop. It didn't take long. "Percel and Hadrum go with you."

Leaving just Ledron and Trajan to ward Denariel. On that task, Sallun and Merrec would count for little—Sallun for his lack of skill with a blade, and the Roach for his lack of will.

"Just the three of us with Na— Her Highness?" Merrec balked, discounting only Sallun. "What if the mutant should strike?"

Percel chuckled. "There goes his fear of heights."

"I'm sure I can manage the skins myself," Kylac offered.

"But may need assistance in the climb," Ledron pressed. "And one who can bear word should something happen to you."

Unlikely, but difficult counts to argue. "As ya sees it, Captain. Though keeping Her Highness out in the open in my absence would indeed be ill advised."

"We could claim one of these lower ledges," said Trajan. "Would put the 'Crag at our backs and give us a better view of the jungle."

As was his habit, Ledron gritted his teeth. "Then to it."

They marched a quarter circuit around the base of the Cindercrag before sighting a low, mostly flat shelf that Trajan and Kylac deemed suitable for those who would remain behind. With a sheer cliff spine above and below, open flanks, and only minimal scrub, the jutting crag afforded clear views that would provide ample warning should the groll attempt to reach them. A thirty-head climb, she appeared— scarcely a leap. But the switchback path they had to follow to reach it cost them almost an hour. By the time they'd settled into position atop the ledge, Kylac wondered if he might have made it to the summit and back in the same time.

With midafternoon upon them, Kylac, Percel, and Hadrum gathered up the half dozen empty waterskins in their possession, slung them over their shoulders, and turned to receive their captain's farewell.

"Move swiftly," Ledron bade them, his hoarse voice and cracked lips providing a further sense of urgency.

And you stay safe, as well, Kylac thought, but surrendered the remark to pity. They'd effectively gone a full day now without drink of any kind. Bearable, mayhap, under friendlier conditions. Not so under theirs. "Back before dusk," he replied instead.

He turned to look at "Fishhook" Percel, who flashed that reckless, lopsided grimace, and at "Fangs" Hadrum, who regarded him with his usual expression of unbridled contempt. *Here we go.*

He assumed the lead from there, backtracking from the defensive ridge along the same trail that had brought them to it—a ribbon of shelf barely a foot wide in some patches, which snaked across the Cindercrag's eastern bluff. Percel followed first, with Hadrum taking the rear. Alone, Kylac could have made much better time. But that decision had already been made, so he tread slowly, allowing his companions to safely keep pace.

Sixty strides brought them to a cleft in the stone that angled upward toward another, higher shelf. Kylac turned into it, and started to climb.

"Where are you . . . ?" Hadrum griped. "You don't intend to scale that?"

The ascent was steep, and littered with loose stones. But there were pits in the stone face in which to set their feet, and tufts of deep-rooted growth in sporadic patches, which they could use as handholds. Treacherous as it looked, they weren't apt to find better.

"What's wrong?" Percel asked. "Were you hoping a rock goblin might fly us to the summit?"

"It's barely more than a gash."

"Or perhaps you'd have the boy carve a nice spiral stair, that those in gowns and speared heels might follow."

"Drink piss."

"I just might, if I had any."

Kylac, silent throughout the exchange, turned back to the rock to conceal a smirk. "We passed other clefts on the way up, but none, I daresay, more scalable than this."

"What good will it do the princess should we break our necks?"

Kylac and Percel shared a glance.

"If you've Merrec's skin," Percel mused, "we may as well go back and swap you for the traitorous Redfist."

Fangs glared in defeat. "A broken neck would be a mercy to standing here any longer with you two." He shouldered past Percel to stand waiting on Kylac. "Well, get on it, then."

Kylac scrambled up to show them how easy it was, then watched the pair follow as best they could—huffing and grunting, but with only a minor slip or two. From there, they inched along the stone lip higher up the bluff until reaching a second cleft, through which they scrabbled as before.

The ledge that trailed from there led only to an apparent dead end, folding back against the cliff to leave them stranded against the flat bluff face beneath a jutting overhang.

Hadrum spat from the height. "Well done."

"Perhaps you should lead then, eh?" Percel suggested in Kylac's defense.

Kylac ignore them both, his gaze scratching across their surroundings in search of a way to proceed. "Wait here," he said, then leapt from the lip . . .

Hadrum gasped, flattening against the stone. Percel, too, stiffened in surprise.

. . . only to catch a pair of jagged knobs farther out along the rock face, thereby arresting his fall.

"You're mad!" Fangs called after him, though his anger couldn't hide the tinge of awe in his voice. "We're not spiders, you know."

Kylac said nothing, but gathered his feet beneath him and, once assured of his footing, sprang higher, to grasp another small protrusion farther up.

"Cork that gravy-lapping hole of yours," Percel bade Hadrum.

"Do you mean to follow him out there?" Fangs asked incredulously.

"I doubt that's what he has in mind."

"Then what's he doing?"

"Stop sniveling for a moment, and I imagine we'll find out."

By then, Kylac had climbed several heads above them, clinging where he could to the meager cracks, gaps, and protuberances the bluff had to offer. Once in line with the pinning overhang, he worked his way toward it, side-scaling along the Cindercrag's pocked face.

Upon reaching the top of the overhang, he shrugged off a length of rope looped over his shoulder, knotted one end around an anchoring rock, and tossed the free length down to his waiting companions, steadying the line over his back.

"Ya can climbs a rope, can't ya?"

Goaded by the taunt, Hadrum was quick to prove that he could. Percel followed. When both had joined him, Kylac retrieved the rope and coiled it again around his shoulder.

"There has to be an easier path to the top," Fangs grumbled. "Or the Breeders would never have reached it."

"And given a day or two, I'm sure we'd find it," Kylac agreed. "But why wind ourselves in endless circles when what we really wants is to go up?"

They proceeded in this fashion for another hour, navigating an array of ledges, gashes, and sheer slopes to claw their way slowly toward the summit. On occasion, they would delve into a defile that revealed pathways snaking inward toward the rock's heart, but these always narrowed or closed, forcing them to climb again and seeming to support Kylac's claim that whatever trail might lead to the summit wasn't one they had time to explore.

"At least, in this direction, we can see what we're reaching for," Percel observed, as they negotiated another tricky ascent. "Crawling back down . . . that will be the real fun."

Hadrum, beside him, made the mistake of looking below. Gripped by dizziness, he lost his footing on one side, and found himself dangling, scrabbling desperately for purchase.

"Percel!" Kylac shouted from above.

Fishhook was already reaching out to snag his partner. Were it not for his swift reflexes and strong hands, Hadrum would have plummeted. As it was, Fangs thrashed there for a moment like a landed fish, nearly pulling them both from the rock's merciless face.

"Whoa!" Percel growled. "Hold steady, now."

Finally, Hadrum calmed, finding his holds and clinging to them with pale knuckles and ashen cheeks.

Kylac called down. "Everyone all right?"

"Stash it, Kronus," Fangs snapped in reply, though his face was buried against the rock, and the tremor in his voice betrayed the frenetic hammering of his heart.

"We're more'n halfway to the top. If'n either o' ya lads wish to remain here . . ."

"Stash it, I say." This time, he managed to look up. "The 'Crag, I can handle. It's the constant distractions I can't stomach."

Kylac withheld comment as Hadrum flashed a glare at Percel and, without a word of thanks, pulled himself on.

"Perhaps next time I let you fall, then, eh?" Fishhook asked. "Your tongue's been wagging since we set forth. I make one small comment, and you yip like a runt fighting for a teat."

"Call me runt again, and you'll have nipped at your last."

With the wind that whistled through the gaps in his teeth, it was difficult to take any of Fangs's threats seriously. Countering that, Kylac doubted the royal guardian's pride could suffer many more beatings, and so preferred not to test it. Should he allow the two men to kill each other, he wasn't certain Ledron would believe he didn't have a hand in it—especially where Hadrum was concerned.

"There's another trail up here," he said, hoping to soothe their frustrations. "Shall I scout ahead while the pair o' ya settle this?"

Hadrum only muttered to himself. Percel shook his head, and said, "On your heels."

Whether subdued by the near-fatal episode, made hopeful by the trail Kylac had found, or set to stewing in their own self-righteous aggression, both Blackfists fell silent for a time. Kylac left them to it, grateful for the reprieve.

The promising pathway wound nearly a quarter turn around the Cindercrag's outer wall, only to end in a gaping crevasse. It took Kylac a running leap to reach the far side, where he used a pair of ropes to fashion a bridge spanning the gap. The others then crossed, hand over hand. Gusting breezes added to the difficulty, and for a time, threats were forgotten, replaced by the camaraderie forged of common peril.

The truce didn't last long. Though the winding path resumed, the winds continued to strengthen, by turns pushing and pulling as if seeking to yank them from the narrow ledge. It wasn't long before Hadrum resumed his grumbling, with Percel then feeling the need to mock him for a wet-nosed Whitefist.

Kylac found himself contemplating leaving both behind, consequences or no.

But he remained patient, respecting Ledron's wishes. Having suffered them this long, he could suffer them a while longer.

By the Eagle's Hour, with the day bending toward dusk, they finally gained a split in the slope that revealed a mostly unobstructed view of the summit, not two hundred paces distant along a broken, twisting trail. Though deeply shadowed here at its mouth by high walls of flanking stone, the path flattened out some forty paces in, offering easy passage—at least compared to the stretches that lay behind or below them.

"At last," Hadrum wheezed through cracked lips, pulling himself up to where Kylac crouched at the mouth of the breach.

"Wait," said Kylac, holding the other back with an outstretched arm.

"For what? The gap to crumble? We won't find a clearer opening."

"Not so clear," Kylac replied, pointing to a set of dark holes in the left wall of the defile, a mere six paces in. "There, where the shadows writhe."

"What are you flapping about? What shad—" His question was cleaved by a startled breath.

"Galamandrytch," Kylac said.

The holes were swarming with them. Blood scorpions, like the one that had killed Ahren. How deep those holes ran, or how many scorpions they sheltered, was impossible to discern at this distance. But with the high walls of the defile blocking most of the waning afternoon light, dozens of the more restless creatures had ventured from their stone dens to explore the trail floor, eager for the night's hunt to begin.

Percel frowned as he joined them. "Well," he said, wiping the sweat from his brow, "how's that for vomit in your stew?"

"Try a torch," said Hadrum. "The fire should drive them off."

A guess and nothing more, Kylac determined, upon searching Fangs's expression. "Should it?"

The Blackfist rummaged through a shoulder sack to produce an unlit brand. Extending it to Kylac, he left no doubt as to who was expected to test his theory.

Kylac took the torch. "Light it."

Hadrum did so, though it took longer than it should have, with his gaze flicking nervously between his work and the straying blood scorpions. With flame at last in hand, Kylac started down the defile.

He tread carefully, eyes marking any movement. The scorpions took no notice of his approach. He realized then that many of them were dead—empty husks littering the rocky ground. When he bent to examine one, he saw that its shell had been cracked in half, and its meaty contents scraped clean.

He checked another, and another. All had been ripped open. Amid the broken pieces, he found the ruined fragments of their bulbous pincers. Only the narrow legs had been left intact, to wither alongside the main body.

As he peered forward, he saw that the path ahead—and in particular the ground around the galamandrytch holes—was littered with their remains.

"What now?" Hadrum asked.

"What preys on galamandrytch?"

"Nothing," Percel replied.

But something had gorged on these creatures. And, judging by the varying discoloration of the sun-bleached husks, it hadn't been a onetime feast.

"Why?" Hadrum asked.

Kylac's only response was to rise and press toward the nest. He held his torch as a shield, careful to keep it downwind so that its black smoke didn't sting his eyes or cloud his view. The few scorpions at his feet seemed to shy at its aura, withdrawing back into shadow. Mayhap Fangs was right.

He placed the flame near the first hole, thinking to chase the scorpions deeper into their rocky hollow.

Instead, the den came to life, with galamandrytch scurrying frantically in every direction. Whether from the heat, the light, or both, some took to spasming uncontrollably, stingers flashing and stabbing at anything within reach. Others soon mimicked their reaction. Kylac withdrew the torch, but the damage had been done. The scorpions were pouring out like a swarm of angry hornets whose nest had been overturned, seeking retribution at any cost and from any quarter.

Kylac found himself backing away to avoid contact. One step, two, three. And still they came, by the hundreds if not thousands, flopping and thrashing as if caught in the throes of seizure.

"I suggest we go around," Kylac advised his startled companions.

"Agreed," said Percel, who gave Hadrum a nudge.

"What if there are other nests like this?" Hadrum groused, nudging Percel right back. Beneath his anger, there was an air of despair. "We've no more than an hour before nightfall."

Which meant, no matter how quickly they reached the pool and filled their skins, they would be finding their way down in the dark, amid a mass of prowling scorpions and whatever else made its home on this rock. Either that, or they descended now, to suffer through another parched night and climb again at dawn.

Kylac ground the head of his torch into the earth. The galamandrytch continued to convulse on the floor of the defile, but at least their frenetic advance seemed to stall.

"We's come too far to retreat, I'd say. But any man feels different is welcome to head back now."

Percel considered, then shrugged. "I'm not going down empty-handed. If I'm to be stung, better today than tomorrow, eh?"

Hadrum glared glumly down the length of the breach, alternately flexing and stretching his gloved fingers—blistered and raw, no doubt, from clutching at the Cindercrag's sharp skin. "To the depths with you both," he muttered, but looked up when turning back toward the evening sun.

16

BY THE FICKLE WINDS of luck, it didn't take them long to find a second breach granting passage to the Cindercrag's interior. Clawing westward around the rock's rugged shell for a quarter-mark, they came upon a broad shelf not far above their heads that lay flat between a pair of jutting stone spires—like a tongue lolling between a pair of tusks. Though crude and rough-hewn, it was immediately evident that this was no natural fissure, but a formation shaped—at least in part—by intelligent hands.

"Well, there," Kylac said as he angled toward it, "this bears promise."

Hadrum, however, stopped short on the barest thread of a ledge—so abruptly that a distracted Percel, bearing down alongside at an overzealous pace, grasped at a hold Fangs hadn't yet relinquished, causing both to lose grip and scrabble precariously for a moment.

"Mother's mercy!" Hadrum swore, as he clung to the stone.

"Suddenly you're a wart on my uncle's elbow? Move on."

Hadrum refrained, instead tossing a nod toward the overhang where Kylac now perched.

"What?" Percel asked.

"Gorrethrehn," Hadrum said.

"Looks clear," Kylac assured him. And it did. The shelf opened onto a wide swath that cut inward over the craggy terrain. Walls and spurs

sprouted upon its flanks, creating folds in the trail, but Kylac sensed
nothing lurking there. It was more than twenty paces in before the
trail finally wrapped from view. A dead end there, mayhap. But, for
all they knew, it opened wide onto a secret meadow lush with fruits
and flowers fed by flowing crystalline streams.

Possibility was the lure of the unknown.

"It's not what you see," Fangs replied. "It's what you don't. Only
the Mother knows what fell rituals took place here."

"Is it their ghosts ya fear, haunting this rock?" He'd known from
the beginning what they were up against. "A mite late now, methinks."

"My gloves are all but torn through. I'd rather not rake my bloody
hands across their poisoned ground."

"All bound to be 'poisoned' from here on in," Kylac said. "But
hang there, if'n ya likes."

"Move," Percel urged, "or step aside." A purposeful glance off the
edge of the lip they clung to left no doubt as to his meaning.

Hadrum glared at his companion, then took a deep breath and
forced himself on. Kylac found it odd that one so proud as Fangs
would admit to being cowed by such irrational fears. But he spared
the spoken thought as the gap-toothed Blackfist climbed toward
him with obvious reluctance—as if waiting for the ancient wraiths
he feared, be they foul creations or the Breeders themselves, to come
bursting out of the sullied ground.

With Percel nudging impatiently at his heels, Hadrum finally
scaled the last stretch of broken slope. Kylac extended a helping hand
as Fangs reached the edge of the tonguelike precipice, only to draw
a sour look for the effort.

"You're blocking the path," Fangs griped, before rolling his eyes
and shuffling to one side.

Kylac shrugged and offered the same hand to Percel, who accepted
it without remark. As Kylac reeled the big Fishhook in, Hadrum
hoisted himself up under his own sagging strength.

"It should feel good to walks for a spell," Kylac offered encouragingly, when he saw Fangs stretching his weary shoulders. "Give
your arms a rest."

"It's your mouth needs rest," Hadrum growled, lisping through the gaps in his teeth. He sniffed. "What's that scent?"

Kylac wasn't certain, though he too had smelled it—faint, yet cloying, like rotting flowers or overripe fruit.

Percel snorted. "Don't smell a thing. Let's just find this pool, shall we?"

Kylac started down the trail, hands itching for the hilts of his swords. He might have drawn them, but didn't want to alarm his companions. The only sounds—aside from the crunching footfalls of the Shadowguard behind him—were those of the breezes that scratched along the rocks or whistled through their cracks. He saw only tiny mites, flitting about the stone, feeding off the lichen attempting to grow there. There was the smell, but that by itself suggested no danger with which he was familiar. Here, it could as easily be a natural fragrance as an unnatural one. And yet, that internal sense—the one he dared not ignore—urged caution.

A steady pace brought them to the bend in the trail in a matter of moments. There, Kylac found neither a dead end, nor the meadow he'd imagined, but a three-way fork with rising walls high enough to obscure his view of where the individual paths might lead.

"Which one?" Percel asked. He knew better than to suggest splitting up. They'd decided long before, near the base of the 'Crag, that exploring separate paths only meant, in all likelihood, getting lost in separate areas. If they had to wander, better to do so as a group.

"Wait here," said Kylac, before climbing the nearest rise. He did so by turns scaling where the gaps were wide, and spanning opposing walls where the gaps narrowed. The first crest to fall beneath his feet revealed little, but he was able to follow its ridged back higher, to an overlook that offered a better view of the land ahead.

They'd come at last to the base of the rock's peak, which thrust like a broken horn into a sky grown ruddy with the first hint of sunset. Here upon the peak's threshold, however, lay a labyrinth, the fork beneath him splintering into a webwork of trails that snaked onward like veins through the Cindercrag's heart. It brought to mind a field of once-muddy earth cracked by the sun, or the splayed pieces of brittle steel smashed between hammer and anvil. Whether suddenly or over ages of time, these footstool slopes had shattered in place, with endless corridors and passageways—some true, some false—now streaming between them.

"What do you see?" Percel called from below, his voice echoing through the narrow canyons until their sharp edges had shredded his words completely.

"Quiet, oaf!" Hadrum hissed in wary response.

"I see it," Kylac said then. To his right—north. Near the peak, but closer to the 'Crag's edge than its center. A jutting spur, and below that, the telltale glint of reflected sunlight. "Eshla's Tears."

"How far?" Percel asked.

"Can we reach it?" asked Hadrum.

One way or another, thought Kylac, seeking to discern the most direct route. Even from this elevated vantage, he found it difficult. Many of the widest-running fissures, open from above, revealed dead-end trails truncated by converging walls of stone. Meanwhile, most of the narrower passageways were roofed almost completely by overhanging ledges, leaving him to guess as to how straight or far they ran. Several tracks emptied out over the edges of bluffs, like the one that had brought them here, while others wound inward to circle upon one another like a nest of hungry snakes.

After observing a general path and committing it to memory as best he could, Kylac scampered back down to rejoin his waiting companions.

"This way," he said, starting down the center fork.

The stony corridor closed quickly, high walls leaning inward to eclipse the day's weary light. Soon, only a crack remained overhead, leaving them bathed in cool, murky shadow. The floor tightened to no more than an angled groove, forcing them to make their way along the sloped base of the adjoining walls. Kylac felt the familiar pressure that always weighed upon his chest when so confined. His lungs felt constricted, and his palms ached. Had his body any moisture to spare, he would have been sweating.

But the fissure opened again as he'd hoped it would, into a wider defile that bent northward. The opening ran a straight course for roughly twenty paces, then jagged left, arced right, and finally folded back in the opposite direction. Two cuts lay ahead, however, in that

elbow bend. Recalling his mental portrait of the terrain from overhead, Kylac chose the left gap and plunged down its craggy throat.

They proceeded in this fashion for half an hour, navigating the
splintered network of tight fissures and rain-widened gullies, guided
by the overhead image branded upon Kylac's memory, and by his
instincts. Twice, they encountered dead ends that forced them to
double back and seek another path. For the most part, however, he
kept them on track, veering doggedly toward the pool's location as
spotted from above.

"Does my nose deceive, or is that stench growing worse?" Hadrum
asked.

His nose was sound. The smell that had greeted them back at the
entrance to this maze had waxed stronger the deeper they'd delved,
unstirred by the stronger breezes found without. Pace by pace, it
had grown more rank, like a festering wound. Though Kylac wasn't
inclined to admit it, he'd more than once used it as a marker when the
way forward was uncertain. Having seen nothing upon this rock to
account for the odor—no profusion of exotic growth or animals—he'd
come to believe it the musk of a larger predator that had settled here.
And few creatures, large or small, could go long without water. If
whatever had eaten those blood scorpions lived upon this rock, Kylac
suspected its den, if it had one, would be found nearer Eshla's Tears.

"Mights be the rock itself," Kylac suggested. "The minerals trapped
within."

"Or your body's stink," Percel added, "since you can't seem to
escape it."

"Or yours," Hadrum snapped. "A man's less likely to be offended
by his own, and you're the only one can't smell it."

Percel shrugged. "I'll be sure to sweeten up just as soon as you
fetch me some rosewater and pumice."

The evening light had taken on a molten cast. Kylac found it
bleeding down through an elevated cut as they followed a bend in
one of the larger, more winding defiles. He slowed and then stopped
for a closer look.

"Thinking we can reach that?" Percel asked.

"Could saves us a fair share o' time and trouble if'n we did. There's a sizable draw across this wall. Reach it here, we'll see the waters 'fore sunset."

"Difficult climb," Percel noted. "But if it means a chance to wash these rusty spearheads from my throat, I'd attempt worse."

Hadrum appeared less certain, swaying on his feet as he eyed the stone face beneath the high cleft with evident distaste. The lack of fluids, coupled with their exertions, had made him light-headed. As usual, however, he stiffened defiantly under Kylac's questioning gaze. "You're the spider. If you can claw your way up there and drop a strand, I'll give it a climb."

A deep undercut ran along the base of the wall. The nearest hold that Kylac might reach was more than a dozen feet overhead—and due to the rounded overhang formed by the cavity, he would have to climb upside down, with nothing to cling to, to work his way up to it.

"Break your neck, and you rot where you lie," Fangs added with a sneer.

"Ya's leave to lap up my blood first," Kylac replied, looking to the opposite wall. The undercut there was much shallower, and the face above more fragmented. Granted, the cracks and shelves it offered were only finger-thin, and his fingers ached as it was from climbing half the day. Also, its slope angled away, so that the higher he climbed, the longer his leap would have to be to cross. Even if he cleared the gap, with his grip somewhat weakened, he might well fail to cling to the other side. Mayhap a foolish risk after all. But then, even with what little he knew about his life's purpose, he doubted it was to die by cracking his skull apart on a wilderness rock not quite large enough to call itself a mountain.

Let's find out.

He backtracked a few paces to find an entry point he liked, then worked his way up at an angle along a series of those narrow ledges. He reached a point level with the opposing overhang, then crawled higher. The rock bit at his skin, tearing blisters. Better that, he supposed, than softer stone and its risk of crumbling.

Upon gaining the angled slab he'd selected as his most likely launch point, Kylac took a moment to reevaluate the task he'd set for himself. The span seemed much farther from above than it had below. With a running start—or even a level base to spring from—it would have been an easy leap. But he would essentially be pushing off from one vertical surface and seeking to clutch another as he fell. Now that he was perched here, measuring his chances, he was less certain he could do it.

"No good?" Percel asked.

Hadrum snickered. "Before the sunset, you claimed."

Kylac looked back to the near wall. He might go higher, he supposed. He'd have to crawl out and around his present position, but there was a pitted hollow twelve heads above him that might serve as an adequate platform. Trouble was, the span would be even greater, and the increased momentum from the longer fall would make the proper landing less likely. He would instead have to aim for the breach itself, where he might land afoot, rather than trying to grip the far wall like a cat clinging to a bedpost.

If he were to miss, and end up striking the canyon floor . . . well, it wouldn't likely be the stone that shattered.

Shards. Stop fencing and makes a move.

He opted for the leap from his present position, and so marked the crags he was aiming for, coiled himself against the slab, and—

A sudden movement drew his eye to the cut in the far wall. Within that cleft, a form had appeared, to crouch upon the lip above his companions' heads, almost directly opposite Kylac's perch. For half a heartbeat, their gazes met, time enough for that single, dreaded word to enter his mind.

Groll.

Before he could draw the breath with which to utter warning, the creature dropped, snarling as it fell atop Percel's broad shoulders. With their attention on Kylac, the mutant had caught the Shadowguard with their backs turned. Only now, as the beast landed on him, did Percel whip his head around.

By then, a clawed hand had raked his throat, rending muscles and tendons and ripping free with a meaty chunk of windpipe. Percel remained on his feet, grasping reflexively at his assailant, but the blood was pouring down his chest like a waterfall in spring, and no amount of flailing was going to wrest his killer free.

Fishhook fell to his knees choking and sputtering, shredded throat tissues fluttering in and out, as useless as gills out of water. Even so, Kylac saw him clutching for his sword hilt, fighting to free the weapon from its scabbard. The groll bore down, clawed feet digging furrows down the length of Percel's back. Percel arched in response to the venom taking root. The groll leaned over and bit his face.

Kylac shoved free of the wall. Rather than catch the far side, he struck it with his feet and propelled himself into a mid-air flip that left him crouched again upon the canyon floor. Hadrum was still fumbling for his flail with one hand, while groping for his gauntlet with the other. But he forgot both and stumbled back as Kylac landed between him and the monster, longsword in one hand, shortsword in the other.

The groll tore free from Percel's face, leaving behind a noseless ruin with the flesh flayed from one cheek. The remaining skin blackened along the course of his veins. If Percel tried to scream, no sound emerged. The mutant swallowed, then thrust his own face toward Kylac in a shrieking hiss.

It wasn't the face of the Ukinh that hunted them—the one that had ambushed him in the sewer caverns back at Wingport, and that he'd intercepted in Denariel's cabin aboard their crippled ship. This creature seemed at once older, and more feral. Shaggy hair grew in bearded clumps around its emaciated body, and small, bony protrusions lined its ridged brow and angular limbs. Its flesh was leathery in the face and torso, but armored with dense plates—like bits of turtle shell—upon its back, forearms, and thighs. A groll, yes, but of another variety. In the eyes of the first, Kylac had recognized a keen intelligence. In this one's, he saw only hunger and madness.

That was all he had time to observe before the slavering creature lunged at him, kicking Percel's body back against the earth and stretching out for Kylac's throat. Kylac stepped back, shielding himself by crossing his blades in front of him. A putrid stench washed over him. The groll swiped madly, its foaming jaw snapping and snarling like a rabid dog's. Kylac parried its strikes, and even launched a few of his own, but the bony shells upon its limbs were strong enough to deflect his blades. Though he chipped at their surfaces, the creature didn't seem troubled by it.

Percel's body shuddered through a series of convulsions and grew still. Hadrum had finally managed to arm himself, but seemed in no rush to join the fray. The groll slashed and shrieked, tearing at Kylac's whirring defenses, as if bent on shredding him into tatters.

And then, as abruptly as they'd engaged, the groll tore away, gnashing its needled teeth in savage frustration. Springing from all fours, it bounded up the near wall, working around to Kylac's back. Kylac whirled to defend himself, but the groll surprised him by turning instead toward Hadrum.

The startled Blackfist froze, then remembered to draw back his flail. But the creature was too close, and all Fangs could do was heft his opposing gauntlet in a desperate attempt to shield his face.

The groll aimed a swipe at Hadrum's exposed waist. As it reached out, Kylac's throwing knife struck the back of its shoulder, causing the arm to retract in reflex. Instead of severing one or more of Fangs's organs, the mutant stumbled into him, knocking him against the canyon wall.

The groll rounded to where it now had Fangs pinned. A second knife struck it in the lower rib cage, and a third caught it in the hip. The creature swatted at the offending blades, knocking them free—wounding itself further in the process. By then, Kylac had rearmed himself with his primary blades and dashed across the intervening ground with swords extended, to force the groll back from his helpless companion.

For the moment, he'd saved Fangs's life. Instead of driving the Ukinh back, however, his strikes seemed only to enrage it. Back it came at Kylac, yowling with the promise of agony, dismemberment, death.

Kylac had faced them all before, and welcomed the challenge to do so again. Thirst and weariness fell away as the energy of battle burned through his veins, igniting his flesh. Faster and faster his limbs and blades moved, resulting in a greater number of nicks and cuts to the creature before him—all building toward the inevitable, climactic moment in which another adversary was laid low to feed the earth.

The beast battled as if possessed of a suicidal frenzy, refusing to turn away. Twice more it tried to come at Kylac from another angle, leaping about the walls of the narrow canyon to descend from above, then diving low to swipe at his legs and feet. Maintaining a mostly defensive posture, Kylac weathered the attacks, watchful for any new wrinkle in skill or strategy that the groll might employ. An impatient fighter might press a perceived advantage, only to discover too late that he'd been baited. But Kylac seldom felt the urge to finish an opponent quickly. The fight itself was what he enjoyed, making him only too happy to prolong it until learning all he needed to about his opponent, allowing *it* to be the one to tire or make that desperate, critical mistake.

Hadrum, thus far, was keeping to the side, shying away whenever the groll skittered or lunged in his direction, using Kylac as his shield. This suited Kylac fine. He preferred the Blackfist not involve himself at this juncture. Acclimating to one opponent's manners and tendencies could prove difficult enough. Factoring in another's—whether for or against—introduced a whole new complexity.

A flail strike came whipping in from over Kylac's shoulder. It was almost as if Fangs had heard his thoughts and decided—even in this—to spite him. The strike forced Kylac to redirect a slash of his own—one aimed for the tendon of the groll's right knee, which might have crippled the beast on that side. Instead, his blade's edge scraped across one of the creature's bony shin plates, causing not the slightest discomfort. Worse, it put Kylac in line for a left-handed swipe that he had to pivot outward to avoid, opening a clear path for the groll to retaliate at Hadrum for the harmless blow that Fangs had landed on the creature's shoulder.

Retaliate the groll did, diving along the path of the retreating flail. Once again, Hadrum reacted in the most obvious fashion—by stumbling backward. This time, however, his heel caught a stone knob in the cavern floor, causing his knee to twist and wrench sideways.

The fall spared him his entrails, for had he not pitched to the right, the groll's swipe surely would have opened his bowels. He hit hard, though, and Kylac heard something pop as Fangs cried out.

Whatever the injury, it would have to wait. Kylac was only scarcely able to slip his longsword into the groll's ribs before it lunged past to have at the downed Blackfist. Fortunately, the wound was deep enough to draw the creature about, forestalling its assault on the weaker of the two men and causing it to reengage with Kylac.

The whirlwind of claws and teeth and bony plates continued unabated. Though blood seeped from the wound in its ribs and a myriad other pricks, scrapes, and cuts, the creature gave no indication of tiring. Its cries of feral rage echoed upon the canyon walls, filling Kylac's ears like shards of glass.

The groll had only one ear of its own, from what Kylac could see—a jagged lobe with serrated edges, black warts, and tufts of coarse black hair. The area where the other might have been was instead grown over with another of those bony shells. When the lone ear pricked suddenly, the groll turned its head, lowering its guard for but an instant.

All the time Kylac needed.

With his shortsword, he swatted the nearest arm wide, which allowed him to plunge his longsword deep into its abdomen, aiming for where its kidney might be. The groll squealed and fell back, but not before Kylac twisted his blade and exited through the side, leaving a large gash. A gout of blood pulsed from the wound, washing down the creature's thigh and forcing Kylac to step back himself, wary of whatever poison or disease that blood contained.

For a moment, Kylac thought the groll meant to throw itself at him anew, so vehement was the thrust of its snout and the ensuing hiss. Instead, it gnashed its teeth and spun away, racing down the length of the canyon in apparent retreat.

Kylac's first thought was to give chase, but he remembered Hadrum, lying there with his damaged knee. Abandoned in an injured state, the Blackfist might fall victim to some menace the moment Kylac let him out of sight.

So he watched the groll speed off until it had vanished behind a jagged stone fold. When the echoes of its scratching claws had faded, he turned to his fallen companion.

"How bad is it?"

"I had a clear shot at its head," Hadrum complained.

"Then ya missed."

"You couldn't step clear for one moment?"

"Mayhap, given warning." Kylac retrieved Hadrum's flail, which the Blackfist had dropped upon the canyon floor. "What o' the leg. Can ya stands?"

"Of course I can stand." Fangs winced as he rose, levering himself up with an obvious effort. Once on his feet, he quickly shifted his full weight to the uninjured leg.

Kylac looked past him, farther down the walled trail, to where Percel lay rigid upon his back, arched in a grotesque pose. "We'll need his waterskins."

"Not with his corrupted blood on them, we won't."

"I wasn't suggesting we—"

A high-pitched yelp came echoing down the canyon, from the direction in which the groll had fled. The cry was sharp and quick, ending abruptly. Its echoes died almost as swiftly.

"What was that?" Hadrum asked.

Kylac looked at Fangs's leg. "We'd have to moves to finds out."

True to form, Hadrum took that as a personal slight, and set forth at once to prove himself capable. The first few steps were ginger ones, but Fangs snarled away the pain and gradually gained confidence. Kylac let him pass, making no move to follow while studying the other's broken gait. The Blackfist would pay for his stubbornness come morning, but Kylac opted not to say as much. If he couldn't move, he was dead anyway.

"Are you coming?" Hadrum asked irritably, looking back.

An easy jaunt brought Kylac alongside. There he remained, allowing his injured companion to set their pace. Though it tore at him not to race ahead, there was little enough to be gained in doing so. He kept his blades in hand, anticipating ambush.

Hadrum huffed and grunted, his progress marked by a heavy, scraping shuffle. Kylac's own footfalls were no more than a whisper. If anything stalked them, its steps were lighter still.

"Which way?" Hadrum asked, when they came to another fork.

Kylac pointed, indicating a rising path through which a wind gusted. The cut curved and folded before the walls fell away, opening onto an elevated spur.

"Waits here."

Kylac proceeded toward the overlook. A stain marked its edge. Blood. That of the feral groll? He crept closer, clear to the lip of the ledge, where the wind strengthened, wailing a lament for the death of another sun. Its light of crimson and gold filled the western horizon. Kylac glanced back to check on Hadrum, then peered out over the precipice.

He was surprised when nothing sprang at him, finding instead the body of the groll, splattered upon a nest of jagged rocks far below. Its stomach cavity had burst—weakened mayhap from the rent in its side—spreading intestines everywhere.

Had it fallen? Could it have jumped? The wound hadn't been so severe. Not for these creatures. Its cry had suggested another enemy. And the spatter of blood upon the ledge told Kylac that the beast had been ripped open *before* it fell. A separate string of droplets ran along a second track, ending at another sheer wall of stone—which itself displayed a fading trail of bloody claw marks.

Whatever had killed it had carried away a piece of it. A trophy, mayhap, or an organ to feast upon.

"Is it there?"

"It's here," Kylac replied, speaking not of the carcass below.

17

"TELL ME IT'S DEAD," said Merrec, a fresh swig of water dribbling from his chin. "Tell me you slew the beast."

Hadrum jerked the skin away from him. "Give it here, if you can't keep it in your mouth. After all we endured, I'll not see you waste it."

Kylac wasn't inclined to argue, though Fangs's sudden grab had caused even more water to slosh from the unstoppered skin. He glanced around at the other listeners—Ledron, Trajan, Sallun, and of course, Her Highness, Denariel—seated before him upon their defensive overlook. Awash with pale starlight, their expressions seemed all the more anxious as they waited on him to finish his tale.

"It never showed," he admitted ruefully. "Not at the Tears, and not during the long trek down."

And a long trek it had been. Hadrum's injury—along with Percel's envenomed corpse—had dissuaded any further attempt at scaling the elevated cleft from which the feral groll had ambushed them, forcing them to navigate the longer, more roundabout path before finally reaching Eshla's Tears. By then, the sun had fully set, leaving the Cindercrag thick with sinister shadows, any one of which might have proven to be the groll—*their* groll—which even Fangs had agreed was most likely responsible for the demise of the other. It had made the climb to make sure *they* didn't, the Blackfist had suggested, slaying its would-be rival so that it could savor their deaths itself.

Mayhap. The notion was as plausible as any other Kylac could conceive. Still, he'd refrained from carrying too far with his assumptions, remaining vigilant against all possibilities.

The font that was Eshla's Tears had been shadowed as well, an obsidian mirror that reflected the cloudless moon and its attending stars. Kylac had resisted the urge to dive in—risks be damned—and had instead studied that broad, placid surface for several minutes at a safe distance. Then he'd inched closer and studied it some more. The surrounding basin was clear, free of boulders, brush, hollows, or crevasses from which to stage an ambush. He'd found pebbles and jagged stones—and little else. There'd been no sign of danger. Yet still he'd waited.

Finally, he'd crept close enough to count the windblown ripples playing across those dark waters and lapping at the sharp-edged borders. There he'd waited again, measuring the pool's rhythms against the brushing breezes. He'd tossed a stone, and then another, each time observing the pattern that resulted, searching for any interference that might indicate a rogue force lurking below.

When there'd been nothing left but to approach the water's edge, he'd done so alone, accepting Hadrum's offer to linger at a distance—to watch his back, the Blackfist had claimed, though both men knew better. With the waterskins remaining to them slung across his back, and with swords in hand, he'd crouched low, reminded all the while of the tarrock ambush that had claimed Brenth on the banks of the Navandi.

But that had been a lowland river, with direct access to the sea. And its smoothly rushing waters had been rushing nonetheless, serving to hide its enemies. In contrast, Eshla's Tears was a placid, freshwater pool cradled by the mammoth Cindercrag. No mindless predator would hazard so high. Any that *had* would only starve for its effort—or be devoured by a mad groll, it seemed. That left only one enemy to be concerned with.

Or so he'd told himself.

When he'd touched the pool, nothing surfaced. When he'd bent low to sniff the waters, nothing lunged for his head—from above or below. Though his stomach had continued to knot in warning, that disquiet might as easily have been born within as without. For all his apprehension, his enemy remained more wary than he.

He'd tasted the waters then, and waters had never tasted so good. Though they'd burned at first against his cracked lips, and had slid down his throat initially like dry leaves scratching against stone, it had taken but a moment for his tissues to recall the feel of moisture and to welcome it. A moment after that, he'd been drinking his fill. An inner voice had warned him not to do so too quickly, else risk stomach cramps. But his thirst had cried louder.

Unable to bear it any longer, Hadrum had joined him, hobbling forward to shove his entire head beneath the pool's surface. Evidently, his fear of ghosts had lessened, else been forgotten. He'd come up laughing and showering himself with spray. Kylac had been more restrained, keeping his gaze moving, his ears pricked, and his blades within reach. He'd found himself wishing that "Fishhook" Percel could have shared in this moment before his death.

The thought had been a sobering one, reminding Kylac of the others in their company, awaiting his return. And so he'd asked Hadrum to fill the skins, one at a time, in between gulps, while Kylac served sentry. For once, Fangs had been too happy to argue. Able to salvage but one of the skins that Percel had carried, they were down to five—less one that would assuredly be drained in short order by those comrades sitting near the Cindercrag's base. Four skins for seven survivors. It would have to do. If he had it correctly from Trajan, there would be additional water sources a day or two hence. Invigorated as he'd felt in that moment, Kylac might have been willing to go the rest of his life without another drop, in praise of their good fortune.

That elation had been tempered almost as soon as they'd turned their backs on the lifesaving pool, replaced by the harsh reminder of the descent that lay ahead. A descent made in the darkness of night through a labyrinth of jagged defiles, over ankle-twisting landscapes, down perilous slopes and sharp stone ridges, stalked by roaming galamandrytch and whatever other creatures might prowl the 'Crag at night. They would be hampered by Hadrum's injury, weighed down by bloated waterskins, and short the strongest of those who'd made the climb. At any moment, the groll might emerge to sever a rope from which they dangled, or trigger a rockslide that might send them to a skin-splitting, bone-splintering end. Else they might wend their way down to the bottom, only to find their companions already dead, and themselves lost in the Ukinhan wilderness.

But what were their alternatives? Wait until morning and hope the others could survive the night? Make the 'Crag their home and live in solitude, learning to dine on the meat of blood scorpions?

So they'd taken their chances, choosing a different trail than the one that had brought them up, and tracing from there the safest route they could find. In the end, their journey had consumed more than half the night. Though it might be said they'd cheated death with every limping stride, those strides had led them inexorably downward, eventually returning them unkilled, unpoisoned, unbitten, to the lower ledge where the rest of their party camped, similarly unharmed. Ledron and Trajan, sharing the watch, had quickly roused the slumbering Denariel to provide her with water before partaking of the same. Merrec had awakened on his own, and grudgingly been permitted a dozen swallows, listening raptly as Kylac shared with them the details of their climb, Percel's death, and the curious tumble of the feral groll.

"Perhaps it was some other beast after all," Merrec observed hopefully. "One that saw a chance to eliminate a rival, but had no particular interest in you . . . or us."

Kylac shrugged. "Mayhap. Or mayhap it's still leery o' me."

That drew an audible scoff from Denariel.

"Her Highness thinks elsewise?"

"Fear has no part in it. But you don't steal eggs back from poachers by flailing about with a maul."

Has she the right of it? Kylac wondered. While his own theory might account for the groll's reluctance to attack his group, it didn't explain why Ledron's had gone unmolested. Did it fear that an assault here might only drive the princess to hurl herself off the ledge?

"Is the creature so concerned with keeping your delicate shell intact?" he asked.

"If not, he'd have killed you all long before now," she assured him.

Kylac studied her expression as best he could in the dim light. The possibility wasn't a new one. He recalled Sallun suggesting something similar weeks ago, back in Wingport. But he had yet to hear it with such ironclad assertion.

"So why not dispatch me and Fangs above? It surely had chances aplenty."

Denariel's eyes gleamed with sardonic amusement. "And what brave champion would have then so gallantly delivered the water to keep me alive?"

Kylac felt a twinge in his gut like the release of a bowstring. Could it . . . ? Had the creature ascended with them to ensure they succeeded? The notion did fit the princess's egg theory, and seemed to better explain events near the summit.

Denariel laughed, as if sensing victory. "You still think yourself superior. Until you believe elsewise, you stand no chance against him."

I'll defer to Your Highness's expertise on feelings o' superiority, Kylac thought. "Makes me wonder what this creature will do with ya whole that it can't do with ya broken."

"Enough," Ledron snapped. It had fast become the captain's favorite word. "We've got what we came for. The rest is guesswork, and avails us nothing in terms of strategy."

"What strategy is that?" Merrec huffed. "Crawl back down and proceed as before?"

"With your lips sewn shut, should you spout discontent. His Majesty may desire your account of things, but I've no use for your tongue before then."

"We'd do better to make our way down in the light," Trajan suggested. "We won't find a safer site below."

Hadrum issued a grunt of agreement. Seemed he was tired of navigating treacherous paths steeped in darkness. After their night's trek, Kylac could scarcely fault him.

"Silence, then," Ledron agreed. "Seek your dreams, or whatever will pass as such. The watch is mine."

HE AWOKE to a sudden spasm, a searing, gut-wrenching agony that had him doubling over on the sharp earth and clenching his teeth to keep from screaming. Opening his eyes, Kylac thought to find the groll's clawed fist buried in his stomach, alternately squeezing and raking at his innards. How could the beast have—

But when he opened his eyes, there was no enemy before him. Just the stone lip where he'd lain down—and suddenly, an open view of the bed of jagged rocks below, layered in the shadows of predawn. His body's violent contraction, he realized, had nearly dragged him over the precipice. Another half roll . . . Might that put an end to the pain now ripping through him?

A scream did escape, then, though it sounded somehow distant. Only when he discovered his teeth still clenched did Kylac realize that the cry hadn't been his own.

Somehow, he found the will to roll over and lurch into a sitting position, still clutching at his roiling entrails. His blurred vision came to rest on Hadrum, hunched over much like himself. Fangs, however, was on his knees, grasping his stomach with one arm while clawing at the stone of their ledge with his free hand. Ledron stood over him, sword drawn, though he seemed uncertain what to do with it. Trajan and Merrec were scrambling to their feet, fumbling for their own blades while rubbing the sleep from their eyes. Another scream tore from Hadrum's lips. Deflected by the Cindercrag's uncaring hide, it echoed out into the moonlit wasteland.

"What's wrong with them?" he heard Sallun ask.

Kylac turned his head. The lookout was seated next to Denariel, both of whom were closer to him than the others. Sallun looked ready to bolt. Denariel, her short hair a sleep-tangled nest, was scowling at the disruption.

"Poison," said Trajan. Though he still blinked furiously, the Tower had found his bearings. His gaze shifted from Hadrum to Kylac. "Groll venom."

"What?" The startled squeak came from Merrec.

"Both at once?" Sallun whispered doubtfully.

Ledron's tone was stronger, his question more direct. "You know this?"

"I've seen it," Trajan responded. He stooped to lay a hand on Hadrum's back, but Hadrum just howled again and fell to his side, where he curled up like a babe in the womb.

"Is it scorpions?" Merrec asked, gaze sweeping the earth about his anxious feet.

"They'd be dead." Sallun's words were choked, his eyes bright with fear. "Were the venom in their blood . . ."

Kylac almost wished it were so. The spasms were coming more quickly now, rolling through him in waves, each cresting larger than the last, wracking his body until he feared his spine might snap.

"It's in their bellies," Ledron explained, "not their veins."

Kylac felt a tortured moan building upon his lips . . .

Instead, his stomach heaved, and a gush of foul-smelling water spilled forth. Somehow, he managed to direct it out over the ledge, to splatter upon the rocks below.

A quick breath, and then he vomited again. This time, he felt his stomach meant to chase after, seeking escape through his gullet. But he found the strength to swallow, which seemed to rein the renegade organ in—though he had half a mind to reach for a dagger and carve it loose.

"That should help," Trajan observed.

The Tower was right. While the sickness still throbbed within, the intensity was much lessened. Kylac felt dizzy, groggy, but at least he was no longer crippled with seizure.

By then, Hadrum was retching as well, spewing uncontrollably in all directions. Ledron and Trajan were quick enough to evade most of it, but Merrec, who'd still been searching for blood scorpions, yelped in disgust as his boots were doused. Only Denariel and Sallun, on the opposite end of the ledge—as well as Kylac himself, alone at the precipice—were fully spared.

"Bloody, festering . . ." Merrec fumed, flinging vomit from his boots.

Hadrum retched a second time, and then a third. Trajan bent to assist him, gripping his shoulder with a steady hand to help control his lurching convulsions.

"Let it go," the Tower urged. "Spit it out."

Hadrum obliged him with yet another wracking heave.

Merrec was still dancing about as if his boots were afire. "Will it get to me?" he cried.

"Be still!" Ledron barked at him.

"Am I poisoned? Shall I shed my boots?"

"Your boots can't harm you," Trajan snapped, "unless maybe you mean to eat them. So cease that craven prancing." He bent back to Hadrum as the Blackfist came up gasping—which gave way to a hacking cough. Bile sprayed and drooled from his lips, but while his stomach continued to lurch rhythmically, it seemed that it had no more filth to summon.

"There," Trajan said. "Give it a moment. The pain should ease."

It took Hadrum much longer than Kylac to reach that point of relative relief. Already, Kylac had drawn himself to a knee. He might have stood, but his innards continued to throb and twist angrily, and he decided it safer to hold his position lest he trigger a renewed assault. Hadrum, by comparison, writhed uncaring amid a rancid stew of his stomach's brewing, with the aimless groping of a soldier mortally wounded on the battlefield.

"You're certain it's not catching?" Merrec asked, scraping his feet on a clear patch of rock. "I thought—"

"Must you continue that warbling?" Denariel asked. Her mere voice ushered a certain calm, commanding the others' attention. "You cannot catch what you already have."

The calm gave way to silence, thick and heavy.

"Have," Merrec echoed. "You . . . but they're . . ."

"*In their bellies*, our good captain said. Or were you too panicked to hear him?"

"I heard. What does that . . . ?" The mercenary's words slowed as Denariel methodically reached for a waterskin, unstoppered it, sniffed, and raised it to her lips.

"Your Highness!" Ledron shouted.

"The harm is done," she replied, and drank.

"She's right," Trajan said. "It makes no difference now."

"The water?" Merrec wheezed.

"Did you hear tell of them feasting up there?" Denariel asked, eyes twinkling with sardonic delight. "Think they slew themselves a nice fat hare, perhaps, and did not bother to share? I might think it, too, if anything more than lichen and grit grew upon this rock."

"But we all drank the water. I'm not . . . we're not . . ."

"We'll know in a few hours—won't we." Denariel took another swallow.

"Fiends," Hadrum growled, his voice thick with agony. "I told you the Tears was cursed."

"By phantom sorceries committed a thousand years ago." Denariel snickered. "My guess? Drag that pool up there, don't be surprised to find a Ukinh's liver resting at the bottom."

Remembered images flashed through Kylac's spinning mind. A splattered groll, its guts splayed open. Bloody spatters on the ledge above, with a trail of drips and smears marking the killer's departure. The dark, placid surface of Eshla's Tears, its fathomless depths shrouded in unknowable mystery.

So much for your egg theory.

Unless . . . Something told him she'd arrived at this latest conclusion a little too quickly. "When did ya knows?"

"A guess, I said." Under his piercing gaze, she raised her chin and added, "The moment I heard your story."

"Yet said nothing?" Hadrum was livid. He tried to stand, but staggered and fell.

"What difference? You and the rogue had already lapped your fill. As had we, since you let us slake our thirst before sharing with us all that had transpired."

"How long do we have?" Ledron asked Trajan.

"A day. If any exceeds that, they'll be the first."

"You said . . . it's not in the veins," Merrec whined.

"Aye," Trajan agreed. "But it'll get there soon enough. Death is slower, but no less certain."

"A rather cowardly way to dispatch us, some mights say."

Denariel smirked. "Cherish that notion, if it eases your agony."

"What, then? Or is poisoning ya 'long with the rest of us but another stroke o' genius?"

"I wonder," said Trajan, peering at Denariel with a discerning eye.

"What?" Ledron prompted.

"Would the beast truly have risked envenoming its prize?"

"You're thinking she's not?"

"Some tell of a mineral that, when consumed, enters the blood and renders a man immune to ingested groll venom."

"Sageryst?" Ledron scoffed. "A sham. Peddled by charlatans and alchemists to the same fools who sniff nagir root and drink thorsbloom."

"Who can know? Few risk treading in lands where they may need it. Fewer still have the means to procure it. But our beloved princess here . . ."

All eyes shifted to Denariel.

"Would you have me apologize?" she asked. "I am a daughter of privilege, you may know, whose father had an explorer's itch. Do you believe he would have traveled with us throughout the Reach without taking certain precautions?"

Therein lies a tale or two, thought Kylac, with more than half a mind to inquire . . . later, when the sensation of his skull being pried apart from within had passed.

Ledron's gaze narrowed. "Does it work?"

"I suppose we'll know in a few hours," Denariel repeated slyly.

"Privilege has its rewards," Trajan acknowledged, with a glint of his own amusement. "So too does a ranger's daring."

"You've partaken of it," Sallun surmised. "When?"

"In my youth, given me by my uncle. Claimed to have harvested it himself."

"Bloody shards," Merrec scoffed. "I had me an uncle of the Sea-watch who claimed to have bedded an entire pod of seamaids. Didn't make it so."

"Uncle Rashad," Trajan added, unflinching. "The Mad Wanderer, as he'd become known."

A man the Tower had mentioned before, Kylac recalled, following Ranson's death, upon his naming of the great banethistle. Though the Blackfist had neglected to mention any familial connection at the time.

"Rashad the *Betrayer*," Hadrum muttered painfully.

Denariel smiled in agreement, hefting her chin. "I believe he owes my father his head."

Ledron was only slightly more circumspect. "A deserter. Not to be trusted."

"Trustworthy or no," Trajan answered them, "he had *my* father convinced that sageryst was effective. Enough so, at least, to see that my sisters and I took it." The grin he flashed at Denariel was somewhat snide. "As a precaution."

"Will it cure us?" Hadrum asked, before buckling at another cramp.

"If not, we may as well open our veins now, and spare ourselves the pain."

Sorely tempting, thought Kylac. "And where did your uncle harvest this mineral?"

"In the only place it grows. The mines of Krathen Ungret."

Hadrum tried again to vomit.

"Ungret?" Merrec echoed.

"But that's . . ." Sallun attempted, and couldn't finish.

"The Ukinhan birthing warren," Ledron finished for him.

"Their lair?" Kylac asked.

"So go the tales," Trajan admitted. "Stumbled across an entrance once, but wasn't fool enough to venture inside. Of those to enter, not one man in twenty comes out again. Whether Ukinha ever haunted those mines, I cannot say. But there are other things that do."

Kylac chuckled, though it caused him to cough. So the creature had intentionally used their thirst against them, driving them to the nearest freshwater source . . . only to poison them. With death in their bellies, they would now have to enter its very den before the sickness killed them off—all but Trajan and Denariel, at least. And formidable a fighter as the Tower might be, he sure didn't seem to fancy himself a match for the groll.

"My apologies, Princess," Kylac said, tipping her a slight bow. "Seems your beastie is indeed more cunning than I'd has wagered." He turned to the others. "But we's come this far. So what say we play its little game out?"

18

THEY DEPARTED THE CINDERCRAG at once. Though the sun hadn't yet risen to light their path, they no longer cared to wait. With its flame akin to a candle now that marked the remaining duration of their lives, every moment mattered.

Trajan led, assisting Hadrum, who with his swollen knee and poisoned belly was scarcely able to tread on his own. Merrec and Sallun followed, with Ledron on their heels, the captain personally escorting Denariel behind or alongside as the terrain permitted. Kylac was once again entrusted with the rearguard. He continued to fare better than Hadrum, finding that the stir of blood caused by movement actually helped to diminish the effects of his illness. The fever, headache, stomach cramping, and dizziness remained, but in a manageable state—provided they didn't worsen. Trajan advised him that, indeed, the more crippling symptoms should lie dormant, for a time.

Gathering strength for the final onslaught before death.

As they crept along the thin, treacherous ledges and through the narrow, night-cloaked defiles, Kylac found it difficult not to regret the few hours of sleep they'd taken. By his reckoning, had they continued directly on down to the Cindercrag's base, they might be miles farther south. Alas, he might as easily regret this entire expedition, for all the power such thinking had.

Slips and stumbles led to a handful of fresh bruises, scrapes, and twisted ankles among the less agile members of their company. None of these injuries, however, were worse than those already endured, and so they counted themselves fortunate upon setting foot once again on the stony flatlands. With a single backward glance, Kylac bid silent appreciation and good riddance to the massive rock and its Tears—which had proven both blessing and curse.

By then, dawn was cresting the eastern horizon in a scarlet wave capped with golden foam. An angry sunrise, Kylac thought, bent on drowning the world. Or mayhap he only felt that way because it looked to be his last.

Though their goal lay south and east, they turned first north and west, forced to round the base of the Cindercrag in order to bypass the headwaters of the Navandi. It seemed doubtful that the tarrocks would still be of issue here. Any that had been herded this far would in all likelihood have turned downriver again the moment the groll had abandoned its waters to climb the 'Crag. Still, it didn't seem worth the risk, now that they could as easily march a short distance farther and avoid the chance that they might be wrong.

They came upon a blackwood elm, its withered limbs dry and twisted. Trajan hacked a branch from the dead tree and gave it over to Hadrum to use as a walking staff. Their pace quickened after that, though not by much. As a company, they were still starved, weary, and wounded, moving only as swiftly as their slowest member would allow.

"We ought to cut him loose," Merrec muttered in Kylac's ear.

Kylac lifted his gaze to where Hadrum hobbled alongside Trajan at the front, setting their pace.

"Would ya suggest the same if'n it were yourself?"

The mercenary puffed his chest. "I'd not ask any of you to risk your lives on my account."

No. O' course ya wouldn't.

"What manner of soldier begs others to die with him?"

"Have you a concern, Merrec?" Ledron asked, glancing back.

"Just seeing that our young rogue is well."

"When he drops, you have leave to check him. Until then, worry about yourself."

I believe he was, Kylac thought, but said nothing.

They found the Navandi along the southwest curve of the Cindercrag, a wellspring driven up from beneath the earth, roaring and spitting in a torrent where it gushed from a breach in the rock's base. A shame these headwaters hadn't been drinkable, Kylac thought, and suspected he wasn't alone in his lament. Ashen stone gleamed like obsidian where touched by spray, the sharper edges worn smooth. South the river ran, for the first hundred paces or so, before a rising berm of rock nudged it eastward, setting it on the path that would carry it across the Ukinhan Wilds clear to the Gorrethrian Sound.

The echo of its emergent rush lingered in their ears as they veered slightly eastward themselves. A southerly course would have been more direct, but the ground that way was buckled and folded, forming peaks and valleys of upthrust stone that would force them to climb and descend, inhibiting their already difficult progress.

As they reached the outskirts of a buttonwood swamp, however, they turned into a ravine that cut south, skirting a line between shattered hill country and lowland bog. Talathandria's Run, Trajan called it, named for an adulterous queen of distant ancestry who, when her faithlessness was discovered, had fled into the wilderness to mate with grolls and become worshipped among them—lying with any mutant, it was said, that brought her the skin of one of her royal husband's bounty hunters. A witch in time, she eventually transformed over the course of many decades into a Ukinh herself. Some whispermongers claimed she still lived, emerging now and then to claim new skins on her own. Even those rangers who scoffed at the legend preferred not to utter the creature's name, and so referred to this stretch simply as the Iron Scar.

Whatever its name, they trekked for an hour, and then an hour more, hemmed by the razored hummocks to the west and by a fringe of rotting jungle to the east. The line between the two was narrow, but mostly unbroken, like a no-man's-land between two armies locked in ageless battle, whose troops were weary of spending themselves one against the other.

Where that truce ended, battle resumed with no clear victor.

Though the hills grew larger to the west, the resulting cliffs loomed like unwilling reserves, reluctant to engage as the frontline ridges were laid low and swarmed over by choking growth. At the same time, the hard-charging jungle was undercut at the roots by waves of stony earth sharp and rigid, which stunted and thinned its strength while giving the ground a permanently choppy appearance—like a battlefield churned to mud and left to freeze.

Farther on, that muddy field became like a wind-whipped sea, as the pits in the stony earth dug deeper, and the ridges between rose higher, sharpening at the edges.

"What manner of terrain is this?" Kylac asked, finding it ever harder to set upon flat ground.

"We're venturing into the Ironshore Wastes," Trajan announced, sweat dripping from his brow.

"Ironshore."

"Bloodrock, some call it, or Spearstone. You'll see. I'd hoped not to tread this way, rounding via the Steppes." His head turned toward the western highlands with what seemed like longing in his gaze . . . before snapping back to reality. "It seems we no longer have a choice."

Kylac wondered what could be so bad as to prefer a path among the barren heights of those broken cliffs. Were it not for the sickening rhythm of his stomach, squeezing and releasing and squeezing again, he might have asked.

Soon enough, he discovered for himself.

Not a mile farther on, they emerged from a scraggly line of growth to gaze upon a vast clearing in which frozen swells had given way to a petrified inferno. Piercing spires swirled high amid razored ridgelines, formations to skewer a fallen man or slice him in half. The stone's skin was pitted and blackened and all but devoid of soil. An ancient seabed, it might have been, given its chiseled, reeflike appearance. But if so, it was an ocean of acid that had roiled upon it, eating at the earth's flesh to leave it eroded and burned beyond recognition.

"We're to cross that?" Merrec balked.

Kylac was loath to cast judgment in this instance. He'd seen spiked moats that might have been easier to traverse.

"As harsh as she looks," Trajan cautioned. "Harder than granite, with edges like a blade. Stick to the slopes, as best you can, and be sure of your footing. One slip here could cost you a limb . . . or worse."

Kylac expected further complaint, for one or more of his companions to beg an alternative. None did. Sallun licked his lips nervously, pale face red with exertion. Denariel's eyes had widened with something approaching fear, but when she caught Kylac looking, she summoned a haughty expression to drive the feeling away. Ledron ground his teeth, displaying only grim resolve, while Hadrum . . . Hadrum leaned strengthlessly upon a weakening staff, too sick and weary and defeated to fuss.

Merrec remained aghast, but seemed to understand that, alone, he would be wasting his breath.

When assured that all were with him—whatever their individual reasons—Trajan resumed his march, choosing his path carefully upon the savage terrain. Now that he saw it, Kylac found the names fitting. Ironshore, for its strength. Spearstone, for those pointed, spire formations. Bloodrock . . . because any foot treading too long here was certain to paint the ground red. Already, he felt the jagged tips and cruel edges sawing at the soles of his soft leather boots. He wondered how far they had to go, but it seemed pointless to ask.

In his haggard state, it was enough to concentrate on the placement of each foot, as Trajan had suggested. He could see where a man who stumbled might easily cleave flesh, crack bone, or shear the former from the latter. For the most part, the slopes were sure and solid, weathered but unbroken. Yet there *were* patches where bits of shale slid hazardously beneath his companions' feet, twisting ankles and knees and making travel that much more treacherous.

Out in the open, the rising sun intensified. The black stone seemed to absorb its blistering heat, releasing it around them in shimmering waves of sweltering humidity. Sweat dripped down faces and limbs, coating their flesh in a boiling sheen. Only the occasional breeze brought anything approaching relief.

Mayhap it was the unrelenting heat, mayhap his implacable illness, but Kylac found himself imagining he was a titan who stood thousands of feet above the earth, treading over what had become a miniature mountain range scorched by fire, replete with knifing

peaks, steep valleys, craggy bluffs, and sheer cliffs. It was all here, a
boundless array of canyons and chasms, spurs and clefts, ridgelines
and crevasses, piercing and clawing with every step. Mayhap the most
rugged, threatening terrain in all of creation, but to him—a being of
such vast, immortal size—a nuisance and nothing more.

Better that than to contemplate the truth.

And yet, chaotic as it all seemed, this land, too, had a rhythm to it.
Even under such duress, Kylac found himself adapting to it, feeling it
in his muscles and bones, to the point where he could almost close his
eyes and know where his next step would take him. Be it a twisting
jag or a slippery downslope, a curling ridge or a cluster of small spires,
it was no different than a bird flapping its course upon the wind or a
ship fighting the waves and currents at sea. Like a spider's web—no
matter how complex or intricate the pattern—there was a sameness of
energy woven through all. To see himself and his company through,
he need only recognize and seize upon the right strand.

Or mayhap delirium was setting in.

Ahead, the twisted, stunted growth of the jungle awaited. As they
neared, a salty, sulfurous stench filled the air. A marsh, Kylac realized.
Dry as this region appeared, water in fact lay beneath this ground. It
would have to, he supposed, to support any growth at all.

The jungle offered patches of shade, but locked away the breezes, so
that their overall discomfort was undiminished. Nor did the meager
profusion of growth do anything to blunt the rocky ground on which
it grew. While branches and exposed roots offered handholds that
hadn't been there before, the company soon learned not to trust them.
Pull too heavily, and the limb might release its tenuous grasp on the
stone, as reliable as a scaling rope during a well-defended castle siege.

Loose rocks were kicked away to reveal small crabs scuttling amid
pools of brackish, rust-colored water. Poisonous, Trajan confirmed,
before anyone could ask, and lacking meat enough to justify the
effort to crack them open. With his stomach wringing at the mere
thought of food, Kylac saw no cause to complain—starvation or no.

Also poisonous were the sponges, fans, and brightly colored fish
found in some of the deeper pools as they went along. Remarkable,
thought Kylac, that even in waters so befouled, in an area as harsh

and inhospitable as this, life had fashioned a home. Fungus and flowers grew side by side at the base of the larger trees, or in tiny plots where soil had settled. Where there was only stone, longer roots had crawled down amid the pits and cracks to set those tenuous anchors that he and his companions knew to avoid. A desolate landscape by most any measure, yet the closer he looked, the more it spoke to him of strength and sheer will.

"How does anything live here?" Sallun marveled, causing Kylac to wonder momentarily if he'd been uttering his thoughts aloud.

"How does anything live anywhere?" Denariel countered. "The Mother is all-nurturing, all-embracing. That is her beauty."

"Beauty?" Merrec scoffed. "I see little enough of beauty here."

"Because men are insatiable. Offer him bread, and he'll ask for a stew to dip it in. Provide that stew, and he'll beg more meats, more vegetables, more spices. Not all that partake of Her bounty are so thankless."

Merrec opened his mouth with what seemed another rebuttal, but a withering look from Ledron caused his bitter expression to go slack, and the words never came.

The members fell silent again, lost in private thought as they focused on their exertions.

An hour or so past midmorning, the illness struck.

Sallun was the first to double over, followed moments later by Ledron, and finally by Merrec. The entire company settled to a halt in a sharp stone hollow while they endured the venom's crippling onset. The spasms were violent, the subsequent retching of an intensity greater than Kylac's, but not quite so brutal as Hadrum's.

Even in the midst of their throes, all kept eye on Denariel and Trajan, waiting for the sickness to manifest in them. By the time Sallun, Ledron, and Merrec had emptied the bile from their bellies, it hadn't.

"Our meager hope, then, is not unfounded," Kylac observed, with as much cheer as he could muster.

"So it seems," Ledron agreed, wiping his mouth with the back of his hand.

"How do we know?" Merrec groaned. "It might only take them longer to—" A vicious dry heave stole the rest.

Trajan disagreed. "The venom seems to be running its course most reliably, following the order in which each of you drank. We'll assume Her Highness and I are spared. Else, what purpose is there in continuing?"

They resumed as swiftly as they could, trudging, lurching, and hobbling in slow, painful progression. Hunger continued to sap their strength, while the sickness left them feverish and dehydrated. That they couldn't become any more ill by drinking the water from their skins seemed of small consolation—though, in truth, it was much needed in order to sustain their weakened bodies.

By noon, they were adrift amid the Ironshore Wastes. No longer visible were the western mountains or eastern swamps—not even stray glimpses through the scraggly, patchwork jungle that surrounded them. The Wastes had engulfed them—engulfed all. Once again, it seemed, they were lost upon an ocean that waited for them to surrender to its vastness. Whether by heat or hunger, the poison in their bellies or the perils all around, exhaustion seemed certain to claim them. Were there swells they could slip beneath in search of the final, jerking breath that would end their misery, Kylac was certain that some among them would have already taken it.

Despite the elements arrayed against them, they pressed doggedly onward throughout the afternoon. Kylac felt his heart racing now, despite their crawling pace. It could sense the death lurking in the blood that pulsed through its chambers, he supposed, and was drumming in denial. Would that denial were enough.

When the day's light began bending toward dusk, he felt a chill settle into his bones, and his fingers started to twitch. He looked to Hadrum, whose skin was pale wax, and whose entire hands were trembling. Fangs caught him staring, but only grimaced before shifting his gaze.

Soon thereafter, the ironshore began to smooth, its fierce ripples subsiding. Soils, though scant, returned to dust the stony earth, forming a thin carpet upon the stone. Thickets sprouted where before only a lone bush would have been hearty enough to take hold. A few hundred paces ahead, trees—actual trees, not just the sad, stunted saplings they'd grown accustomed to—loomed tall, straight, and proud, with skirts of foliage about their base, and overarching limbs laden with leaf and moss.

"Are the Wastes behind us?" Kylac asked.

"Near enough," Trajan replied, "or at least, the finger we had to cross. We call this the Spinewood. There are other names for it—the Riddled Lands, the Forsaken Forest, the Blackfell Hollows among the more pleasant."

Kylac nodded with understanding. "Another fell region o' death and danger. Can I assumes we're getting close?"

"Another hour to the cave mouth, give or take."

Kylac wondered how certain the Tower could be about this. Was the recollection of his prior excursion to the forbidden area so vivid? Was it maps he'd committed to memory? How sound could those charts be if the region was so seldom traveled?

As Kylac weighed his doubts against the sureness with which Trajan had guided them thus far, the Tower considered Kylac and then Hadrum carefully, as if measuring their condition. "I do hope you'll be with us to see it," he said, "though you may end up wishing elsewise."

Cactus and other spiny plants came to dominate the thickening woodland. At times, Trajan had to forge their path through the clawing brush with his axe. When questioned by Ledron as to the wisdom of such a loud, brutish approach, the Tower's response was much as it had been concerning the Ironshore Wastes. "Had we time to skulk our way around, we would."

So they barreled onward, raked or pricked with every step. When twilight overcame them, they fashioned firebrands per Trajan's instructions—harvesting branches safe to burn, avoiding those whose smoke would prove harmful. The humidity clung to them like a damp blanket, yet Kylac continued to feel the warmth leach from his body. Hadrum, he saw, was shivering, though sweat still bathed the Blackfist's skin. He noticed also that his veins and Fangs's had begun to swell, appearing red and angry beneath the pale flesh around hands and wrists. Their extremities would die first, it seemed, as the body began its inner retreat from the venom's relentless assault.

As the hardland forest thickened, so too did the mournful symphony of chirps and moans, shrieks and wails, raised by invisible creatures. All inedible, of course. Though that seemed just as well. Even had they the time and means to catch something, few were in any condition to stomach it. All that mattered now was this mineral—sageryst—and the desperate hope that it might counteract the poison's effects as capably as it shielded against them. Were it to function only as a preventative, and not as a cure . . .

The thought trailed away as they stumbled sometime later across a clearing marked by a surprisingly cool breeze. Kylac traced that wind and found that it came from a crescent-shaped hole in the earth—a dark vent into some subterranean space.

"Is this it?" Sallun asked. Whether hopeful or fearful, it was difficult to tell.

Trajan shook his head as he knelt beside the breach. "It's not the entrance we seek, but study it closely, and train your eye for others. The ground above the mines is riddled with shafts and sinkholes. Some might only snare a foot. Others will give you time to scream your lungs empty and draw another gasp to scream again. Not all reveal themselves so openly."

Particularly in the dark. Though many did. Every so often, they would stumble across another clearing. Sometimes, Trajan would march them around the perimeter, wary of what lay at its center, hidden beneath the brush. Others were plainly marked by those chill breezes gusting up from beneath the ground, reeking of sulfur, rotting mushrooms, and things for which Kylac had no proper reference. Each time they passed another of the forbidding openings, its foul breath raised the hairs on his flesh.

He wasn't the only one so affected. The entire land, it seemed, had come to share his shivering sense of disquiet. The cacophony of predator and prey throughout the twisted wood had died to almost utter stillness. An unnatural calm cloaked the region in its stead, eerie with its false sense of peace. Like creeping across an hours-old battlefield, Kylac thought, before the crows and flies had descended en masse. Where, amid gaping corpses and silent ghosts, one could almost hear the din of battle and the faded echo of men's screams.

The imagined caterwaul, underscored by the pulse pounding in his ears, reached a crescendo as they came upon a gouge in the earth that plowed down toward a yawning cave mouth. Kylac knew before Trajan had raised his hand in halt that their destination was at hand.

The Tower looked them over, so Kylac did the same. Pale, wan, haggard, to a man. Hadrum in particular looked no better than a corpse, swaying on his feet. But even Denariel and Trajan were sweat-streaked and gaunt, limbs hanging as loose as a stringed puppet's.

"We'll need more torches," the Tower said.

So they set about making them, scouring the nearby brush for branches that might serve. All assisted save Hadrum, whom they left slumped against a wall of the stone furrow that sloped down to the cave mouth. Kylac could have easily joined him, for all the strength and energy left to him, but preferred to keep moving. If these were his final hours, he wasn't going to spend them lying about, waiting for the end to take him.

"That should suffice," Trajan said, when each of them had secured a bundle of would-be brands. They coated the heads in what pitch remained to them, ultimately discarding the last few sticks for which there was no supply.

"Are they enough to see us through?" Ledron asked.

"Only the Mother knows."

They turned toward the cave mouth, with their sacks full of torches, near-limp waterskins . . . and little else. Retrieving Hadrum, who groaned at being hauled again to his feet, Trajan guided them down to the opening. The Tower paused briefly upon the threshold to peer up at its looming rim, then passed beneath its shadow.

The ground, uneven before, turned craggy almost at once. The floor itself remained relatively smooth, but was littered with loose rocks fallen from the ceiling. Many were too large to kick aside, and so had to be tread upon or stepped around. Another unwelcome obstacle, but they'd come to expect nothing less.

An arid chill rushed to embrace them, filled with those rank smells sampled above. Hours earlier, it might have proven a welcome relief from the intense heat, stench or no. Now, it only set Kylac's teeth to chattering. Nor could he seem to keep his arms from shaking—from his fingertips to his elbows. He felt the same affliction in his lower legs, though his weight upon them lent some semblance of stability. He found himself grasping his sword hilts, vainly seeking to steady his suddenly unreliable hands.

They'd ventured no farther than twenty paces when the shadowed sunlight surrendered to deep blackness. Trajan stopped, drawing their first torch and bending to light it.

"I'll not trouble to list the terrors that may haunt us," he said, striking flint with steel. "Suffice to say that silence will serve us best. Should any hear a skittering," he added, his gaze finding Kylac's, "do give warning. There's a nasty beetle here that attacks in swarms, a bite from which will turn living flesh to leather. Karatikuus, they call it."

"Deadskin." Sallun said, and shivered. When the others looked at him, he added, "I've heard claim it's the same toxin by which a Ukinh strengthens its hide, and mends so quickly."

Finally, a spark caught, and Trajan's torch flared meekly to life.

"Anything else?" Kylac asked.

"Debris and tremors will threaten your footing, amid pitfalls like those I spoke of above. Yet this tunnel is said to serve as the labyrinth's spine, opening again to the southeast. Cling to it, we'll find the sageryst—and may just find ourselves closer to home when we emerge."

"*If* we emerge," Merrec muttered glumly.

"Beetles, tremors, tunnel," Kylac echoed. "And the rest as we go."

19

Into the tunneling cavern they plunged, grouped close within the meager globe of light cast by the firebrand clutched in Trajan's fist. Beyond, the stale air thickened, congealing in the absence of sun and sky. Though he couldn't see the jagged ceiling of stone hanging above their heads, Kylac felt its suffocating weight, growing heavier with every step that carried them steadily downward, deeper into the island's black bowels.

The cold that permeated the cave strengthened its grasp, scraping at Kylac's bones and numbing his flesh. He could no longer seem to control his shivering limbs—a fact that didn't bode well should the groll choose to abandon caution and strike now from out of the depthless dark. With his vision limited, he turned to his other senses. But his ears were ringing, his nose overwhelmed with unfamiliar scents, and his extrasensory awareness muddled by the wracking, feverish chills pulsing through him in relentless waves. His belly had begun to churn again with a resurgent nausea, cramping painfully in steady rhythm. Despite the penetrating cold, his brow was soaked with sweat, and his blood aboil.

By all appearances, Hadrum remained even worse off, stooped and staggering. So that Trajan could focus on leading them, Ledron had tasked Merrec with keeping the failing Blackfist upright. Merrec had griped, of course, but may as well have complained to the rocks at his feet. Hadrum himself had resisted initially, recoiling from the mercenary's touch as if it were blighted. But resistance required a strength that Fangs couldn't maintain. He slumped now against Merrec's shoulder like a moldy blanket, a burden the Redfist bore with evident distaste.

The others poisoned—Ledron and Sallun, as well as Merrec—were not quite so stricken. They at least could still sustain their own weight, while maintaining a mostly steady pace and direction—or as much as the terrain and their weakened condition would allow.

As they staggered onward, Kylac instinctively counted his paces, marking their path should they end up having to retrace it. There were no real landmarks to memorize, only enveloping darkness and a floor whose scabrous, rock-strewn surface was revealed one patch at a time by the flickering torchlight. So he noted instead any shift in direction, and the count at which it occurred. *At forty-two paces, veer north. Nineteen paces, straighten to the west. Thirty-seven paces, hook south. Twenty-five paces, jag west. Eighty-eight paces to the cave mouth.* He tracked these segments in reverse, in both sequence and direction, so that he wouldn't have to flip the entire progression all at once upon turning back. *At seventy-four paces, curl west. Forty-two paces, veer north. Nineteen paces, straighten to the west. Thirty-seven paces, hook south. Twenty-five paces, jag west. Eighty-eight paces to the cave mouth.*

The effort was largely unnecessary, he suspected, as they were primarily trekking due east or west, if coming back—with many of the turns forced upon them only because Trajan was tracing the curve of the tunnel's southern wall as a reference. But that wall was in fact riddled with other, branching offshoots. Should something happen, and they find themselves groping this way again in utter darkness, it might not be so easy to discern a side cave from the main one. Better to map the details as he went along. A simple enough matter, for one with his training. As the chain lengthened, he simply dropped the unnecessary pieces, marking only the step counts and the north–south shifts in what would be a westerly course. *Fifty-five, south. Seventy-four. Forty-two, north. Nineteen. Thirty-seven, south. Twenty-five. Eighty-eight to the cave mouth.* He repeated the string as a litany with every step, adding rhythm and cadence—like learning the lyrics to a tune. *Fifty-five, south. Seventy-four. Forty-two, north. Nineteen. Thirty-seven, south . . .*

If nothing else, it gave him something with which to occupy his mind, to distract him from the venom's gnawing effects and the elsewise boundless repetition of their journey.

He'd marked eleven segments—some six hundred and twelve paces in all—when their torch guttered weakly, having consumed the pitch-coated length to reach the small, bare haft by which Trajan clutched it. Darkness closed round like floodwaters as the flames withered, but was driven back as the Tower lit the head of their next brand from the dying tendrils of the first. The discarded stub glowed feebly for a moment, then vanished in a well of black.

Fresh light in hand, they proceeded.

Soon thereafter, Kylac noted a rising heat. Yet his shivers only grew stronger. *The poison,* he thought, *stewing in my veins.*

He believed as much until Denariel said, "That warmth . . . where is it coming from?"

The echo of her voice was startling, though it was swallowed quickly by the dark.

"A vent," Trajan replied, more quietly. "Said to lie at the warren's heart. Some manner of volcanic rift. Near to where the mineral we need will be found."

Kylac took note. Should they become separated, he might follow the heat to its source.

"Are we getting close, then?" Merrec dared to whisper.

Trajan ignored him.

"How does one consume this sageryst?" Kylac asked.

This, the Tower answered. "Grind it up, drink it down. Nothing could be simpler."

Compared to what they'd been dealing with, sure. Though Kylac had neglected to carry with him an alchemist's mortar and pestle. Nor was there any great assurance that, in the end, they would still have water in their skins or strength enough to lift them.

The windless air grew dank, the walls themselves trickling with salty moisture—the one Kylac could see, at least. *The very stone sweats.*

Not from the heat, of course, though it seemed that way. The setting soon reminded Kylac of the tunnels inside Mount Krakken, through which he'd delved to face the dragon Killangrathor. Though the great beast was said to have been the last of its magnificent breed, he couldn't help but wonder if another of the monsters might lurk somewhere below.

Sharp stone spears emerged before them, hanging above their heads like icicles. Gazes turned skyward, but as before could see nothing of the ceiling to which the formations were rooted. They might have been six-feet long or sixty, though judging by their slim width and the shape of stalactites he'd encountered in the past, Kylac's wager would have lain with the former. Which meant the tunnel itself was narrowing—at least from its size at the cave mouth. Whether that made any difference whatsoever with regard to their journey was more difficult to guess.

He was admiring a particularly strange, double-tipped spear when an ominous rumble led to quakelike reverberations. Trajan paused, bracing as if to draw his axe, so the others froze alongside. Kylac wondered at the wisdom of doing so beneath so many daggers of stone, but chose not to speak of it, instead keeping silent overhead watch while loose rocks rattled at their feet.

"Not so terrible," Merrec said, when the trembling had subsided.

They had time enough merely to draw breath, however, before it began again, twice as violent as before. Kylac heard cracking overhead, and didn't hesitate.

"Back!" he shouted, as a stalactite broke free to shatter upon their left flank.

He observed the others as they reversed past him. Ledron did so while shielding Denariel from the silt and dust and bits of shale raining from above. Sallun scurried after them, head ducked low. Trajan backed away more cautiously, eyes lifting to mark the path of falling debris.

Merrec was the last to respond, but did so by shoving free of Hadrum and scrabbling back in a panic. Hadrum fell toward a fringe of darkness, where he dropped like a sack of grain. Kylac started after him, but was forced to dodge as another stalactite came crashing down, splintering into a thousand fragments. Another clipped his shoulder when he tried to redirect.

Trajan, seeing this, slowed his own retreat, trying to thread the border between those racing from harm's way, and those still in it, so that none would be deprived entirely of the torchlight.

"Quickly!" the Tower barked, withdrawing another pace. Kylac knew that, when forced to choose, the Blackfist would cater to his captain and princess.

Kylac finally managed to lunge forward to squeeze Hadrum's arm. Fangs regarded him with glazed eyes. Kylac dropped low, grabbing that arm and drawing it over his own shoulders. Stepping forward with one leg for the required leverage, Kylac pressed himself to his feet, hefting Hadrum in the bargain.

Trajan's firebrand no longer lit their path, but its glow was still a beacon amid the encroaching black. Kylac tread after it, all but dragging Hadrum with him.

Then the ground beneath them shifted. Kylac tilted toward Hadrum as a crust of stone that masked a hidden sinkhole crumbled beneath their weight. His stomach lurched as he found himself falling. He grasped reflexively for the lip of remaining stone, then tried to catch his companion. But Fangs, weakened beyond any clutching of his own, slipped away like a slab of butchered meat, vanishing soundlessly into the sudden void.

Kylac counted nine heartbeats before the Blackfist's voiceless descent ended abruptly with a splattering smack.

After checking his hold, he hauled himself out of that black pitfall, fighting a plummeting sensation of his own. Stepping carefully amid a debris-littered floor invisible at his own feet, he hastened after his remaining companions.

He found them huddled together within a niche in the tunnel's wall, aback of any visible stalactites or other obvious dangers. A fresh layer of dust darkened the stubbled, sweat-streaked faces that marked his arrival.

"Hadrum?" Ledron asked.

Kylac glanced at Merrec, then shook his head.

The temblor had subsided, though it had yet to cease. The tunnel still groaned and cracked in irritation.

"Tremors, you said," the mercenary snorted, glaring at Trajan. "The earth is collapsing around us."

"Then rot here, if you prefer. It's your blood we came to cleanse, not mine."

"And your throat the groll will rend when we're gone," Merrec muttered. The others glared at him, but all knew the situation. "Kronus there is the only reason the mutant hasn't killed you already."

A strange fact, given how Kylac felt. Though he'd proven more resilient to the groll's venom than Hadrum, his own condition was fast deteriorating. Were the Ukinh to engage him now, it might not find him so formidable an opponent.

"Can we proceed?" Ledron asked Trajan.

The Tower shrugged. "Only one way to know."

So they set forth again, with Kylac having to adjust his step count for this particular segment, based on how many paces he guessed they'd retreated. When he came again upon the dual-pronged stalactite he'd noted earlier, however, maintaining its grip upon the ceiling, he was able to discard his estimate and take up his count from before.

Of meager consolation, but any was better than none at all.

As they proceeded, it struck him that the reverberations still rippling through the stone had become constant. Volcanic tremors, in his experience, waxed and waned, which left him to wonder if this wasn't something else entirely. Landslides, mayhap, or cave-ins, triggered by the larger quake. It might take some time for the earth to settle. Now and again, he heard what sounded like distant roars, like some great creature bellowing amid the depths. But it could as easily have been the earth, grating and grinding against itself. The sounds here were as foreign as the smells, and, though unpleasant, Kylac would assume them harmless until they proved elsewise.

The narrowing of the tunnel he'd observed before continued. Before long, the walls on either flank became visible, as did the ceiling. The earth grew wetter, as well, invaded with briny moisture. Support beams appeared, thick wooden ribs bracing overhead spans of lagging. Many sagged or bowed, seeping mineral water, looking more hazard than help. That they remained at all after so many centuries seemed a marvel. Kylac touched one in passing, and found it petrified, more stone now than timber.

Twice more, quakes forced them to halt their advance and take shelter within shallow depressions in the walls, while dust and shale fragments cascaded from the ceiling. But neither was worse than the first, and their journey on both occasions resumed swiftly.

They were some two thousand paces in, already on their fourth torch, when their forward trek came to an abrupt end.

A wall of granite and clay blocked their path, the tumbledown remains of a cave-in. It appeared to have happened recently. A haze of dust still choked the air, while the stones themselves displayed clean planes and sharp edges. But of course it had happened recently, Kylac thought, for the timing was yet again too perfect to be anything less than the groll's work.

"Seems your beastie remains busy."

Denariel seemed to agree, her sudden chuckle echoing with derision. "Your move, Captain."

Sallun's face reflected a sheen of disbelief. "The groll did this? How could it . . . could it possibly . . . ?"

Kylac was wondering the same. Amid the clogging mound, support beams lay mangled and splintered. For all its strength and cunning, the mutant couldn't have wrenched those mineralized pillars free, or caused the quake that had brought the ceiling low.

Could it?

As if in answer, there came another of those roars from the earthen depths, seeming to emerge from a dozen tunnels and vents all at once, making its location impossible to pinpoint. This one, however, was loud and near enough for Kylac to determine that it was no crushed sigh given off by the crumbling earth.

There was life in that cry.

All froze as the monstrous echo subsided. When it had, Sallun's and Merrec's faces were terror-stricken. Even Denariel's mocking grin had vanished.

The muscles in Trajan's forearm flexed as he gripped their torch. "Jaggeruunt," he whispered.

What's a jaggeruunt? Kylac wanted to ask, but the grim horror etched upon the lines of Trajan's face suggested silence.

The Tower waited a moment longer, then approached the blockage. Kylac, meanwhile, had taken note of a gaping side tunnel that veered in from the southwest. A heat seemed to be emanating from it, as well as a fetid odor unlike any he'd smelled before now.

He was drifting toward it when a couple of midsized rocks rolled from the broken mound, to tumble toward their party. Pulled free by Trajan, Kylac realized, who was testing the landslide's thickness. One of the bouncing stones forced Kylac to step aside. Another caught Merrec a glancing blow against his shin.

"Bloody maggots!" the mercenary hissed.

The jaggeruunt's cry came again, louder than before. This time, it seemed to emanate chiefly from the cave that had caught Kylac's interest.

Trajan joined him at the mouth of that breach. Upon reaching out to brush its inner lip, he withdrew his fingers as if burned.

"It's near," the Tower said, then turned toward Ledron. "We must go. Now."

"Where?" Sallun asked.

"Back. Else into one of these other tunnels. Perhaps we can work our way around."

Ledron's jaw clenched.

"Can it not be killed?" Kylac asked, tapping the hilt of his longsword.

The next cry shook the cavern, filling his ears with fury and torment. Stones danced and rolled from the wedge of shattered earth that blocked their path. The floor began to tremble.

"Try, and your flesh will become mortar for these stones. Captain."

"The tunnels," Ledron agreed.

Trajan nodded, gripping Denariel's arm with his free hand and all but flinging her back the way they'd come. Ledron, Merrec, and Sallun followed. Kylac hesitated, peering into the quaking depths of that mysterious cave mouth, tasting its warm, fetid breath and listening to a shrill, grating rumble now echoing from within.

He considered lingering long enough to at least glimpse the creature, if not to test his blades against it. But he wasn't going to glimpse much when left alone in pitch darkness, and was hardly feeling his best. Giving him little choice but to bank his curiosity in this instance.

He caught up to the others nine paces to the west, where Trajan's torch probed a north-facing fissure barely large enough for him to squeeze through.

"A smaller vein than most," Ledron observed.

"May it dissuade the beast from giving chase," Trajan said, and ducked inside.

Denariel cast about, then entered on his heels. Ledron had her back, motioning for Sallun to have his. Merrec looked at Kylac. He seemed about to suggest something, when a staggering roar rattled the earth at their feet.

His face a mask of fear in the deepening shadows, Merrec dove into the cleft. Amid the rumbling blackness, Kylac followed.

20

The darkness and the quaking gave chase, nipping at Kylac's heels as he trailed his companions through the narrow passage. He wasn't entirely sure why he bothered. His lungs burned, and his vision had begun to blur. With his health worsening, he was reminded with every step that these could be his final moments—no longer hours, but moments. Did he wish to exhaust them in frantic flight through these cramped corridors? Or would he find truer peace turning about to engage the thing that hunted him, meeting death with defiance?

Dogged by uncertainty, he obeyed his instincts, which told him that the true fight lay before him, not behind. Blindly confronting the jaggeruunt would cost him time and energy better spent in pursuit of the sageryst. Aside from that, these others still depended on him. He wasn't going to forsake the promise he'd made to safeguard them from the groll simply to chase some prideful notion of a warrior's end.

His pride in his word was stronger.

Mayhap ya should stop giving it so freely, he thought.

The tunnel they'd entered widened, but continued to curl and twist, intersecting with other passages every few paces. A veritable honeycomb lay before them, now that they'd abandoned the warren's spine. Trajan was displaying no hesitation in choosing one branch from the next, but that had more to do with the burrowing pursuit of the creature that hunted them, Kylac suspected, than any navigational prowess the Tower might possess in this labyrinthine dark. They jogged where they could, and strode swiftly where they couldn't, setting caution aside in order to escape the known threat behind them.

That driven pace seemed to fulfill its intended purpose. Little by little, the cracking and grinding of the jaggeruunt's passage, along with its trumpeting cries, diminished in strength. It happened quickly enough, in fact, that Kylac wondered if the creature had ever actually caught their scent. Mayhap theirs was an accidental brush. Or mayhap, as Trajan had hoped, the beast had clung to a wider branch of tunnels, deeming these foreign intruders unworthy of its effort. He could scarcely even guess without knowing more about their invisible foe.

When the tunnel widened enough to allow three abreast, he closed ranks with the others and decided to ask. "Care to tells me what we're running from?"

A distant roar clawed at the craggy walls in powerless frustration. Trajan glanced back, then eased his reckless pace.

"A creation of the Breeders," the Tower replied.

"Naturally." *Or* unnaturally. "For what purpose?"

"To dig these caverns, perhaps." The Tower's breathing was labored. "An earth-rending behemoth, set to core amid the earth's cracks and fissures."

"Ah." That was why that other passage, near the cave-in, had been warm. It had only recently been dug, or at least expanded. He thought of the basilisks encountered alongside Torin beneath the ruins of Thrak-Symbos—an age ago, it seemed. "We seem to have outpaced it."

Trajan finally stopped. To catch his breath, Kylac supposed, though it was also about time to light a new brand. The current one was fast succumbing to the darkness. "Lumbering, yes, but invulnerable. Should it find us, it would grind us all into pulp."

"So it wasn't the groll that blocked the tunnel?" Merrec asked.

Trajan scowled, but saw that others shared the mercenary's question. "When the Breeders were no more, the jaggeruunts burrowed underground to fathomless depths." He shook his mane of hair. "I did not count them among the perils we might face."

Which might better explain the Tower's concern. If even the rarer dangers were manifesting . . .

"You're suggesting the mutant awakened it," Ledron said, "flushed it from below."

Baiting it to lash out and destroy the main tunnel, Kylac thought. The brutish jaggeruunt may have performed the work, but it was the groll that had directed it, forcing them into the maze of smaller caves in which they now found themselves.

"We made the right choice," Trajan insisted, as the new torch flared to life. "These passages will return us to the primary tunnel at some point. We need only find the right trail."

Spoken with great confidence—for the sake of his listeners, it seemed to Kylac, as he met the Tower's gaze. He hoped there was something more to it than mere bluster.

Their trek resumed, though they proceeded this time more deliberately than before, taking pause at each tunneling fork to discern what they could of its path. Which was little. A tube veering right might loop to the left. A vein wrapping left might twist to the right. Sometimes, separate offshoots reconnected farther on, making the time spent in selecting one from the other a wasted effort. Other branches simply rejoined the trunk from which they'd split, carrying them in a complete circle. Else Trajan would guide them down a long, winding tube that led only to a wall of rock and a vertical shaft too steep and narrow to climb, leaving no choice but to retrace their steps.

There seemed neither logic nor pattern applied to the warren as a whole, and no clues to indicate what lay even three paces beyond their meager light. The best Kylac could do was to memorize those passages they'd already traversed, preventing them from repeating past failures.

"Dead end," he remarked at a three-way split, when Trajan started to the left.

The Tower looked to the right. Kylac shook his head. "That one brought us here. We try the center, or double back twelve paces to the fork on our left."

Trajan appeared doubtful. "You're certain? None of this looks familiar."

"We's been here already," Kylac assured him. "Twice."

Trajan clenched his jaw in frustration. "Bloody shards. Am I as lost as that?"

They took the central tunnel. Better that than intentionally backtrack over covered ground—never mind that the opening behind them might as easily lead forward as the one ahead.

This time, fortune favored them. Though it weaved and curved with almost every step, the vein continued unbroken for nearly fifty paces. At the next junction, they hung right, and again at the next. A dead end forced them to redirect, but Kylac spotted a fissure hidden in a fold of the wall that opened onto a parallel tunnel larger and smoother than the one they followed, allowing them to progress in their easterly course.

The rumbling caused by the jaggeruunt had all but faded. Its occasional cry still echoed out of the dark, but the huffing and grinding had settled enough to alleviate that particular fear. Kylac had begun to sense their luck had turned, that fate might see them through this after all.

Then a new sound arose—a faint, shrill scratching.

"Listen," warned Kylac, holding up the others.

He met with fretful expressions. Denariel's gave way quickly to annoyance. "To what?"

Would that it were merely a ringing in his ears. But Kylac knew elsewise. Amid the breathing of the caves, the scratching grew louder, with the tone and cadence of rushing waters. A moment later, Sallun's ears pricked. Then Trajan's.

"Just the wind," Merrec suggested nervously.

Ledron hissed at him, scowling as he, too, strained to hear.

By then, there was no mistaking the swelling sound, a fierce skittering rising fast on their heels.

Trajan confirmed it. "Karatikuus."

And so they ran, faster than before, loping through the darkness with pounding hearts and sweating limbs. The labyrinth persisted ahead of them. Each time the tunnel split, Trajan selected the largest opening and drove down its gullet. All the while, the intensity of the skittering grew, approaching from every direction, reverberating about the jagged walls until Kylac imagined them aswarm with pincered little creatures, armored in obsidian shells.

Then the encroaching tide revealed itself at their backs, and the time for imagining was past. Kylac glimpsed them as the vanguard came around the corner, like foam scudding on a wavecrest. Not obsidian, as he'd assumed, but iridescent, glinting green and silver in the dim fringe of their torch's light.

"Will fire slow them?" he asked.

"No," Trajan huffed.

"Then ya'd best run."

His companions turned their heads, looking back as the screeching of a thousand tiny legs crescendoed, filling the tunnel behind them. There, the emerging beetles surged like floodwaters, leaping and crawling over one another in waves, swerving around corners, splashing over mounds and jags, stray bodies flinging up like bits of spray. They covered the floors, the walls, and eventually the ceiling as more and more rushed in, to lay claim to every inch of rocky earth.

Eyes widened. Merrec whimpered. Then all were whipping back around, racing forward in reckless haste. A stumbling, lurching sprint over uneven terrain ensued. Their formation seemed to hold, though only Ledron did anything to maintain it. The Head drove Denariel before him, a step behind their long-legged leader and torch-bearer, Trajan. Sallun and Merrec were stride for stride a pace or two back, each casting desperate, rearward glances at Kylac, who, though he could have overtaken them, didn't. He'd sworn to shield them, and shield them he would . . . though he wasn't sure how.

He could hear the beetles, and feel them gaining ground, but knew enough to keep his eyes forward. Merrec did not. One too many frightened looks over his shoulder distracted the mercenary from a ragged hump that jutted from the tunnel wall.

"Eyes ahead!" Kylac shouted in warning.

Merrec turned too late. The protruding rock clipped his thigh, spinning him out of control. He gasped, then grasped at Sallun like a man about to drown, seizing a fistful of the lookout's cloak and dragging him down from behind.

Kylac heard a snap of bone and watched Sallun collapse awkwardly to one side. The young lookout yelped in pain, reaching reflexively for his ankle. Already, Merrec was scrabbling madly to his feet, clawing and crawling his way forward at Sallun's expense, looking at Kylac with a mix of fury and terror—and lacking any apology—as he shoved the injured lookout aside to continue on his way.

Ledron glanced back at the commotion, but ran on. As did Trajan. Their concern was for Denariel. Only Kylac stopped, dropping to a knee at Sallun's side.

"Grab my arm," he urged.

Even that simple motion caused Sallun to squeal with fresh pain. Kylac saw the weird lump in Sallun's boot. His lower leg was not just cracked, but splintered.

"Go!" the lookout cried.

The light around them was retreating, fleeing down the tunnel with Trajan. At their backs, the darkness approached like a spreading pool of blood spilled at night in a black alley.

"Ahh!" Sallun howled when Kylac tried to drag him to his feet.

The black pool spread, dividing and taking form as a horde of green-and-silver deadskin beetles. The sound of the insects' skittering was like the shriek of a blade scraped against heavy plate.

Kylac drew his swords.

"What are you doing?" Sallun asked, when Kylac stepped over the downed lookout to crouch between him and the arriving swarm.

The karatikuus were large, of a size like a child's fist. Large enough to strike. Kylac met them the only way he could, blades dicing upon the floor, killing a dozen with every stroke. And his strokes came quickly, so that scores died within just a few instants. As guts oozed from the slivered shells, the nearest beetles converged, cannibalizing the exposed remains of their comrades. The tide seemed to collapse upon itself, and, for half a heartbeat, it appeared it might actually be stemmed.

But scores dead did not account for the hundreds pouring after. Though the floor before him thickened with bloody insect pulp and the crush of those gorging upon it, karatikuus at the edges leaked past, skirting his flanks. Kylac saw them, felt them, as they swarmed over his boots, rushing to reach Sallun.

The lookout wailed as their pincers tore at him.

"The princess!" Sallun wept. "Your duty . . . is to Her Highness!"

Kylac growled and redoubled his effort, sweeping his feet across the ground to send dozens flying, stomping on others to crunch their shells and splay their innards. But the spreading carnage seemed only to incite the others. Delay as they might to feed, nothing within his immediate power was going to deter them all. Nothing he could do would turn them about or keep them at bay.

"Go! Go!" Sallun insisted, jerking and writhing as the beetles nipped at his flesh. He tried to say it once more, but a karatikuus had crawled into his mouth, strangling him from within. While gagging on its armored body, he managed to produce the dagger Kylac had given him, offering it up with a trembling hand.

Kylac cursed and hopped back over his young comrade, opening the lookout's jugular with a flick of his trailing wrist and the long-sword gripped loosely in that hand. He knelt, jabbing his shortsword into the earth for the heartbeat he needed to retrieve and sheathe Sallun's dagger. An instant later, he could scarcely see the lad beneath the churning blanket of deadskin beetles smothering him beneath the departing light.

Departing, not departed. Something had caused his surviving companions to hold up. Kylac turned and ran, beating beetles off his legs and out of his cloak, shedding the garment when he realized just how infested it was. By some miracle, he had yet to be bitten. *Because they're too busy devouring their own . . . and Sallun.* Candle, he might have been called, with his unruly, flame-colored hair and those freckles like sparks upon his waxen cheeks. Or Skulks, as Kylac had known him originally, before rescuing him from Ulflund's pack in Wingport. So much had the lad endured on this journey, only to have it end like this. *I should has listened to that greasy barkeep,* Kylac reflected. *I should has let him be.*

Quickly enough, he came upon the others, and realized why they'd stopped. The trail they followed had opened into a broad, pocket cavern. But there it ended. Trajan and Ledron were searching frantically for some opening amid the creased walls, while Denariel, seeming small and frightened for the first time, hugged herself in the center of the chamber. Merrec, he found curled low against a niche in the far wall, the Roach shrinking into it as if seeking to escape back into his mother's womb.

"Is there no exit?" Kylac asked as he arrived.

"Do you see one?" Ledron barked.

"What about that?" He pointed with his shortsword to a hole in the ceiling, some four heads above them. A natural chimney leading upward into more darkness.

"Heft me up," Ledron commanded Trajan.

The Tower obeyed, dropping his torch and locking his hands to form a stirrup. Ledron stepped into it, and with a heave from Trajan's powerful shoulders, was able to squirm his way into the void.

"I can't see where it goes," he called down, his voice muffled within the tube of hollowed rock.

"It's that or the way we came," Trajan reminded him. "I'm sending Her Highness up."

Denariel didn't object. By the sound of their approach, the beetles had finished feasting upon the first course, and were eager for the second.

As she clawed her way up into the chimney, a torch flared above her. Ledron, it seemed, had managed to ignite one of the brands he carried.

"There's a pocket here," the Head called down, "but it narrows farther on."

"Just go!" Trajan urged again. "Kronus."

"Send Merrec," Kylac said.

The Roach, reaching a level of awareness to overcome his panic, all but lunged out of his chosen corner. The Tower, however, scowled that fierce glare of his, and made no move to offer aid.

The first beetles appeared at the mouth of the cavern, probing like eager wavelets.

"Let's go!" Merrec pleaded.

Trajan lifted the mercenary, then beckoned again for Kylac, who sheathed his blades.

"How will you follow?" Kylac asked, as he stepped into the Tower's interlocked hands. A larger flow of beetles washed in, spreading along the chamber's edges.

Trajan tossed him skyward like the others. Merrec cleared a path quickly enough, scurrying after Ledron and Denariel. Inside the pocket that Ledron had observed, Kylac quickly braced himself in a seated position, hands reaching down.

"Jump!" he shouted down.

Trajan glanced around at the deadskin beetles filling the lower chamber. From Kylac's vantage, the floor and walls seemed to ripple with their swarming, green-and-silver bodies.

With the upturned look Trajan gave him, Kylac feared the Tower meant not to join him.

But then the big man crouched and leapt high, arms outstretched. Kylac caught him by the elbows, and there strained to hold him. Pulling with his back and pressing with his legs, he managed to haul the Tower high enough for Trajan to grasp the rocky sides of the vent.

When safely situated, the Blackfist inclined his shaggy head in gratitude. "After you."

Kylac turned at once, fighting to keep his breathing steady as the walls gripped him like those of a tomb. He could still hear the scratching and screeching of the karatikuus giving chase. Ahead, Merrec was struggling to thrash his way through a crook in the chimney's passage. The vent narrowed at the same time, as Ledron had warned, making it doubly difficult to navigate. With Ledron tugging roughly from the other side, however, the Roach finally cleared the obstacle, huffing and cursing as the jagged rocks pierced and scraped at his skin.

Behind Kylac, Trajan inhaled sharply.

"What is it?" Kylac asked.

"Just go," the Tower urged.

Kylac measured the narrow gap ahead and angled himself accordingly. Though it took some creative maneuvering, he passed through with minimal difficulty. Barely three feet beyond that bend, the vent opened into another, level tunnel. That's where he found Ledron, Denariel, and Merrec, taking stock of themselves and one another.

"Come!" Kylac hissed, peering back into the chimney.

Trajan, wide and burly and long as he was, seemed to be wedged within the narrow bend. Only his head, an arm, and half of his broad chest poked through. The other shoulder appeared caught on a crag.

"Hold there," Kylac bade him, freeing a dagger and reaching back down the hole. "I'll chisel ya free."

The Tower winced, and then winced again. "No time," he said. "Go."

Kylac jabbed at the stone, chipping at the corners that had the Blackfist trapped.

"Damn it!" Trajan snapped. "It's too late!"

Kylac jabbed again. A small chunk of rock fell away. From the resulting gap emerged a deadskin beetle. Kylac withdrew reflexively, then pierced the insect on the tip of his blade before it could bite Trajan's face.

But he saw in the Tower's pained expression that there were others, nipping at him from below. Kylac could hear their skittering excitement, and hesitated.

"Go, I thay."

Thay? Trajan looked down at his tongue, which appeared to shrivel and harden while Kylac watched, as if all the moisture was being sucked out of it. When he looked up again, the whites of his eyes were shot through with reddening veins. His cheeks and brow crinkled at the edges, while deepening seams spread throughout.

"Will trap 'em here," he wheezed. "Long ath I can. Thee her home."

Kylac stabbed another beetle as it emerged from the hole at Trajan's throat, then slashed that throat in the bargain. By then, the Tower's skin felt more like deerskin hide, and little blood seeped out. So he plunged his dagger into the Blackfist's eye, deep into the brain. Trajan stiffened. A twist, and it was done.

Kylac pulled free of the hole, cursing and chipping at the stone lip to send bits of rocky debris sliding down, helping to bury the Tower's face and further plug any gaps between his body and the walls of the chimney. A temporary shield at best. The karatikuus would engulf and devour him quickly enough, and their pursuit would resume.

The remaining three looked at him. Ledron, Merrec, and Denariel— for whom it seemed all would indeed be asked to surrender their lives.

"Bring the torch," said Kylac, and turned right, embarking down the tunnel.

21

Nᴏɴᴇ ǫᴜᴇsᴛɪᴏɴᴇᴅ ʜɪᴍ, initially. Numb with shock, it seemed. Content to follow him—or anyone else, more likely than not—so long as he led them *away*. Ledron jogged in step with Denariel, a guiding hand upon her back, while the torch crackled weakly in his other, flame whipping and snapping like a windblown pennon. Its glow lit the ground and walls in a dim globe, and, at Kylac's back, cast his shadow before them, where his ready blades stood out like the spines of some demonic creature. Etched in light, that shadow stood out sharply against those into which they delved, whose writhing forms withdrew only reluctantly into nooks and crevices, behind crags and corners, as the group pressed them, then reappeared as swiftly behind Merrec, as if to consume any possible path of return.

The Roach himself kept glancing back, seeming to fear that they might consume *him*, too. *Take him, if'n ya can stomach the taste,* Kylac bade the trailing darkness. Long had he tolerated the mercenary— even been amused at times by how deep and unabashed the Redfist's greed and selfishness ran. With what Merrec had done to Sallun, however . . . it seemed now to Kylac that they'd suffered the mercenary quite enough. Were circumstances any better, he might have taken the pleasure to gut and flay the craven himself.

Instead, he trained his dizzied focus on the path ahead, picking their route amid the coring black. His step counts were long gone. He relied now on his inner compass and instincts alone. How they might ever find their way out again was of little consequence compared to their need to outpace the karatikuus and find their way to the warren's heart.

"You'd do better to surrender me now," Denariel commented, after several moments of uncertain progress. "Should you leave me to him, perhaps he may spare you."

Speaking of the groll, of course. Kylac ignored the suggestion, as did Ledron. Mayhap Merrec took this to mean they were considering her counsel, for he called forward, asking, "What will it accomplish for us all to die at Her Highness's feet?"

Kylac responded through gritted teeth. "In your case, a swifter, cleaner passing than ya'll find at mine." He turned his head for Merrec's reaction. The Roach had the audacity to look surprised, and put forth a wounded expression. At the same time, his eyes beaded darkly. *He takes my meaning well enough,* thought Kylac. Should the mercenary redeem himself, Kylac might indeed ease his dying as he had some of the others on this journey. Elsewise, there were ways in which to prolong a man's suffering, even one whose life promised already to be short-lived.

"What direction do we follow?" Ledron asked. There was a hesitancy in his normally sure voice, as if wary of the answer.

"Heat and smell," Kylac replied. "They should lead us to the core." It wasn't a complete lie. Furnace-like breezes brushed his fevered face, carrying the scent of sulfurous gases finding vent amid the cracked earth. They were close. But, being this close, the heat and stench were thick all around—in each tunnel and every gap and fissure. What he thought lay just ahead might as easily be lurking beneath, beside, or behind them.

"Can you see well enough?" Ledron asked, bringing the torch forward.

"Well enough," Kylac assured him, nudging him back. In front, the harsh light might blind him in spots—from which a cunning adversary might launch an attack. Better to have less light and short warning than too much and none at all.

Their ragtag company hurried on because it was all that was left to them. There was no time to mourn, no time to rest, and no purpose in doing so. Their only hope was to keep moving as swiftly and for as long as they could, begging mercy of whatever gods might chance to hear them this close to the Abyss.

The shrill clawing of the deadskin beetles had died to a whisper. A momentary triumph, it seemed, though Kylac held his pace. Should he allow their group to slow, he might not get them moving again—himself included. If the beetles didn't catch up to them, the venom in their veins would. Rest was no longer an option, lest it become permanent.

The twisting corridor widened abruptly, and, for a moment, Kylac thought they'd stumbled upon the warren's spine at last. Alas, it proved but a cavern, though much larger than the one from which the four of them had climbed. He could tell by the altered echo of their shuffling footfalls, and because it felt suddenly as if a great weight had slipped from his shoulders. An open space, and vast, it was to Kylac like a breath of fresh air.

Instead of arcing along its wall in search of the nearest opening, Kylac plunged directly ahead, into the void. Shallow craters appeared upon the floor at their feet, forcing him along the narrow webwork of ridges that ran between them. He wondered what the appearance of these hollows might indicate. Would that Trajan were there to tell him.

Their steps brought them to a wall on the far side. Veering south, he found another corridor, and ventured into it. If any still questioned his course, they did so silently. Mayhap his decisiveness had convinced them. Mayhap none wanted to know the truth.

The corridor this time proved short, leading to another pockmarked cavern. He crossed it as he had the last, only veered east, again taking the nearest side tunnel. His sense—based again on echoes, subtle wind currents, and his observations of the terrain that lay behind them—was that these caverns were interconnected by multiple thread passages, and that therefore it scarcely mattered which one he chose. All he knew with relative certainty was that they needed to be heading south by east, and that, if they continued to do so, they must eventually spill back out into the main tunnel from which this forsaken leg of their journey had begun.

Unless, of course, his venom-addled senses had failed him somewhere along the way.

The possibility weighed heavier with every step, every bend, every worming exit that led to but another cavern or passage. Surely they should have reached the spine by now. Was there no chance he'd gotten himself turned around during their flight? A half step measured at the wrong angle was all it might have taken to knock his inner bearings off kilter.

But that way lay doubt, and the last thing he needed was to start turning circles north, south, east, west in hopeless desperation. Better to cling to the path he'd chosen, and see it through.

Another tunnel led to another cavern, which brought them to another tunnel. And then, abruptly, there it was, widening around them with those telltale ribbed arches. The warren's spine. A river compared to the series of narrow streams down which they'd been flowing. His patience rewarded, Kylac breathed a silent sigh of relief, pausing there at the confluence between empty stream and barren river while Ledron grunted approvingly and reached to light a new brand.

"One left, after this," the captain informed them.

Kylac nodded. What else to say? Their light would last until it didn't . . . just like the rest of them.

"Is this it?" asked Merrec, peering out from the mouth of the smaller tunnel. "Why have we—"

The question was cut short by a sharp, quick gasp. Kylac turned his head to find Merrec with a startled expression upon his face—an instant before being yanked backward into darkness.

Kylac lunged, shielding Ledron and Denariel while peering back into the smaller tunnel. By then, Merrec was wailing in fright, his cries echoing helplessly within that rocky tube.

"Captain?" Kylac asked.

"Shards!" Ledron swore, fumbling the unlit torch and burning himself with the other. "What now?"

"It's him," said Denariel.

"Go!" Ledron barked, as he stooped to retrieve the fallen brand.

By that command, the Head might have meant for them to flee forward, down the spine. But Kylac took it as permission to double back. And so he did, determined not so much to rescue Merrec as to settle matters with the groll, for once and all.

That must indeed have been Ledron's will, for the torch followed, lighting his path with its withering curls. Denariel hurried alongside, as if afraid to be left alone in the dark. She actually started to outpace the captain, until he clamped a restraining hand upon her arm.

Their journey didn't last long. As they rounded a crook in the passage less than twenty paces in, Kylac caught sight of Merrec's feet— just as they were snatched skyward from view. Another chimney, he realized. He and his companions gathered beneath it. The ceiling hung low enough that he might squirm his way into it . . . but once inside the narrow vent, how to bring his weapons to bear?

Kylac's hope for pursuit faded along with the departing echoes of Merrec's screams, which grew ever more panicked, then peaked with a curdling shriek of pain. A quicker end than he deserved. Or so Kylac thought, until the cries continued, one after the other—a staggered string of yelps and yowls amid a steady, gut-wrenching wailing.

"So kill him and be done with it," Ledron muttered grimly.

"A show of strength," Kylac observed. "To tell us what's in store."

Ledron snorted. "Means to finish us itself, does it?"

"And savor the moment, it seems, after so long a wait."

"A fool's errand, Captain," Denariel offered. "As it was from the first."

"Soon ended." A surge of defiance burned through Kylac, fueling his confidence. The straits were dire, but a vessel rocked was not a vessel capsized. This turn seemed to him a break in the storm. "To confront us directly, it must abandon the shadows." His hands flexed around the hilts of his blades. "That's all I ask."

Denariel rolled her eyes and shook her head. Her fearlessness, he admired. Her dour, defeatist attitude, he would as well do without. A paradox, this woman. Death meant little to her, it seemed, so long as she could boast of being right.

He led them back, ushered even then by Merrec's unrelenting screams. Ledron lit the new torch as they went. Its fresh flame filled the narrow passage, chasing shadows over the sharpest crags and into the deepest crevices. For a few brief moments, the darkness retreated. As they returned to the main tunnel, however, it gathered again in heavy folds, weighing heavily upon the fringes of their small globe—like a lone candle surrounded by night.

They turned east, into the belly of that darkness, keeping clear of the scabrous walls. Clefts, jags, support beams—easy places from which the groll might strike without warning. If the creature were to step forth and meet them, as Kylac believed it must, he was determined that it should happen out in the open, free at last of guile or surprise.

Sickness, exhaustion, hunger, thirst—he could no longer recall a life without them. They assailed him with every step . . . sapping strength, eroding confidence. He was the world's greatest fighter. He would have to lie dead, defeated, before he believed elsewise. Was this truly to be his fate? To drudge his way through this infernal tunnel until his legs gave beneath him? Should that happen, would it be the venom that savaged him from the inside out, or the groll that shredded his helpless body from the outside in?

He struggled to stay alert, keeping an eye out for those ambush points. But his head throbbed, and his stomach churned. His legs dragged, and his arms shook. His vision blurred, and the light seemed to dim.

His thoughts drifted, conjuring recollections of faces, locations, and events of his past—and others that had never been. Names eluded him, so that it became harder and harder to tell memory from fantasy. Friends, foes, and misbegotten images of nonexistent strangers hounded him like a rabid throng, laughing at him—or weeping; it was difficult to tell. Some bled, many from wounds delivered by his own hand. The spirits of victims, he supposed, returned to escort him into the afterlife. It caused him to wonder, would he be as formidable a warrior there as he'd been here?

Ghouls and phantoms, he told himself. Fevered imaginings without power or substance except that which he granted them. But that understanding kept falling farther and farther to the back of his mind, shoved aside by fanciful matters that demanded attention, seeming of great importance. The frog on the end of his fishing pole, whose

skin turned orange when he dipped it in the river. The battlement of
wet sand that collapsed as it dried, drawing sentries made of colored
glass down amid windblown dunes, while an army of camel-riding
jesters and boar-mounted scarecrows swept near to trample them.
The maiden with pink hair and pleasant smile, who didn't seem
to realize that her legs were being devoured by a swarm of yellow
mites. Kylac pointed, to show her. When he looked back up, her face
had been replaced by Sallun's, beneath a hood of cresting sea waves.
As those waves fell forward to cover the lookout's eyes, Sallun and
ocean alike melted away, falling into a smoking chasm from which a
blistered moon fought weakly to rise. The cliffs forming the chasm
began to quake, and—

"Kronus!"

The earth jolted and the cliffs fell away. He looked up . . . into the
dirty, unshaven face of a man with an intense gaze, clenched jaw, and
a once-shorn head giving rise now to fields of stubble in horseshoe
formation around a bald pate. Ledron. The head of a torch—his
blistered moon—flared brightly before his eyes.

"Not yet, lad." The peak in the captain's throat jabbed as he spoke.
Streams of sweat streaked his brow. "We're nearly there."

A woman scoffed. "Forget it, Captain. He's as good as gone."

"And yet the groll still hides. It knows better than you do, I think."

Denariel. The woman's name was Denariel. His was Kylac. He
blinked, and made no move to resist when Ledron's gloved hand
reached up to pat his cheek none too gently

"Where are we?" Kylac asked.

"The core, or near enough. Can you not feel it?"

The captain pointed to the ground, which Kylac now realized was
trembling beneath his feet. The earth was humming here, alive with
restive movement. A crack and a hiss betrayed the sudden release of
steam nearby.

"Not so far now," Ledron insisted. "But I need you to focus."

"Focus," Kylac echoed. His tongue felt thick and heavy. He used
it to lick his lips, and nodded.

His blades were still in hand. Whatever his state when Ledron
had been prompted to act, he hadn't dropped them. And he was still

on his feet, so he hadn't fallen. Had either occurred, he would likely be having this conversation with the groll instead.

He scanned the darkness for the creature, blinking and yawning to further wake himself, twirling his swords to test his uncertain reflexes.

"Here," Ledron offered, unstoppering his waterskin.

"Save it," said Kylac. "We'll needs it for the sageryst."

His response must have satisfied the Shadowguard captain, for Ledron eyed him only briefly before stepping back, withdrawing himself and his torch.

Denariel shook her head. "Then you still mean to play out this farce?"

"'Til the jesters and scarecrows descend," Kylac told her.

The princess fronted him a queer expression, smooth brow furrowing in puzzlement. Then she tossed her hair and looked away, to make it clear she didn't care.

They resumed, one step, and then another. Before him, Kylac watched the tunnel floor sway from side to side like a ship riding a broadside current. Within moments, the fever dreams attempted a return. Here, a stream of withered rosebuds spilled from a cleft in the wall, turning to ash as they touched the floor. There, a lavender imp perched upon an upthrust crag. With the cheeks of a squirrel and the teeth of a beaver, it set to preening itself with a forked tongue. Kylac willed the creature and other nonsensical imaginings away, while making various attempts to induce wakefulness—biting his tongue, clenching his fists, tapping his legs with his blades.

Oddly enough, the best results came in closing his eyes, forsaking his vision altogether to rely on his other senses. Forced to listen, smell, and feel his way through the void kept him more in tune with his real surroundings, and helped to keep his growing madness at bay. Every twenty strides or so, he would crack his lids again for a glimpse of the terrain ahead, but only to reassure himself that he hadn't died somewhere along the way.

He'd taken nearly a thousand steps in this manner, pacing and directing himself according to his companions' footfalls, straining to remain vigilant against any perceived threat, when he heard Ledron inhale sharply beside him.

"Is that . . . ?"

Kylac allowed his eyes to open. He found Ledron first, then followed the captain's gaze toward the northern wall of the rocky corridor. There, a vein of blue-tinged mineral glimmered faintly in the dim torchlight, gashing the tunnel's skin like a ribbon waterfall trickling down a cliff.

Ledron blinked and rubbed his chin with the back of his fist. "Come. This may be it."

Kylac, less trusting of anything his gaze revealed, could only hope the captain was right. Though his first steps toward the narrow vein caused the world to lurch so suddenly that he felt he might roll completely upside down, he closed his eyes and pressed on, entrusting muscle memory to compensate for his reeling equilibrium. It must have worked, because five paces after that, he found himself near the wall, half a step behind Ledron, who bent close to the rock with the torch. The vein of mineral remained, glinting now like a frozen river in sunlight, its thin, crystalline depths a penetrating sapphire.

"Well?" the captain asked, turning to Denariel.

The princess shrugged. "Mine was a crushed powder, dull and sandy."

"But glittered like this, surely." Ledron ran a finger along the seam of mineral, determined, desperate. "The color . . . this has to be it."

"So try it," Denariel suggested. "Though harvesting it from that thread might prove challenge."

"There will be more," Ledron said. "Farther on, if we—"

Above their heads, the wall crumbled. Amid the showering debris, a form dropped. Kylac had the presence to shove Ledron aside—so that the captain narrowly cleared the path of descent—before raising his longsword to deflect the groll's initial swipe.

The mutant came at him as it had in the sewers of Wingport, savage and relentless. Kylac's weapons seemed to work themselves, driven solely by instinct. So much for not being taken unawares. He was on his heels, the earth like the deck of a storm-tossed ship. Ledron was down and not getting up, fallen torch seething against the earth, while pelting stones continued to cascade around him. Denariel was behind Kylac, still breathless with shock. As a shield he served, between her and the groll, but not for long, as he retreated steadily toward her.

She seemed to realize this, and moved to clear his path. She did so hastily, and stumbled. The resulting motion sent her staggering backward toward the wall—only the wall wasn't there. A gaping side tunnel awaited her. Though she flailed in a frantic attempt to halt her momentum, she fell, then continued falling, spilling toes over crown along a descending, chute-like path. As suddenly as that, the tunnel devoured her, with only scraping, grunting, gasping sounds marking her trajectory as she tumbled down its lightless throat.

The groll pressed its attack for another heartbeat, then dove after her, plunging into the chute's depths.

Kylac hesitated—dizzy, winded, his thoughts a muddled, roiling mess. *Your duty is to Her Highness . . .* Sallun's parting words. *See her home . . .* Trajan's. *May the bards make me a liar and a leper . . .* His own.

The next thing he knew, he'd sheathed his shortsword so that he could retrieve the torch at Ledron's feet. The captain was still unconscious—dead, mayhap. There was little time to check, and none to revive him.

The princess, Kylac thought. Such rudimentary notions were all his mind could process. Defend Denariel. Slay the groll. With torch in one hand and longsword in the other, he set after them.

22

THE TUNNEL EXIT TOOK SHAPE ahead, a curtain of inky darkness framed by the sharp-edged ring of stone that formed the cave mouth. Beyond that veil, the earth thrummed and cracked and hissed, trembling with tumultuous activity, awash with the stench of sulfurous vapors. The lair of a dragon, if Kylac didn't know better. And mayhap he didn't. So far beneath the earth of this foreign isle, his normally sharp-sure senses reeling, who was he to say? With creations like grolls, tarrocks, and jaggeruunts running amok, it might well be the Breeders had something more in store. Something shackled and forgotten, mayhap, burning with a thousand-year-old hunger, straining even now to tear free . . .

He might have slowed as he neared the tunnel mouth, easing cautiously across its threshold. He might have held his present pace, trusting to hope that the groll was not awaiting his arrival as it had in the Wingport sewers, ready with a headsman's swipe. Instead, he punched through in a diving rush, tucking and rolling with longsword warding his right flank, and flaming torch his left.

But the expected ambush failed to materialize. As Kylac uncoiled following his roll across the piercing ground, he spotted his enemy not at the cave mouth, but off to one side, crouched over Denariel's prone body.

The groll hissed at his emergence, possessively warding its long-sought prize. And inspecting the damage, Kylac realized. Denariel lay sprawled, unmoving, bruised and scraped, with blood oozing from her nose and ears. Dead? His chest tightened, and his stomach heaved strangely. Had the tumble killed her? Had the groll? At a distant glance, there was no way of knowing.

The mutant was almost tender in its attentions, gently straightening the princess's skewed limbs before running a clawed hand across her brow. Kylac looked for any twitches or spasms in Denariel's muscles, but observed none. Hopeful signs, both.

Heat and moisture filled the sulfuric cavern, the bounds of which stretched beyond his meager globe of light. From what he could see, fissures both narrow and wide raked the cavern floor, giving vent to scalding clouds of steam. A hazy, perilous landscape. One more reason to finish this quickly.

He turned and wedged his torch into a crevice in the near wall. The groll hissed again, but this time sprang at him. More than a dozen feet between them, and the creature covered that distance in a single leap. By then, Kylac's shortsword filled his empty torch hand, enabling him to bring two blades to bear.

His dizzied senses tightened with urgent focus, a flood of fresh energy channeling along the currents of his body. It gave him a strength and speed that he wasn't sure he still possessed. A strength and speed he would need. For the groll seemed every bit as anxious for this moment as he was. It had used the weapons available to it during his company's trek across its lands, yes, but had never expected Kylac to succumb to them—nor even wished him to.

It had expected and wished for this.

A fevered imagining, mayhap. But experience had taught Kylac to trust his intuition. His ability to anticipate the thoughts and motives of his opponents had never failed him before. Questionable as his instincts might be in this situation, it was too late to begin doubting himself now.

The ravaged texture of the cavern floor made footing treacherous, so Kylac did his best to hold his ground, keeping his back to the torch lest the groll decide to snatch it from the wall and leave him in darkness. Even in those conditions, the mutant would find him a capable opponent. But with the board's pieces arrayed as they were, the Ukinh needed no further advantages.

So the monster pressed him where he stood, swiping and jabbing from every conceivable angle—and some that Kylac wouldn't have thought possible. A result of its shapelessness, he decided. Varied though his past opponents had been—be they demons, basilisks, elves, or men of most every ilk—all had been confined by a set form and size, limiting their height, weight, reach. Account for these combat-critical attributes correctly, and there was little an enemy could do to surprise or unbalance him. The groll, however, seemed a different creature with each foray, hulking and brutish one moment, small and sinuous the next. By turns it sniped, then pummeled . . . dodged, then barreled . . . whipped, jabbed, slashed—but never in any discernible sequence. As he'd learned in Wingport, it wasn't apt to repeat a movement or combination previously used, giving him no routine to mark or counter, and thus no knowledge from which to craft an advantage.

The groll had learned, too. It was the surest way to explain why the edges of Kylac's blades had yet to scratch its skin. The mutant had discovered firsthand just how damaging those edges could be, and so made sure to avoid them now, blocking and swatting the weapons by their sides or blunt spine as needed, else evading them altogether. Try as he did to alter the angles of his cuts—to attack, shield, and parry as erratically and unpredictably as his opponent—Kylac couldn't seem to score a meaningful hit.

He edged to his left—and felt the ground give beneath his foot. He only narrowly drew back before a piercing whistle hailed the eruption of a steam geyser through the collapsing crust of earth. The stone at the edges of the blast crumbled inward, forming another fissure. The ground's sloping pitch caused the blast to be directed away from him. Even so, a wash of superheated vapors seared the flesh beneath his tunic, and drove him back nearly to the cave mouth.

The groll shied in the opposite direction, allowing a veil of steam to pass between them as the geyser subsided. Kylac counted two full heartbeats before the mutant reappeared, come lunging through that

lingering curtain before it could dissipate. He did well to repel the
mutant's strikes in that moment, while coming to terms with the
new danger. In addition to the pitfalls he could see, the room might
well be riddled with those he couldn't, hidden beneath his feet by
patches of thin stone where the steam hadn't quite eaten through. A
single misstep . . .

The groll arced high, then swept low, giving him no time to
dwell on it. A spray of slaver flecked Kylac's cheeks. His face began
to tingle. He half expected it to burn. Instead, it quickly grew numb.
Touch it, and your mind will drift toward madness, Sallun had said of a
groll's venom. Privately, Kylac laughed. Judging by his mind's earlier
wanderings, madness was already rapping at his door. The venom in
his belly was of far greater concern. By rights, it should have claimed
him already. *A day,* Trajan had said. *If any exceeds that, they'll be the
first.* By Kylac's tally of hours, he'd achieved that, or near enough to
make no difference.

One more feat for the bards to embellish in everlasting song.

But none would learn of it if he failed to escape this fiendish
chamber, and soon. His fight in the sewers hadn't lasted so long—
more than half of which had been fought with daggers alone. Two
shortswords had enabled him to quickly maim this same creature
and drive it hence. With longsword in hand, he should have killed
the beast thrice over already, and been well on his way.

Thus far, he'd nicked the creature, and nothing more.

The venom had dulled him, weakened him, slowed him. It gnawed
at his cramping entrails. It blurred his vision, disrupted his balance,
addled his thoughts. That he'd withstood the groll this long was a
testament to his training, his will, his preternatural anticipation.

Or was the creature merely toying with him? Amid their frenetic
exchanges, Kylac caught gleaming flashes of the assailing Ukinh's
baleful eyes, the one feature that remained unaltered. While its flesh
hardened or grew malleable as needed, while its limbs bulged or
shriveled, while its head and shoulders puffed or shrank, those eyes . . .
those eyes stayed constant. Bright, slitted orbs, they appeared now and
again between strikes not with crude bloodlust, but grim, calculating
intelligence. He saw hatred in those flashes, yes. He saw fury and

a seething hunger for vengeance. But beneath all of the animalistic savagery he might expect, Kylac also recognized an abiding calm, a grim confidence, a certainty that the desired outcome to this struggle was already decided.

A realization, strange and unsettling, slipped over Kylac's shoulders like a cloak of ice. He couldn't win this encounter. He might have, had he ended it sooner. But his best chance had already passed, and the longer this played out, the smaller that chance grew. His unblemished success as a fighter was due as much as anything to his ability to outlast any opponent. Well, for the first time, he'd engaged with one that had the skills and the patience to outlast him. At full health, never. But he might as easily wish for a third sword arm. As matters stood, be it now or later, he would falter.

And his enemy knew it.

His veins tingled with an unfamiliar feeling. Dismay? It tasted like dirty ash. And glowing at its fringes, the embers of fear. Kylac bit his tongue in defiance. Die he might, but not afraid. Never afraid.

So he found himself in a situation like never before. He would simply have to react as never before. He would have to do the one thing he'd always avoided—the same thing the groll was avoiding now. Become impatient. Reach for an opening that wasn't yet there. The pit fighters he'd known in Atharvan would call it a swipe from the knees. Spitting from the gallows, a Parthan outlaw might say. Let those who learned of it later describe it as they wished. Succeed, and he might emerge victorious. Fail . . . well, he would only be hastening the inevitable.

Of course, now that he was decided, he still had to devise a specific maneuver. His options seemed limited. The groll's defenses were perfect, like the groll was perfect. Fast, powerful, indefatigable. Such an amazing creation, he realized, in a way he hadn't before. Intelligent, determined, dutiful—

His blooming appreciation gave way to a sudden notion. Denariel. Its true devotion was to recapturing Denariel . . . for whatever purpose fueled its primal need. To deliver her to the Grenarr for ransom, he supposed. Was that not the original plot? It would have a difficult time doing so, lacking a ship or any contact with the seafaring raiders that Kylac was aware of. Mayhap none of that mattered. Mayhap it would possess her for possession's sake, knowing only that it must ward her because that was the task it had undertaken.

Little of which concerned him now, except that Kylac believed, were its prize threatened, the mutant would respond.

Assuming, of course, she wasn't dead already.

A whirring feint-attack-feint combination backed the groll up a half step, giving him the space he needed to make his break. Abandoning the torch wedged into the wall at his back, he dashed toward Denariel, where she yet lay unmoving.

The groll gave chase, springing after him. It caught him easily. Kylac turned to engage it mid-leap, blades thrusting. The groll dodged one and slapped the other aside. Kylac ducked a retaliatory swipe, curled his torso to avoid a snapping snout, then brought up his longsword to slash at the groll's leg. The Ukinh deflected the flat of the blade with its knee, but had to withdraw an intended counter when Kylac's shortsword jabbed upward toward its exposed chin, instead leaning away and using its free hand to push the uppercut aside.

A furious cycle of advances, blocks, pins, parries, feints, dodges, spins, hacks, slashes . . . all at what would surely appear to others a mind-numbing speed. Kylac himself was becoming dizzied by the effort—hardly fair, since he'd been dizzy from the outset. He found himself grunting, panting, wincing, and holding his breath by turns, where normally he would have settled by now into a smooth, comfortable rhythm as sustaining as it was draining.

Throughout it all, he continued to retreat toward Denariel. The groll, he was sure, could smell his desperation, else it would have stamped out the torch, he suspected, before launching itself in pursuit. Unless it wished for the torch to remain, so that Denariel would have light should she come to. Shards, who knew? And why was Kylac having to contemplate these matters—sometimes belatedly—when instinct and reaction were normally all he needed?

A tremor rattled the earth, and small geysers of steam vented throughout the chamber. A discolored trail to his right marked a crumbling vein of superheated stone. Foul vapors hissed from the breach, unleashing fresh, shimmering waves of clear liquid fire. The cracking, hissing tumult gave rise to an echo from the earth that might have been a furious, trumpeting cry.

Denariel stirred. Her brow furrowed, and a soft moan escaped her lips. Alive, though she didn't wake. Kylac was nearly upon her. As for what he should do when he reached her . . . he really wasn't sure. He might wound her, in hopes of distracting the groll. But would it? And could he make himself harm her—his own ward—in the first place?

The venting gases from the latest eruptions spawned a new idea—a better idea. The more he considered it, the more he liked it. Above all, it *felt* right, the solution he'd been looking for, the chance he needed. But how to execute it?

He cast glances at the ravaged ground around them, his gaze scratching and clawing but never drifting far, returning always to the beast with which he danced. Damn, but this Ukinh was persistent. Relentless in its savagery, yet steadfast in its emotions. A moment's frustration was all Kylac needed, yet the Breeders' most beautiful, most seamless creation refused to yield him even that much.

And then he spied it, a veined patch of earth whose jagged lines appeared ashen in the torchlight, of lighter, yellowed hue compared to the black stone foundation through which they ran. Stained with whatever mix of sulfurous gases were eating away at this cavern's underbelly. A crust of stone ready to collapse.

Or so he hoped. If he could but lure the groll over it . . .

But this wasn't some mindless creature to be led along by the snout. Of the scenarios that played out in Kylac's mind, none ended with the Ukinh doing his bidding. It was pressing him now should he have aims against the princess. But how did he mean to draw it away from her? More likely, it would remain beside her, shielding her, when he redirected. Since it was Kylac who teetered at the precipice, what cause had the groll to force the action?

Kill her.

Kylac growled at the suggestion.

You owe her nothing.

He must not even consider . . .

She despises you anyway.

But it mattered not what she thought of him. It never had. He'd promised Ledron, promised himself . . .

A mercy, like the others. Sallun. Trajan. If'n ya die, the groll claims her.

Swat as he might at the justifications, they kept on him like a bothersome fly. Killing Denariel seemed the only sure way to incite the groll—if not spurring it toward vengeance, then at least removing any reason it might have to remain at her side. He and his enemy would be free at last to face each other unfettered, to scratch and claw about the chamber until one of them was no more . . .

His heel brushed against Her Highness's foot. That mere, brief contact drew a snarl from his opponent. And in that instant, Kylac decided upon his course.

"'The Monster and the Maiden,' is it?" he teased, adding a laugh as he weathered the groll's spiking aggression. "I know not what version they tells upon these shores, but on mine, the poor lass breeds only maggots."

He pressed an offensive only to abruptly withdraw, reaching back for Denariel's neck with his shortsword and running its spine along her throat.

The groll knew his blades were single-edged, too dull along the spine to so easily split skin. But it lunged anyway to disrupt the strike and push him clear. Kylac fell back, losing grasp of his shortsword, and the pair of them went into a roll. He drew a dagger—Sallun's dagger—to replace the lost blade. Mayhap the groll had misjudged which edge he'd used, Kylac thought as they tumbled. Else it might have thought he'd used that spinal edge in error. More likely, it recognized his bluff, but wasn't going to let him linger in that position, lest he change his mind.

Whatever the truth, they were committed now, ensnarled on the ground in a furious exchange of claws and teeth and slashing blades.

Directly over the veined patch of weakened earth.

It held their weight, stronger than he'd imagined. Just as well, since Kylac hadn't envisioned wrestling his enemy into the snare. A lure and a well-timed leap were more along the order of what he'd expected. He'd underestimated the force of the groll's flying tackle, and now here they were. That was the problem with expectations—they too easily bred disappointment.

Which meant adapting. But how? The ground here *was* soft. He could feel it shifting beneath them. The creases deepened, marked by those yellowed veins. It might take another quake. It might take no more than their continued struggle. But the earth here would give, and he'd best be clear when it did. Whatever damage the steam might do to the groll's flesh, he was quite certain it would do far worse to his own.

But those veined creases might as easily have been the strands of a spider's web, with the way the groll had him pinned. The creature had sliced itself half a hundred times on his warding blades, yet showed no sign of relenting. He'd lopped a pair of envenomed claws from the fingers on its left hand. He'd shaved a slab of meat from its side and even scored a deep puncture where a man's kidney would have been. The groll, for all its thrashing, had yet to slip past his defenses in any meaningful way. A single scratch would kill him, as Sallun had told it, but surface tears in his sleeves, boots, and breeches would not. By that measure, he was still the better fighter, still capable of—

The earth rumbled. A shrill whistle emerged from a stone fold at his right, accompanied by that blistering heat. The moment for reaching had come. He dropped his longsword, heard it clatter upon the ground. The groll leaned toward the exposed flank. Kylac engaged its shift in momentum, rolling to that side. His dagger came arcing around in pursuit. The groll's head and neck shrank, avoiding a blow that might elsewise have driven into its temple. But the strike ended where it had been aimed all along   a hard stab into the whistling breach.

The flagging ground crumbled—not downward, but upward—as the pressure below burst through, given escape. Kylac felt the skin of his hand blister as he snatched it away. The dagger left behind vanished in a geyser of steam. So too did the groll, where it lay along that seam of broken earth, an anguished shriek ripping from its maw.

23

THE GROLL'S INHUMAN SHRIEK seemed to sharpen as it echoed throughout the cavern, like frozen shards being driven into Kylac's ears. Kylac himself was rolling aside, snatching up his discarded longsword and fetching a new dagger before flipping to his feet. The movement left him lightheaded and wobbly, yet neither could dull the thrill of imminent victory.

The heat of the geyser held him at bay, so he threw a glance toward Denariel, who was pressing herself from the cavern floor. The Ukinh's scream, it seemed, had finally brought her to.

"Stand fast!" he called to her, on the chance she was lucid enough to understand him—and willing in this instance to obey. He didn't wish to lose her to one of the chamber's pitfalls.

But her awakening won only that momentary notice, for by then the geyser was dissipating. In its place crouched the groll, stretched between the edges of the new fissure, its green-black hide scalded a deep shade of red. Sallun's blade had fallen into the chasm, but had done its work. The Ukinh's eyelids fluttered, revealing blood-red orbs blistered in their sockets—blinded, given the way the beast's head turned frantically from side to side.

Kylac stepped forward to put his longsword through its heart—but hesitated. Between its steam-ravaged flesh, precarious perch, and suddenly desperate movements, the creature had become somehow pitiable. Its scream had died, but a soft mewling remained, hissing and gurgling from deep within its throat. The sound caused Kylac's chest to ache with inexplicable guilt. Who was he to willfully destroy such a rare and wondrous creature? What threat had it ever truly posed them?

"No!" Denariel cried. She was on her knees, rising unsteadily, one hand reaching out to him.

The mutant perked, neck twisting and craning, its ruined gaze searching. It snarled, then pushed off the near edge of the chasm to cling to the far lip. With a heave, it pulled itself up until its arms had straightened below it. Legs curled to either side, feet grasping the stone lip at its waist. From that perch, it sprang backward, a rear somersault that placed it before Kylac once more.

Kylac reacted instinctively. His desire to kill the creature may have waned, but he couldn't have it lunging after Denariel, either. So his longsword lashed out, cleaving its left foot at the ankle.

"No!" Denariel screamed again, stumbling toward them as the groll shrieked and collapsed over its wounded leg. A clawed hand swiped out blindly, only narrowly missing Kylac's own leg as he slid back, out of reach.

"Stop! Stop!" the princess pleaded as she staggered near.

Kylac continued to retreat from the writhing groll, arms outstretched to prevent Denariel from coming too close. He wondered as he did so what it might take to bridle the beast, suspecting that, even blinded and hobbled, it stood a better chance of navigating this warren than they did on their own. If he were to spare its life, might it agree to lead them clear?

"Away from him!" the princess shrieked. Then, as she fought to squirm past, "Let me go!"

The groll hissed, but ceased its attacks. It crouched there on hands and knees, head tilted, chest heaving, as a fresh rumble boiled beneath the cavern floor. Already, the color of its hide was darkening, returning to normal. The membrane covering its eyes was no longer bubbling, and the gush of blood pumping from its severed ankle had slowed to a trickle.

"Please, Highness," Kylac said, shifting from one flank to the next as she sought vainly to sidestep him. "Stay back."

The new rumble built steadily, in strength and in sound. Not like the others, which had rattled the earth without warning.

"Monster!" Denariel yelled. "Monster!"

Kylac could make no sense of her raving. He was too sick, too dizzy, too focused on the groll and the oncoming tremor. A crackling filled his ears, like lightning, only unbroken, welling up from below.

Then the ground buckled. A pillar of rock surged skyward amid a spray of steam, smaller chunks and debris raining from its sides. The cavern shook so violently that Denariel fell, and Kylac nearly fell with her. The groll flipped over, onto its backside, to face the thrusting pinnacle, the head of which appeared then to split wide around a central void ringed with shards of diamond-flecked stone.

From that void emerged a deafening roar, and again the chamber shook, rattling stones from the ceiling. As they clattered around him in a dusty shower, Kylac realized that this was not a spear of rock, but a slug-shaped leviathan that had breached the cavern floor, its cataclysmic arrival opening a fissure that had all but torn the chamber in half.

The jaggeruunt.

The torch guttered where it was wedged into the wall, sprayed by dust and silt. Shadows deepened. Kylac's pulse throbbed in his ears, echoing the creature's name like the beat of a war drum.

Jaggeruunt . . . Jaggeruunt . . . Jaggeruunt . . .

Its circular maw squeezed in and out as it scented the air, rings of diamond-edged teeth flexing rhythmically. It then crashed to the floor, which cracked and splayed beneath its massive bulk.

And turned toward them.

Once again, Kylac obeyed his instincts, driving his left shoulder into Denariel's midsection and hefting her like a sack of grain. "No!" she squealed again. Her fists beat against his back. Her lower legs kicked. She arched and squirmed, but Kylac's forearm clenched fast around her thighs, his own burning from the added weight as he staggered toward the cave mouth.

"Unhand me!"

With the way she thrashed, Kylac wasn't certain he could do so—not without slicing her on the edge of the blade still gripped in that hand. Nor did he intend to try until he'd hauled her clear. The earth quaked beneath his feet, loose fragments bouncing, larger plates bucking. He risked a glance over his empty shoulder. All he saw or could sense was the looming mass of the charging jaggeruunt, its armored bulk carving furrows in the earth, steam spitting and spraying from either side as broken slabs shifted and fell around it.

When Kylac stumbled, he judged he'd gone far enough, and hurled Denariel from him as he dropped to one knee. She landed unceremoniously, grunting in surprise, defiance, and at least some measure of pain. But Kylac had no more time to worry about her scrapes and bruises than his own. He whirled at once to face the pursuing jaggeruunt, blades raised in feeble defense.

The jaggeruunt's bellow rocked the already reeling cavern. Kylac found it aimed not at him, however, but at the groll, crouched where he'd left it, braced on all fours—two hands, a foot, and a scabbed stump. Its head was cocked as if listening to their retreat, though Kylac would be astounded if it heard anything over the din. The jaggeruunt's pulsing maw opened toward it . . .

But tasted only empty earth as the groll sprang aside, opposite the direction Kylac had fled with Denariel, all but vanishing within the edge of darkness that fringed their torchlight.

The jaggeruunt's disappointment reverberated amid the jagged walls, between floor and ceiling, and within the splitting chambers of Kylac's skull. The creature itself reared and swatted from side to side, shattering boulders or sending them tumbling. Kylac sidestepped the bone-crushing clatter, coughing as he inhaled a thickening cloud of dust.

Bracing as the jaggeruunt's great head swung toward him.

He knew at once how absurd he must appear, how useless it would be to scratch at this burrowing behemoth with anything less than a siege engine. But Denariel was still down behind him, scrabbling amid a pile of loose rock, her efforts sagging as fear and awe took twining hold of her limbs. He might veer to either side in an attempt to draw the beast, but if it failed to follow, only open ground would remain between it and the princess. Better to stand before it, he thought. A gnat, mayhap, but even gnats could prove distracting.

The ground heaved in protest as the stone-devouring juggernaut lurched forward. A fissure at Kylac's feet widened, forcing him to adjust his stance. Before the creature could gather its momentum, however, it halted and swung about. Kylac realized why when he spied the groll, reappeared behind the beast, hissing in challenge.

The jaggeruunt roared and whipped about, bathing Kylac in a warm gust of mineral-laden breath. So near was the passing brush of that monstrous maw that Kylac caught sight now of the progressively smaller tooth-rings concealed inside the first. He might have reached out and raked them with his longsword, had he wished. He didn't, and the creature ignored him, forsaking the enemy at its snout to bend back and pursue the one at its tail.

"Get away!" Denariel yelled. Surprised by her sudden concern, Kylac turned to find her rising at last to her feet. He also found her looking not at him, but across the cavern at the groll. She stepped in that direction, only to stumble on a loose stone and pitch forward onto hands and knees. "Get away!" she cried again.

Though fast-recovered from its burns, the groll was still sightless, judging by the erratic twists and turns of its neck. It perked to the sound of Denariel's plea, yet held its ground until the last moment, waiting until the jaggeruunt was upon it before lunging clear as it had before, a one-legged leap bearing it away from the torch and the cave mouth leading from the cavern.

Again the jaggeruunt gorged on empty stone. And again it roared its displeasure, thrashing in place, spitting shattered bits of rock while rearing its head in search of a new target.

"Away!" Denariel shrieked at the behemoth, stumbling still, but climbing doggedly to her feet. With the first semblance of sustained balance, she staggered forward. "Leave him be!"

The jaggeruunt swung toward her. Whether attracted by sound, scent, or vibration, Kylac couldn't say. He knew only that she was staggering in the wrong direction, toward the great slug rather than away from it.

Denariel hesitated in belated realization of this, freezing as that giant, constricting maw with its powerful, grinding tooth-rings bore down on her.

Kylac raced toward her, sheathing his weapons as he did so. Useless as they were in this fight, better to have his hands free.

His flying lunge knocked her flat again. He'd intended to remain standing in her place, mayhap even bait the creature in the opposite direction. But his own balance failed him, spilling him down on top of her.

They fell into a shallow fissure between ridges of broken stone. Kylac recognized at once that it wouldn't save them. Should the jaggeruunt turn toward them, its weight would crush the flanking ridges, the fissure floor, and them with it.

The cradling earth shook them until Kylac's teeth rattled. Showering pebbles and grit sought to bury him. But the dreaded impact never came, as the jaggeruunt's grating mass veered in the direction from which they'd come, rather than the direction in which they'd landed.

Enabling them to survive another charge.

Kylac pushed to his knees, uncertain he could survive another. His stomach had become a pit of angry adders, all of them writhing and choking and striking, and his hazy vision refused to clear. Tracing the jaggeruunt's new path, he was unsurprised to find the groll once more at the head of it, luring the beast on. The mutant was its true target, Kylac realized, the mutant that had goaded it from the depths and provoked it still. He and Denariel were of no real interest to the colossal worm. How else to explain why they were still alive and not fleshy stains seeping into the cracks of the earth?

It did *not* explain why the groll continued to bait the creature, but that was no great mystery. Addled as he was, even Kylac could see that the mutant was trying to give Denariel a chance to escape—believing it would run her down later, no doubt. As for the princess's actions . . . there he was flummoxed. He'd gathered during their voyage that she didn't loathe her beastly captor the way Ledron and his Shadowguard did, but to throw herself in harm's way for its sake . . . by what reckoning did that make sense?

His head hurt too badly to ponder it. All he understood, as Denariel wrestled him in an attempt to rise, was that he shouldn't let her do so. Let the groll play catch-the-mouse. Even limping around on one foot, it was better suited to the game than they.

"Flee," he said, though the word sounded slurred. Was his tongue to blame, or his ears? "The tunnel . . . we has to . . ."

The princess continued to grapple, grunting and snarling, throwing fists and hurling elbows. A hundred and one holds he knew to lock down or incapacitate an opponent, but his body had become sluggish, unresponsive, and he couldn't seem to apply any of them. He couldn't even move his forearm when Denariel opened her mouth to bite it, clamping down hard.

A tickle, compared to the other pains radiating through him. And so he ignored it, using that moment in which the princess focused on biting him to grasp and twist her thumb in such a way as to pin her fast. She would have to be willing to break the digit before—

Denariel growled and yanked. The bone snapped. The princess yelped as she slipped from his grip and pulled away, to chase after the jaggeruunt.

His disbelief complete, Kylac found the strength to lurch to his feet and totter after her, one arm clutching at his burning intestines.

Though blind and maimed, the groll seemed to note their struggle—even while scuttling from left to right and back again, keeping but a pace or two ahead of the jaggeruunt as it weaved across the cavern floor in pursuit. For when Denariel broke free and rushed again to join the conflict, the groll slowed, hissing at her in apparent frustration.

His head splitting and spinning, Kylac wondered: How long could they persist at this?

The mutant appeared to regard the same question, for it ceased its hobbled scampering to crouch beside the great rift that had opened upon the jaggeruunt's emergence. After a brief moment in which it peered down into that steaming gulf, it turned its back to the chasm and stood, slowly straightening.

The jaggeruunt roared, accelerating.

"No!" Denariel yelled. The Ukinh's blind gaze turned to her, and she screamed again. "No!"

The jaggeruunt's head withdrew into its body upon final approach, then sprang forward, seizing the motionless groll square within the center of its clenching maw. Blood squirted, black as ink, as meat and bones were minced and shredded in a single, pulsing bite of those multilayered tooth-rings. Its pace unslowed, the worming behemoth continued then over the ledge, diving headlong into the chasm, bearing its meal and its own grinding bulk into the steaming blackness below.

24

Hɪɢʜ ᴀɴᴅ sʜᴀʀᴘ, Denariel's wail pierced the tumult.

The jaggeruunt descended amid thunderous reverberations, trumpeting its satisfaction. In the chamber above, the earth cracked and grated, steam hissed, stones clattered. But it was the princess's cry that cut Kylac to the core, like glass shards filling his chest, and cold steel raking his spine.

She fell as she climbed the rugged slope leading up to the chasm's edge. Facedown, she began to sob, cradling her broken thumb, her desperate denial become a wracking, wordless plea.

Kylac staggered after her, legs bending awkwardly beneath him. With the way her crumpled form continued to claw strengthlessly toward the fissure's edge, he half feared she meant to cast herself into it. *Let her do so,* the damaged part of him whispered, *and toss yourself in after.*

He slipped as she had, dropping near her feet. A wrenching spasm set the adders inside his stomach to panicking, their fanged bites piercing. His jaw clenched, and he couldn't seem to make its muscles relax. He nonetheless had the presence to reach up and clutch Denariel about the ankle, thereby stalling her ascent.

"No . . ." she whimpered anew, then turned and shrieked at him. "*No!*" Like that, her strength returned. She began kicking him with her free leg, then slid back to batter him with her good fist. "No! No! No!" she echoed. "You killed him! You *killed* him!"

And she sobbed and thrashed and snarled, broken thumb and all. Kylac was too weak, in too much pain, to do more than cling to her ankle, grasping it as he might a lifeline amid raging seas. That's how it seemed to him—surrounded by black, stormy swells that stung and burned, numbing nerves and seizing muscles, tossing him up and down and from side to side, relentlessly pummeling . . .

A rock came to Denariel's fist, black and jagged, flecked with tiny grains of gleaming mineral. Funny that *these* he should see so clearly. He watched them rise overhead, like stars in a dark firmament. A shadow fell over him, eclipsing the meager light, as the princess took aim . . .

The shadow dropped, and so too did Denariel, with a grunt and a sigh. The star-speckled rock rolled harmlessly from her limp grasp. Though it took Kylac another moment to realize it, her struggles had ceased.

"Hardly a fitting end, Kronus."

Kylac turned his head to find the man casting the shadow. Ledron. The Head's blurry face was bruised and filthy, with a smear of blood leaking from one ear. Elsewise, he seemed to have recovered quite well from the attack in the tunnel.

"A dragon, you bury in its den," Ledron went on, kneeling to check Denariel's injuries. "But you would let a pampered waif smash your skull?"

Was that what she'd intended? And for it, the captain had knocked her unconscious. "Ya . . ." Kylac protested. The sound of his own voice screamed through his brain. "She . . ."

"We don't have time to wrestle with her," Ledron explained. The captain dug into a pouch while turning toward him. "The jaggeruunt may return."

Would that excuse satisfy the princess when she came to? In either case, Kylac was too sick to argue. He couldn't seem to stop staring at the discarded, mineral-flecked stone.

"Here, open your mouth."

Kylac rolled onto his back, propped upon his elbows . . . but found himself capable of little more. Spasms caused his jerking limbs to seize uncontrollably. So Ledron bent over him, squeezing his rigid jaw muscles to force them open. Sand and pebbles poured from a tiny pouch into his mouth. His tongue burned. Had he been able, he might have spit it out.

"Be still, you fool," Ledron warned him, grappling with a water-skin. From the distant depths, the jaggeruunt bellowed. The chamber shivered in response.

The water was warm, but welcome, helping to wash the burning from his mouth. It proceeded down his throat, carrying with it the scraping sands. Kylac coughed and snorted, and some of the burning spread to his nose. Ledron responded by pouring him a fresh mouth-ful of the tasteless grit—sageryst, he presumed—chased by another mouthful of water. This time, he swallowed, and managed to keep most of it down.

A tingling warmth spread through his neck and around to the back of his aching skull. The frantic drumming of his heart soon began to slow. Within moments, his muscles seemed to relax, gripped only intermittently by those violent twinges.

"Better?"

His vision still swam. His pulse throbbed in his ears, and his stomach still wrenched and churned, pricked and strangled by those invisible serpents. But when he straightened his fingers, they responded. When he stretched his toes, they did, too.

"Come," said Ledron, grasping his arm and pulling him to his feet.

There Kylac swayed, while the captain bent carefully to scoop up Denariel and heave her over his shoulder.

"She . . ." Kylac began, wrangling his uncooperative tongue. "Why so . . . distraught?"

Ledron shifted, adjusting her deadweight upon his back. "Come," he said again.

Before he could take his first step, Kylac's longsword slipped from its sheath, snapping out to block the captain's path.

"What the bloody . . . ?"

"Ya didn't . . . didn't . . ." Kylac swooned, but managed to remain upright. "Answer, Captain."

Ledron glared, then shook his head. "I couldn't say—not for certain. But I fear . . . The groll may have seduced her while she was
in its clutches."

"Seduced. That . . . the groll. It . . ." The pieces had been laid out
before him, but his mind couldn't seem to make them fit.

"Difficult to fathom, I know. But it's happened before, to others who
found themselves under the creatures' delusion-spawning influence."

Grasp as he might, Kylac could draw nothing from his experience
to dispute the claim. Delusion-spawning influence, was it? *Touch it,
and your mind will drift toward madness.* Was it possible? Could the oils
of a groll's skin, its saliva, its blood, induce such a delirium? Amid a
churning sea of thoughts, Kylac recalled his own sudden admiration
of the mutant—an admiration so intense that it had prompted him
to stay his hand when he might have slain the creature.

"Not saying it's common," Ledron added, "only that it's been
observed. I cannot explain her behavior elsewise."

Kylac felt himself nodding. Or was that but another tremor of
his body?

A rumble shook the earth.

"We should go," Ledron insisted.

Kylac lowered his blade, unsure how he'd raised it to begin with.
A warrior's instinct. His body's recollection of an action performed
with innumerable repetitions. Something about the matter still didn't
weigh as it ought. Might the Shadowguard captain be seeking to
play him false?

Ledron must have seen this in the frown that weighed upon his
cheeks and brow. "Save your strength," he urged. "Let the brume in
your head clear. We've not escaped this abyss quite yet."

The captain shifted his burden once more, then departed, marking
carefully each step set upon the treacherous ground. Kylac lingered
momentarily, then sheathed his longsword.

Mayhap he should have chosen his own steps with greater caution,
for he'd managed not two strides before the tingling in the back of
his skull swept forward, causing the cavern floor to tilt abruptly. The
jagged ceiling rolled overhead, and the torchlight dimmed.

Kylac's final thought as the blackness gripped him was to wonder what mineral Ledron had actually fed him.

25

Hᴇ ʙᴜʀɴᴇᴅ ɪɴ ᴛʜᴇ ʙʟᴀᴄᴋɴᴇss, and there came to know pain.

In life, he'd been well acquainted with its physical forms. It had been his study, his art, his father's will that he devote himself to learning and later applying its myriad methods. Blood flow, air flow, joints, nerve trails, pressure points, internal organs—so many interwoven elements and processes of the body to understand. And for each feature, each function, a dozen or more techniques by which to alter, disrupt, or end it. Bloodletting, strangulation, paralysis temporary or permanent, blunt trauma, acute trauma, acids, poisons, hand weapons, ranged weapons, no weapons   he'd come to know them all.

Some might say he'd never been given choice—that, had he grumbled or balked, he might have been cast out like so many other pupils deemed inadequate under his father's tutelage, disowned and fed to the streets. But that wasn't so. There'd always been a choice, even when the only other option was death.

And he'd made his—albeit for his own reasons. He'd never acquired his father's callousness and loathing, never developed that unslakable thirst for vengeance, never tasted that disdain and derision for all of human life. Nor, when the truth had been revealed and the opportunity presented, had he cozened to the notion of spilling blood for anything so empty as a purse of coin or jewels. Rather, he'd discovered early on that his sheer aptitude for personal combat fostered in him a fascination that wouldn't be denied. When a bird learned it could fly, 'twas only natural to see how high and far it could go.

Thus had he spent the rest of his days seeking the bounds of his potential, finding none.

In death, however, it wasn't physical pain that welcomed him, but a soulful anguish more difficult to comprehend. It was fathomless emptiness and innumerable sorrows, gnawing solitude and a million spirit-wrenching torments. His identity had been stripped away. In its place, he was no one and he was everyone—past, present, and future. He was a withered crone arguing with herself in the burrow beneath a great tree, surrounded by beetles and glowworms. He was a bitter warlord, brooding on his latest victory in a crumbling tower lashed by rain. He was a Powaii elf, strapped to a woven mesh as an A'awari elf hacked off his foot and fed it to a savage press of bloodthirsty faces. He was Torin, pining for a lass who wasn't Marisha, and then Marisha, whose heart ached for an absent lover who wasn't Torin. He was a king and a peasant, a queen and a waif, a lord and a leper, a general and a brigand, a master and a slave, a maiden and a whore, a squalling infant and a withered bag of bones.

He wasn't always human, either. By turns, and all at once, he was a wolf, a fish, a worm, a flea . . . But in pain. No matter his essence, always in pain. He bathed in molten rock and in frigid seas. He tasted raw earth and chafing wind. He knew yearning unfulfilled, desire unsatisfied, aspirations unrealized. He experienced failure and disappointment and unnecessary cruelty . . . barbed betrayal and curdling greed . . . cold whim and flaming anger . . . envy, jealousy, spite . . . these and countless dark sentiments akin to them wracked the formless shell he'd become, as both victim and perpetrator. He hated and was hated. He cast aside and was himself discarded. He begged and was denied, prayed and was ignored. He hungered . . . only to laugh as another starved.

Ageless eons of suffering he knew, without beginning or end. Devouring and devoured by the tempest of eternity.

Until the engulfing horror fell away, like a maelstrom losing grip. Through the black he swam, toward a fierce red glow. The radiance brightened and split—

And suddenly there was light above, tangled greenery all around, and a stony bed beneath. Though blurred at first, the images quickly came into focus. Vision, he recalled. Earth, jungle. The Sundered Isle. The Ukinhan Wilds—

He lurched forward, twin shortswords in hand from the scabbards at his waist. Kronus. His name was Kronus.

"Ah. Rejoining us, are you?"

Ledron. He turned toward the voice. The Shadowguard captain hovered at his left over a narrow stream festooned with brambles, a crude wooden spear in hand. A pair of rainbow-colored fish lay unmoving on the bank beside him, lidless eyes entranced by the freshly risen sun. The day was new, but already warm, with just a hint of salt-and-flower breeze.

Across from him sat Denariel, propped against a stump, bound and gagged. Dirt and leaves peppered her ratted hair. Grit and soil had been wiped from her face to reveal bruises and scrapes. A wrap and splint had been used to immobilize her left thumb. Her fierce gaze stabbed at him through the thin veil of heat and smoke rising from the cookfire that separated them.

"I had my doubts," Ledron admitted. "I've known breathing dead to sleep for years . . . and others that never wake at all."

Kylac closed his eyes, and for half a heartbeat the roaring vortex threatened to suck him back in. But then it was gone, moving on like some funneling storm cloud, black, shapeless tendrils clawing out from its edges. A fever dream, he decided, blinking a few times to be sure, though he wouldn't soon forget its ravaging brush.

"Her Highness . . ." Kylac rasped, his leathery tongue thick in his throat. His thoughts felt much the same, swollen with concern, raw with mistrust.

"Tried to stab you when she came to," Ledron explained. "Left me little choice." The Head drove his spear into the stream, but huffed in disappointment and withdrew only dripping water at its tip.

They were outside the warren. Which meant . . . "Ya carried us both clear."

"Her, then you, a few strides at a time. Give praise that Trajan was right about the warren having a southern exit."

"How long?"

"Seven hours, I'd say, to the cave mouth. Another two to find this stream."

"Nine hours?" And here Kylac remembered thinking the captain had poisoned him, willfully or elsewise.

"I'll not lie," Ledron said, "I'd hoped you'd rouse sooner." He jabbed again with his spear. This time, he sneered in triumph and drew forth another rainbow-colored fish.

"Ya might has left me."

The speared fish wriggled and thrashed. "At the time, you were our only viable food source. I wasn't going to leave you for the kara-tikuus or jaggeruunt."

Was that a jape? From the flat tone, Kylac couldn't be certain. He looked again at Denariel. The sight of her present condition continued to trigger in him a nagging suspicion. "Will your king not punish ya for treating his daughter so sorely?"

"I live according to his judgments." As the fish's struggles slowed, Ledron speared the pair caught earlier, then approached with all three. "As it stands, I shall honor the stars merely to see his court again—even if it is to face the lash."

As the captain reached them, Denariel lowered her smoldering gaze to stare at the soft leather of her boots. Kylac studied her a moment longer, then sheathed his blades. Was the fact that he still wielded them not reason enough to dismiss any lingering doubts? None of Ledron's claims lay beyond belief. This notion of the groll having seduced her with its toxins . . . bizarre. Yet even this, he'd already deemed plausible. If he among all could be so awed by another's fighting prowess, who was to say someone like Denariel, with her professed appreciation for nature's many varied forms, would be immune to an even deeper emotional connection?

He would question the princess herself about it, he determined, as the opportunity arose. Until then, he would attribute his uneasiness to the physical turmoil his body had so narrowly survived.

"Are we safe here, then?" he asked, making another scan of their surroundings.

"Not as yet," Ledron admitted. "But my head is a fog, and my strength gone. Should we tread farther without food, *you* will be carrying *me*."

Not likely, Kylac thought, given his own starvation. They'd been three days now without eating—three days of hard march, intense heat, and violent struggle. Even with his recent rest, his legs felt like shapeless sacks of grain, his head a feather twisting in the breeze. Serpents no longer battled in his stomach—just worms squirming over and through hard-packed earth. Their digging intensified as Ledron filleted the first fish. "Do we knows if'n those are edible?"

"Prism fish," Ledron grunted, holding forth a chunk of raw meat. His grim look spoke the rest. *Does it matter?*

Kylac took the fillet. White, tinged with iridescent flecks of pink. Unlike any fish on his shores, but that in and of itself told him nothing. He sniffed, and learned as much. *Krakken's blazes,* he thought, and gave rein to his hunger. Careful of any bones, he gulped it down. The taste was foul, and the texture curdled his throat. At the same time, he couldn't recall a morsel he'd ever enjoyed half so much.

Ledron had paused to observe him, as if waiting to see if he might retch it up or keel over at that very moment, on that very ground. "Are these all for me?" Kylac asked, goading.

"Just the one." The captain turned back to the half-eaten fish, to fillet the other side. "You want more, spear them yourself."

Kylac was sorely tempted to do just that . . . though it might be wiser to await his belly's response to this first nibble. Should he tolerate it without ill effect, he could try for more.

Ledron gave him the second fillet, which Kylac wolfed down as before, this time withdrawing a pair of sharp, thin bones along the way. Even so, he finished before the captain had set his knife to the next fish. This one, Ledron ate himself. Only then did he take the third and shuffle over to crouch beside Denariel.

The Head loosened the knot behind her neck and slid the gag from her mouth. Denariel worked her jaw momentarily, then bit down on the piece of fish that Ledron held before her. She chewed and chewed with sour face and downcast gaze—then abruptly lifted her head and spat the mouthful at Kylac.

"What the . . . ?" Ledron grunted, drawing back.

The volley fell short, landing at Kylac's feet.

"Murderer," she snarled, bits of raw fish clinging to her chin.

Kylac could only regard her with bemusement. "Was it I, then, carried your precious beastie down into that fissure?"

"You blinded him, hobbled him. Your blades, your work."

She wasn't entirely wrong, Kylac supposed. But then, the mutant had seemed plenty spry enough to evade the jaggeruunt, even on one foot. As he remembered it, the groll had given its life to save hers. Had she not been too stubborn to run . . .

"Dawning winds," Ledron muttered, which he followed with a heavy sigh. "It's done and passed. Let it go."

The princess ignored him, her hatred aimed clearly at Kylac. So be it. The captain was correct in his assessment, and Kylac wasn't going to waste his breath apologizing or defending himself. "If'n I recall," he said instead, "that pet o' yours killed a lot o' your father's men. And at least part o' ya willed it to happen."

"They knew the risks."

"As did your beastie, I'm sure."

She spat again at his feet.

"Enough," Ledron snapped. "Are you to be fed, or not?"

Denariel's snorting laugh carried a touch of madness. "Like some mare or mule? Go on, then, Captain. Feed me."

Ledron regarded her dubiously, then offered her another bite. She took it as before, chewed, then promptly raised her chin—higher than before—and spat once more at Kylac. This time, he had to move his shin to avoid being struck, at which Denariel grimaced in victory.

"Of all the knuckle-minded . . ." Ledron grumbled, rising in disgust. "As you will, Highness." He ate the remainder of her first fillet in front of her, then flung the half-carved fish by its tail toward Kylac. "Have yourself a second helping, Kronus."

Kylac saw no reason to refuse. The princess's pain and anger had clearly usurped her hunger. Mayhap, in time, she would come to see past whatever seduction had overtaken her. In the interim, he wasn't going to let good meat—if good meat it was—go to waste.

He shaved the remaining fillet from the fish's carcass with his own blade, and consumed it without displaying any visible hesitation. That didn't mean he lacked concern for Denariel's own hunger, or how long it might be before it could be addressed. "How much farther to this outpost Trajan spoke of?"

"Unless I'm mistaken, we've one more jungle to pass through, and a bank of foothills to climb. Twelve leagues, maybe. Due east. Without incident, we could be there by nightfall."

Without incident. Kylac knew well enough the narrow likelihood of that.

And yet, with Denariel's groll no longer pursuing them, one might safely hope that the worst of this death march lay behind them.

"The possibility is stirring," Kylac said, "but unless *I'm* mistaken, nightfall won't wait for us." He gathered his weight, and took gingerly to his feet. Even that careful movement triggered a moment's lightheadedness. His thighs threatened to cramp, and his stomach snarled. *Ya's endured worse,* he encouraged himself, thinking at once that it might be a lie. "Shall I carry Her Highness? Seems it's my turn."

"Her Highness will walk," Ledron said, as his knife severed the bindings at her ankles. "And Her Highness will keep pace. Else I shall present His Majesty with Her Highness's head, with regret that her body was eaten by tarrocks."

Denariel's glaring eye, directed at Kylac, shifted to measure the captain's seriousness. When Ledron didn't blink, she did. "Her Highness shall look forward to returning home," she replied haughtily, "to see that the chivalry of her valiant protectors is justly rewarded."

"Until then," Ledron said, crouching again to replace Denariel's gag, "Her Highness shall remain blessedly silent."

The princess offered no resistance, save for the gleam in her eye that vowed retribution.

When finished knotting the gag in place, Ledron grasped her by her elbow and hauled her roughly to her feet, leaving her wrists lashed behind her back. "We're agreed, then. Let this day's march be our last."

THE SUN'S CRAWL across the sky outpaced their own across the earth. Night fell. Still they marched.

They agreed to do so without a word between them. Easier it might have been to nestle amid a circle of rocks or sprout of hedge and give rest to strained muscles and aching bones. Denariel limped, though she did her best to hide it. Ledron favored an ankle, and winced with every other stride. Even Kylac's joints had drawn an ache along the way. But stopping to rest meant huddling though another night, sleeplessly watching for the approach of some hungry animal. It meant the possibility of fresh conversation, or even silent companionship, among they who had no more use for one another. It meant waiting that much longer for their ordeal to end.

So they kept grinding along in the moonlight, leading by turns, less a trio of comrades and more a loose formation of seeming strangers headed vaguely in the same direction, lost to their private demons and the tapping of whatever flagging energy source kept them on their feet. Denariel's strength was clearly fueled by hatred, sorrow, a hunger for reprisal. She'd eaten nothing throughout the day—not the berries they'd foraged, the roots they'd unearthed, or the raw eggs that Kylac had brought down from a nest. Whenever something was offered, she would merely glare at the food, or he who extended it, else look away, ignoring her warders altogether. Ledron seemed driven by the same duty-minded purpose that had compelled him from the outset—on the surface. A layer or two below, Kylac sensed the pangs of loss and disgust that jabbed at the captain, threatening to tear free. The Head would persist in his duty, but its fulfillment could no longer bring satisfaction. The price paid was already too great.

Kylac was less prone to such sentiment, seeing little enough use in dwelling on what couldn't be helped—not now, at least, while their own fates were still in question. He fed instead, as he so often did, on the vitality that surrounded him. No matter where he turned his senses, he found life in motion. The brush of wind that rustled leaves, stirred needles, or swept over stone. The sheen of poison on the tip of a thorn beneath a bright orange blossom. The scent of decaying flowers amid those in full bloom. The frenetic activity of insects bustling along the boles of trees or burrowing around their roots.

The flight of a startled thrush, its heart beating as fast as its wings. The presence of larger creatures that stalked these lands, and the cold chill of their calculating gazes. The intensity of emotion radiating from those he traveled with, like the heat from a fire. Life teemed as always with its tiny marvels—sights, sounds, and sensations both pleasant and foul, surprising and expected, bizarre and mundane, venerable and fleeting. An endless profusion for Kylac to experience, like a song sung in rounds, or a tale without end.

It all seemed new to him, in a sense. And in a sense it was. One didn't come as close as he had to death and walk away completely unscathed. Hand in hand with that near destruction came a sense of rebirth, of experiencing the world as if for the first time. Much felt strange and unsettling—much that had once been familiar. He might have been alarmed by this, but chose instead to focus on just how raw and vibrant, how *alive*, the world seemed.

And how pleased he was—aches, uncertainty, and all—to be a part of it.

Were it not for their condition, the trek might have been an easy one. The ground amid these higher, southern elevations was dry and mostly even. The forest they'd passed through had been dominated by mahogany trees and largely devoid of tangling groundcover. Even the foothills, through which they climbed now, rose in smooth, measured steps, lacking the sheer ridges and harsh slopes like those shaping the Cindercrag or the western heights along the Iron Scar. In fact, little of what they'd encountered that day matched the savage wilderness through which they'd trekked north of the Ukinhan warren. Streams were plentiful, the waters fresh. Of the various small foods Ledron and Kylac had sampled, none had caused sickness. Kylac had felt predators marking their progress—from the trees earlier, from stony dens now—but none attacked. Here and there, he spotted a bush that Trajan had taught them to avoid. By the balance, however, it was as though passing through the warren had carried them into another land entirely.

Some of that was a ruse, he knew, a calm belying the dangers that lurked behind this boulder or that, waiting to catch them unawares. This was still an untamed land, a border region on the edge of a hostile frontier. It belonged to neither civilized man, nor bestial mutant—and was therefore subject to either. Like those who strayed into the no-man's-land between warring armies, travelers here were either desperate or mad.

So said the wide-eyed expressions of the sentries who received them when finally they reached the wooden walls of the outpost dubbed Bitterwood. Surprise and suspicion made for a cold greeting, initially, but gave way quickly when the rheumy-eyed outpost commander, still yawning with interrupted sleep, was presented with Ledron's token of rank and informed of the identity of his royal charge. At that point, the yawns ceased, and stern postures turned suddenly servile. Commander and guardsmen fumbled all over one another to see them through the gates and usher them into the warmth and safety awaiting them behind the stone-and-timber palisade. A collective awe fell about the trio like a blanket, with questions and courtesies vying for the visitors' attention amid a general excitement such as this garrison, Kylac suspected, had seldom known.

Ledron, of course, had no patience for their fervor. A few grumbled instructions had the post commander ordering the curious Redfists back and calling for a meal of stew and sausage to be prepared. The commander then summoned an escort to accompany him in personally leading Her Highness and the captain of His Majesty's Shadowguard to his quarters, ordering a steward along the way to fetch fresh linens and anything else Ledron or the princess might require.

Kylac, meanwhile, was shown toward the barracks, his own care entrusted to a pair of Stonewatch soldiers—one with a sagging belly and bowlegged gait, the other with pointed chin and pinched shoulders. He accompanied them without complaint, finding it odd that Ledron should dismiss him with scarcely a nod . . . then recognized the wisdom in sparing Denariel his presence for a time, here where it seemed unnecessary. Mayhap she would eat now without being overcome by the urge to spew it at him.

"Shall it be cider or ale?" the pinch-shouldered Redfist asked him, upon seating him at a table in a narrow food hall adjoining the barracks.

"A cup o' both, if'n ya has it to spare. Ya can saves my sausage for the morning, though. A trencher o' stew should suffice."

"Whatever pleases you, the commander said."

It would have pleased him more not to be served or waited upon, but in this instance, Kylac lacked the strength to argue. As he leaned forward upon the rough wood of the table, he realized he would do well to remain awake long enough to eat.

He did so by recounting the steps of their journey in his head, reflecting now on the fates of the many lost—the many he'd failed. While he did so, his attending soldiers whispered to one another in the hall's moon-limned outer doorway, but mercifully chose not to ply him with questions. Through an inner doorway, he heard the snores of other garrison Stonewatch, mayhap a score, slumbering in the adjacent hall.

When his stew came, he wolfed it down, wondering as he did so how Ledron and Denariel were faring. Had the latter succumbed to her appetite? Or did she mean to continue starving herself in protest? A part of him wanted to take pride in having seen her safely through such a horrific trek, against such terrible odds. And yet, with her heart broken and so full of spite, he couldn't help but feel that he'd failed her, too.

When the meal and drink were finished, he followed his guides into the inner barracks to claim his pallet. As he lay down, he thought of the journey that yet lay ahead, and where it might lead.

Then sleep took him, and he thought no more.

26

THE BARGE STRUCK HOME with a jarring thump. Within the cabin, Ledron and Denariel lurched in their seats, while Kylac stood to pull aside the moldy canvas covering a rain-streaked window. Amid the downpour, receiving dockhands hurled mooring lines from the wharf, while bargemen dug their poles in against the current. The river strained, reluctant to release them, but as the lines looped about cleats and drew taut, its persistent tug relented.

Their stay at Bitterwood had been brief—just a single night's rest, though no rest had ever felt so good. Following their morning meal, a detachment of Stonewatch had ridden them half a day to the river, loaded them onto this barge, and set them on their way that same afternoon. Two nights and two days, he'd been told, would see them to Avenell, the home city of King Kendarrion.

Two nights and two days it had been, during which Kylac had spent most of his time pacing the deck undisturbed while watching the land drift by. Whether the crewmen had been instructed to leave him be, or whether they chose to do so of their own accord, they'd made no effort to engage him—which suited Kylac fine. Able to sit, stroll, stretch, recline, or exercise as he pleased, his health and spirits had improved rapidly. The river, running wide and straight, had treated them much more kindly than the sea. Its rush was fast, yet smooth, and whatever threats lurked beneath its surface had for the most part remained hidden. He'd spied the snouts of tarrocks periodically, their armored eyes gleaming balefully in the moonlight. And he'd seen serpents dangling from the trees, camouflaged amid curtains of vines. But each had kept to its own domain, disinterested mayhap, or knowing better than to threaten.

It had helped that Ledron and Denariel kept to the cabin where he did not. The captain had emerged only as far as the doorway, and only for brief moments when the princess required privacy. Denariel herself hadn't ventured even that far. Without their bitter company to befoul his mood, Kylac had quickly made peace with the events of this mission—a success, despite its terrible failures—and come to feel better about his prospects upon these wild shores.

He'd rejoined them in the cabin less than an hour ago to escape the torrential shower still seeking to drown the world outside. No words had been spoken. Ledron had looked up, reaching for a dagger, before relaxing with a curt nod. Her back to the doorway, Denariel hadn't bothered to turn, sulking upon her corner cot. There the three of them had sat, listening to the streams battering the cabin roof. Hunkered in that shared space, yet as far from one another as the moon from the sun.

A meaty fist rapped at the cabin door.

"Come," said Ledron.

The door cracked inward, with the bargemaster thrusting his narrow face through the opening. "She's fast, sir. Captain Ruhklyn has brought an escort contingent."

Ruhklyn, then, would be the barrel-chested soldier at the head of the mounted company Kylac now observed through the cabin window. Its members had gathered at the edge of the pitted roadway where the dock met land. A quick count revealed eleven men, all in leather, surcoat, and ebony gloves of the Shadowguard. Only Ruhklyn went unhooded, revealing a sharp crown of orange hair around a horseshoe hairline, with a beard forked to match. Both burned bright amid the rains.

"Captain, is it?" Ledron muttered. "Assemble the crew in flanking columns. Kronus will lead us out."

He looked to Kylac, who dropped the canvas drape and nodded. "When you're ready."

They gave the bargemaster a moment to assemble his crew. While listening to the shouted orders and responding footfalls, Kylac allowed his gaze to shift to Denariel, who stood wearily, as if hefting a yoke. Somewhere over the past two days, the fire had gone out of her, trampled by a grim resignation.

Kylac felt a strange pang at its loss.

She refused to turn under the weight of his gaze. Realizing this, Kylac moved toward the doorway, giving her his back.

Mayhap a bit of her fire still smoldered after all.

The columns had assembled by the time Ledron had ushered her forward to stand at his heels. Drawing the hood of the cloak provided him at Bitterwood, Kylac led them out into the rain. With only four bargemen on either side—the whole of their crew—it wasn't much of a tunnel, but enough, Kylac supposed, to help shield them from whatever danger Ledron feared. An assassin's arrow, mayhap, poised to loose the moment Denariel emerged. After Ulflund's betrayal, there was no knowing how deep or wide the Grenarr's infiltration ran, nor what they might resort to with their abduction attempt foiled.

But Kylac sensed no danger, just the pummeling rains. By the time they stepped from the barge onto the dock, their cloaks were drenched. By the time they slipped past the dockhands to stand before Ruhklyn's company, that wetness had begun to soak through.

"Captain Ledron," Ruhklyn boomed, drawing to full height upon his steed. The big brown mare snorted and pawed the earth. "The delay in your arrival had us sick with worry."

"Eased by the pride of promotion, I trust."

Ruhklyn's smile caused the braided prongs of his beard to flare outward. "A conditional appointment, pending your return. With glad heart shall I be relieved of the burden."

Tension radiated from Ledron's clenched jaw, the only response to Ruhklyn's feigned respect.

"Grieved I am, however, to learn of your losses. Fifty of our finest . . . *Lytherial's Chariot* . . ." The rival captain shook his head. "A price I'm not sure His Majesty was prepared to pay."

"Something only His Majesty can decide," Ledron growled. "Must Her Highness drown while you recount your sorrows?"

"Forgive me. We've brought a carriage—"

"I see it there, behind this wall of horseflesh. May we pass?"

For but a moment, Ruhklyn's eyes narrowed, green eyes gleaming like a viper's. Then he inclined his head and nodded to the soldier on his left, who nudged his horse aside.

"No salute for your returned captain?" Ledron asked, as he guided Denariel through the opening.

"When relieved of mine own rank, brother in arms."

Ledron tossed back a glare before redirecting his focus on the awaiting carriage. Ruhklyn's forced smile held up at his back. Trailing now, Kylac eyed the rival captain until finally the redbeard's gaze shifted to meet his. All at once, the smile vanished.

The carriage driver opened the door. Ledron searched the interior before allowing the driver to assist Denariel in entering. While she did so, the Head looked about sourly, seeming as pleased as Kylac at the prospect of riding along in that wheeled chamber, but seeing no better alternative. He wasn't going to have the princess riding out in the open. And he wasn't going to let her out of his personal reach.

"Suspects them, do ya?" Kylac asked, after Ledron had waved the driver back to his bench.

"Everyone."

"Shall I ride up front? Tell me our course, and I'll ensure they follow it."

Ledron shook his head. "Take the far window. I'll take the near."

At least we'll be sheltered from the rain, Kylac thought as he sprang aboard. For all the good it did them, with water dripping already from every layer.

No sooner had they settled in—Ledron beside Denariel, Kylac across from them—than the carriage jerked forward. Rain thrummed upon the rooftop, and dripped from their sodden garb. Ruhklyn's voice boomed in command, and mounted Shadowguard fell in alongside, further obscuring Kylac's view of their surroundings. Beyond, curious onlookers peered at them from beneath awnings and pavilions— fishmongers and merchants, artists and craftsmen, those peddling or purchasing wares despite the heavens' glum mood.

He was given to observe little else as their carriage rolled and jounced along a thoroughfare paved with crushed gravel that seemed to cut a straight path inland from the river's edge. Shops and stalls alternated with taverns, inns, stables, and foundries. Many used bright signs and pennons to compensate for drab, weathered siding. Or mayhap it was merely the rain-spawned haze that made them seem so, sapping color and luminance. A bustling port, if not a large one, Kylac decided. Few buildings stood taller than two stories, and space between them was broad and plentiful. Passing traffic was light—lighter than usual, he assumed, given the heavy rains and their armored escort, for which others diverted or pulled aside. But even if the numbers of those he saw were doubled, he'd be surprised if the city were to boast a population half as large as Wingport's—a mere fraction of those held by the larger cities with which he was familiar.

He might have asked, but had no desire to spark conversation. Once the princess was delivered to her father, he would have plenty of time to explore.

As the road started to wend and climb, marketplaces and plazas gave way to lanes of manses and clusters of cottages, with parks, gardens, and streams nestled in between. Somewhere amid the highest elevations, no doubt, he would find Kendarrion's palace, overlooking the city like a tree skirted by toadstools. Even with his view limited by the carriage walls and the line of flanking Shadowguard, Kylac felt familiar already with Avenell's design, dictated like most cities' by the lay of the land, its methods of commerce, and concerns for the security of its citizens.

His explorations—geographically, at least—would surely be minimal.

A vast spread of lawn preceded a spiked moat and the drawbridge that spanned it. The clatter of wheels and hooves dulled upon thick oaken planks. A single guard tower spanned the main gate of the curtain wall. Beneath its arch, the hammering rainfall ceased . . . only to resume on the other side, where an inner courtyard served home to a smattering of industrious Redfists. Many paused to take in the scene of arrival, and murmurs spread.

Thereafter, a high stone wall with wrought iron gates opened to receive them. Here the palace grounds awaited, whitewashed cobblestones laid down between colorful garden rows filled with benches and statuary, ponds and fountains. Kylac glimpsed caretakers crouched amid the plots and hedges, rain spilling from brimmed hats as they pruned and weeded. A young nobleman chased a maiden who frolicked teasingly around the bole of a fruit tree, wet gown clinging to her lithe frame. A pair of robed planners—architects, mayhap, or landscape artists—held discourse beneath a nearby gazebo. One gestured outward, a rolled parchment clutched in his fist, while the other ignored him, distracted by the young lovers at play.

The carriage rolled beneath another stone archway and into the next courtyard, where red-gloved Stonewatch patrolled the inner grounds and ramparts. Skirting a massive fountain at the heart of the square, the carriage turned until the view from Kylac's window was overtaken by the outer wall of a keep draped in banners, bedecked with painted shields, and fronted by a broad splay of crescent-shaped steps.

Their journey ended not at this main entrance, but inside a cavernous stables around back. There, amid the smells of hay and horses and oils and tack, Ruhklyn bellowed a halt, and they were finally given to emerge.

From the stables, Ruhklyn and his attending patrol escorted them through a series of halls and corridors until they came at last to a mid-sized audience chamber three levels up, lined on one side by windowed alcoves. Plush bench seats filled those bays, and tapestries softened the walls. High-backed chairs, divans, and multicolored cushions were clustered before a hearth at the back of the room, and a squat dais overlooking three rows of velvet-lined benches formed its head. Not the king's primary receiving chamber, given its relatively plain dressing and design, but rather reserved for more personal gatherings of the royal family and its visitors.

Ruhklyn's guard ring held up in the center of the room, keeping them hemmed, while a tall, bony steward in emerald robe turned from one of the window bays, fleshless hands wringing before him.

"Ah, Your Highness—" He hesitated, alarmed by Denariel's bruised condition. "Of great relief it is to see you."

"Is Her Highness not allowed to sit?" Ledron grumbled at Ruhklyn.

"We are to await the pleasure of His Majesty," the flame-bearded captain replied.

Something in the Blackfist's tone—the lack of apology, mayhap—caused the nape of Kylac's neck to itch.

"Word of your arrival reached His Majesty in council," the steward explained with greater reassurance, though his hands continued to wring. "He shall not be long detained."

"How is he?" Denariel asked.

"Distressed, Your Highness. Despite the circumstances, the Grenarr have stubbornly held your father to the terms of the accord. And here you are, returned just a day before the wedding."

Accord? Wedding? The words piqued Kylac's interest, as did the hint of reprimand that had crept into the steward's voice.

"I speak of my brother. How fares Thane?"

"Alive, if not whole, Your Highness. Or so the Grenarr emissary assures us."

"And my father believes her."

The steward blinked as if confused. "Your father sees little choice. As long as . . ."

He trailed off as the man who could only be Kendarrion swept into the chamber, a pair of attending Shadowguard in tow. Without slowing, he shoved aside the nearest of Ruhklyn's company, forcing his way into their inner ring. Denariel turned, and seemed to shrink, recoiling ever so slightly as her father reached for her, then enveloped her in a crushing embrace.

The king's eyes closed, his seamed face a contorted mask on the verge of tears. He was not a large man, though his layered robes lent him added girth. Even so, the strength of his arms seemed in that moment sufficient to bend iron or shatter stone. A daughter lost, suddenly regained. Kylac felt the heartache, the relief, radiating from him without any concern for those who witnessed it. Formality, protocol—the world itself—meant nothing. All he knew was the child clenched in his arms, an irreplaceable treasure he might never again let go.

Initially hesitant, Denariel reached up to return the embrace,

gripping her father with urgent need, burying her face in his shoulder
as if there to hide from the horrors she'd endured. A father fair of skin,
Kylac noted. Suggesting Denariel's *mother* had been of dark flesh . . .
else signifying some other paternity unaccounted for.

For a long moment, they clung to each other undisturbed. The
emerald-robed steward wrung his hands. Ruhklyn smirked sourly.
The rest seemed unwilling to breathe, fearing the intrusion it might
cause.

When at last Kendarrion opened his eyes, he drew back to study
his daughter—blood-born or not—at arm's length.

And slapped her full across the face.

The steward winced. Shadowguard stiffened. Kylac, so seldom
surprised, did well to keep his blades sheathed. Beside him, Ledron
had tensed, but held himself in check. Kylac resolved to do the same.

No simple task, as Denariel raised her splinted hand to her stricken
cheek and he took note of her wounded expression.

"The latter is for your brother," Kendarrion said, "and all you
nearly cost us."

Ruhklyn's sneer caused Kylac's fingers to ache for his sword hilts.
Were heads to roll in this, he knew already which would topple first.

When he looked back to Denariel, the hurt that had registered was
gone, buried beneath the more familiar, iron-willed pride. Lowering
her hand, she hefted her chin to face her father squarely. "Would that
I had stirred such strength in you long ago."

"Fool, child. Have you no sense of the consequences wrought by
your deeds? Of the lives put at risk? Your people. Your own brother.
Tossed like dice."

"I've returned, haven't I?"

"And those squandered to see you home safely, what did their
deaths gain us?"

Kendarrion's gaze shifted to Ledron, whose report, set down at
Bitterwood, had been delivered already by advance courier, laying
out for the king and his advisors the details of their voyage. Kylac
had taken no part in that official statement. Only now, in the heat
of this exchange, did he wonder at the full breadth of information
it contained.

"I took a chance, Father, which is more than you have done."

The king shook his head with grave sadness. "You speak of strength, yet with your every defiance, you weaken—"

The rasp of steel stole his words as the Shadowguard at his back whirled to meet a new retinue, this one led by a bald, black-skinned woman draped in a blue-and-yellow tabard over long, loose sleeves. Tall she was, at or above six heads. As swords crossed to block her entry, she grinned to reveal polished ivory teeth, and raised her hands in a placating gesture.

"So keen in their duty, your Shadowguard," the new arrival hailed, her smooth voice marked by a deep, penetrating timbre. "I would think those at my back sufficient for Your Majesty's comfort."

Indeed, those accompanying the ebon-skinned newcomer were Blackfists themselves, three in number, hands on hilts as if begging for a chance to draw. Their grim glares cast a stark contrast to the unarmed black woman's rapacious smile.

Kendarrion bristled. "You've keen ears, Sabrynne."

And a formidable figure, beneath that shapeless tabard. Though it might hide the precise cut of limbs and muscle, the garment couldn't veil the jutting curves of her chest, the bold arch of her back, the width of her shoulders, or the squareness of her jaw. "Meaning no insult, Your Majesty, but this castle is not so large as to stem a tide of whispers. And my master, the Great Grendavan, bade of me word be sent the moment the Princess Denariel was returned."

"I have only just now greeted her myself. I would have sent for you straightaway."

"Doubtless. May I enter? I fear the glint from your Shadowguard blades is rather blinding."

A daring woman, this Sabrynne, given the barely bridled fury of the elite soldiers by whom she was surrounded. Else a woman who believed herself above personal threat. Kendarrion's steward had made mention of an emissary. Despite the unusual physique—or typical, for all he knew of the Grenarr—that certainly seemed to describe her. An enemy allowed into their midst.

But why? How did her presence here piece together with Denariel's abduction?

The Shadowguard lowered their blades at a gesture from their king. Sabrynne, that bright grin still raising her cheeks, stepped forward, formless garb failing to fully mask the strength and grace of her movements.

"Princess," she said, with a polite bow. "Forgive such crude observation, but you appear a mite trampled. I trust you suffered no critical harm during your time in the wilds?"

Black-gloved fists throughout the chamber flexed around ready hilts. Kendarrion himself reddened angrily. "My daughter is in no condition to present herself. She will do so on the morrow, as stipulated."

"My overlord will be so pleased. But if Your Majesty will again forgive me, the miraculous timing begs a certain wariness."

"What wariness, Sabrynne?"

"This is indeed Her Highness, Princess Denariel, is it not? It would be most . . . *unsettling* if my master were to learn that I allowed a decoy to stand for her at the altar."

Denariel spat at the emissary's feet. "Take that to your altar, you tar-skinned devil."

Before matters could escalate, Kendarrion stepped between them, facing Sabrynne, warding his daughter at his back, and raising his hands to bestill any reaction from his Shadowguard. "Stand fast!" he shouted to his men, then leveled his glare at Sabrynne. "You would raise talk of suspicion? Then do your part, emissary, to alleviate mine. What I have sworn to deliver, I shall. See to it that your overlord does the same, lest tomorrow end in blood."

Sabrynne, her grin never faltering, bowed in apology. "If I have called into question Your Majesty's honor, I beg forgiveness. Rest assured, I shall report my discourtesies to my master, and ask that my tongue, if it offends him, be removed. I meant only to express my delight at hearing that Her Highness has been safely fetched in time to—"

"Fetched?" Kylac echoed. Speaking of tongues, he'd held his long enough.

Kendarrion glanced at him in annoyance. Shadowguard gazes flicked his way before turning forward again. With a pronounced craning of her sleek, sinewy neck, Sabrynne seemed to notice him for the first time.

"I beg the young sir's pardon?"

Kylac ignored her, speaking solely to Ledron. "Fetched, she says. That the way of it?"

Ledron's jaw clenched.

Sabrynne continued to smile, though her gimlet eyes held a piercing gleam. "A Shadowguard *hatchling*, Your Majesty? He appears to be missing his gloves. Or has he yet to earn them?"

"A stray, discovered on the road," Kendarrion replied dismissively. "Of some assistance, my captain tells me, in escorting my daughter home."

"Ya claimed she was abducted," Kylac reminded Ledron.

The Head replied without facing him. "Let it be. You don't understand—"

"Hence my concern. Enlighten me."

"My," voiced Sabrynne, with a jackal's delight.

Her amusement stoked Kendarrion's frustration. "You will be paid according to your services, boy," he snapped at Kylac. "Elsewise, these matters are beyond your *concern*."

"If'n he neglected to tells ya, I signed on not for gold, but for her"— his gaze flicked to Denariel—"to see her reunited with yourself. Am I to gather now that I found her in Kuuria o' her own accord? That I *fetched* her here against her will?"

The princess looked up. For the first time in days, their eyes met. Rage and loathing, no less than before, thrust at him like flaming pokers. But something more burned now amid the hate. A crack of confusion. A hint of vulnerability.

What has I done?

Tension gripped the air. Shadowguard gaped at him. Others, like Ruhklyn, looked to their king for a call to action. Kendarrion's mouth twitched, but formed no words as he grappled with his emotions, royal gaze shifting from Kylac, to his daughter, to Ledron, to his steward, to Sabrynne. Of all present, only the graceful emissary still seemed certain of herself, even as she tilted her shorn head to one side in question. "Are these the tales with which Your Majesty rallies outlanders to his cause?"

A flush colored Kendarrion's cheeks. Embarrassment, though it swiftly gave way to fury. Toward Sabrynne. Only, the emissary was untouchable. So the king whirled upon Kylac.

"I will not be questioned in my own hall by some impudent sell-sword," he said, drawing Denariel close beside him. "Captain Ledron, escort him from my sight."

"At once, Majesty."

But Kylac brushed aside his cloak to casually reveal the hilt of a shortsword. "If'n ya please, Captain. Not until I's heard some answers."

Ledron froze.

"Shadowguard!" Kendarrion barked.

Swords leapt from their scabbards, and the ring tightened by a collective step. Kylac crossed his arms, bringing palms to rest atop the pommels of his weapons. His shoulders began to tingle.

"Hold!" Ledron shouted, raising his hands in a desperate bid to stave off bloodshed. The surrounding Shadowguard wavered. "Majesty, a moment's council. I beg you."

Kendarrion looked as if his favorite jester had just spit in his stew. "Remove him, I say, and the captain of my Shadowguard says no?"

"We may ask him to leave, but we'll not force him."

The king's lip curled dangerously.

"If ever I've served you, please. I've seen too many of my brothers felled."

"That is *your* failing," Ruhklyn scoffed, "not ours."

Ledron turned to Kylac.

"Go ahead," Kylac urged softly. "Let 'em try."

Kendarrion's skeletal steward had retreated as far as he could, into the recess of the nearest window bay. Across the ring of Shadow-guard, Sabrynne had also crept back, tucking her hands within the long, loose sleeves of her shirt, ears still joined by that predatory grin.

"I will have the runt in shackles," Kendarrion insisted, "else your own head on a pike. You choose, Captain."

Ledron looked again at Kylac, his expression beseeching. But Kylac would have none of it. He was far too disgusted with himself at the prospect of having dragged a helpless maiden—as it now seemed—back into a situation she had willfully sought to escape. At the heart of that decision lay a deceit played upon him by the captain and his Shadowguard. A failing of his own making, yes, but any opportunity to rectify matters began with a discovery of the truth.

The Head must have taken some measure of this, for his gaze was the first to falter. Shoulders sagged before squaring with resolve. "Then I must advise my lord to withdraw himself and Her Highness to safety." His hand gripped his sword hilt, though he was wise enough not to draw it. "Arys," he added, addressing the Blackfist nearest the doorway. "Send for reinforcements."

The king sputtered in disbelief. "You number more than a dozen."

"And what Your Majesty has asked will require at least a score."

"Best make it two," Kylac suggested. "In fair warning, for carrying my carcass from those tunnels."

Ledron studied him. "Arys, make it so."

Arys looked to his king. "My lord?"

Seeming to lose confidence that this was some manner of bluff, Kendarrion nodded absently. As Arys departed, sounding an alarm, the king stepped back toward the dais, drawing his scowling daughter with him.

"Ridiculous," Ruhklyn said. Hefting his ready sword, the flame-bearded giant stepped slowly around Ledron and into the center of the ring, positioning himself to both face Kylac and shield his royal charges. "Give word, my lord, and I shall bleed the whelp."

"No," said Ledron. With an upraised arm meant to fend off the rival captain, he pivoted to face Kylac squarely. "If he is to kill any of us, he will kill me first."

"Ya believe I won't?"

"I believe I executed my duty to my king, my people. If death is to be the price, let me pay it."

Kylac's fingers tapped his pommels. Should the captain account for his lies with his life? Difficult to decide without knowing the precise nature of those falsehoods, and how deep they ran.

The slap of leather-soled footsteps against castle tile preceded the return of Arys and another half dozen Shadowguard. And behind them, a dozen more. Kylac paid little heed as they filed into the chamber and fanned wide, sealing off the exit. His only focus was

Ledron, weighing, calculating, determining the guardian's fate.

A fountain of energy climbed his spine and cascaded over neck and shoulders, begging release. He might kill every one of these men and free Denariel to roam as she pleased. Would she thank him for that? He tried to imagine it, but could only envision her glaring and shrieking and cursing the day he was born.

Another ten Shadowguard arrived, faces anxious as they crowded in, pressing the inner ranks forward. They couldn't yet know what threatened, but seemed eager enough to meet it. Forty-five soldiers in all. There weren't enough rugs in the room to soak up all the blood.

"You have your numbers, Captain," Kendarrion noted, from behind a wall of bodies now. "Take the boy into custody, if you would."

"I's never been one for dungeons." Rank with emotion, the chamber had become. Amid the expectant stares and sweating palms of the Shadowguard seethed the king's ire, Sabrynne's curiosity, the steward's trepidation, Ledron's stoic resolve, and Denariel's antipathy. The time had come for some fresh air. "Let us talk later, when all are a mite less riled."

A backflip landed him feetfirst atop the nearest window bench. The steward cringing there let out a startled yelp. Several of the Shadowguard leaned back in surprise. Still facing them, Kylac launched a sidekick that shattered the latch between the dual casement windows, causing them to burst outward. A gust of wind and rain swept into the room.

With a snarl, Ruhklyn charged   only to trip over Ledron's outstretched leg. Face-first, the rival captain fell. But his rush had incited the others, and in the next breath, a wave of Shadowguard surged toward the window.

Kylac ducked outside onto a rain-slicked ledge. As the first swords thrust after him, he dropped to a stone terrace extending from the second story below. Shouts rang. Hopping the terrace balustrade, he hit the lawn, arresting his momentum with a forward roll. Already, the shouts were spawning echoes. He peered up at a covered turret and found a sentry there pointing down at his position.

He veered right, skirting the castle wall, making for a nearby orchard. Commotion, alarms—let them have their little uproar.

Kendarrion's troops could buzz about like hornets until their wings fell off. In a thousand different places could he conceal himself, in a hundred different ways. So that he might spare them, he wouldn't allow them to catch him.

Into the orchard he sped, lashed by rain and self-reproach, as the cries of futile pursuit gathered in his wake.

27

Starlight slipped through the arrow loops in the stone wall to form slivered pools on the chamber floor. The heads of those pools, arched to a point, scratched at the edge of an old, burgundy rug run through with spirals of faded gold. A sun-bleached tapestry hung from the far wall, flanked by fraying banners. The bed was large, but its blankets smelled of must, and the wardrobe wide, but had been gnawed by rats and was layered in dust. Tarnish coated the brass candle holders on the bedside table, while scratches and clouds marred the full-length mirror standing in the far corner. The chamber pot was chipped and made of clay.

Though every necessity had been provided, no shrewd guest would feel welcome here.

Kylac hid between wardrobe and outer wall, where the gathered shadows lay thickest. For nearly an hour had he waited, cloaked in stillness. The sporadic rains had finally ceased just before dusk, and the clamor of the evening's search had subsided. The palace grounds and castle halls still swarmed with patrols, and both Shadowguard and Stonewatch remained on fullest alert. But in this secluded pocket of the rear keep's eastern wall, activity was minimal.

Upon reaching the orchard hours earlier, he'd had half a mind to simply keep going. Scale the walls of the palace grounds and slip out into the city. Disappear among its citizens and be rid of this entire affair. He'd clearly involved himself in a matter that he shouldn't have. In what way would it benefit him to kick up a greater fuss? Especially when the apparent victim would sooner see him flayed and roasted on a spit then receive his apologies.

But therein lay the crux of his unease. Throughout this journey, he'd believed Denariel's hatred of him to be misguided, a byproduct of her spoiled nature or a lack of willingness to truly understand his. He couldn't fault himself for that, and so had wasted little concern over it. As long as *he* knew he was doing her a service, she could thank him however she wished.

The revelations in Kendarrion's meeting chamber had changed that. He'd done Denariel no service, and she had ample reason to despise him for it. If it wasn't too late, he felt beholden to make amends.

He stood slim chance of doing so, however, without better knowledge of the situation. His rash action in siding with Sallun, and assumed understanding in joining up with Ledron, was what had led to this. With a piece or two of the puzzle still open to interpretation, and at least a few others missing entirely, his first task would be to gather the full story.

After a moment's consideration, he'd determined just where to get it.

Or so he'd supposed. After discerning this chamber's location and stealing into it, he'd believed the most difficult portion of his mission accomplished. But the quarters had been empty, leaving him to wait . . . and wait . . . and wait . . . until he'd begun to wonder if he hadn't made another mistake. A whisper overheard was only as reliable as the mouth that uttered it. The information might have been wrong, or even staged to steer him false. Though the latter seemed unlikely, his target might have been transferred or detained without common knowledge. Even truthful gossip had a way of souring over time.

Patience, he'd urged himself silently, and did so again, leashing his doubts. For every possibility of error, there remained an equal likelihood that he'd chosen correctly. His father had taught him early on how perilous a lack of patience could be, and how often success was but a matter of waiting out one's opponent. If it took all night, he would try again on the morrow.

The air cooled, and darkness deepened. Sounds softened and bled away. Kylac half slept as he stood there, resting his eyes and thoughts, adjusting his stance to keep muscles fresh.

Waiting.

Then voices approached, a dim murmur answered by a harsh grunt. His eyes opened. Peering around the edge of the wardrobe, he spied torchlight seeping beneath the chamber door. A hand worked the latch. Freeing a knife from its sheath, Kylac leaned back.

Four figures, three of them armored. Only one entered, sandaled feet brushing against the woven mat set down upon the threshold. The others posted themselves outside the door as it closed, sentries and jailors both.

The lone occupant lit a bedside candle before shedding her sandals and stepping to the wardrobe, soft on her feet. Kylac remained still, breathless, as the doors opened. The woman shed her tabard, then pulled her loose shirt overhead. As it came free, Kylac appeared behind her, pressing a hand over her mouth and laying a knife against her throat.

"I'd has words with ya, Sabrynne," he hissed in the emissary's ear. "But quietly. Yelp for your guards, and ya'll have one less tongue to offer your overlord."

He waited for the cords in her neck to slacken, and for taut muscles in her torso to relax. They did so more quickly than he would have thought. Slowly, he released his muffling hand, keeping the blade in place.

"Beg aid of the vipers against the adder?" the emissary asked softly. Though she didn't turn, Kylac caught the insidious grin that stretched her black lips. "Darr's hatchling, I presume."

"Ya saw clearly enough what His Majesty thinks o' me."

"Or what His Majesty would have me *believe* he thinks of you."

A woman accustomed to lies within layers. Kylac nearly grinned himself. "Ya thinks me a pawn in this. And mayhap I's been. So tell me, what game are we playing?"

"Asks the pawn of another pawn?"

"I's heard their account. Now I'll hear yours. And see what truth might be sifted between them."

"Ah, but where does the game begin?"

Kylac could speed the conversation, he supposed, by sharing what he thought he already knew. But why give Sabrynne opportunity to let him cling to false assumption? "Wherever ya please, until I's heard it all. Thane," he added, when the emissary remained silent. "What is this about the prince?"

"Darr's son, as I am told."

Kylac's blade pressed deeper. "These halls are filled with voices, Sabrynne, but all speak the same. Raiders, they calls ya. Reavers, slayers, vermin. They say your skin is a curse and that your hearts beat only pus. Would ya say nothing to refute them?"

"Pus, is it? Nudge that blade much closer, and I suppose we'll learn."

From the lack of tension in her smooth voice, Kylac's threat had already exhausted itself. He could either slit the emissary's throat and seek his answers elsewhere, or find another way to draw the other out. "Is your grievance so flawed that ya'll not even try it on me?" He stepped back, withdrawing his knife. "Ya do has a grievance here, don't ya?"

Sabrynne cocked her head, no doubt wondering if Kylac meant to plunge the blade into her back. Slowly, she rounded to face him. "What do you care of our grievance?"

"Outlander, Kendarrion named me, and outlander I am. Must the king's enemies be mine? I's yet to decide."

The black grin broadened, lips curling to reveal the pink tissue underneath. "You seek to profit where you may. A swine rooting for truffles."

"I's been called worse. By any name, a better friend than enemy."

Sabrynne licked the corner of her mouth, crossing arms etched with lean muscle over her ample bosom. Even in dim candlelight, Kylac could see every fibrous cord beneath the sleek, black skin of her shoulders. If this woman served as an emissary, how strong and seasoned were the Grenarr who served as warriors?

"The tattoo," Kylac noted, gesturing with his knife toward the shark's fin inked upon her neck—hidden earlier by the collar of her tabard. "Has it any significance?"

"A symbol of the sea. Of the perils our people have endured. The perils we mean to escape."

"The land holds perils of its own, from what I's seen. This one in particular."

"As my people well know. It was *our* forefathers who settled this island, not theirs. Ours who drove the savage creations of the long-lost Gorrethrehn inland to make its shores inhabitable. The isle of Grenah, we named it. The Addarans came later, refugees and castoffs from their own far-flung lands. A battered people, dispossessed, upon whom we took pity. We bade them welcome, opening our settlements to them, sharing our resources. More came, to find similar welcome. And still more. For more than a century we toiled together, side by side. But as time progressed, prosperity fostered greed, which spawned disputes, which culminated in war. By then, we Grenarr were hope-lessly outnumbered. Betrayed by those we'd once rescued, we were driven from the land, banished to the seas and a scattering of barren atolls. For nearly two centuries have we persevered, surviving as we may, taming the ocean, yet never forgetting the homeland that was taken from us."

We. The woman spoke of events generations old as if she'd lived through them. Despite the calmness of her recitation, it was evident that the enmity of her forebears burned deep. "So ya'd reclaim it. Drive forth the Addarans as they did you. Take your revenge."

"So say the Addarans, for fear and betrayal is what they know. A piece is all we ask. A mere toehold upon which to cultivate crops, raise livestock, build lasting homes upon sturdy soil. A means by which to sustain our children, to give them a better life than the sea alone can provide. We've asked their rulers for this. Begged and bartered for generations. We've much to offer in trade, given our mastery of the sea. But they will concede us not a scrap—not a single plot or parcel—for fear that we would try to take more."

This much, at least, matched to some degree the tale Ledron had fed him in Wingport. A stalemate between the land-dwelling Addarans and seabound Grenarr. The stories differed, of course, in who was to blame, each omitting mention of his crimes and cruelties against the other, neither acknowledging the other's claim upon this land.

Elsewise, the foundation was the same. So he decided to forge ahead and prod for the next piece. "Ya needed something more to barter with, then. Something Kendarrion wouldn't refuse."

"His son," Sabrynne confessed. "The crown prince, Dethaniel. Aye, we took him. In an effort to end the bloodshed between our peoples. To better induce his father to hear our proposal."

"Which was?"

"A sliver of land upon the northeastern peninsula. As far as possible from their principal settlements here in the south. A region barely inhabited, held chiefly to ensure that we do not. Of no great cost for all we can offer, and to ensure Dethaniel's safe return. A fair accord by any measure."

"Ransom, some might calls it."

"Perhaps. But no lives lost, and countless saved."

"And the princess?"

"To seal the accord—"

"Ransom."

Sabrynne smirked, bowing slightly. "To entice Kendarrion and his ilk to keep the peace, she will wed our overlord himself, Great Grendavan the Eighth."

"A hostage."

"A queen, to rule at our overlord's side and unite two nations. Befitting, really, as her mother was Addaran, and her true father Grenarr."

He should have welcomed the information, for the answer it served to Her Highness's unresolved parentage. But the emissary's smile took on a wolfish cast, triggering in Kylac an inner alarm. "By choice?"

The smile became sad. "Cruel, this world can be. One more reason to end this bitter feud between our peoples."

A ravishing. Which would best explain Kendarrion's fury toward these people—and Denariel's. A story worth exploring, but not one he wished to hear secondhand. Should Sabrynne try to rationalize *that*, he might have to check her veins for pus after all. "So how did Denariel end up in Kuuria?" he asked instead.

"Did she? We know only that she disappeared shortly after the terms of the accord—"

"Ransom."

"—were settled."

"Abducted, I was told."

The emissary shook her head. "An accusation we weathered, initially. But the trail confirmed what our spies had reported: that she had sailed forth in willing secret, attended by a captain of the king's own Shadowguard, conveniently enough."

Ulflund. The captain named renegade by Sallun and Ledron. And renegade he may have been—at least against the king—if he'd thrown in with Denariel somehow. "And your overlord's response was, what? To await her return?"

A feint. A chance for Sabrynne to lie to him.

"My master feared it a ruse," the emissary admitted, and did well to seem pained by it. "A game Darr was playing to safeguard his daughter. The king claimed that this wayward captain had been dismissed from service even prior to his desertion, for failing to prevent Dethaniel's capture, but could not say where he and the Princess Denariel might have gone. The Great Grendavan determined that further inducement was required. It thus fell upon me to present Kendarrion with his son's ring finger, to accompany the signet ring delivered earlier as evidence of his initial seizure."

Capture and *seizure* seemed tame words for abduction, but Kylac decided to let them go. "Kendarrion's response?"

"Word by then had been received. Denariel meant to petition the aid of some cousin—an Emperor Derreg—the distant ruler of some distant land. Her disgraced captain had assembled a handful of so-called Loyalists, a crew of mercenaries, and a beastly Ukinh to serve under her command. They did so, the king assured us, without his commission, in defiance of his personal wishes. He only learned of it because an informant in Denariel's company had betrayed their circumstances and destination with a delayed report. On the chance this information proved true, an elite company would be setting sail aboard their fastest ship to give pursuit."

"Still ya disbelieved him?"

"We wished him speed and fortune in her retrieval, and bade him send Dethaniel's royal finger with the pursuers, along with a threat to hack the prince into further pieces if the wedding did not take place as planned—in the event that Denariel should require further persuading."

With such brutal honesty, Kylac was inclined to believe her. Moreover, the fragments fit. Ledron had truly held Ulflund a traitor to king and crown. By extension, would he not have held the runaway princess a traitor to her father and brother? Thane's severed finger might have humbled her, accounting for her resentful cooperation in returning home. Shards. Given the slaughter of her cohorts in Wingport—most by Ledron, the remainder by Kylac—what choice would she have had?

Lass should have told me, he thought. Had she confided in him, he might have found a way to help. But what cause had she been given to do so? He'd already slain her Shadowguard captain. To her, he was but another mercenary—not unlike the one who'd already betrayed her. She couldn't know that he'd been misled.

That he'd acted too quickly, too blindly, to learn what he'd truly stepped into.

"Difficult this must be," Sabrynne allowed, "through a father's eyes. My master is unsurprised that the terms have proven easier to accept than abide."

Even now, the emissary was unconvinced that Kendarrion meant to follow through. To her, the entire episode of Denariel's disappearance was more likely a subterfuge the king himself had orchestrated. "How deep can a man's machinations go?"

Sabrynne's eyes gleamed in the candlelight. "No further, I pray, with my master arriving on the morrow to claim his bride."

"And does your master truly mean to return the prince?"

"How long would our claim upon these shores last if he did not? We will honor our side of the accord—"

"Ransom."

"—and trust that Kendarrion's love for Denariel will entice him to honor his."

Of some question, that. If the king was willing to trade this half-daughter for his presumably trueborn son, might he also sacrifice her for the sake of his progeny? As much as Sabrynne sought to downplay the Grenarr threat, it seemed clear that any concession granted now would increase the danger to Kendarrion's people gen-erations hence. "Anything more?"

"A question of my own, if I may. Do you mean to interfere?"

"Should I?" Kylac shook his head, genuinely conflicted. "It's not for me to correct this world's ills, even if'n I could identifies them."

"Keen interest you've shown, for one content to stand aside."

"Calls it umbrage. I won't tolerate being played false."

Sabrynne's dark head bobbed with understanding. "Have I been truthful enough?"

"I'll let ya knows." Sheathing his knife, Kylac turned toward the door.

"The guard," Sabrynne warned.

"The windows are too narrow," Kylac explained, as he tripped the latch and opened the door.

All three Shadowguard remained, facing him as he emerged. He punched two in the throat, leaving them doubled over and gasping for breath. The third managed to grasp the hilt of a sword before being driven to his knees with that same arm bent behind him. All three lay slumped in forced slumber before any could raise a moan.

"They may has questions when they wake," Kylac acknowledged, with Sabrynne peering at him from the doorway. "Answer them as ya will."

And like a stray whisper, he ventured down the hall.

28

Tʜᴇ ɢʀᴇɴᴀʀʀ ᴀʀʀɪᴠᴇᴅ at daybreak.

As the dawning sun crested the horizon, Whitefists blew seashell horns within their towers, sounding the alert. Bells rang throughout the city, taking up the cry and spreading unspoken word to all corners and districts within moments. A grim awakening for those only beginning to stir. The enemy had been sighted.

That or a hurricane, thought Kylac, as he climbed the southern seawall upon a flight of lichen-covered steps. He glanced up at a cloudless sky, where stars were fading amid the brightening heavens. Yet, upon the wharfside district visible across the bay, vendors in the midst of opening shops and assembling stalls were reverting course, stowing wares and securing possessions, battening down as they would against a storm. Others, refusing to be cowed, carried on as if planting a battle standard, boastful of their courage and disparaging of those giving heed to caution. Despite those taunts, fishing boats being readied for launch were tied fast, and those in the harbor already set sail swung about as if realizing they'd forgotten their nets. Traps and poles along the shore were withdrawn, and an inland exodus begun.

The southern seawall had been erected atop a thick stone jetty that arced south and east from this main shore to form harbor and serve barrier against the sea's more violent intrusions. Atop its weathered heights, Kylac gazed out upon a smattering of vessels riding ocean swells colored jade by the morning twilight. Small, coastal rigs, creeping about like fleas on a hound's pelt. Save one. Bearing from the east, the sleek black vessel approached with the rising sun at its back, riding a stream of molten gold. A giant beetle, this one, its dark carapace bristling with sharp ridges, piercing spines, and serrated edges. The fleas scattered before it, scurrying to either flank when failing to outrun it, where they were brushed aside by the great wake billowing behind it, unworthy of its attentions.

For several moments, Kylac observed its approach, while warm waves crashed against the seawall and the jetty on which it was built, touching his cheek with salty spray. Other onlookers had joined him by then, more curious than afraid. Urchins like himself, for the most part—homeless souls with little to lose and less to protect. Some murmured bitterly about Kendarrion's cowardice, how he would sell their lives for that of his own son. Others shook their fists in the air and hollered outright threats, vowing the peace would never last, that they would kill any tar-skin foolish enough to set foot upon their shores.

Toothless bluster, for the most part, though Kylac wouldn't discount the anger and frustration that fueled it. One didn't erase centuries of fear, hate, and misunderstanding simply because a pair of kings might clasp hands in forced truce.

As the Grenarr ship neared the mouth of the harbor, mobilizing soldiers rushed to meet it—Whitefists atop the seawall, Redfists along the inner shore. The beetle maintained its speed and heading, gaining size and definition, seemingly undeterred by the thickening cluster of armor-clad bodies, or by the loaded catapults, ballistae, and other armaments being readied to receive it. As with their emissary, Sabrynne, these Grenarr believed themselves untouchable. Making the Addaran response a display of strength for the city's pride, nothing more.

Or so Kylac presumed. And yet, he took note that the Seagate, as he'd heard it called, had yet to be dropped low enough to permit a vessel with near as deep a draft as the one driving toward them. Stretched between squat stone anchor towers north and south at the corners of the bay's mouth, the great chain—with iron links as

long and thick and twice as heavy as a man—appeared sufficiently
strong to forbid the windblown passage of any ship when drawn as
taut as it was now. Though dipped at its center below the waterline
to permit the egress of smaller, local crafts, the barnacle-encrusted,
seaweed-laden Seagate remained set to serve its longtime purpose of
repelling any would-be maritime invaders.

Might Kendarrion have had a change of heart?

"Clear the wall!" a voice rang out. A company of Seawatch approached at Kylac's back with bows in hand, sweeping onlookers aside
as they raced along the battlement. "Clear, in the name of the king!"

That drew more mutters and curses, but the Whitefists weren't
pausing to argue. The jeers they ignored, but when a rangy codger
threw a mussel at the company commander, the commander had him
apprehended and forcibly dragged back down an access stair. When
another pair rose up in defiance of the codger's rough treatment, a
brief scuffle resulted in one of them tumbling over the rampart, to
smash against the jetty rocks at the outer base of the wall.

As blood seeped from the broken body, it seemed for a breath that a
full-force riot might erupt. But with more and more soldiers arriving,
the protestors settled for howling in outrage, even as they scurried to
get clear. Meanwhile, a resounding clank echoed ominously from the
Seagate's flanking anchor towers, signaling the release of whatever
locking mechanisms were housed within. A shrill, rhythmic groan
followed hard upon, marking the slow, grinding turn of hidden drums
unreeling massive lengths of chain. Amid a clattering keen, the Seagate sagged, its own weight hauling it downward, into watery depths.

So much for the king's resistance.

Realizing what little good his blades could accomplish here, Kylac
himself made a show of cowering as the trampling Whitefists ran by.
For pity's sake, he paid cursory respect to the overzealous protestor
sprawled lifelessly upon the jetty below—committing the unfortunate
wretch to memory on the chance no one else had—before claiming a
place in line among the departing civilians. Time to position himself
where the true conflict would be centered.

No great mystery, given the activity upon the wharf, where a
Stonewatch contingent was clearing the docks around the largest

slip in the harbor while establishing an inland cordon against those citizens who'd begun to gather. As Kylac reached the base of the seawall stair and began the long loop around the bay, he noticed also a commotion higher up within the city, suggesting the movement of a company from the palace grounds. A welcoming retinue, likely as not, dispatched to receive the new arrivals.

He hastened his pace, keeping to the edge of the well-worn road-way, hood raised to obscure his face. Not that he expected anyone to recognize him. But, with so many soldiers bustling about, there seemed no cause for unnecessary risk. As their number and frequency increased, he took to slipping in and out of the light flow of civilian traffic making its way in either direction. Now and then, when he felt a passing gaze weighted with possible interest, he would duck behind a horse, a wagon, a clutch of fellow travelers, vanishing as needed.

All the while, he marked the continued approach of the Grenarr vessel, which was fast transforming from beetle to bird of prey. Its angled prow, towering masts, and thick lines were raked and taut, like a falcon in descent. A jutting bowsprit served as beak, and the armaments bristling upon its decks as talons. Like any predator, full of power and grace. Much larger it now seemed, here within the harbor, than it had upon the broad expanse of the coastal tides. Should it decide to attack, it wouldn't easily be felled.

For all its harsh appearance, however, the enemy ship slid into port without a hint of aggression. Kylac had rounded the western loop of the jetty by then, turning east upon the mainland side of the bay. Still half a mile distant, he again hastened his stride, surrounded now by a thickening stream of civilians flowing toward the docks in either curiosity or protest. His progress slowed as the press thickened, coming to a halt at a human wall thirty paces out. With alleys to either side similarly clogged, he took to the rooftops—also inhabited, though not as heavily. There, he slithered unerringly among the distracted onlookers, too sleek and swift to draw much notice, finding ways to blend and disappear when he did. A mere eddy amid a churning river, he saw little risk of causing greater stir.

For their part, the Grenarr appeared kind enough to wait on him, showing no sign of making ready to disembark. Sails had been furled, and mooring lines tied fast. But no planks had been lowered, and no crewmen come forth. He could see sentries in the nests and ratlines, but there they perched, observing the mob come to greet their arrival, awaiting some further command.

Stonewatch soldiers peered back at them, those assembled on the wharf who weren't engaged in keeping the crowd at bay. Their collective stance was nonthreatening, but neither had they been ordered to set aside their pikes and spears. Impassive though they might seem, Kylac could taste their emotions on the wind—a stew of indignation and hostility tinged with fear.

His rooftop course led him to a sharply sloped corner perch overlooking the dockside plaza. The turret's height and pitch would discourage any from joining him, but the distance was too great to hear much in the way of any words that might be exchanged. Given the size of the retinue descending through the city, and the furor attending it, he'd be unsurprised to find Kendarrion himself amid the train. Either way, Kylac desired a seat closer to the imminent proceedings.

He took a moment to calculate the various methods by which to make that happen. Penetrating the guard ring would be difficult, though not impossible, given the distraction of the crowd. He might subdue a Redfist posted outside the cordon, and make use of the uniform to join the soldiers within. Else he might attach himself like a barnacle beneath the dock, or even to the belly of a carriage as it passed over a bridge or drainage hole.

He settled on a far simpler course, descending from one perch while taking aim at another. Down on the dock, at the outer edge of the Stonewatch cordon to one side, stood a large loading arm. In service to the adjacent berth, yet near enough to observe the welcoming. A pack of teenaged youth were clambering up the post, trying to claw their way to the top, finding little success. Kylac would just have to show them how.

By the time he'd descended and skirted the heart of the crowd, the royal retinue was arriving—a train of six carriages surrounded by threescore soldiers—which served to draw the throng's attention. Kylac used that diversion to worm his way through those milling

along the edge and to reach the loading arm. A disheveled youth
with a buck-toothed sneer had managed to scale it with the aid of
his companions, where he now jeered and hurled epithets at everyone and no one. While his street-tough comrades argued as to who
should go next, Kylac sidled up to the base of the post.

"Room for another?" he asked.

Giving them no time to respond, he shimmied his way to the
top, where Buck-tooth greeted him in openmouthed surprise. When
that had subsided, the young thug furrowed his brow as if preparing
to object. Kylac looked him in the eye, grimacing as he presented
a knife, twirled it in his fingers, and jammed it into the beam on
which they sat.

"Filthy tar-skins," he spat. "I'll flay every one o' them."

The thug studied the embedded knife, the post Kylac had so effort-
lessly scaled, the leery gazes of his friends below, and decided to let
the newcomer be.

There Kylac roosted, of no particular notice amid the swarm of
humanity, waiting for the display to unfold.

He didn't have to wait long. After parting the crowds to lead the
carriage train safely onto the dock, the attending troops set about
reinforcing the cordon. When the wall of Redfists had doubled in
thickness, Captain Ruhklyn motioned to the pair of Shadowguard
warding the lead carriage door. The door opened, and out stepped
Kendarrion.

"Traitor!" the people cried. "Craven!"

"Burn them in their box!" one man urged. "Make it a floating
coffin!"

The king seemed hunched and sluggish in his movements as the
chorus of displeasure and derision rained upon him. Nonetheless, he
ignored the jeers and catcalls while mustering the strength to step
forward, escorted by a personal guard ring twelve strong, until he
stood facing the larboard side of the docked ship, there to await the
pleasure of his enemy.

Kylac looked back to the remaining carriages, but no other bodies
emerged. Not Denariel. Not Ledron. He wondered if the latter was
even now watching over the princess, or if his absence indicated

something more notable. Had events of the prior afternoon left the Head in disfavor? Gazing down from his overhang at where Ruhklyn stood beside the king with proud chest and jutting, fork-bearded jaw, Kylac found himself measuring what, if anything, the rival captain's prominent presence here might suggest about Ledron's standing.

Contemplating what effect it might have on his actions.

After several moments of no discernible movement from the Grenarr, the crowd's energy waned, anger giving way to uncertainty. Gradually, an expectant hush stole through their ranks, dulling their roar to a murmur. Though the citizens clustered here numbered in the thousands, far more had chosen to hunker in their homes or head inland to higher ground and greater safety. Many of those who'd chosen to place themselves in the line of fire had to now be wondering, which was the wiser choice?

When the sun had slipped fully from the sea, the Grenarr at last showed signs of activity, lowering a gangplank by which to descend from the maindeck. As the plank touched down upon the dock, the crowd rediscovered its voice, taking affront, it seemed, to even that sliver of befouled wood making contact with their shores.

The first Grenarr to venture forth proved to be a pair of hulking brutes standing well over seven heads in height, scant dress revealing the impressive cut of heavily muscled limbs and torsos. Each carried a harpoon eight feet in length, capped with a barbed head. Though some within the crowd hollered all the louder, many were duly intimidated, sapping the overall uproar.

Behind the pair of guards came a man taller still, yet leaner, accompanied by one who, at six-and-a-half heads, appeared short in comparison. Both were strong of jaw and broad of shoulder, though tunics and leather pauldrons revealed a lesser measure of skin. Their physiques were imposing nonetheless. By the standard of her fellows, the stately Sabrynne now seemed almost a dwarf.

As did Kendarrion, when the enemy quartet settled before him, half-naked guards flanking the more modestly clad pair at the center. Though outnumbered three to one by the king's attending Shadowguard, it was the towering Grenarr contingent that appeared the more formidable.

After a momentary standoff, the tallest among the Grenarr bowed low to Kendarrion, then raised his arm in an expansive gesture toward the crowd. His voice boomed in declaration. "People of Avenell, you honor us with your welcome."

A swell of boos spawned a cascade of threats. The Grenarr leader weathered both with a broad smile, as if accepting an ovation.

"And Your Majesty, Kendarrion," he added, when the furor began to wane, "a gesture most noble, to greet us personally."

Kendarrion's stance was frigid, though his glare was molten. He seemed to chew his response before he uttered it. "With pride and purpose, we receive you, Great Grendavan, in hopes that the enmity of our forebears should be resigned to the past."

He closed the statement with what seemed a growl, and again the throng roared its displeasure. Insult heaped upon injury. It was clearly taking every measure of restraint Kendarrion could manage to observe propriety here, when it looked as if he would sooner leap forward and throttle the overlord standing before him. The anger of the crowd added nothing to his own.

"I had hoped that Her Highness, Princess Denariel, might be here to join us," Grendavan admitted. "If I may, are preparations in order for this night's ceremony?"

Again the protests rang. Kendarrion did nothing to stem them, allowing them to play out before answering. "All is being attended to. Her Highness is making ready to execute her duty."

"A duty not without reward." The overlord grinned slyly, drawing a fresh wave of outrage. "Nonetheless," he amended, again project-ing his voice to the masses, "I understand your fears. Change breeds uncertainty. We too are wary, afraid of what lies ahead. And yet, just as we draw warmth from the dawning sun of this new day, allowing it to burn away brume and shadow, we are also hopeful. To that warmth, that hope, should we cling. Despite the troublesome cir-cumstances by which this union is wrought, I stand convinced that your people and mine, and the children of these lands, will come to celebrate this day."

The crowds murmured and groaned, but seemed to be quieting overall, anxious mayhap to hear Kendarrion's rebuttal. "Is this the

whole of your delegation, then? I was informed there would be more."
A passive reply, which drew more ire from the crowd.

"A mere twoscore have I brought. Family, nobles, captains, to serve
as witness. If it please Your Majesty, they await my signal."

"Bring them. My chief seneschal has been instructed to see to
your comfort."

"And safety, I trust. Surely Your Majesty sees the confidence we
demonstrate in placing ourselves in your care."

Ostensibly, yes. But if Kylac had understood it correctly from
Sabrynne, Dethaniel would not be returned until *after* the wedding
ceremony. Thus, it was in Kendarrion's interest to see to it that all
went as planned, if indeed he meant to see his son again.

The king mustered a curt nod. Grendavan leaned toward the
shorter attendant beside him, who turned to face the ship, placed a
hand in his mouth, and gave a shrill whistle. Almost at once, a line
of Grenarr appeared atop the gangplank and began to make their way
down—males mostly, but with a handful of females among them.

Much of the crowd began to disperse. Odd. Should it not stoke
their fury to witness this greater number of Grenarr welcomed so
freely to their shores?

"Festering coward," Buck-tooth muttered beside him. Kylac turned
as the young thug lowered himself by his arms before dropping to the
dock below. Accompanied by his small band of urchins, the hardened
youths strolled away.

Kylac realized then that most in attendance had come solely for
blood. Despairing now of finding it, they could stomach no more of
this farce. They'd thought to see these marauders spitted over a fire,
near enough to hear the screams and smell the charred flesh. Surely
that was the only way their king would ever willingly receive them.
Instead, those still watching saw the Grenarr escorted in small groups
to the empty carriages, which had been brought to convey them safely
and comfortably through the city to the royal palace. A far better
treatment than many Addarans could ever hope to experience, yet
extended openly to their most hated adversaries. Appalled, they were
turning away, looking to slake their bloodthirst elsewhere.

Plenty remained, raising their voices as if to compensate for those departing. But their objections were no match, it seemed, for their king's will. Though he seethed at Grendavan's reassuring smile, Kendarrion remained resolute in the love he bore his son, and would therefore do nothing to jeopardize the prince's life.

Further words were exchanged between the rival rulers, but Kylac couldn't make them out. The spectacle portion of this was over—at least until the wedding, he supposed. All that remained between now and then was a matter of logistics best discussed privately.

When all was said and done, the company of Redfists wrangling the crowd opened a path through which Ruhklyn's Shadowguard ushered the royal train. Grendavan and his towering guards had entered the last of the empty carriages, in line immediately after Kendarrion's. The shorter Grenarr attendant remained behind, striding back up the gangplank as the train set forth.

It was this man whom Kylac's gaze followed when the carriages had rolled clear. He took note of the stubborn protestors who set forth on foot in pursuit of their king, as if their harsh words might gain sway at some point along the city route. He saw the line of Redfists that remained planted along the inner edge of the dock, a deterrent against any who might seek to threaten their unwelcome guests while in port. But it was the ship itself—specifically the number and positions of those left behind to patrol it—that held his greatest interest.

In the hours since his mooncast conversation with Sabrynne, Kylac had found plenty of time to consider the situation—chiefly what he could live with, and what he could not, before he put this matter behind him. If Kendarrion was determined for them to eat the meal the Grenarr had prepared, so be it. But did that mean they had to partake of it precisely as it had been laid out?

If he was to attend this feast to conclusion, Kylac intended first to season a dish or two to his taste.

A vague plan formulating in his mind, he dropped from his roost and melted into the dockside crowd. He still had plenty of information to gather, and only the daylight hours in which to do it. Come nightfall, he would act, and the course of this adventure would change.

With a tingling anticipation brewing in his veins, he set forth under the rising sun to make ready for the pending darkness.

29

"ANYTHING TO REPORT?" Kylac asked, his voice deep and gruff as he climbed into the crow's nest beside the Grenarr lookout.

"Nothing," the lookout grunted. "The night is—"

Kylac's knife bit into the back of the sentry's neck, severing his nerve tether. As the victim's useless legs buckled, Kylac caught him around the mouth with one hand while slicing his throat with the other. The blade slipped through the man's leather hauberk as if it were wet parchment, dragging deeply enough to part the flesh and veins beneath, yet leaving the windpipe intact. Breaching a man's airflow might reduce the chance of scream or shout, but often led to noisy sputtering and choking as throat and lungs fought to repel the invasion of fluid. Dying this way was cleaner, quieter, and virtually painless.

It was the best Kylac could offer him.

He held the body long enough to control its spasms, to make sure it didn't thump or thrash about in any way that might reveal itself over the creaking of the ship, the gusting of the wind, or the breaking of waves against the dock's pilings. Unlikely, at this elevation, with the sentries below focused on their respective fields of view as trained. But the night was young, and his work only just begun. Too soon yet to risk a rogue echo or any other mistake.

When the lookout had bled his way to lasting darkness, Kylac propped him back up and drove a shortsword through the front of his neck and into the mast, pinning him in place, hilt bracing his chin. Undetectable from below, given the dark clouds, new moon, and harbor brume. For anyone not standing in the crow's nest, it might not have been noticeable in the brightest day.

He descended along the mast, doing nothing to hide his movements from any who might glance up at him. He still wore the uniform taken from one of the off-duty sentries found in the hold—the one whose turn it was to initiate the current guard rotation, though it scarcely mattered. That was the danger with uniforms: wearing one, each man looked much like the next. At a distance, in these conditions, the sleeveless tunic, leather hauberk, and wind-resistant cloak not only offered protection against chill breezes on a cool night, but allowed him to impersonate whichever of them he chose. The others would now perceive him to be the crow's nest lookout he'd just killed, rotating down to relieve the starboard sentry. His shorter stature and slimmer build would betray him up close, of course, but by then it would be too late for whomever he approached.

Murder, most would call it, to take a life so unawares, a man who'd done nothing to directly threaten him. But murder was a part of the natural order, at times, and certainly a price one risked when accepting a soldier's calling. Many who would decry assassination as a craven's business thought nothing of setting ambush for an opponent, or raiding and plundering as they pleased. Grendavan had left no greenhorns aboard his vessel, only bloody-handed veterans who'd themselves become strangers to pity, and thus had little right to ask for it. Regardless of how this feud had begun, one didn't take part in abducting a king's son or terrorizing a populace without anticipating the possibility of reprisal.

Justifications, yes, meant to assuage the twinge of regret that knotted in his stomach. But even if Kylac were to grant these men a chance to defend themselves in open challenge, what good would it do them? They couldn't stand against him, alone or together. Circumstances dictated that they die in the most expedient manner available, so as not to draw notice. Departing this world so peacefully wasn't an option he might have afforded them elsewise. Shards, the pair in the hold had bled out without ever waking. Would any future fate have been so kind?

"Anything to report?" he asked of the starboard sentry, as he had the man above.

Like his comrade, the soldier replied almost without turning. A moment later, his blood poured in a black wash over his black skin. A broken neck would have been swifter, but these men were of a height to make that method more challenging and less certain. As before, Kylac's smothering hand muffled any startled objections, while the victim's paralysis ensured minimal struggle. The sentry atop the sterncastle was hidden from view by the climb of decks. Sentries larboard and fore gazed out into the night. Kylac lowered the corpse into a crook of shadow beside the nearest deck stair, checked again on the other positions, and started forward.

He'd spent the waning piece of his afternoon observing the placement and rotation of the ship's skeletal guard contingent, committing their routine and its timing to memory. He'd then crept aboard to verify that no others lay in hiding. Eavesdropping on snatches of conversation, shadowing the crewmen's steps where practical to do so, he'd learned all he needed to. Seven aboard, not counting their commander—Tormitius Shorecleaver, given the passing talk among his men—who remained closeted in his cabin, opening the door only to receive the hourly shift report. One sentry at each primary point of the compass, plus the one in the nest. The final pair in their berths belowdecks, allowing two hours' rest for every five spent at watch. He knew each man's pace, the timbre of his voice, and his disposition toward each of the others. More than sufficient to execute this task.

With the first shift change following sunset, he'd emerged from his concealment to make this the final rotation of the night.

Wiser they would have been, he thought, to reverse the order of that rotation. Leave the least vulnerable sentry, high in the crow's nest, to oversee the relieving of each guard before descending to rest. Not that this could have stopped him, but it would have made his work this night more interesting. Instead, Tormitius's concern was that the crow's nest lookout be fresh, vision undulled by consecutive hours of watch at each of the four quadrants below. So it was that Kylac had been able to eliminate the off-duty pair sleeping in their hammocks, take the uniform of the one headed topside, then proceed immediately up the mast to kill the overhead sentry first—leaving only a sightless witness to his successive kills.

Granted, these pirates might never have believed that anyone could so easily board their vessel without being detected, much less slaughter them one at a time without a whisper of alarm being raised.

Kylac had overcome greater challenges—under less favorable conditions.

He completed his loop from bow to larboard rail to sterncastle, killing each sentry under the guise of his replacement. Their attention focused inland, none of Kendarrion's dockside troops took notice. Or, if any had, they hid well their reactions to it. Kylac doubted them capable of such discretion. Even if they *were* to suspect something, none would dare approach the Grenarr vessel, Kylac assured himself, without explicit authorization from Kendarrion or Grendavan—or both.

Only one remained to discover what he'd done.

He descended the starboard staircase leading down from the sterncastle, affecting the crisp, heavy gait of the last pirate to give homage to his blade. Arravus, by name, though one of his crewmates had called him Scar. Upon reaching the outer door to the captain's quarters, he rapped as he'd seen another do the hour before—a single knock, then two in quick succession, followed by one more.

Fingering his knife, he waited.

His actions brought no response. Kylac frowned. Three times had he witnessed this routine—twice from afar, once up close. In each instance, the reporting sentry had been received by Tormitius straightaway. So what should he do? Knock again? Wait?

On an impulse, he tried the latch, and found it unlocked. He pressed inward, his back against the door. Unbarred, the portal swung open, creaking softly on oiled hinges. Darkness awaited him inside. Had the commander exited while Kylac was occupied? Not by this route, insofar as Kylac had seen. But mayhap there were other hatchways within. He'd seen at least one while prowling the lower decks that might lead up into the rear of this cabin. If so, the commander might be anywhere.

He waited for several moments there in the cracked doorway, a dim beam of shrouded starlight laid across the floor. Outside, waves lapped against the ship's hull, while winds whistled through the rat-lines, tugged at furled sails, and plucked at taut stays like the strings of a lute. He heard the distant murmurs of those making business or mischief along the wharf, punctuated by the occasional shout, or by the shriek of gulls warring over some scrap of fish. Yet he heard nothing within—nothing louder than the steady beat of his own heart. He smelled oak and teak, hides and ink, seasoned leather and musty linens, an array of spices both foreign and familiar, and the faint scent of burning lamp oil—but of the cabin's occupant, they revealed no useful sign.

Finally, with his vision attuned to the darkness, he slipped inside, shutting the door behind him. An antechamber awaited, used at times, at least, as a navigation room. Maps and charts were spread across a table, nailed to the walls, or rolled up and stowed in cubbies and bays. Those he could see depicted sea lanes and the hazards that formed them. There were schedules, tide tables, and logs of a nature he assumed to be nautical, but which might have been indecipherable to any but the Grenarr.

And no one there to tell him their meaning.

When convinced of this, he ventured deeper, toward a curtained opening separating the antechamber from the primary quarters within. He slowed as he reached that cloth partition, creeping low to look for anyone standing to either side. A dim glow revealed the light of a lantern somewhere beyond—he could hear it and other metal implements scraping as they swayed upon iron hooks—but that light illuminated little else.

Standing sideways, he drew his longsword and used it to brush back the curtain, half expecting to trigger some trap or ambush. Neither manifested. Again he hesitated. If Tormitius had truly escaped to parts unknown, then he was wasting time with this cautious approach. Nonetheless, his instincts urged patience. He had yet to identify all of the strange smells stewing in this unfamiliar cage—a blend of herbs, waxes, oils, and incenses that could well hide a man's musk. And those were merely the physical scents. Among them lay the odors of death and deceit, thrumming in the stale air, pulsating in his veins.

He stepped inside the main chamber—dominated by a lavish bed, but filled as well with all manner of furnishings and accoutrements. A broad bank of glass squares formed a window at the rear of the cabin, though only a diffuse light was allowed to pass. Chests and lockboxes of various size squatted here and there, while along the walls stood closets and cabinets filled again with cubbies, hooks, and pegs bearing all manner of jewelry, clothing, weapons, tools, and instruments.

And on the floor on the larboard side of the bed—beside a cramped writing desk cluttered with vellum, compass, and stoppered inkpot—lay a flung hatch.

Kylac hastened toward it, casting sidelong glances as he did so. A sure sign that the commander had fled, likely in a rush.

Almost too sure.

He took the bait nonetheless, crouching low, peering at the rungs of the ladder as they faded into progressively deeper darkness. After a moment's consideration, he sheathed his longsword, then placed himself upon the ladder, facing astern, exposing his back to the chamber above and the darkness below.

He'd expected the ambush to come from below, but heard the whisper of movement and felt a sharp twinge in his neck warning of danger overhead. He continued as if oblivious to both . . . until the dart flew from its hollow pipe, reeking of poison. An abrupt duck allowed the dart to sail past, but as he resurfaced, his ambusher was at his back. A blade fell, aimed at his right shoulder in a swipe meant to cleave his torso into angled halves. Twisting to that side, he flung his body flat against the edge of the hatch, inside the weapon's arc, so that the sword swept past his face and away from him. As it did, he drew a knife with his left hand and planted it to the hilt in the sandaled foot of his assailant.

The assailant howled, stooping reflexively. Kylac released the knife, leaving it buried, and gripped the pirate's forearm, pinching nerves that caused him to fumble his sword. As the weapon dropped down the hatch, Kylac emerged, rising and circling so as to face his enemy, his own longsword drawn and pointed at the shark fin tattoo on the side of the commander's throat.

"A fair attempt, Tormitius."

The so-called Shorecleaver bit short his screams, but grimaced and huffed in obvious pain. When he bent toward his foot to remove the knife, Kylac pricked the pirate's neck with the tip of his longsword.

"Ah. Let's leave it a moment, shall we?"

Tormitius glared at him through eyes glazed with pain and defiance. "Is my master dead?"

Kylac slipped free of the confining hauberk he still wore. "The Great Grendavan? Why would ya think that?"

The pirate's gaze registered surprise, then anger, as he took in the youthfulness of his captor. A routine expression with which Kylac was familiar. "Kendarrion's pet assassin, I presume," Tormitius spat, gesturing vaguely at the blood pooling around his foot. "Come to finish the task."

"Not quite. Your overlord lives, so far as I'm aware."

"Then you came in search of the prince, thinking to find him stashed in our hold."

"I imagined y'all wiser than that, though I'd be lying if'n I denied having myself a look."

The Shorecleaver straightened somewhat as shock settled in to partly numb his agony. Muscles throughout his black body bulged and strained. He'd have done better to relax and accept the pain, rather than fight it, but such was the body's instinctive reaction. "Then what—"

"Grendavan left ya in charge. His chief lieutenant, to hear your men speak it."

"If you think to ransom me—"

"Your overlord would sooner use ya for chum than grant an exchange. Is that what ya would tells me?"

A reluctant nod. Brows pinched over bloodshot eyes. "So why haven't you killed me?"

"Should this night go as planned, I shall likely has need o' ya."

Tormitius managed a harsh chuckle. "Like the horgworm serves the killifish, so will I serve a landsnake like yourself."

Kylac didn't need to know what a horgworm was to surmise that it couldn't be trusted. "We'll discuss how cooperative ya may be on the morrow. For now, all I ask is, do ya know where the king's son is being detained?"

By the time Tormitius thought to lie, it was too late. The shift in his gaze and sudden pause in breathing had given him away. He seemed to realize this. "I'll see to it you find him in pieces, in payment of your king's treachery and cowardice."

Treachery and cowardice. Kylac might have laughed at the irony. "I see ya staked yourself in the garderobe," he observed instead. A fitting answer as to why he hadn't smelled the man. "Tell me, how did ya know I was coming for ya?"

Tormitius swooned on his feet, the throbbing and blood loss of his wounded foot taking their toll. Pride gave him a sudden measure of renewed strength. "Your knock. You used signal from the daylight hours."

Alerting the commander at once that something was amiss. For all his preparation, that detail had escaped him.

Alas, the elusiveness of perfection.

Nonetheless, his objectives here were complete—the ship secured, the first mate apprehended, and Kendarrion's troops privy to none of it. Of course, it wouldn't be long before the gulls descended in flocks upon the bodies abovedecks, which would surely draw the notice of any spies Kendarrion might have charged with watching the enemy vessel. But stowing them all below might itself draw unwanted attention, and would require time Kylac didn't wish to waste.

"What now?" Tormitius snarled, managing to sound contemptuous despite his state.

Retrieve his shortsword from the sentry in the crow's nest, collect evidence of the kills, and proceed to the palace before the completion of the wedding ceremony. But first . . .

"For yourself? Back to the garderobe."

He was behind the other before the pirate could do more than flinch, longsword sheathed, arms wrapped under the Shorecleaver's shoulders and over his neck, putting him to sleep. He then slid his knife from Tormitius's foot, dressed the wound to stanch further blood flow, and bound him wrist and ankle with thongs of leather taken from Grendavan's wardrobe. Upon relieving the pirate of various weapons stashed about his person, Kylac deposited him, trussed and gagged, into the garderobe as promised.

He wedged an iron bar against the door as further safeguard before shedding his Grenarr cloak and tabard and leaving them on the bed. Slower it would be to creep through the city wearing those, and time would soon become a factor. The Starling's Hour drew near.

The hour marked for Denariel's wedding.

30

HE FOUND ONLY A THIN CLUTCH of protestors outside the palace grounds. Fewer than threescore, gathered loosely before the barred double gates of the outer stone wall. A mere tenth of the angry throng held at bay by the spiked moat of the curtain wall. Here, most looked more like mourners, robed in black, bearing candles and long, sorrowful faces. While one or two of the more boisterous ones hurled shouts or fought to raise chant or cheer, the others would continue to murmur or hum softly, often making beseeching gestures toward the night sky or whispering their private prayers. For Her Highness's safekeeping, and for their own. For wisdom and foresight for His Majesty. For the courage and peace of mind that might see them through this bitter act of treachery.

Kylac wondered if any of them had ever manifested such desires through prayer alone. He'd eluded death too many times to completely discount the possibility of gods of some fashion looking after him from Olirian fields, but it seemed foolish to rely on it. Why wait for some heavenly overseer to give ear and grant a request that he could more readily attend to himself?

With that thought in mind, he veered off through the darkness, scaled the wall at a section where the sentry's back was turned, and proceeded like a shadow across the expanse of gardens beyond. He moved quickly, bolstered by a lack of fear, using hedgerows, statuary, and the shroud of night to mask his approach. The palace sentries were on guard first and foremost against mobs and rioters, not some solitary rogue of uncertain purpose.

The inner wall presented no greater challenge, though it stood twice as tall, thrice as thick, and boasted a dense guard ring upon its ramparts. Once he'd scaled its height and slipped past a small pack of Stonewatch caught up in an argument over whether peace with the Grenarr might prove to be a blessing, he descended to the courtyard beyond. Regiments patrolled the grounds, making sweeps in carefully drawn patterns of which Kylac made swift study. Even the thickest armor had its chinks.

Exploiting those weaknesses, he wound past a string of fountains, probing along dead angles, to reach the palace face and skirt his way around the eastern side. He found there the leeward side of a tower too high and sheer to scale—and proceeded to scale it, slithering into an open window near the top.

His inward descent carried him through chambers empty and occupied, down stairwells straight and twisting, and along corridors broad and narrow. He followed the most expedient route, if not always the most direct, creeping across rooftops, leaping to adjacent outbuildings, even sliding down the chimney of a cold hearth. He traveled invisibly, even when in plain view, posing by turns as a blacksmith's apprentice collecting iron oddments, as a chandler's boy making a delivery of fresh candles, and as a maimed scullery lad hauling a bucket of vegetable scraps to a hog trough. Such roles rarely drew suspicion. And suspicion itself wasn't all that difficult to overcome. Self-assurance had a way of deflecting disbelief.

His final disguise had him donning the robe of an acolyte and joining a line of other youths of various ages, ceremonial lantern in hand, singing a hymn as he marched slowly from a cathedral ante-chamber. Though his presence there drew an odd look from one or two of the other choral lads trying to place his face, he sang all the prouder, nodding at them to do the same. He'd already arranged for this with the choir master, taking the place of a senior lad come down with a sudden illness earlier that afternoon. Kylac didn't keep many coins on his person, but those he did were of significant value. A silver fist had been more than enough to sway the lad to feign a rasp within his lungs and proclaim Kylac his cousin. The family's stature among the city's nobility had ensured that few questions were asked—though it seemed the fact that he could sing was all the disgruntled choir master had really cared about.

When their procession had ended, they were arrayed across a dais at the head of the cathedral floor, behind a golden pulpit and beneath a vaulted ceiling upheld by magnificent arches of polished mahogany. The architecture of the hall was resplendent, breathtaking, with intricacies chiseled from shining marble, carved from gleaming wood, wrapped in glimmering satin, wreathed in precious metal, and bedecked with sparkling gemstones—the whole of it almost blinding in its radiance.

No less radiant was the attire of those Addarans in attendance, draped one and all in their most opulent finery, each trying to outshine the next. For the ladies of the court, shimmering weaves competed with glittering jewels, free-flowing locks, and the vibrant colors painted over their powdered faces. For the noblemen, it was pressed fabrics, badges of heraldry, braided ropes depicting various empty honors, cropped hair, and trimmed beards. Soldiers lining the outer edges of the chamber wore their medals of rank and achievement, ceremonial sashes, and the color of glove from which to draw their name—be it Blackfist of the Shadowguard, Redfist of the Stonewatch, or Whitefist of the Seawatch. Their weapons glinted, devoid of nick or scratch, and their armor of leather and mail gleamed as if newly worn.

Neither sheen nor luster, however, could mask the darkness befouling the faces of those whose gazes weighed heavily upon the Grenarr contingent gathered near the foot of the dais. Swarthy, brutish savages, their expressions seemed to say. Though others smiled bravely or with an affected air of grace and reconciliation, there was no mistaking the consensus. The Grenarr were a plague, a pestilence. A man might spare a roach, but not because it was worthy of his pardon.

Kylac was struck by the force of their rancor—their seething hatred and intense loathing. To his eyes, Grendavan's brood looked human enough. Crudely garbed, by comparison, but no less deserving of air, sustenance, and shelter than any member of this city's prideful flock. But then, he'd never watched a cherished family member or beloved neighbor be robbed or ravished or killed by one of these pirates. Were he to do so, he might feel differently.

Had he any family or neighbors to speak of.

Still, it seemed senseless to blame an entire clan for the actions of an individual—to damn a man for the color of his hide because another wearing the same had once wronged you. But men seemed determined to wage war against one another. To that end, he supposed it was as valid a reason as any.

A philosophical question, but also a practical one, as he weighed the most likely level of response here. The civilians in attendance were to have been relieved of all weapons before entering the cathedral, but Kylac could smell the metal and oil of their hidden blades. He doubted the Shadowguard had screened them all that closely, not when the Grenarr had been permitted their weapons. *For ceremonial purposes,* Grendavan had suggested, as well as a deterrent against any rogue action from the crowd. Difficult to deny him this when Kendarrion had himself used these justifications to insist upon the presence of his armed guard ring.

The result was a tinderbox dry and hot, just waiting for a spark.

Of greater concern were those fronting the dais itself—those more intimately involved in the proceedings. It seemed all who might have been present were. Ledron beside Denariel, Ruhklyn beside Kendarrion, along with a dozen chosen Shadowguard. The most loyal they would be, and thus the most eager. Opposing them, Grendavan and his towering kinsmen—men and women selected as carefully for their own loyalty and combat skills, Kylac didn't doubt. Twoscore adherents who would be swift to defend their overlord, and slow to surrender, despite odds here of roughly two to one against them—not counting civilians. Behind and to one side stood their emissary, Sabrynne, grinning as if at some private jape.

Their fates, Kylac reassured himself, would depend in no small measure on their own actions.

The choir's hymn ended. As the echoing refrains dissipated into the void of the overhead rotunda, a priest emerged from an open passageway at the head of the dais. His seamed face was stern, and his back hunched, as if it were all his frail body could do to bear the weight of his lavish robes and opulent headpiece. Bushy tufts of hair sprouted from his age-spotted brow, while white wisps clung to his neck beneath what appeared to be a bald head. He pressed his bony fingertips together as he came to stand behind the central altar, where rested a three-pronged candelabra, its large central candle flanked by two smaller ones, all unlit.

Kylac's own position left him to overlook the priest's right shoulder, so that he could no longer see the old man's expression. But he felt the venom in the holy man's gaze as it shifted stage left ever so briefly to take in Grendavan and his Grenarr retinue. The priest made a sign with his fingers that might have been a ward or a curse, then turned stage right toward his king with an air of palpable disapproval.

Kendarrion nodded stiffly.

"We beseech the Fair Mother Eriyah to bear witness to this occasion," the priest intoned with surprising strength of lung, "that Her nurturing light might sap a measure of the darkness that overshadows this deviant union."

Not the typical preamble, Kylac decided, looking for Kendarrion's reaction. The king nodded again, seething in his gold-trimmed finery.

"Have we a maiden fair, strong of voice and mind, who would submit to the bond of marriage?"

Even bathed and painted and clothed in gown and jewels, the princess wasn't what Kylac would call fair. But then, it was hard to see past that terrible pout. If ever expression alone had the power to destroy, Kylac had no doubt but that all present would be lying now beneath a heap of fiery rubble.

"We do," said Denariel.

"Have we a man," the priest snarled, and gave a hacking cough to clear his lungs, "who would submit to the bond of marriage?"

Grendavan lifted his head and bellowed proudly, "Strong of voice and mind. We do."

Whispered murmurs spread through the audience. The priest focused on Denariel. "Let them step forward."

No ceremonial pomp here. Straight to the thrust, this holy man.

For the best, Kylac supposed, for all concerned. If it had to be done, the swifter the better.

Denariel climbed the steps toward the altar, leaving Kendarrion and Ledron behind. Her movements bespoke no hesitation—though, to Kylac, her bravery felt forced. Resigned to carry out this farce, determined not to let her enemy smell her fear.

Grendavan approached from the other side, towering over the priest, the altar with its candelabra, and the diminutive princess, grinning merrily.

"Kneel," said the priest, his head turned this time toward the Grenarr overlord.

Grendavan gave a slight bow before doing so. Kneeling, he was nearly eye level with Denariel, standing across from him. When she knelt in turn, she seemed but a child again. Courageous. Dutiful. But a child nonetheless.

The priest observed her momentarily, then beckoned for a pair of young acolytes standing by with lit tapers. They stepped near, one beside Denariel, the other beside Grendavan.

"With permission, Your Highness," said the priest, his voice soft with sympathy, "I would forgo the Maiden's Prayer, the Gift of Oils, the Supplicant's Song, and the Obeisant Caress, in hopes of preserving the sanctity of these most sacred rites."

Denariel blinked. Surprised, and in no small measure relieved. "As Your Holiness deems best."

"Forgo what rites you would, old man," Grendavan agreed, "that we may sooner consummate this union according to *our* traditions."

The murmurs this time were more vocal. A noblewoman gasped. The overlord's smile betrayed a wolfish gleam.

The priest took the flaming taper from Denariel's attending acolyte, and bent toward her. "My noble lady, I ask only what is required. Your honorable vow—to which all in attendance must mourn to bear witness—that you hereby agree to wed and thus serve this man, until death intervenes. If you would, then speak the words, and with this candle light your own, as a symbol of your intent."

"Until death intervenes," Denariel echoed, staring daggers at Grendavan. Accepting the taper from the priest with a hand splinted to protect her broken thumb, she lit the nearest candle within the candelabra. As it took flame, she blew out the taper and returned it to her attending acolyte.

The priest regarded the wisp of smoke from the acolyte's taper with a heavy sadness.

"Is the ceremony ended, then?" Grendavan nudged.

The priest whirled on him, snatching the taper from the acolyte on that flank as if he might seek to drive it like a stake into the overlord's eye. "As I will not ask her to sully our sacred oaths on you, nor will I hear them profaned by your black lips. I ask only if you mean still to take this noble lady as your wife, with what promise you can give to cherish, defend, and sustain her as befits a woman's honor, until death intervenes. If you can speak these words—under the gaze of the Fair Mother Eriyah—then do so, and with this candle light your own, as a symbol of your intent."

As Grendavan reached for the taper, the priest turned away, clutching to it like a mongrel warding a bone.

"The words, if you dare speak them."

The overlord smirked, and placed a hand to his chin. "Hmm, have I cause then to reconsider? A profound burden, women can be. I of all men should know, having four sea wives already and too many concubines to count. Would you request that I forsake their needs by taking on the needs of this one?"

The audience roared in outcry. Soldiers throughout the room stepped forward, hands gripping the hafts of their weapons. Ruhklyn started toward the dais until Kendarrion restrained him.

"Silence!" the king bellowed, a shout fueled with pain and fury. "You have been summoned here to bear witness, not protest! Captain Ledron," he said, "see to it that any man or woman here who looses their tongue again is held upon charges of treason."

Ledron, grinding his teeth beside the king opposite Ruhklyn, gave a curt nod as the furor dimmed. "As you will, Your Majesty."

"Proceed," Kendarrion barked, drawing Ruhklyn forcibly back.

"Forgive me, good king," Grendavan bade, rising beside the altar with a suddenly benevolent mien. "Addarans, my future brothers, your forgiveness, too, I beg. A jest it was. A poor reaction to perceived discourtesy. I am reminded that my vision of our future, an image clear and crisp, is yet mist-shrouded for some. Rather than taunt those with a clouded view, I should seek to brighten it, to bring it into focus." He turned to Denariel, and bowed deeply. "My lady, if you would help me mend the rift between our peoples, to put an end to this brewing enmity, I would serve you, yes, until death intervenes."

With the priest distracted, the overlord snatched the taper away from him. Swiftly, Grendavan knelt, and lit his end of the candelabra. He then pinched out the flame of the taper and submitted it to his attending acolyte with an expression of utter reverence.

Stricken, the young acolyte seemed unable to respond, except to turn to the priest in question. Gazes followed, to find a tremor rattling the priest's frame. A seizure, it appeared, and Kylac wondered if the old man was set to die where he stood.

"Finish it," a fuming Kendarrion instructed.

The priest recovered himself well enough to wave at the acolyte. His motion seemed to snap the boy out of his trance. Quickly, the lad accepted the dead taper and stepped back.

"If your vows be true," the priest rasped, his voice now tremulous, "let your lights be joined, and your union recognized."

Denariel took a moment to glare at her father before touching the priest's arm with a reassuring hand. She then removed her candle from the candelabra, and waited for Grendavan to follow. Moving slowly, so that the Grenarr overlord might mimic her movement, she took aim at the larger candle still unlit in the center. As the flames of their opposing candles met, the wick of the central candle took fire.

"United," Kendarrion called out, "until death intervenes."

"United," the crowd chanted as one, in solemn, begrudging tone, "until death intervenes."

Denariel replaced her flanking candle in its holder, and waited for Grendavan to do the same. When he had, she took to her feet beside the altar, and watched the overlord rise across from her.

Kendarrion stared up at his daughter, his eyes gleaming with regret. "Captain Ledron," he said, "you are hereby relieved from my royal daughter's service. Her safety is now her lord husband's concern."

Ledron, stone-faced as he regarded those at the altar, offered no response.

"Captain Ruhklyn," Kendarrion said, "the gallery is dismissed."

"Sergeant," Ruhklyn echoed to a Redfist near the double doors at the back of the cathedral. "Release the gallery."

Kylac had seen enough.

"One moment, Sergeant," he called, stepping forward from the line of singers at the back of the dais.

He strode smoothly toward the altar, drawing odd looks of surprise and confusion, but nothing so serious as alarm, dressed as he was in his choral robe. The restless stir of the crowd, uncertain whether to remain or depart, offered a gentle commotion to help cover his approach. As he neared the priest, he raised his bare hands before him in a placating gesture. The priest scowled in disapproval, but turned his questioning gaze toward the choir master, who could only gape at the old man, perplexed.

Kylac stepped past the priest, proceeding toward the newlyweds. He smiled disarmingly at Grendavan, who regarded him with bemusement, and was allowed to settle a little more than arm's length from the princess, hands folded loosely at his waist.

Denariel gasped softly in recognition, before her brow furrowed in familiar distaste. "What do you want?"

"I's come to apologize."

"Kronus." A breathless mutter from the foot of the dais. Ledron, too, had recognized him.

"A selfless thing ya's done here. I knows now ya had other plans."

"Kronus?" Kendarrion echoed, glancing at Ledron before squinting toward Kylac.

"Would ya truly submit to him?"

"All right, pup," said Grendavan, approaching at his back as if to shoo him away, "the deed is done. Bid your farewells and be gone."

Kylac remained focused on Denariel, piercing her with his unrelenting gaze, until at last her face flickered with uncertainty. At that, he smirked with reassurance. "'Til death intervenes."

"Seize him!" Kendarrion hissed.

Too late. Kylac's left hand flew beneath his acolyte's robe, grasped the hilt of his longsword in a reverse grip, and thrust the blade straight up behind him, driving its tip through Grendavan's jaw and higher, into his brain.

The room seemed to freeze, its occupants transfixed in collective shock. From the crowd came only startled gasps and strangled yelps. Denariel staggered back a step. Ruhklyn, who'd been lunging toward the dais, halted midstride. Without so much as a glance at the dead man skewered on the tip of his sword, Kylac turned from Denariel to regard the gawking assembly—particularly Grendavan's guards and kinsmen.

"None other must die," he suggested.

But the alternative outcome, it seemed, had been decided. First to recover, the Grenarr were reaching already for their blowguns. Kylac couldn't be sure that he'd be their target. As likely as not, they would retaliate against Denariel or Kendarrion.

Something he wouldn't allow.

Ripping his longsword free in a motion so smooth that Grendavan remained standing, Kylac sprang atop the altar, knocking aside the flaming candelabra as he leapt toward the Grenarr. A shortsword came to hand with his second bounding stride. With his third, he tossed the weapons in the air before him—a further distraction, but one that also let him swap hands, the shortsword caught in his left, the longsword in his right.

As suddenly as that, he was upon them.

The swiftest to draw their blowguns were the first to lose those arms, some at the elbow, some at the shoulder, some at the wrist. He hadn't the time to punish them equally, and so took more flesh from some than others. The limbs fell, drawing the weapons with them. He smelled poison upon those weapons, amid a pungent aroma of fury, fear, and fountaining blood.

Chaos ensued. Behind him, Grendavan's corpse had finally toppled. Screams and shouts erupted from the crowd, the bulk of which turned toward the exit in a rush. Ruhklyn diverted his own rush toward the Grenarr, roaring for the Shadowguard to join him. Those nearest the enemy entourage were only too eager to heed his call, shoving civilians aside as they drew their swords and joined the fray. Ledron bounded toward Denariel, a human shield, calling for a clutch of

Shadowguard nearest Kendarrion to defend their king. At the back of the dais, the horrified choir master and his singing lads funneled through the rear passageway, back toward the priest's quarters. The priest went with them, only to turn about near the clogged portal, crying out a condemnation upon those spilling blood in his blessed cathedral, entreating them to stop.

Few heard the holy man's pleas. Fewer still paid them any heed. The gallery was in a mad panic, stampeding toward the exit doors. Stonewatch stationed there fought back the press in a futile effort to open those doors, which were hinged to swing inward. A handful of civilian observers fought against the surge, drawing their smuggled knives to join the fight against the Grenarr—complicating Ruhklyn's own, more organized attack. Snatching Denariel by the arm, Ledron was drawing her and Kendarrion clear, backing toward the side wall opposite the melee, establishing a defensive line of dutiful Blackfists in rearguard. Kylac observed all of this while still at the center of the enemy entourage, ducking Grenarr blades, dodging fists and spurts of blood, doing his best to evade their howls of sorrow, cries of pain, and calls for vengeance. He was no longer attacking, only defending himself where necessary, for the greater threat was now posed by Ruhklyn's Shadowguard, converging from all sides like a pack of rabid dogs, squeezing down like a noose.

A Grenarr woman stabbed at him with a blade reeking of venom, snarling through a mouthful of filed teeth. Kylac dodged her swipe and left her behind, feeling a twinge of pity despite her savagery toward him. Having anticipated this likely slaughter, he might have taken greater steps to avoid it. But a full slate of considerations had necessitated the risk. None of the Grenarr present, he supposed, be they male or female, were any less complicit than the next in Grendavan's scheme. And not a one had entered this hall without being fully prepared that bloodshed might result.

There was one, however, he was determined to spare if he could. One who'd shown no pretense, confessing readily to her people's machinations. One—the only—among the Grenarr who hadn't drawn a blade. She shrank back instead amid the civilian throng, as if hoping to escape notice, distraught over what she was witnessing.

"This way, emissary."

Sabrynne blinked, eyeing the smears of blood that painted Kylac's swords. A Blackfist lunged at them. With a scissor block, Kylac caught the blade that reached for the emissary's throat, turning it aside before twisting it free of the assailant's grasp. Disarmed, the guardian retreated, in search of another weapon.

"Best if'n we don't tarry."

Sabrynne nodded dumbly and took to Kylac's heels. Kylac turned at once, veering toward the center aisle, circling around the rim of soldiers bent on crushing inward upon the Grenarr contingent. A few noted him and turned to intercept, but quickly found themselves seeking blades lost upon the floor. Kylac left them in his wake, unharmed.

Carving a nonlethal path, Kylac escorted Sabrynne onto the dais, where she reflexively met the sightless, cross-eyed stare of her gruesomely slain overlord.

"Ya can lie down beside him, if'n ya wish, else follow the choir." He gestured in the direction of the singing youths' mass departure, adding, "I'd recommend the latter."

Sabrynne's gaze narrowed. Kylac couldn't quite read what he saw there. Surprise? Suspicion? That and more, Kylac supposed, as the emissary looked again at Grendavan. It couldn't be easy to hate a man and owe him your life at the same time.

"For the name o' Dethaniel's location, I'll even hold back the first wave."

As if in response, Ruhklyn caught sight of them, from deep within the melee against the Grenarr. Walled off from the dais by his own men, the captain settled for pointing them out, hollering for a pursuit.

Sabrynne grimaced. "You would never reach him. Even if you knew how to find—"

"Then the truth should cost ya nothing. Here they come."

The emissary retreated a pace, crouching with instinctive anxiety as the imminent charge coalesced. "Blackmoon," she whispered, then straightened in challenge. "If you would meet your doom, seek the pretender's son amid the Blackmoon Shards."

Kylac inclined his head, bidding farewell with a final warning. "Should any o' those lads ya follow come to harm, ya'll wish they hadn't."

Sabrynne glowered, then turned and fled, drawing a fierce scowl from the priest as she slipped through the inner exit. Kylac, true to his word, held his ground against the initial clutch of Blackfists giving chase. Seven in all. Kylac danced with them, shed them of their weapons, let another four, five, six close round, then slipped free of their ironclad formations, taking new aim. Ruhklyn's Shadowguard had all but overwhelmed the twoscore Grenarr with their own, superior numbers.

Time to end this.

Placing his back to those under Ruhklyn's command, he shot toward those under Ledron's. They resisted as best they could, forming a tight phalanx with their swords and armor. Kylac darted through them all the same, finding seams where there were none, forcing gaps amid walls of steel and iron. Slapping weapons aside, taking care not to draw blood, he squirmed his way under, over, and past them until he'd slithered beyond their ranks to where Ledron had Kendarrion and Denariel hunkering within an alcove against the side wall.

The Shadowguard captain came forward to engage him, but seemed to understand that it was only a formality. Kylac disarmed him as he had so many others, brushed Denariel aside when she stepped in to shield her father, and slid up behind the king to place a bloody shortsword at his throat.

31

"A WORD, YOUR MAJESTY. If'n I may."

"What are you doing?" Denariel cried.

Her coiled stance told Kylac she was prepared to lunge, but the blade at her father's throat—along with a fretful confusion—held her in check. The same could be said of the nearest guardsmen, who formed a tight arc around him, but hesitated to press any closer. Those he'd disarmed were retrieving their weapons, scowling with embarrassment and the promise of retribution as they rejoined the ready ranks. Save for Ledron. The Head stood in a frozen crouch, arms outstretched, palms down, in a gesture urging calm.

"Would you just stand there?" Kendarrion sputtered at his captain, incredulous.

"Ever seen a pack o' men disemboweled over the same ground?" Kylac asked. The image seemed to give those around him further pause. "Your captain spared my life. A deed that also paid for his falsehoods. Should he confront me again, however, Your Majesty shall watch him wrestle his comrades here over the tangle o' loose entrails."

He hoped it wouldn't come to that. The Head's only lie, insofar as Kylac could recall, had been to blame the Grenarr for Denariel's abduction. And how great a lie was that, when they had in fact initiated all of this by abducting her brother, Dethaniel? Given his own culpability in assuming the truth rather than questioning it, Kylac, after much reflection, had decided to spare the faithful captain.

If he could.

"You don't want to kill him," Ledron assumed. "Else His Majesty would be dead and yourself long gone."

"Doesn't mean I won't," Kylac warned, as some of the bolder Blackfists advanced a step. "So ya mights want to rein these lads in."

Stonewatch at the mouth of the cathedral had finally managed to wrest open the doors, allowing the gallery observers to spill through the breach. Several carried injuries, having been shoved aside or trampled in the crush. Few noticed the predicament their king was in, concerned only with escape. Others saw, but hastened out anyway—or tried to stop, only to be forced along by shepherding soldiers.

More and more of those soldiers, however, were turning, drawn by the about-face and sudden hush of those walled around Kendarrion. Among those engaged throughout the cathedral floor, word spread that their king hung upon the edge of a blade, carried by murmurs, shouts, a tap on the shoulder, or a tug on the arm. With the civilians emptying, and many of the soldiers wavering, the intensity of the surrounding tumult gradually softened.

"Stand fast!" Ledron commanded, as the guard ring continued to tighten with the press of those assembling at their backs.

The last to notice were those positioned across the hall where the Grenarr had stood—where the carnage lay thickest. Though the massacre was complete, they hacked and stabbed at their slain enemies, reacting to every twitch or moan. While some thought to help pull aside their wounded comrades, most hovered like vultures. Blood spattered their bodies and faces, and dripped from the edges of their blades to join the pools and rivers spilled across the floor.

Ruhklyn stepped clear as he caught sight of the standoff. "Clear this room!" he hollered, when a straggling civilian bumped into him. As his men worked to obey, he advanced slowly toward Kylac, chest heaving, murder still flashing in his eyes.

"Impetuous whelp," Kendarrion fumed. "Kill me or not, I'll have you tarred and flayed for what you've done here."

Even with his obstructed view, Kylac sensed full well the butchery he'd triggered—the spread of mutilated bodies, severed limbs, gaping mouths, and unseeing eyes. He fought back another twinge of regret. Yes, he'd expected the Grenarr might be slaughtered. But so had they, else they would not have armed themselves with their poisoned darts and envenomed blades. Upon final reckoning, some of this was their choice, some of it was not. Such was the nature of life—and death.

"I waited for Your Majesty to intervene," Kylac answered, knowing that it wasn't their deaths that concerned Kendarrion, but rather the consequences thereof. "Ya didn't. So I did."

"Fool," snarled Ruhklyn, shoving his way through the ranks of soldiers to join the inner circle. "You've started a war."

"My son," Kendarrion growled, choked by the threat of tears. "You've killed my son."

He sagged, then started to thrash, heedless of the shortsword at his throat. To save the king from himself, Kylac rotated grip, using the dull edge to press even tighter, cutting off Kendarrion's airflow.

"No!" Denariel squealed.

"Your son might yet be spared," said Kylac, "though his breaths may indeed be measured against ours. Shall we continue wasting them?"

"Ashes are ashes," Ledron agreed, halting Ruhklyn with a forcible swat across the chest. His gaze was steeled, his jaw clenched. "So let the rogue explain himself."

Breathless, Kendarrion finally ceased his struggles, allowing Kylac to ease his grasp.

"Their emissary bears word of his treachery," Ruhklyn advised Ledron, pointing his bloodied blade at Kylac. "A fiend *he* set loose."

"With cause, I'm sure," Ledron insisted. "As he surely had cause for slaying Grendavan before our eyes, and not secretly at some other juncture."

With Ledron commanding calm, and the final echoes of the gallery's departure fading into stillness, reason was at last finding purchase amid harsher emotion, raw anger ceding ground to a more sensible curiosity.

"I might has killed him silently," Kylac acknowledged. "But this gives us witnesses—enough, I hope, to supplant whatever rumors would elsewise seek to condemn His Majesty."

That was one excuse. The other had been his desire to overcome the king's skepticism concerning his abilities. To undertake the next stage of this mission, he needed Kendarrion and the king's closest advisors to believe that he might actually be able to succeed in what he intended. And, for that, he knew they would need to observe his skills and his daring firsthand.

Ruhklyn snorted. "And you're fool enough to think the Grenarr will care? His Majesty will be deemed accountable regardless."

"Why kill him at all?" Kendarrion demanded. "Better it would have been to ransom him in exchange."

For the ill befallen your daughter, thought Kylac. *For Sallun and Trajan and the others.* Outwardly, he shrugged. "Dance with knives, and you're bound to be pricked."

"For that, you doomed my son?"

"As for the emissary," Kylac pressed, eyeing Ruhklyn, "your men will no doubt bring her to heel. Should they fail . . ." He shrugged again. "What's one more spy in your midst?"

Fast as he was, Kylac knew well the futility in seeking to hunt down and silence rumors. Easier it would be to collect dry leaves in an autumn wind. Whether through a direct chain of clandestine communications, the strands of whispers threaded together from a web of informers, or merely some status report *not* delivered on schedule, the Grenarr would be alerted to this turn of events. Better in this instance, it seemed to Kylac, that they learn precisely what had taken place, conveyed firsthand by one of their own.

Ruhklyn was unappeased. "And if she's already halfway to the harbor? We've no ship that can catch theirs."

Keeping his shortsword around the king's throat, Kylac sheathed his longsword in order to produce a small pouch, which he tossed at Ruhklyn's feet. "Have a look," he urged.

Ruhklyn didn't move, so Ledron snatched it up, loosened the drawstring, and reached inside . . . to remove six flayed pieces of black skin, each tattooed with a shark's fin.

"Grendavan's vessel is ours," Kylac announced. "The only skin missing belongs to the chief lieutenant. Our captive. A lone wolf who will lead us to the Grenarr den—mayhap in time to prevent

Dethaniel further harm, provided we act at once."

Ledron handed the throat skins to Ruhklyn, who dropped them to the floor with evident distaste.

Kylac turned his eye upon Denariel. "Your daughter risked much, Your Majesty, to fight for the future o' your people. In that, I served her poorly. So let me atone for my misdeeds. Permit me, and I will rescue her brother, your son the prince, or give my life in the attempt."

Denariel glared at him, gently rubbing her splinted hand with the other. "Why should we trust you?" she asked. "Why not kill you now before you complicate matters further?"

Kylac released his hostage, eliminating the most obvious answer to that question with a gesture of faith. Kendarrion turned, retreating toward his daughter while massaging his throat. Ruhklyn waited a heartbeat more before lunging forward, sword leading, with Kylac seemingly distracted by the royal pair. But as the petulant Blackfist completed his stride, he found the tip of Kylac's longsword—freshly unsheathed—pricking his barrel chest.

"Ya can't stop me," Kylac boasted, his eyes still fixed on Denariel, "so why not aid me?" He turned his head to face Ruhklyn, who held his breath in stiff-necked fury. "I's started a war, ya says. Alas. So let me finish it."

32

A WARM WIND GUSTED EAGERLY against Kylac's back—the same wind that filled the black sails billowing behind him, thrusting their vessel forward upon the waves. *Vengeance*, the Grenarr called her, and Kendarrion had seen no reason to rename her. She rode the swells seemingly without effort, knifing through the windblown crests and gliding along the glazed troughs. Where *Denariel's Return* had seemed to battle the ocean, rocking and wresting in its progress, *Vengeance* rose and fell to a smooth, peaceful rhythm, at one with the heartbeat of the seas.

Overhead, the afternoon sun shone brightly through a cloudless sky, its light causing the waves below to sparkle. Kylac squinted against the brilliance, the hood of his cloak pulled forward to shade his eyes. Standing at the bow rail, he saw only endless ocean before him. Rather than the confinement he'd felt upon his first voyage, however, this one bespoke nothing but opportunity.

They'd lowered sail and set forth that very dawn, the first since Denariel's ill-fated wedding ceremony. Though Ruhklyn and others had urged forbearance pending further deliberation, Kendarrion was nothing if not single-minded concerning his son. Deliberations among the Addaran king and his royal council would indeed commence at once. Apologies and additional concessions would be put forth. But so too would Kylac's proposed rescue attempt, on the chance that, upon word of Grendavan's demise escaping their shores, Prince Dethaniel should be made to suffer the wrath of Grendavan's lieutenants and sons.

The captive Tormitius had promised as much when informed of his overlord's demise. He'd also cursed them for cowards and refused to be of any aid whatsoever when questioned as to *his* knowledge of Dethaniel's imprisonment. At that point, Ruhklyn and other dissenters had renewed their objections, but Kylac's confidence had been unflappable.

"Before we're done, he'll tell me everything we need to knows."

And if he didn't? Well, *Vengeance* herself was not without clues. While they had yet to fully sift through and decipher the many charts and logs found within the ship's navigation room, it seemed certain that, once they did, they would have a fair idea of how to retrace her passage to where Dethaniel was being held.

A place dubbed the Blackmoon Shards, if Sabrynne had spoken true.

In the meantime, Kylac was less convinced than others that the prince would be punished for the outrage committed under Kendarrion's roof. The account gleaned from Sabrynne in the emissary's quarters had led him to believe that the larger plan to bring peace between the warring nations was greater than one man. The desperate risk Grendavan had assumed in personally coming ashore seemed to underscore this belief. Slay Dethaniel as a mere act of retribution, and the Grenarr would at the same time relieve themselves of their most valuable bargaining chip, reverting to the previous stalemate. Even if those were the instructions left behind by Grendavan prior to setting foot on Avenell's wharf, would his successors choose to follow them through?

Whatever the enemy's contingency plans, there was a chance that the response would ultimately benefit Kylac's effort. Massing for a retaliatory assault might draw ships away from those guarding the prince. Or, rather than uniting the Grenarr, Grendavan's death might as easily result in confusion and infighting, buying time for their expedition while a new leader emerged to make a final decision about the prince's fate.

A murky future didn't always portend doom.

As if in evidence of this, they'd found the ship's hold to be well stocked with provisions—a minor boon, since none had wanted to spend the time or draw the attention that extensive additions to her cargo would bring. Only a handful of barrels and crates—ale and water and select foodstuffs—had been wheeled aboard during the predawn hours, while the greater focus had been to settle upon a crew. Kylac had insisted upon meeting each man that Kendarrion or his captains recommended, to gauge their character as best he could for what might be required of them. There was no accounting for where this voyage might lead, and he didn't wish to be saddled with another like "Roach" Merrec, "Fangs" Hadrum, or "Blowfish" Ranson.

"Winds like these, we should reach the Baravian Atolls within a week," said Ledron, as he approached at Kylac's back. "We'll learn then whether your friend the emissary lied to us."

The remark carried with it a sting of accusation. Kylac shrugged it off before responding with a barb of his own. "Or whether your scholar saw chance to swindle us."

Ledron's frown deepened. "What cause would he have to do that?"

The king's coin, mayhap? When the name of the location provided by Sabrynne had proven unfamiliar, Kendarrion had swiftly set about seeking a historian who could place it. After much ignorance and confusion, a member of the royal circle had turned up a slack-jowled cartographer who claimed knowledge of "Blackmoon" referring to the Baravian Atolls—those, it seemed, upon which the Grenarr had initially taken refuge when driven from Addaranth generations before. While none had any reason to discredit the mapmaking scholar or his assertion, Kylac had misliked the reek of opportunism that had emanated from him while accepting payment.

Rather than say as much, however, and risk delaying their departure on the account of added uncertainty, Kylac had bridled his suspicions, trusting in other means of ferreting out the truth during the course of their voyage, should it prove that one source or the other had led them astray.

As his silence lengthened, so too did Ledron's irritation. "If you've reason to believe we're sailing in the wrong direction—"

"Ya said yourself their navigational records suggest an easterly course."

"*East* leaves ample room for error. Particularly over a great distance."

"Shall I renew discourse with our prisoner?" Kylac offered, suggestively tapping a sheathed sword hilt.

Ledron stiffened. "You are not to visit him without my leave."

Of course not. Because doing so would stretch the bounds of His Majesty's conciliatory nature. Kendarrion had poorly hidden the fact that he still envisioned this enterprise unfolding as a prisoner exchange—Grendavan's chief lieutenant for the crown prince, Dethaniel. Unlikely, in Kylac's estimation, but that debate could wait.

He dipped his head in deference to Ledron's authority. "Then it seems the information in our possession is all we have to acts upon. What more we needs will boil free in time."

Ledron's jaw clenched. "I suppose I'll have to trust you on that."

Within his cowl, Kylac smirked. The captain was less bitter than he pretended. Neither he nor his king had objected when Kylac had requested that Ledron be the one to lead their expedition. Who better suited to act as Kylac's handler, the king had agreed, than the man whose boot had scraped him up from those outland shores? Left behind in Avenell, the disgraced captain might likely have been dismissed, if not jailed or executed. Steeped in such utter disfavor, he needed a chance to redeem himself—and he wasn't likely to find a better opportunity than this.

As for trust? A double-edged blade. Kylac harbored no doubt that, depending on how matters unfurled, Ledron would offer him to the Grenarr as a human trophy in reparation for his action against Grendavan—whether or not Kendarrion had given any specific command to seek that course. Allies they might be in this, but only to a point.

"The captain metes out faith in his comrades most grudgingly, I's observed. Even those o' equal rank."

"Ruhklyn is a dog. To entrust both His Majesty and Her Highness to his command . . ."

On that count, Kylac was more sympathetic. He, too, had felt a certain pang at leaving Denariel behind. Not so much in concern for her safety as the unfinished business between them. Freeing her from her would-be marriage had done nothing to earn her forgiveness for the death of her Ukinh companion. And she'd been livid when denied a position among their crew, holding Kylac more responsible than Ledron, Ruhklyn, or her father for their joint, steadfast refusal. Oil upon the flames. Much like Ledron, Kylac was here seeking to atone for a perceived failure. If returning her brother didn't reconcile that debt, then nothing would.

"As Her Highness's acting shadow, I might worry more for Ruhklyn. Care to tells me the story between the two o' ya?"

Ledron shook his head. He did not. "It troubles me that Sabrynne evaded capture," he admitted instead, openly this time. "The spider swept out the window may be the very one to bite you in your sleep."

"Or as easily be devoured by owl or snake." Where would the Grenarrian go? What great harm could she cause? "She is but one woman."

"As you are but a single, half-grown man," Ledron snorted. "And consider the trouble you've wrought."

"Anything else gnawing at ya?"

Again, the clenched jaw. "I just feel as if we may have missed something."

Truth unfettered, Kylac felt the same, but had yet to fathom what it might be. It could be any number of matters—or a brace of them. A mission thrown together as quickly as this, fraught with such urgency and uncertainty, was like fishing with a tattered net. "The misgivings of a new adventure, my friend."

"This is no adventure," Ledron snapped, "and I am not your friend. We find His Highness and return him to His Majesty. After, we are well rid of each other. Agreed?"

Without waiting for an answer, Ledron turned and stormed away. More bitter, mayhap, than Kylac had initially believed.

But he refused to let the other's resentment cloud his own outlook. His was a life of action and reflex. *There is only so much a man can plan for,* his father had preached. *The rest is tumbling with the die that is cast.* Let Ledron and others fear the unknown. To Kylac, it was life's very breath.

With his gaze on the horizon and the wind at his back, Kylac filled his lungs, savoring the moment and the boundlessness of the next.

Here ends Book One of the *WARDER* trilogy.
The adventure continues in Book Two:
The Blackmoon Shards